Jeffrey Dahmer, Gemini
smooth talker with a dual personality, sexually conflicted, preoccupied with thoughts of death

Timothy McVeigh, Taurus
precise and obsessive, easily influenced by friends, has a skewed vision of the world

Edward Gein, Virgo
meticulous, habitual, secretive, adapts well in places of confinement

Charles Manson, Scorpio
possessed of a free spirit, controlling, magnetic, and egotistical

Ted Bundy, Sagittarius
attractive, charming, and irresistible, as well as arrogant, conceited, isolated, and depressed

John Wayne Gacy, Pisces
deceptive and eccentric, a chameleon with a reputation for loving children

Lee Harvey Oswald, Libra
a dreamer, a loner, intense and emotional, a seeker of fame

Lyle Menendez, Capricorn
materialistic, capable of making long-term plans, ruled by reputation, career—and mother

Plus in-depth profiles and astrological readings for:

David Berkowitz, Wayne Williams, Andrew Cunanan, Perry Smith, Charles Starkweather, Richard Speck, Gary Gilmore, Dean Corll, James Earl Ray, and more

D1444183

ZODIAC
OF DEATH

*Profiles and Horoscopes of
50 Notorious Criminals*

Don Lasseter and **Dana Holliday**

BERKLEY BOOKS, NEW YORK

ZODIAC OF DEATH

A Berkley Book / published by arrangement with
the authors

PRINTING HISTORY
Berkley edition / October 1999

The Penguin Putnam Inc. World Wide Web site address is
http://www.penguinputnam.com

ISBN: 0-425-17146-9

BERKLEY®
Berkley Books are published by The Berkley Publishing Group,
a division of Penguin Putnam Inc., 375 Hudson Street,
New York, New York 10014.
BERKLEY and the ''B'' design
are trademarks belonging to Penguin Putnam Inc.

PRINTED IN THE UNITED STATES OF AMERICA

10 9 8 7 6 5 4 3 2 1

Contents

Introduction

"**I** guess I was born under a troublesome star," said actor Joel McCrea, playing the role of Wyatt Earp in the 1955 movie *Wichita*. His comment reflects an age-old belief held by millions of astrology followers: that stars, planets, constellations, signs of the zodiac, the moon, and the sun provide insights into and influence human destiny.

If astrologers can develop horoscopes that reveal correlations between heavenly bodies and the destinies of commoners and kings, leaders and followers, might they not also unlock the mysteries of criminal behavior by tracing the astrological influences in the lives of notorious killers? Studies have uncovered startling observations related to killers and their horoscopes. For example, an extraordinarily large number of serial killers were born under the signs of Gemini and Sagittarius. "Son of Sam" David Berkowitz, Jeffrey Dahmer, and Wayne Williams are Geminis, while Ted Bundy, Richard Speck, and Charles Starkweather are Sagittarians. Of course, this doesn't mean that everyone born under these signs is destined to become a homicidal maniac. It is necessary to calculate the exact time and place of birth for each person and then to examine the alignment of planets, the relationships between signs, and many other factors in the subjects' charts, before any possible explanations for criminal behavior can be considered.

And yet many remarkable conclusions surface in the horoscopes of killers. A proportionately large number of women who take lives are born under Aries, while Aries men who become murderers usually seek out women as their victims. Two notorious mass murderers, James Huberty and George Hennard, were born only four days apart in the sign of Libra. The 50 profiles and horoscopes of notorious killers contained in the text of this book illustrate other similar findings.

Astrology, the complex study and interpretation of how signs and planets influence human affairs, is the basis for horoscopes drawn by amateurs and experts throughout the world. Most people know the sign of the zodiac under which they were born. Nearly everyone has, at one time or another, glanced at the daily horoscopes carried by most major newspapers. More than a few readers marvel at the seemingly accurate application to their own lives, especially if it's encouraging news, which it usually is. But serious students scoff at these "forecasts," refusing to even call them horoscopes. Accurate astrology, they point out, must be based on specific individual data including precise birthplace, date, and time of birth within four minutes.

It is often surprising to discover how many different types of people read horoscopes. Astrologers serve clients in all walks of life: the famous and infamous, laborers, entertainers, business executives, service professionals, athletes, even political leaders. It was widely reported that President Ronald Reagan may have been guided in certain decisions by information his wife obtained from an astrologer.

From the beginning of human history, men and women have sought meaning and guidance for the conduct of their lives. Ancients studying the relationship of earth to the cycles of heavenly bodies discovered what appeared to be correlations between cosmic activity and social interaction. Gradually, astrologers learned to use data related to the position of planets, the sun, moon, and signs at the exact moment of an individual's birth. When this information is linked to the longitude and latitude of the place of birth, the combined data can be calculated into intricate patterns from which horoscopes for any person or event can be produced. The study has evolved into an intricate system through which an astrologer can identify and interpret the specific influences that affect an individual's life.

Most professional astrologers emphasize that horoscopes do not foretell the future or predict unavoidable events. Instead, the charts identify influences that may be used to guide one's life, to make decisions, to understand and cope with relationships, to select the optimum time for implementing plans, or to deal with one's own strengths and weaknesses. Horoscopes do not reveal any fatalistic or unpreventable future etched in stone. It is not a crystal ball. Instead, the science offers an understanding of factors that point to potential events, thus offering assistance in selecting a path to cope with these circumstances.

Critics of astrology point out that no scientific evidence exists to support the belief system. Perhaps not, argue astrologers, but by the same logic, there is little scientific evidence to support belief in any of the major religions. Absence of authenticated facts, events, or persons idealized in various theological entities certainly doesn't diminish the faith believers hold in those religious tenets, or in their deities. Shouldn't astrology be treated with the same open mind?

If the moon can pull our massive oceans into tidal patterns, couldn't it be possible that the same moon or other parts of our solar system could pull or push the behavioral patterns and cultural circumstances of these tiny inhabitants of earth called humans? A vast number of people seem to think so. Astrology predates some religions and is given prominent mention in the Bible. Arguably, faith in either one should not be rejected.

For readers who are new to the complexities of astrology, the next paragraphs offer a brief explanation of basic guidelines. For a more detailed lesson, refer to Appendix A at the back of the book.

The twelve signs of the zodiac begin with the spring equinox, approximately March 21, the time of new life and rebirth. The chapters in this book are divided by these twelve signs:

Signs of the Zodiac

Aries	(March 21–April 21)
Taurus	(April 22–May 20)
Gemini	(May 21–June 20)

Cancer	(June 21–July 22)
Leo	(July 23–August 22)
Virgo	(August 23–Sept 22)
Libra	(Sept 23–Oct 22)
Scorpio	(Oct 23–Nov 21)
Sagittarius	(Nov 22–Dec 21)
Capricorn	(Dec 22–Jan 19)
Aquarius	(Jan 20–Feb 18)
Pisces	(Feb 19–Mar 20)

Being born within any one these date ranges makes the person a "native" of that particular sign of the zodiac.

An astrological chart takes the form of a circle divided into twelve, pie-shaped slices called *houses*. Lines between the pie shapes are called *cusps*.

First, the position of the planets in the solar system at the time of a person's birth are identified. Then, the longitude and latitude of the person's birthplace are plotted into the astrological chart. The planets, for the purposes of astrology, include the Sun and Moon as well as Mercury, Venus, Mars, Jupiter, Saturn, Uranus, Neptune, and Pluto. The calculations not only discover which houses these planets influence, but also identify the location of these heavenly bodies in relationship to the twelve signs of the zodiac at the moment of the subject's birth or at the moment of other important events in the progressing life of the subject. As an example of the use of house characteristics, if the astrologer studies the chart and sees influential planets in the subject's eighth and twelfth houses, involving death, investigations, secrets, and prisons, the resulting interpretation might suggest a need to evaluate that information and look for ways to stay out of trouble. Of course, this is a very simplistic view. A professional astrological analysis will lend deeper, essential details.

Among the many influences a horoscope may disclose is the potential for criminal behavior, even murder. Following are profiles and horoscopes of 50 notorious killers revealing the astrological influences related to their lives and crimes. If these criminals were born under "troublesome stars," could more specific knowledge have been used to guide them away from their paths of violent, bloody murder? Might horoscopes have been helpful in counseling them prior to the killings and possibly averting the tragedies? Social scientists continually search for methods of crime prevention. Perhaps they should open their minds to the possibility of adding one more tool to their arsenal.

With a track record of nearly 50 centuries, astrology should not be arbitrarily discounted as a useful tool in analyzing the makeup of people who descend into the abysmal depths of murder. Thousands of homicide victims die each year in the United States. Any tool to help understand and prevent murder must be given a fair chance to work.

ZODIAC
OF DEATH

ARIES

Aries is an aggressive, combative sign ruled by Mars, the planet of violence, stabbing, shooting, and explosives. A disproportionately large number of women who become killers are born under Aries, while Aries men who turn to murder often seek out female victims. People born under Aries are endowed with physical energy and enthusiasm that can turn deadly when the planets are misaligned.

Kenneth Allen McDuff

Thursday, March 21, 1946, 1:30 P.M.
Rosebud, Texas • Time Zone: 06:00 (CST)
Longitude 096° W 59' • Latitude 31° N 04'
Placidus Houses • Tropical Zodiac

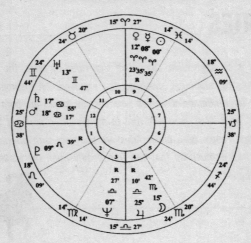

The dreadful fear felt by death penalty advocates—that killers released from prison will repeat their crimes—was proven valid by Kenneth McDuff, who turned the nightmare into reality. After being condemned to death for committing three heinous murders, McDuff dodged execution five times before Texas officials eventually *granted him parole!* And he killed again, torturing, raping, and strangling at least two women. Authorities suspected him of being responsible for several more deaths. His outrageous blood spree resulted in sharp changes to parole laws in the Lone Star State.

In his youth, McDuff earned a reputation as a schoolyard bully and scofflaw in Rosebud, Texas, south of Waco. A dropout after the ninth grade, the tall, muscular rowdy faced his first prison term in March 1965, having been convicted of multiple burglaries. A judge sentenced him to only nine months for crimes that probably should have earned him several years behind bars. This marked the first of many lucky breaks handed him by the jurisprudence system.

Upon release, McDuff resumed his hell-raising lifestyle. On August 6, 1966, he and an accomplice kidnapped 16-year-old Edna Louise Sullivan, along with her two male companions, age 17 and 15. In a rural pasture, McDuff used a pistol to savagely execute the boys as they lay in the car's trunk. The terrified girl, just slightly over 5 feet, 110 pounds, trembled in fear while both men sexually assaulted her. Finally, McDuff tortured and strangled her to death with a broken broomstick.

Soon afterward, the accomplice, suffering guilt and fear, confessed to Fort Worth sheriff's deputies. He named McDuff as the killer. Arrested, McDuff denied his involvement, blaming everything on his partner. In a trial for murdering Robert Brand, one of the boys, the jury heard McDuff's testimony but noticed that he rubbed his knuckles each time he disavowed his own culpability. They convicted him on November 15 and recommended execution in the electric chair. Prosecutors decided not to try McDuff for the other two murders. After all, how many times could the killer be electrocuted? The decision turned out to be a tragic one.

Prior to each of five scheduled execution dates, sometimes within hours, lawyers and judges managed to obtain stays. McDuff's extraordinary luck continued when the U.S. Supreme Court invalidated death penalty statutes across the country. Texas soon re-enacted the laws, but couldn't apply them retroactively, so McDuff received a new sentence of 20 years, with *eligibility for parole!*

Despite a long record of behavior problems in prison, McDuff came close, several times, to gaining enough parole board votes for release. In an attempt to improve his chances, he offered a bribe to a parole official. Caught in the felony, which could have extended his prison stay, he slipped away from punishment once again when officials chose not to take judicial action.

Apparently ignoring McDuff's negative attitude, and brushing off desperate pleas from police and prosecutors, parole officials granted the killer a release on October 11, 1989, to live in Temple, Texas, with his sister. Within three days, the strangled body of an alleged prostitute turned up on the outskirts of town. Exactly one year from his release date, McDuff landed in jail again, and could have been imprisoned for parole violation. But pressures from the federal government to reduce overcrowding in prison persuaded officials to give McDuff yet another chance. His incredible string of luck continued.

The fortunate ex-con enrolled in a Waco college, with the help of a government loan, and lived in a campus dormitory. Usually dressed in tight jeans, snap-button shirts, cowboy boots, and an ever-present cowboy hat, the 43-year-old "student" looked out of place. He spent most evenings in a dreary section of Waco populated by prostitutes and druggies. Arrested for drunk driving, McDuff admitted to his parole officer that he used booze and drugs, a clear violation of his conditional freedom. Nevertheless, he benefited from a generous decision not to revoke his parole.

Suspicion fell on McDuff when a pair of prostitutes vanished from the mean streets of his hangout area. Police observed his pickup truck speeding downtown with a female passenger apparently trying to kick out the windshield. But he escaped arrest.

In late December 1991, a young woman named Colleen Reed, 28, vanished from an Austin self-service car wash. Witnesses noticed two men cruising the area in a late-model beige Thunderbird, the exact model and color McDuff had recently purchased. Two months later, a convenience store clerk, Melissa Northrup, with whom McDuff had temporarily worked, was kidnapped from the store, not far from the dormitory where McDuff lived.

That same week, McDuff's mother, who had always protected him and denied that her son could kill anyone, filed a missing-person report on him. His beige T-bird had been abandoned at a motel near the convenience store. In February 1992, the strangled body of a prostitute was found buried in a shallow grave near his dormitory. She had last been seen at the dorm residence while McDuff still lived there. Then, in April, a fisherman, looking around a gravel pit stumbled upon the grisly, disemboweled remains of Melissa Northrup, the convenience store clerk.

McDuff's luck finally ran out in April 1992, when his cruising buddy, who'd been with him in Austin on the night Colleen Reed disappeared, spilled the beans, and linked McDuff to the woman's brutal rape and murder. He informed authorities that McDuff had told him his brand of desire for women was to "use them up."

With the help of some remarkable police work and the television show *America's Most Wanted*, a swarm of police detectives captured McDuff in early May outside Kansas City, Missouri, where he'd been working as a trash hauler. He faced two trials in 1993 and 1994, and heard judges hand down death penalties for the murders of Melissa Northrup and Colleen Reed, even though the latter's body was not found until well after the trial, in October 1998.

No one knows how many women McDuff slaughtered. As he waited for his date with the executioner, he was not a popular man in prison. Inmates who might have received early paroles served longer terms in prison as a result of laws changed due to McDuff's crimes.

On November 17, 1998, at age 52, Kenneth McDuff paid for his crimes. He was executed by lethal injection.

Horoscope for Kenneth Allen McDuff
Born March 21, 1946, 1:30 P.M. CST, Rosebud, Texas
Source: Birth certificate

Outrageous decisions by justice system officials, who repeatedly set Kenneth McDuff free to kill and kill again, are evident in his twelfth house of prisons as well as in his ninth house of courts and legal matters.

Astrological explanation for this remarkable failure by the system begins with two potent planets. Mercury, exerting an element of control over McDuff's twelfth house, is in opposition to Neptune, the planet of confusion. This negative aspect sets up the opportunity for McDuff to benefit from indiscriminate, illogical decisions made by parole officials and judges to release him even after he'd been sentenced to death. Another factor that contributed to his incredible luck with the courts is the influence of Jupiter on his ninth house of legalities. Jupiter bestows the most luck of any planet, and in McDuff's chart it occupies the sign of Libra. Libra represents fairness and justice, which was frequently capsized in McDuff's criminal career.

McDuff's ninth house, the strongest in his chart, contains three planets: Sun, Mercury, and Venus, all of which are found in Aries. Their relative configuration within this sign causes the personality characteristics they rule to take a negative turn. The Sun governs ego and sense of power, which became destructive facets of McDuff's personality. He compensated for low self-esteem by becoming a troublemaker, an Aries characteristic, inevitably placing him in legal jeopardy, a ninth-house matter. Mercury governs his thoughts and manner of speaking, which turned offensive and belligerent. Venus influences his impulses and desires, which evolved into lustful depravity. Typical negative characteristics of Aries include hostility, anger, and aggression. McDuff displayed all of these as a youth and continued to indulge in undisciplined, childish outbursts throughout his life.

In addition to being influenced by Mercury, McDuff's twelfth house comes into play once more with the residency of Saturn and Mars. Saturn amplifies his feelings of insecurity and inadequacy. Mars, the planet of war and savage behavior, infuses him with the potential for violence. Sexual deviation enters the picture due to the placement of Mars in relation to Venus, which signals McDuff's inclination to savagely use women for only one purpose: to satisfy his greedy lust, then to dispose of them. Also, his fifth house of sex is ruled by Pluto, the planet associated with kidnapping. Further substantiation of carnally perverse tendencies in McDuff are seen by his Moon, ruler of women, being in the sadistic sign of Scorpio. Such a configuration suggests that he would not hesitate to rape, then kill his female victims.

Regarding the placement of Saturn in McDuff's twelfth house, it is interesting to note that Saturn rules Capricorn. Attached to each sign is a slogan or phrase. Those who know Capricorns might feel goosebumps when they hear that McDuff often bragged that he liked to "use women up." Capricorn's slogan is, "I use."

In committing his final crime, McDuff elected to take along a pal. His seventh house of partners is ruled by Saturn, one of the planets dwelling in his twelfth house of self-destruction and prisons. McDuff's choice of partners certainly turned out to be destructive when his cohort informed police of his and McDuff's joint involvement in rape and murder. Saturn's ruinous impact within the twelfth house foreshadowed McDuff's destiny of confinement in prisons for long periods of time.

Ironically, McDuff's powerful ninth house contains influences that helped lead to his capture. In addition to ruling legal matters, the ninth house also governs the effect of television on one's life. The popular television show *America's Most Wanted* was an important element in terminating McDuff's life of violent crime. The ninth house, governing law, finally saw justice do the right thing by invoking the legal process of executing this savage killer.

George Walterfield Russell, Jr.

Wednesday, April 2, 1958, 12:50 A.M.
West Palm Beach, Florida • Time Zone: 05:00 (EST)
Longitude 080° W 03' 13" • Latitude 26° N 42' 54"
Placidus Houses • Tropical Zodiac

George Russell made maximum use of his near-genius intelligence, glib tongue, captivating personality, and good looks to repeatedly evade justice. Depite the fact that he was one of the few African Americans residing on Washington state's affluent Mercer Island, Russell easily mixed with everyone in the community. Surrounded by Lake Washington, which forms Seattle's eastern border, the island offers a haven from city evils. All through high school on Mercer, Russell attended parties in the lavish homes of his classmates, and made jokes about being the "token black." He bragged about his mother teaching in college, and his wealthy stepfather being a rich, well-known dentist. Russell also expressed interest in joining the ranks of law enforcement. He spent much of his spare time running errands for and chatting with local cops, becoming their de facto mascot.

No one suspected that the epidemic of home invasions by an elusive cat burglar on the island was none other than the popular, affable George Russell. His exploits continued for years, beginning in his high school days and continuing on into his thirties.

While Russell's peers attended college and moved into responsible professions, he seemed caught in a time warp, never maturing. Very much a Svengali, he attracted pubescent female teenagers, dazzling them with his vocabulary, elegance, generosity, and controlled sexuality. Using his knowledge of police procedures, and his acquaintance with many of the local officers, he impressed the immature girls by pretending to be a plainclothes agent, claiming that he worked undercover in narc raids with various law agencies.

Gradually, officers he knew began to suspect his activities. A string of arrests for minor offenses confirmed their fears. But no matter how many times cops nabbed Russell for misdemeanors or borderline felonies, he always came up with slick alibis. By talking fast and feigning regret, he was able to persuade judges to let him off with warnings or suspended sentences.

Russell's source of income mystified his circle of friends, who were unable to guess that he burglarized homes, sold drugs, and ran endless con games. When Russell's mother walked out of his life, leaving him with his dentist stepfather, who soon remarried, George escalated his night raids. Sometimes he entered homes for nothing more than the thrill of standing near sleeping residents. To him, it represented his superiority, his ability to win "the game."

Other nights, Russell could be seen gliding among the crowds on dance floors of restaurants and bars which catered to young crowds. Employing his personal magnetism, he could walk past long lines in front and avoid paying the cover charge. Inside, he would hold court at his reserved table near the disc jockey. Patrons assumed Russell held some special status or was a manager. Impressionable dance partners fell in love with him, and he moved in with one for several months. She didn't know that he had already impregnated a teenager, who had an abortion. And she recoiled in astonishment when Russell turned cold and began abusing her. Sometimes he would deliberately break her possessions, or flatten her tires in revenge for some imagined slight. She would always know he had done it when she found his "signature." Russell would leave a Snickers candy bar at the scene, a statement of his snickering contempt for his victim. It became apparent to the disillusioned paramour that George Russell actually hated women.

A barmaid in Russell's favorite hangout didn't fall for the

sleazy, oily VIP role in which he reveled, and felt appalled at his manipulation of women. She verbalized her hatred for Russell, warned female customers, and convinced the manager of the night spot to permanently eighty-six him. He confronted her with boiling fury and threatened to kill her. No one paid attention. They just assumed that good old George was venting his hurt feelings. Anyway, he wouldn't be able to carry out his threats because the woman he despised moved out of the state.

With his lifestyle of keeping no permanent residence, Russell needed few possessions, and he carried all of them in a blue sports bag. That made it easy to crash on the couch or floor at various friends' homes until his welcome wore out. Hanging out at his favorite coffee shop, he met four gullible teen girls, just out of high school, who had rented an apartment for the summer. It didn't take long for George to become a surrogate big brother to them, move in, and eventually share a bed with one.

By 1990, Russell had been arrested 24 times, but served only short sentences. None of his intimates even guessed at the rage festering inside him. Certainly, no one connected him to the shocking discovery on June 23 of a nude female body lying near a trash compactor adjacent to the club where the barmaid he hated had worked. Mary Ann Polreich, in her early twenties, had been strangled, savagely beaten, and violated by a foreign object in the anus and vagina, *after death!* Her killer had gone to the trouble of posing her body face up with one hand clasped over the other on her chest, as if she were lying in a coffin.

George Russell, always chummy with the police, even offered tips and suggestions during the intense, prolonged investigation.

Seven weeks later, a 13-year-old girl discovered the body of her mother, Mary Ann Beethe, 36, grotesquely posed in bed, wearing nothing but red high heels, her face wrapped in clear plastic, her knees raised and spread apart. The victim had been battered and bludgeoned to death. The killer had left a shotgun inserted in her vagina, and the unspeakable act had been performed postmortem. Investigators labeled the death scene "pure evil." They would find that Beethe had been a habitué of the same nightclubs as Russell, and was a close friend of the barmaid George had threatened.

On the last day of August 1992, the landlord of Andrea "Randi" Levine, 24, found her nude body in her apartment, spread-eagled, arms clutching a book titled *More Joy of Sex,* and a plastic sex toy jammed into her mouth. From her head to her toes, 231 shallow stab wounds shredded Levine's skin. Her death had been caused by a blow to the head with a blunt object. The victim had also been a frequent patron of the nightclubs where George Russell played his games, and witnesses later revealed that he'd visited her at home several times. She'd previously been victimized by a mysterious cat burglar.

At first, none of the murders seemed to be connected, but exhaustive investigation finally linked them. In September, a young woman found herself accidentally locked out of an apartment late at night, in the same complex where George Russell lived with the four teenage girls. A black man offered to help her, then brutally fractured her skull with a stone. She survived.

Long hours of investigation finally led to George Russell. He tried to use the same tired, unctuous tactics to dance away from the growing evidence, but he'd burned too many of the police officers too many times over the years.

Found guilty of all three murders, Russell received a sentence of life in prison without the possibility of parole. In the annals of crime, Russell is considered an anomaly in his selection of victims. Most serial killers seek out strangers of their own race, but Russell had previously met all three of the white women he killed. Typical of sociopaths, or antisocial personality disordered criminals, he never demonstrated remorse, and still speaks not of his innocence, but of the paucity of evidence used to convict him. The cold stone enclosure of Walla Walla State Prison in southeast Washington will be George Russell's home for a long, long time.

Horoscope for George Walterfield Russell, Jr.
Born April 2, 1958, 12:50 A.M. EST, West Palm Beach, Florida
Source: Charmer, *by Jack Olsen*

In many professions, personality makes the difference between success and failure. George Russell used personality to succeed in crime. On the surface, he appeared to be affable and outgoing, with open, optimistic charisma. His persona was "life of the party." These characteristics can be traced to the influence of Russell's Sun and Mercury in Aries. The Sun governs his ego while Mercury shapes his thinking and manner of speaking. Since Aries is a fiery, active and energetic sign, both his speech and the way he presented himself to others would reflect these qualities. Russell's ascendant, Sagittarius, governs his personality and temperament through rulership of his first house. Sagittarius is the most optimistic and friendly sign of the zodiac. Finally, Jupiter, the ruler of Sagittarius, is found living it up in Russell's tenth house. As the tenth house represents the public perception of him, Russell seems to be overflowing with humor and good will, bringing nothing but fun and games to his friends. But underneath all this joviality lies a very different story of dark, brooding bloodlust.

The cold and calculating planet Saturn occupies Russell's first house of personality. This alignment colors his behavior with patience and cunning. He used these traits during his furtive night visits to explore potential victims' homes and apartments. Since Saturn is the most materialistic of the planets, and influences Russell's second house of money, it is to be expected that he began his criminal career with clandestine burglaries.

The murders of women, which came later in his life, are foreshadowed by Russell's Mars opposing Uranus. This most negative aspect, heated by the violence of Mars, indicates the stabbings and beatings he inflicted on his victims, brought on by the pressure of Uranus occupying Russell's eighth house of death. Mars is nestled in Aquarius, the Uranian-ruled sign that bestowed on Russell the hidden traits of icy detachment.

The other occupant of Russell's house of death is Pluto. In mythology, Pluto is the god of the underworld. In astrology, this planet represents obsession/compulsion, which describes the addicting fascination with death that gripped Russell. Pluto sits in opposition to Venus, creating the worst possible aspect. As Russell's Venus rules the fifth house of sex, his perceptions of sex and death are intrinsically linked. All of the murders he committed were sexually oriented. Russell's bizarre habit of lasciviously displaying his victim's bodies after death relates to Uranus, the planet of quirkiness and eccentricity. It also points to the exhibitionist grandstanding of Leo's influence over his eighth house.

All of Russell's victims were women. The Moon, ruler of women, makes a square aspect to Russell's Sagittarius ascendant. This negative configuration explains the difficulties he had in relating to women on anything more than a superficial basis. It might account for his ability to impress young girls, overwhelming them with his flamboyant personality. His repeated lies about his background and associations with affluent people, and his attempts to enhance his own self-esteem are negative characteristics of Sagittarians. This pattern is significant since the Moon, with its profound involvement of women, governs his eighth house of death. The Moon is in Virgo, one of the signatures of serial killers. Coinciding with this placement, another signature of serial murder is Sagittarius, Russell's ascendant.

For years, Russell evaded being punished for his crimes by utilizing a remarkable glibness. The fast-talking, slick alibis Russell used when questioned by police and judges are portended by his Moon in Virgo. Virgo is a Mercury-ruled sign, and as such relates to communication.

The tenth house, representing Russell's reputation, is the strongest one in his chart and is occupied by two planets, Jupiter and Neptune, while being governed by Libra. Jupiter's presence shows Russell's desire to be important and influential in the community. Neptune's influence provided him with the skills of a con man. Lies and deception are Neptunian traits illustrated in Russell's outrageous exaggerations regarding his accomplishments and status. Libra, the ruler of his midheaven, is a fun-loving and affectionate sign. Russell adopted these qualities to enhance his popularity. But the superficial facade soon gave way to expose the real George Russell, a homicidal sexual predator.

The twelfth house, which governs prisons, is ruled by Jupiter, which aided Russell by providing protection and good luck. As a result of its influence, Russell escaped the death penalty, and was sentenced to prison for the remainder of his life. With his Jupiter in the sign of Libra, his punishment was astrologically appropriate. Libra represents the scales of justice.

Judias Buenoano (a.k.a. Judy Goodyear)

Sunday, April 4, 1943, 7:10 P.M.
Quanah, Texas • Time Zone: 05:00 (Central War Time)
Longitude 099° W 45' • Latitude 34° N 18'
Placidus Houses • Tropical Zodiac

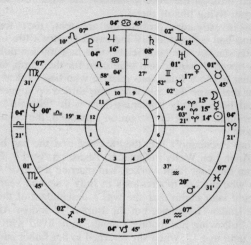

Dubbed the "Black Widow" by news media, Judy Buenoano sat on death row for over thirteen years, convicted of killing her Vietnam veteran husband, Air Force sergeant James Goodyear. He died at age 37 in 1971, as a result of being systematically poisoned with arsenic. Seven years later, Judy legally changed her surname, and the names of her two sons and daughter, to Buenoano, the Spanish translation of Goodyear. Apache Indians spoke Spanish, and she frequently mentioned being a descendant of that tribe.

Buenoano may never have been brought to justice if her boyfriend hadn't survived an attempt to murder him. In June 1983, he drove to a restaurant to join Judy, 40, in a party for employees of her beauty salon, called Judi's Fingers and Faces, in Pensacola, Florida. After the meal, she told him she would like to stay with the girls a little longer. Judy instructed her lover, John Gentry, 37, to leave and meet her later at her upscale home. First, though, she slipped a package of marijuana into his coat pocket, whispering that it was for her teenage son. Ever obedient, Gentry left, walked the block to a lot where Judy had persuaded him to park, started his car, and switched the lights on. The explosion would have killed him if most of the lethal force hadn't been expended through the Ford's sunroof. He sustained serious injuries from flying bits of metal.

When investigators probed the incident, they found that Buenoano had surreptitiously increased Gentry's life insurance, for which she was the beneficiary, to a half million dollars. Detectives traced dynamite and wire used for the bomb, and found a trail that led to a Buenoano relative who had worked on Gentry's car that same day. Evidence also turned up suggesting that Judy had been slowly poisoning him with "vitamin" pills she urged on him. As the investigation expanded, the sleuths found even more.

Tracing Buenoano's life, they learned that she had been born Judias Anna Lou Welty in Quanah, Texas, on April 4, 1943. Her father, an itinerant farm worker, had married a Native American woman who died of tuberculosis in Judy's second year. Buenoano would later claim that she was a descendant of the famous Apache leader Geronimo, but the Bureau of Indian Affairs denied it. Following her mother's death, Judy lived with a grandmother until age 12, when she returned to her father and his new wife, who lived in Roswell, New Mexico. Buenoano, whose veracity would often be challenged, said that her father and stepmother abused her, and she fought back one day using a skillet as a weapon. Arrested and detained for two months, Judy refused to go back to her home and spent the next two years in an Albuquerque educational detention center, where she earned a high school diploma in 1959.

Two years later, Judy bore an illegitimate son she named Michael. In 1962, she married James A. Goodyear, an Air Force sergeant stationed in Roswell, and he legally adopted her little boy. He also fathered another son and a daughter. After the family moved to Orlando, Florida, in 1967, the military sent Sgt. Goodyear to serve a hitch in Vietnam. He survived combat, but three months after his return home, Sgt. Goodyear fell ill with an unexplained body-wracking malady. Vomiting, aching in nauseous pain, suffering delusions, and rapidly losing weight, he was hospitalized in critical condition in September 1971 and died three days later. The widow soon collected insurance and benefits worth more than $100,000. She used part of the money to buy a home in Pensacola.

Single again, Judy met and became involved with Bobby Joe Morris, 35, a husky Pensacola swimming pool construction contractor. They lived together until he moved to Trinidad, Colorado. Shortly afterward, Judy's Florida home inexplicably burned, she collected $90,000 in fire insurance and immediately followed Morris to Colorado. Once again living with Morris, without marrying him, she assumed the use of his last name. The following January, he experienced a drastic health change, reeling with attacks of nausea, convulsions, weight loss, and diarrhea. Doctors couldn't isolate the cause. Judy, working as a nurse in the hospital, lovingly tended to him, often bringing tropical fruit juice and holding his head up so he could drink it all. Morris died on January 28, 1978, while medical experts scratched their heads, saying the cause of death remained "obscure."

Buenoano wanted to have the body cremated, but Morris's family insisted on conventional burial. The "widow" collected about $30,000 from life insurance companies and moved her brood back to Florida to an even nicer home in Gulf Breeze, near Pensacola.

Buenoano's first son, Michael, joined the Army in 1979, but was discharged after a few months. Living again with his mother and two siblings, he fell sick in November, lost over 40 pounds, and suffered paralysis of all four limbs. Admitted to Walter Reed Hospital in January 1980, he was treated for a number of conditions, but no diagnosis was ever pinned down. One doctor suggested the possibility of toxicity from lead poisoning, but couldn't be certain. Transferred to the Veterans Administration hospital in Orlando, Michael was released to the care of his mother. The very next day, while riding in a canoe with Judy and her younger son, an "accident" occurred in which 19-year-old Michael, weighed down with leg and arm braces, drowned. Judy Buenoano produced three insurance policies that paid a total of nearly $100,000.

The parking lot explosion that nearly killed John Gentry spurred detectives into an intensive probe of Buenoano's background. When they discovered the long list of mysterious illnesses suffered by men in her life, and three deaths, they arranged for the bodies to be exhumed. Pathologists found enough arsenic in the remains of Bobby Joe Morris to kill eleven

men. James Goodyear's internal organs had been also been ravaged by arsenic.

Buenoano faced juries in three different trials. She had told
inconsistent stories about the drowning of her son, and signatures
on the insurance policies had been forged. The prosecution presented a bundle of circumstantial evidence in March 1984, which
resulted in a conviction for first-degree murder. The jury had
mercy on her, though, and recommended a sentence of life without parole for 25 years.

The trial for attempted murder in the car bombing of John
Gentry earned her another twelve years tacked on to the life
sentence. But jurors felt that the evidence against the relative
who had worked on Gentry's car was insufficient to prove he'd
installed the bomb, so they found him not guilty.

In 1985, Judy Buenoano heard a third jury convict her of killing her husband, James Goodyear, and a judge condemn her to
die for it.

After appealing the death sentence for over thirteen years, Judias Buenoano, now frail at 54 and without the glamorous
makeup she'd always used, nervously grimaced while guards
strapped her in the three-legged oak chair called "Old Sparky."
On the last day of March 1998, which would have been her late
son's 37th birthday, she became the first woman to be executed
in Florida in 150 years.

Horoscope for Judias Buenoano (a.k.a. Judy Goodyear)
Born April 4, 1943, 7:10 P.M. Central War Time, Quanah, Texas
Source: Birth certificate

The astrological explanations for Judy Buenoano's extraordinary
life and crimes virtually leap off the page. Aries, her natal Sun
sign, represents a fiercely competitive and assertive nature. Aries
is crowded with three powerfully influential planets: the Sun,
Mercury, and the Moon. Their arrangement in her seventh house
of marriage and romantic partners flashes a red light of pending
disaster for the lovemates of this imperious and lethal woman.

First, the Sun accounts for Buenoano's colossal ego, her urge
to dominate her mates, and her need to exercise powerful authority. Adjacent to the Sun, Mercury endows her with persuasive ability, a sharp tongue, and a restless irritability. Finally, the

Moon lends turbulence to her emotions. Making matters worse, an opposition between the Sun and Neptune, the most negative aspect, indicates a festering alienation between her desires and those of her husband or partner.

The doomed husband and the boyfriend succumbed to Buenoano's use of arsenic. Poison is an affiliation of Neptune, which is found lurking in her twelfth house of secrets.

Buenoano attempted to kill another lover with dynamite. Explosives are governed by Mars, which is negatively aligned with Venus in her eighth house of death. This ominous alignment planted the seed for Buenoano's plan to kill a loved one for money. Violent Mars rules Scorpio, the sign of greed, and dominates Buenoano's second house of money. Greed plus money, mixed with violence, added up to death. The "Black Widow" could see no reason why she shouldn't blow up her lovemate in order to satisfy her lust for insurance payoffs.

Venus and Uranus occupy significant positions in Buenoano's eighth house, revealing a serious preoccupation with financial gain through lethal means. Venus, the planet of love, is found in her sign of Taurus. Since Taurus is associated with money and material possessions, this configuration increases her deep affection for riches. Uranus signals eccentricity. Buenoano's attitude toward death and money are quirky indeed, as exemplified by her peculiar choice to kill her paralyzed son by drowning him. Uranus not only occupies her eighth house of death, but also influences her fifth house of children, so it follows that she would have no compunction about murdering her own child if it would result in profit for her. One more effect of Uranus, a positive one for Buenoano, comes from that planet's favorable alignment with her ascendant, Libra. The result is Buenoano's good fortune in repeatedly collecting on insurance policies, and in escaping justice for years.

Buenoano's midheaven sign, Cancer, involves obtaining a desirable home (as purchasing jewelry is to Taurus and acquiring automobiles is to Mars). Thus, each time she received her ill-gotten monetary gains, Buenoano bought a newer and grander house to impress acquaintances. The midheaven indicates her standing in the community.

Another insurance scam worked by Buenoano involved arson. She torched one of her Florida homes, and was successful in defrauding the insurance company. Arson is a crime associated with Mars and Aries.

Buenoano's careening ride along a path of murder finally came to a screeching halt when she was convicted and sent to prison. Appropriately, Neptune, the planet ruling poison, is found in the twelfth house of prison. Poison had played a major part in her destiny; it was her tool in murder, and the thing that led her to death row. But her own death came by a far different method.

Uranus, in its alignment with her ascendant, had provided a certain amount of good luck. But that eccentric, unpredictable planet also rules electricity, and reigns powerfully over her eighth house of death. Judy Buenoano was executed by electrocution.

Herbert Mullen

Friday, April 18, 1947, 6:06 A.M.
Salinas, California • Time Zone: 08:00 (PST)
Longitude 121° W 39' 16" • Latitude 36° N 40' 40"
Placidus Houses • Tropical Zodiac

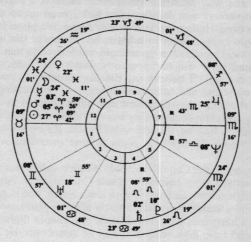

"**I** want you to kill somebody," a demonic voice shrieked at Herb Mullen on October 12, 1972. The diabolic words came to him at his parents' home in Santa Cruz, California. In Mullen's mind, the voice sounded like his father. No one knows whether the ghoulish demand might have been seeded by something Mullen read in a newspaper, since another serial killer, Edmund Kemper III, had recently claimed three of his eventual eight victims in the hills around Santa Cruz. Not to be outdone, Mullen would take the lives of thirteen men, women, and children.

Born on the 41st anniversary of the region's most cataclysmic event ever, the 1906 San Francisco earthquake and fire, Mullen was mentally troubled by the connection. It grew to extreme importance in his mind when newspapers carried a self-styled forecaster's prediction that an even greater quake would crumble the Bay Area on January 4, 1973.

Mullen firmly believed that "the Great Creator" might be persuaded not to inflict the earthquake, if he, Mullen, would offer a few lives in sacrifice. "We human beings," he said, "have found murder decreases the number of natural disasters and the extent of the devastation of these disasters: therefore, we will always murder."

How and why Mullen formed these ideas is a mystery. His Catholic parents sent him to parochial school up to the tenth grade. Young Herbert became a Boy Scout and played baseball on a Little League team with his father as coach. His home life seemed ideal, centered in an upscale neighborhood that included a lake and park. But he apparently didn't see it that way. He would later say, "I believe my parents consciously intended to retard my social and sexual awareness. . . ." Expanding on this imagined cruelty, he speculated that other children avoided socializing with him because they worried about dire consequences. According to Mullen, the kids would think, *If I help him to enjoy life a little bit, his father is going to have me killed in my next life.*

Unhappy in the Catholic schools, Mullen celebrated when his family moved from Salinas to Santa Cruz in 1963. Attending a public high school, he bonded with other males, one in particular, and found a steady girlfriend. Shortly after he graduated in 1965, Mullen's happiness plummeted like a bird shot in flight when his best friend from high school died in an auto crash. He mourned all summer.

Struggling with recovery, Mullen attended a community college, then transferred to San Jose State. In 1967, he convinced his high school steady to marry him. After she agreed, doubts assailed her due to his drug use, his violent outbursts, and his choice to avoid military service as a conscience objector. The engagement ended.

By 1969, Mullen had decided he wanted to study Asian religion by traveling to India. This didn't disturb his parents, but something else bothered them profoundly. Mullen had developed a habit of obsessively imitating every move made by his brother-in-law and parroting his every word. A psychiatric examination diagnosed the odd behavior as *echopraxia* (imitating movements) and *echolalia* (parroting words), both being symptoms of schizophrenia. Mullen voluntarily entered a hospital for treatment that lasted six weeks. Uncooperative and resistant, he checked himself out.

During that summer of 1969, Mullen drifted aimlessly, behaving in a bizarre manner, his large dark eyes blazing with inner fires. He told anyone who would listen that strange voices ordered him to do odd things, such as shaving off his bush of black hair, burning his genitals, or making homosexual advances to an acquaintance. He obediently complied with the demands. On Halloween day, he was again committed to a psychiatric hospital, where he received antipsychotic drugs. Doctors reluctantly discharged him four weeks later with little optimism for any improvement. The next summer, in Hawaii, Mullen's bizarre fantasies of death and symptoms of schizophrenia led to another mental hospital stay. His parents paid for Mullen's return to Santa Cruz, where police arrested him a few days later for what appeared to be drug-influenced behavior. A judge once again sent him to a mental ward, where he stayed a short time.

The next two years of Mullen's checkered life saw him working part-time menial jobs while drifting aimlessly in San Francisco. In September 1972, broke and homeless, he returned to his parents, who were distressed by his disjointed verbal expressions. When he physically assaulted his father, they considered long-term hospitalization, but California had drastically reduced the availability of such facilities. Mullen's delusions grew more fragmented and the voices plagued him constantly, demanding death.

On October 13, 1972, while driving his old '58 Chevy through the Santa Cruz mountains, Mullen spotted an elderly man walking by the roadside. After braking to a halt, and asking a few questions, Mullen clubbed the derelict to death with a baseball bat and left the body barely concealed. Before October ended, he picked up a hitchhiking student, just as Edmund Kemper was doing during the same time period. Mullen plunged a knife into her body twice and hid the corpse in a canyon.

In early November, Mullen visited St. Mary's Church in Los Gatos, a short drive north of Santa Cruz, and sat at the confessional. No one knows what he said to Father Henri Tomei, but everyone in the region learned what he did next. Mullen violently stabbed the priest to death.

With the date of a forecasted earthquake looming closer, Mullen's mind grew more frenzied. He needed more victims to forestall the disaster, and images of an old high school drug-dealing acquaintance, John Gianera, floated in his turmoiled mind. Mullen drove to the hills and knocked on the door of a cabin, but a woman inside told him Gianera had moved. He located Gianera and used a newly acquired pistol to execute the dealer and his wife. Then Mullen returned to the cabin and took the lives of the woman and her two children. He knew he had acted wisely, because the victims' voices entered his fevered mind and told him so.

The predicted earthquake didn't happen, so Mullen figured the sacrifices he'd offered had worked, and more killings would prevent other disasters. In late January, while hiking in the woods, he barged into a camping tent, confronted four teenage boys, and ordered them to leave. When they tried to talk to him, he opened fire, killing all four. In February, still driven by telepathic messages, Mullen pulled his Chevy station wagon over near an elderly man working in his yard and shot him to death. Finally, a witness who had seen Mullen commit murder called the police with a description of the car. He was apprehended a few minutes later.

Slugs recovered from several of Mullen's victims matched his gun, so Mullen went to trial in July 1973. His lawyer, who also defended Edmund Kemper, told jurors that Mullen was insane, and therefore not responsible for his acts. The jury, after listening to extensive psychiatric testimony, disagreed and found the defendant guilty of eight second-degree murders and guilty of two first-degree murders in the deaths of James Gianera and his wife. The judge sent him to prison for life.

Horoscope for Herbert Mullen
Born April 18, 1947, 6:06 A.M. PST, Salinas, California
Source: Birth certificate

Herbert Mullen's chart brings to mind a pressure cooker ready to explode. Four planets—Mercury, the Moon, the Sun, and Mars—are bottled up in his twelfth house, which governs secret activities and resentment, as well as places of confinement and restriction. Adding to this potential eruption, three of these planets are found in Aries, the sign of aggression and hostility. As Aries natives crave freedom and independence, the twelfth house of confinement is the worst possible place for them. The stress created in Mullen's psyche by these crowded, conflicting pressures partially accounts for the inner voices that drove him to murderous binges.

Examination of the influences exerted by this trio of planets in Aries makes it apparent that Herbert Mullen's destiny seemed dismal. Mercury, governing mental processes, strongly contributes to his mental derangement. And, by sitting in opposition to Neptune, Mercury creates the worst possible aspect for mental stability. The hallucinations Mullen experienced are also a function of Neptune, which clouds thinking and impedes rational thought.

The effect of the Sun's placement in his twelfth house eroded Mullen's self-confidence, making him even more vulnerable to the other influences.

Mars, laden with violence, lit the fuse leading to Mullen's behavioral explosion that ended thirteen innocent lives. This planet of war and physical force occupies a place in opposition to Neptune, creating another extremely dangerous aspect in Mullen's chart. Considering the Mars/Neptune opposition, it is not at all surprising that Mullen's inner voices ordered him to kill. Mars governs shooting as well as stabbing, and Mullen did both to various victims while on his rampages. Neptune rules drugs, and it can be seen that Mullen's mental deterioration was accelerated by his abuse of narcotics.

The Moon's presence in the twelfth house, instead of helping the situation, adds to the problem by being situated in the hypersensitive sign of Pisces. Emotions, the province of the Moon, are tossed about on the rough seas of Pisces sensitivity, so Mullen's range of feelings experienced extreme turbulence. His fourth house, in which matters of the father are found, is also governed by the Moon, ruler of the subconscious mind, explaining why the demonic voices plaguing Mullen sounded to him like the voice of his father.

Saturn is the most powerful planet in his chart. Unfortunately, Saturn represents depression and fear. Mullen's irrational phobias relating to pending earthquakes or other natural disasters is a function of Saturn's presence in his fourth house of home and father. This alignment also contributes to his feeling of being tightly controlled. Mullen complained about his parents' intent to retard his social and sexual awareness. His subordination to his father, combined with fear, also caused the demonic voice to sound like his father. The combination of a powerful, afflicted twelfth house and a dominant Saturn means that frustration would be paramount in his life. Mullen would be unable to free himself from his own bondage.

The first house, representing Mullen's personality, temperament, and disposition, is ruled by Taurus, his ascendant. A Taurus personality under stress is stubborn and unyielding. Adding to this inflexible attitude is the square aspect the ascendant makes to Pluto, the planet ruling obsession. A square aspect indicates an obstacle that is difficult to overcome. Mullen's solidly fixed and obsessive/compulsive personality is aggravated by this negative Plutonian influence. His resistance to accepting help during his confinement in a psychiatric hospital, and refusal to change, is shown by his first-house configurations.

This most melancholy picture comes full circle after the commission of his murders. Mullen's anger and hostility represented by his Mars/Aries combination, bursting out of confinement, resulted in the murder of thirteen victims. He ended up in prison for life. Prison is a twelfth-house concern, where, if he were treated for his mental illness, he might be able to cope. If not, all his energy could simmer into another eruption, causing perhaps as much harm to himself as to others.

TAURUS

People born under Taurus tend to be stubborn and inflexible. Two well-known dictators—Adolf Hitler, born on April 20, 1889, and Saddam Hussein, born on April 28, 1937—are both natives of Taurus, with only eight days separating their birthdays. It therefore comes as no surprise that Hussein has openly expressed his admiration of Hitler. Remarkably, two other Taurus natives, suicide cult leaders the Reverend Jim Jones and Marshall Applewhite, were born within four days of each other in 1931—Jones on May 13 and Applewhite on May 17.

Timothy McVeigh

Tuesday, April 23, 1968, 8:30 A.M.
Lockport, New York • Time Zone: 05:00 (EST)
Longitude 078° W 41' 26" • Latitude 43° N 10' 14"
Placidus Houses • Tropical Zodiac

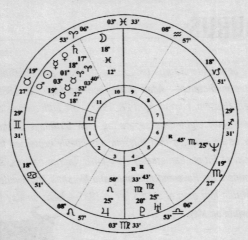

Not until April 19, 1995, did most Americans seriously consider the possibility that a citizen of the United States would ever commit a violent act of terrorism on American soil, cold-bloodedly massacring scores of innocent people in the name of an abstract political cause. Timothy McVeigh changed all that when he parked a Ryder rental truck crammed with 4,000 pounds of fuel oil and fertilizer explosives adjacent to the Alfred P. Murrah Federal Building in Oklahoma City. He activated a fuse, then sped away in a battered old Mercury. Minutes later, at 9:02 A.M., a massive earth-rattling explosion disintegrated the building's front half, ripping out a vast crescent-shaped section. Nine stories of glass, steel, and concrete plunged downward, compressing everything and everyone in its path. On the other side of Fifth Street, and within a block's radius, windows shattered and walls crumbled. Cars parked at the curb were tossed around like toys. From as far away as 50 miles, people felt shock waves.

Of the 168 victims who perished that day, 19 were small children. A photograph of a fireman holding the limp body of a child touched hearts across the nation. More than 500 additional people sustained injuries, many of which left permanent damage.

News media across the nation blared the stunning story all day and into the following weeks. Americans gathered around television sets and wondered what kind of a maniacal monster could have sacrificed so many lives. Had some foreign power finally infiltrated the United States?

The national attention would soon swing from suspicions about a Third World terrorist and look homeward. Shortly before the sun reached its zenith on the morning of April 19, an Oklahoma highway patrolman signaled Timothy McVeigh to pull over on Interstate 35, several miles from the site of the bombing. The 1977 Mercury Marquis driven by McVeigh had no license plate.

Trying to talk his way out of a ticket, McVeigh explained he was driving from another state, and maybe the plate had fallen off. But when the officer noticed that McVeigh had a gun with him, he arrested the crestfallen driver.

Meanwhile, in the lethal carnage of the Murrah building, while the search for bodies continued, investigators located the Ryder truck's vehicle identification number. Tracing it back to the agency, they obtained a description of a man who had rented the truck. Using a composite drawing, the FBI connected it to Timothy McVeigh, who was in Noble County Jail in Perry, Oklahoma. When television cameras focused on McVeigh, wearing an orange jumpsuit, being led out of the small town jail to be charged with the bombing, a wave of relief swept the nation.

Born in Pendleton, New York, Timothy McVeigh was reportedly a happy, good-natured child. His father had proudly used a video camera to record such events as little Tim climbing onto the lap of Santa Claus, playing with his toys, or pretending to drive a tractor. In his early childhood, McVeigh lived with his parents and two sisters in upstate New York. But when he reached age 15, his parents divorced and his sisters moved to Florida with their mother. The boy and his father remained in New York, where McVeigh quietly withdrew into himself. If he had any interest in the opposite sex, he concealed it. With intelligence well above average, he earned a scholarship to college. But after a short period of attending a community college, McVeigh dropped out.

A newfound interest occupied most of his time. McVeigh

learned the techniques of survival in the wilderness and concentrated on knowing everything possible about firearms, almost to the point of obsession. His father would one day tell a television reporter that Timothy seemed to be preparing for a nuclear holocaust. Increasingly, while earning his living by flipping burgers at a fast-food joint, and later as a security guard, the younger McVeigh spoke to his small circle of friends about harsh injustices perpetrated by the government.

Considering his mistrust of the government, acquaintances were surprised when McVeigh joined the Army at age 20, along with a few close buddies. The comrades were assigned to the same basic training unit, which tightened the bond among them. Military service gave McVeigh the opportunity to sharpen his weaponry skills and hone his survival interests. While serving at Fort Riley, Kansas, McVeigh met another soldier thirteen years his senior, who would eventually be convicted of involvement in the Oklahoma City bombing.

Adapting quickly to Army procedures, McVeigh earned a rapid promotion to sergeant. Operation Desert Storm took him to the Mideast during the Gulf War. As an armored vehicle gunner he earned a Bronze Star. McVeigh began to consider making the Army into a career, but when he volunteered for special training to become a Green Beret, he failed to make the grade. Other soldiers saw his extreme disappointment, and later speculated that McVeigh's life turned downward at that point.

Disillusioned, McVeigh left the Army and drifted without purpose, growing even more resistant to what he regarded as government oppression. "We have no proverbial tea to dump," he wrote to a New York newspaper. "Is civil war imminent? Do we have to shed blood to reform the system?" Reunited with ex-Army pals, McVeigh became radical in his gun-freedom activism, speaking fervently against laws designed to limit the availability of certain weapons. At the same time McVeigh was reaching his flash point, a deadly incident in Texas galvanized various dissident groups into anti-government action. A Waco sect calling themselves Branch Davidians held out against an FBI siege in 1993 until a disastrous fire killed 76 of them, including their leader, David Koresh.

The tragedy electrified Timothy McVeigh. From then on, he spoke of little else. One of his sisters revealed that in early 1995 he said, "There's going to be a revolution. . . . I know I'm going to be ready. . . . You'll see in either April or May something big is going to happen."

In his trial, two years after the Oklahoma City bombing, McVeigh did not take the stand. Prosecutors called witnesses who testified that McVeigh had revealed his plans to destroy the government building. The Ryder agent pointed to McVeigh as the man who had rented the truck. Other evidence linked McVeigh to the bomb ingredients. When the jury found him guilty as charged in eleven counts of murder and conspiracy, relatives of the victims wept in relief.

At the final hearing, McVeigh finally spoke, but only to cryptically quote a Supreme Court justice who had said, "Our government is the hope, the omnipotent teacher. For good or for ill it teaches the whole people by its example."

McVeigh's puzzling words did not serve to sway the federal judge. He issued the sentence, saying, "It is the judgment of the court that the defendant, Timothy James McVeigh, is sentenced to death on each of the eleven counts of the indictment."

McVeigh settled into a federal prison cell on death row. Where the Murrah Federal Building once stood, photos, flowers, stuffed toys, and other mementos of 168 victims decorated the fence around the knoll. Thousands of visitors filed by each month in reverent silence. In December 1998, work started at the site to build a permanent memorial.

Horoscope for Timothy McVeigh
Born April 23, 1968, 8:30 A.M. EST, Lockport, New York
Source: The All American Monster, *by Brandon M. Stickney, p.44*

What drove Timothy McVeigh to commit the heartbreaking terrorist act that took 168 lives? Experts in criminal behavior have produced few answers. But astrological analysis points an accusing finger at the overwhelming influence of McVeigh's friends and acquaintances.

By far the most revealing section of Timothy McVeigh's chart is his eleventh house of friends and social interaction. It is crammed with five planets, revealing that the people who surrounded him prior to the bombing influenced almost every facet of his life.

The five planets, in order of importance, are (1) Saturn, structure and organization; (2) Venus, comradeship; (3) Mercury, thinking, talking, and communicating; (4) the Sun, ego and the male sex, and (5) Mars, aggression, initiative, and interest in explosives. Although all five are weak, due to their relative positioning within the solar system, this weakness becomes important because it transposes the characteristics associated with each planet. For example, the Sun represents ability to lead, so a *strong* Sun would suggest a powerful leader, while a *weak* Sun conversely implies poor leadership ability. In McVeigh's case, it is probable that his friends, all male, would be the leaders, and McVeigh the follower. Their suggestions or ideas would grow in his mind, and eventually McVeigh would believe the concepts were his own.

Saturn's significance relates to its co-rulership, with Mars, of the military. During McVeigh's hitch in the Army, bonds with pals grew, and two of them would eventually be considered co-conspirators in the bombing. Military training played another role as well in helping McVeigh accumulate the knowledge needed to execute the stunning crime. Saturn also involves rules, regulations, and hierarchy, all of which would not only be a part of military life, but would also become the focus of McVeigh's rebellion against the government. The weakness of this planet caused McVeigh to align himself against rules, instead of becoming a staunch supporter of law and order. Incidentally, more Saturn is seen in its effect on McVeigh's eighth house of death, portending the wasting of 168 lives and his own sentence to die for the murders.

Venus is the planet of affection and friends, which reinforces the importance to McVeigh of bonding with comrades, especially in the Army. The weak aspect of this planet suggests that he depended on his buddies, instead of being needed by them.

Mercury, ruling communication and speech, relates to the activities of this circle of companions in sharing radical philosophies against established authority. The men discussed and planned methods of retaliating against the government, with McVeigh listening and following the ideas of his stronger cronies.

Mars, the planet of warfare and weapons, rationalizes McVeigh's decision to battle what he perceived as oppression against the Branch Davidians, with whom he sympathized. It is no accident that the Oklahoma City bombing took place on the anniversary of the lethal raid in Waco, Texas. McVeigh planned it that way. The red planet's energy also accounts for McVeigh's use of an explosive as his weapon of choice. If Mars' position had been stronger in his chart, McVeigh might have chosen to fight a real enemy, instead of cowardly destroying the lives of innocent people who had never harmed him in any way.

If Mars fires McVeigh's need to wage war in the name of revenge, his desire to do so is represented by the planet Pluto. A notable characteristic of Pluto is cooperation with others. In McVeigh's chart Pluto sits in a strong and harmonious aspect to Mars, which supports the allegations that McVeigh planned and executed the terroristic bombing with extensive help from co-conspirators.

Another astrological influence revealing McVeigh's tendency to be dominated by the ideas and actions of others is the position of the Moon. The Moon, ruling his emotions and his subconscious mind, is in Pisces, the most suggestible sign in the Zodiac. With the Moon in Pisces, McVeigh would be easily persuaded by associates who appealed to his emotions. McVeigh's outward personality is ruled by the sign of Gemini, which is his ascendant. Gemini people adapt to existing surroundings and influences, rather than creating original ideas and activities.

One other important facet of McVeigh's chart involves the composition of Taurus, the strongest sign in his chart. As already mentioned, the Sun, Mercury, and Mars are crowded into his eleventh house of friends. That trio's influence also stems from their occupation of key positions within the sign of Taurus. Positive Taurus qualities are stability and practicality, while its negative characteristics are fixation and obsession. Again, McVeigh succumbed to negative control. It is unclear exactly when he and his friends conceived the idea of retaliation bombing, but whenever it was, he became obsessed with the notion and fixed on its cruel, death-dealing implementation.

In the final analysis, the position of Saturn and Venus in the sign of Aries led to McVeigh's capture. Haste and impulsiveness are Aries features. In spite of all the planning carried out with his comrades, McVeigh's foolish haste and carelessness, specifically the absence of a license plate on his getaway car, caused him to be captured and brought to justice.

David Joseph Carpenter

Tuesday, May 6, 1930, 9:16 P.M.
San Francisco, California • Time Zone: 08:00 (PST)
Longitude 122° W 25' 06" • Latitude 37° N 46' 30"
Placidus Houses • Tropical Zodiac

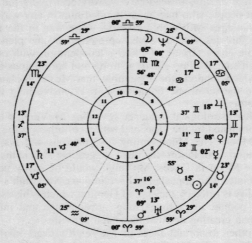

In the same scenic hills and coastal shoreline between California's Golden Gate Bridge and Petaluma—where a pedophile would later snuff out the life of little Polly Klaas in 1993 (see the profile for Richard Allen Davis)—a fiend stalked state park trails in 1979 and 1980. Eight hikers lost their lives to the so-called Trailside Killer. David Joseph Carpenter was convicted of murdering five of the hikers, four women and one man, who lost their lives in Mt. Tamalpais State Park and Point Reyes National Seashore Park. In addition, a separate verdict condemned him for killing two women in the forested hills near Santa Cruz, 60 miles south of the landmark bridge.

Carpenter had served nearly 20 years in prison for sex crimes when he launched his ruthless serial killing spree only months after being paroled to live in San Francisco. Several of the victims were raped before they were killed.

Carpenter never strayed very far from his place of birth. Born in the sparkling "City by the Bay" on May 6, 1930, he was raised and educated there. A little sister joined the middle-class family four years later, but it appeared that Carpenter's mother may have wanted her first child to be a girl. She reportedly treated her son as such, making him take ballet lessons, dressing him in "sissy" clothing, and carefully screening out any boy who might have been his friend. As a result, classmates teased him mercilessly and often cornered him after school to inflict beatings. It would later be revealed that Carpenter also suffered physical abuse at home. He began stuttering at age 7, and would be plagued with the disorder his whole life. Observers noted that he always had great difficulty articulating the word *mother*.

With a knot of anger possessing him, Carpenter translated his inner turmoil to an obsessive sex drive. At age 10, recalcitrant and disruptive in school, he ran away to a mountain cabin owned by his parents, but was dragged home for more punishment. By the time Carpenter turned 12, his parents had sent him to a state hospital as a result of his sexual misbehavior. After dropping out of high school, he molested two young relatives, an 8-year-old boy and a little girl, only 3. The California Youth Authority incarcerated him for testing and observation until after his eighteenth birthday.

In 1952, now grown to his full height of 5 feet, 10 inches, weighing about 160 pounds, and already starting to go bald, Carpenter ended a short stint as a Coast Guardsman and took a job with a shipping company as a purser. Not an attractive man, with his high round forehead, full-lipped pouting mouth, upturned "Porky Pig" nose, and dark, humorless eyes, he still managed to attract a few women. He married one of them in 1955, and with his strong, frequent sexual demands, fathered three daughters within five years.

Apparently unsatisfied by marital sex, Carpenter offered a ride to a friendly female co-worker in July 1960. He drove her into the heavily forested grounds of The Presidio, a military reservation overlooking the Golden Gate. When the shocked woman rejected his request for sex, Carpenter attacked her with a hammer. A military policeman interrupted and saved the seriously wounded victim's life. Sent to federal prison for fifteen years, during which his wife divorced him, Carpenter was released early, paroled in April 1969.

Married a second time, Carpenter succumbed to his overwhelming sexual urges again in January 1970. Deliberately rearending a car, he confronted the female driver and forced her at knifepoint into the hillside brush, where he openly admitted he wanted to rape her. A struggle ensued in which he slashed her, then backed off and allowed her to escape. The next day, in Santa Cruz, he carjacked a woman, took her to the cabin where he'd hidden as a young runaway, sexually assaulted her, and sped away in her car. A third attempted rape, in as many days, failed.

In February, he repeated the carjack rape with another woman, and forced her to drive him to a town in central California. The police caught up with him in Modesto. Tried and convicted, Carpenter served seven years, part of it in tough Folsom Prison. The state paroled him in 1977, but because his crimes had violated conditions of his previous release, the federal government sent him to McNeil Island in Washington state for two more years. Paroled again, on May 21, 1979, Carpenter was assigned to a halfway house in San Francisco.

Within three months, a man fitting the description of David Carpenter began killing female hikers in the trails and woodlands of Tamalpais Mountain. The first victim was executed with a shot to the back of her head while she knelt in a secluded glen. Eight weeks later, the second woman was violently stabbed to death. That same day, Carpenter received medical treatment for several cuts to his hands.

In March 1980, yet another woman died on the mountain from stab wounds. A hiatus of seven months passed before a young couple vanished from a trail in picturesque Point Reyes. Then, in the final few weeks of 1980, four more women were accosted and murdered. Two of the corpses weren't found until late November. They'd been stripped nude and executed with .38-caliber slugs. A few yards from the pair of tortured bodies, investigators finally located the decomposing remains of the missing couple, also dead from .38-caliber bullet wounds.

The killer changed location in March 1981. He found a ready supply of hikers in the verdant hills near Santa Cruz, the coastal resort where serial killers Edmund Kemper and Herbert Mullen (see separate profiles) had spread death and terror during the previous decade. Carpenter, dressed in a gold-colored windbreaker, appeared on a hiking trail, blocking the path of a youth and his girlfriend. Producing a handgun, he boldly announced that he planned to rape the girl. She lunged toward him and he shot her to death, then critically wounded her companion. Several witnesses saw him speed away from the park in a small red car.

Up to that time, Carpenter's homicide victims were strangers. In May, he persuaded a young woman he'd met at his workplace to take a ride to Santa Cruz with him. Her nude, raped body was found three weeks later with a bullet hole through one of her eyes.

A widespread investigation, which had overlooked the paroled sex offender through bureaucratic loopholes, finally zeroed in on David Carpenter. A case built on circumstantial evidence became considerably stronger when an investigator found the .38-caliber handgun Carpenter had given to an ex-con buddy. Ballistics proved that bullets found in the victims' bodies came from Carpenter's gun. Although detectives suspected him of multiple murders throughout the state, in regions where Carpenter's work took him, they began legal proceedings by charging him with two killings near Santa Cruz. Found guilty, he was condemned to die.

Subsequently, Carpenter also was convicted of killing four women and one man in Marin County, on Tamalpais Mountain, and at Point Reyes Park. Five more guilty verdicts of capital murder, delivered exactly four days after his 58th birthday, sent Carpenter to San Quentin's Death Row. The prison, holding more than 500 condemned men, sits on San Francisco Bay, just a few miles from the once-again peaceful and safe trails winding through the hills above the Golden Gate.

Horoscope for David Joseph Carpenter
Born May 6, 1930, 9:16 P.M. PST, San Francisco, California
Source: Birth certificate

An obsessive and deviant sex drive doomed David Carpenter from an early age, and eventually sent him on a brutal quest for satisfaction through rape and murder. The violent planet, Mars, is one of the rulers of Carpenter's fifth house of sex, saddling him with an enormous sex drive. But his fifth house also holds a weak Sun lounging in the sedentary sign of Taurus. Astrological calculations of distances and angles between these planets expose this weakness. Thus, Carpenter's character traits stemming from the Sun would be feeble and pallid. This means he retreated into feelings of inadequacy and very low self-esteem.

The conflict between these two extremes caused frustrating internal anguish. He constantly fantasized about sexual adventures with women, a result of the Moon and Neptune making a conjunction within Virgo and dwelling in his ninth house of dreams. The Moon represents women, while Neptune is the planet of fantasies, delusions, and deceptions. That latter ingredient, deception, added another sick twist to Carpenter's mental agitation. He probably deceived himself into believing that women deserve harsh treatment. Neptune also creates the possibility that Carpenter held exaggerated ideals about women, and when that balloon was punctured by rejection, he deluded himself into thinking all women are sluts who deserve to die. This is reinforced by the Moon ruling Carpenter's eighth house of death.

Desperately longing for sexual satisfaction, but plagued with his sense of inadequacy, and fueled by violent Mars, Carpenter felt compelled to feed his lust by forcing women to submit to his aberrant desires. The pitiless brutality that spewed forth in Carpenter's treatment of female victims stems from Pluto, the planet of cruelty and sadism, crouching in his eighth house of death, under the Moon's rule. An even deadlier element is added by the negative aspect found in Pluto's alignment with Mars and Uranus. Mars brings in shooting and stabbing, while Uranus is associated with irrationality and unpredictability. Both planets are in the volatile sign of Aries, creating an incredibly dangerous arrangement.

To be afflicted with stuttering certainly didn't help alleviate the dilemmas plaguing Carpenter. In his chart, Mercury rules the signs of Gemini and Virgo, and all three relate to communications, or in this case, problems in communicating. Carpenter's difficulty in saying the word *mother* also comes from Mercury in its conjunction to Venus, which rules his tenth house of mother. Both planets' alignment to the Moon in Virgo depict an obstacle—his stuttering—which is difficult to overcome.

On the subject of maternal influence, the Moon's position in relation to Venus, ruler of mother, suggests serious difficulties. Distrust, misunderstanding, and problems in communication between Carpenter and his mother were foreseeable.

Carpenter selected the secluded coastal mountain trails to stalk, rape, and kill his victims. His Sun sign is Taurus and his Moon sign is Virgo. Both of these relate to earth, which may have lured Carpenter to mountains and forests. In addition, Saturn is in Capricorn, another earth sign. Since Saturn resides in his first house of personal interests, the outdoors would probably appeal to him.

Mars enters the picture again in ruling Carpenter's twelfth house of prisons. The combative red planet helped pave a path for murder that Carpenter followed all the way to Death Row. With merciless Pluto hovering in his eighth house of death, and co-ruling his twelfth house of prisons, it is probable that this cruel planet will turn on Carpenter and finally bring about his own end.

Jeffrey Dahmer

GEMINI

A remarkable number of serial killers, including Jeffrey Dahmer, David Berkowitz (Son of Sam), and Wayne Williams, were born under the sign of Gemini. Symbolized by twins, Gemini reflects the dual nature of these murderers. Their Jekyll-and-Hyde personalities helped many of them escape detection for long periods of time. When influenced by negative planet alignments, Gemini natives are not only two-faced, but also superficial and undependable.

Jeffrey Dahmer

Saturday, May 21, 1960, 4:34 P.M.
Milwaukee, Wisconsin • Time Zone: 05:00 (CDT)
Longitude 087° W 54' 23" • Latitude 43° N 02' 20"
Placidus Houses • Tropical Zodiac

By 1991, the nation had grown accustomed to accounts of bizarre, cannibalistic serial killers such as Ted Bundy, Ed Gein, and John Wayne Gacy. News watchers were nevertheless stunned when they learned of Jeffrey Dahmer's gruesome crimes. How could such a good-looking young man, who seemed so shy and polite, be involved in these hideous sex murders? And could it be true that he actually ate the flesh of his victims? Monsters capable of such behavior should be ugly, deformed, repulsive. Dahmer, who stood a little over six feet tall, had the blue eyes, wavy blond hair, full lips, and perfect features of a model. He looked more like an all-American athlete or a movie actor.

Born on May 21, 1960, in Milwaukee, Wisconsin, Dahmer was an only child for six years until a little brother arrived to steal his parents' attention away from the older sibling. Soon after Jeffrey started school, the family moved to a posh neighborhood filled with huge manicured lawns just north of Akron, Ohio. This ideal setting should have been one of serenity and contentment, but angry disputes between Dahmer's mother and father kept his home life constantly unsettled.

Young Dahmer's classmates were puzzled by his odd obsession with death. From the woods surrounding his home, he collected remnants of dead creatures, which he kept in boxes or jars. He seemed to take a certain pleasure when an unfortunate animal became "roadkill"; at these times, he took advantage of the opportunity to cart home severed limbs or heads.

In school, Dahmer sought attention by screwball behavior and abnormal pranks. Trying to impress his male peers, Jeffrey sneaked booze into classes and sipped it behind the teacher's back. He didn't bother to show off for girls, though. By the time Dahmer reached high school, he realized that his sexual thoughts focused exclusively on other boys. Private fantasies reeled through his mind in which his fascination with homosexuality and death blended into demonic scenarios, all enhanced by booming heavy metal music.

Tension in Dahmer's home reached the breaking point in June 1978, shortly after he'd completed high school. His mother and father separated, both leaving the home and deserting Dahmer. Living alone for several weeks, he felt that neither parent wanted him. Driven by loneliness, he picked up a teenage hitchhiker and brought him to the house. After drinking some beer, Dahmer didn't want his new pal to leave. When the opportunity came, he bludgeoned the visitor, then strangled him to death. After concealing the body for a few days, he retrieved it and surgically removed the limbs. En route to a dump site, Dahmer barely escaped arrest when a traffic officer pulled him over and noticed bulging trash bags in the car. Shrugging it off, the officer cited Dahmer for reckless driving and let him go. Frightened, Dahmer returned home to bury the body parts in his backyard. He kept the victim's head for use in playing out sexual fantasies, and finally disposed of it, too.

A short stab at attending college soon fell into an alcohol-induced shambles, so Dahmer joined the Army in 1978. Assigned as a medic in Germany, he functioned well for a time, but his alcoholism and split personality caused fellow soldiers to avoid him. Unsatisfactory duty performance earned a 1981 discharge for Dahmer before he had served his full term of enlistment.

In civilian life, Dahmer drifted aimlessly in an alcoholic daze, with stops in Florida and Ohio. A belligerent drunk, he frequently fought with other bar patrons. Jobs lasted only until employers grew impatient with his chronic drunkenness and absenteeism.

Dahmer's grandmother, who lived in a Milwaukee suburb, offered him a room in her home so he could make a new start. For a short time, Dahmer appeared to be escaping his inner torment through Bible study and work. But the powerful magnet of his dark fantasies soon drew him into an underworld of gay sex. At bars and bathhouses, Dahmer found the companionship he needed. Police arrested him for public sexual behavior in 1986 and 1987, after which he agreed to seek counseling while on probation. He maintained steady employment at a chocolate factory while continuing to live with his grandmother. At night, he dreamed of sexual encounters with helpless men or dead bodies.

To live out the fantasies, Dahmer experimented with drugging his sex mates. When they awoke and complained, he lost his membership in a gay bathhouse. Dahmer took the next step in September 1987 by slipping powerful drugs into a young man's drink. As Dahmer recalled it, he woke up locked in a nude embrace with a dead man. Initially, he concealed the body in his grandmother's basement, then chopped it to pieces and put it in plastic bags to be picked up by garbage collectors. He kept the skull as a sex toy for several months.

Drawn to dark-skinned males, Dahmer picked up a Native American, 14, and brought him home. After drugging and strangling the youth, Dahmer used the corpse for sex and hid it until the next Sunday, when his grandmother attended church. In the charnel basement, he dissected the body for easier disposal, once again retaining the skull.

Repeating the pattern several times over the next year, Dahmer made up excuses to keep his grandmother out of the basement. Now 28, he needed a place of his own so he moved to an apartment in September 1988. Within days he lured a young boy into his new quarters, drugged him, and took nude photos. The boy staggered home and collapsed. Emergency medical treatment revealed a heavy drug dosage, and the boy reported being with Dahmer. Police arrested him at work, but his innocent face and convincing lies earned Dahmer conditional freedom in a work release program.

Alarmed by the near-miss of being sent to a hard-time prison, Dahmer took a hiatus for several months. But in March 1989, he met a handsome African American in a gay bar and left with him. This time, Dahmer not only kept the skull, from which he

had boiled and peeled away the flesh, but also retained the severed genitals.

By March 1990, Dahmer's ostensible good behavior ended his
part-time incarceration, and he moved to another apartment,
where he could listen to his head-throbbing music, watch tapes
of bloody horror movies, and bring home gay young men to kill,
use for necrophilic sex, and dismember. He perfected his lure of
offering them payment for posing nude, and even started a photographic collection of the human game he bagged. In some of
the pictures, the subject had already been murdered.

Growing weary of drugging his victims, Dahmer decided to
use a razor-sharp knife to cut their throats. In September, he
added a new twist with his eighth and ninth victims. After stripping flesh from the bones, he cooked and ate it. As the list of
young victims grew, Dahmer's experimentation became increasingly bizarre. While one victim still lived, Dahmer drilled a hole
in the teenager's brain to inject acid. He decorated the growing
collection of skulls with paint.

In May 1991, police responded to a complaint about a boy,
14, seen wandering naked outside Dahmer's apartment. When
the officers arrived, they found Dahmer trying to control the
drugged youth. Again, Dahmer's clean-cut appearance and
smooth talk convinced the cops that they'd simply interrupted a
gay lovers' quarrel, so they left. The whole police department
was later embarrassed when the boy turned out to be Dahmer's
thirteenth murder victim.

Victims number fourteen through seventeen succumbed to
Dahmer's lethal orgies over the next few weeks. In July, he
brought home a street-wary African American, 32, who deftly
avoided drinking the drug-laced cocktail. After Dahmer impa-
tiently snapped handcuffs on him, the intended victim escaped,
ran several blocks, and yelled for the police. A pair of officers
took him back to Dahmer's apartment, and found a mind-
numbing collection of photos, skulls, and body parts. Following
a brief scuffle, they arrested Jeffrey Dahmer.

With his sanity as a key issue, Dahmer stood trial in early
1992. The sickened jury decided that the defendant knew very
well what he was doing, and understood the consequences.
Found guilty, Dahmer faced life in prison without parole, since
Wisconsin had no death penalty.

The life sentence turned out to be relatively short. On November 28, 1994, a fellow inmate overruled the state and gave Dahmer a summary execution by beating him to death in a prison washroom.

Horoscope for Jeffrey Dahmer
Born May 21, 1960, 4:34 P.M. CDT, Milwaukee, Wisconsin
Source: Birth certificate

The lyrics of an old song speak of "fascination turned to love." Jeffrey Dahmer found a sickening new twist to the concept. His morbid fascination with *death* apparently turned to love, as indicated by the power of Venus in his chart. The planet of beauty and harmony endows the recipient with affection, but in some cases the love can turn to a ghastly excess of perverted pleasure.

In Dahmer's eighth house of death, Venus lounges like a painted harlot. As the ruler of Dahmer's Libra ascendant, Venus held the power to seduce Dahmer into becoming personally involved in death in several ghoulish ways. The strength of the harlot is seen in her grip on Dahmer's ascendant, which governs his first house, the domain of his physical body, personal appearance, and most important, his special interests. So, Dahmer's mind and body, under the beguiling influence of Venus, festered with a peculiar interest in death that turned to fascination, then to love. In its role as a component of Taurus, Venus gives intensity and compulsion to his growing depravity. The total configuration of his chart suggests that Dahmer was truly in love with death.

The Sun, planet of ego and self-confidence, also resides in Dahmer's eighth house of death, accompanied by Mercury, ruler of mental pursuits and intellect. Under the Sun's omnipotent strength, Dahmer gained a sense of personal power through his intimate flirtations with death. As his experience and knowledge about dying increased, so did his ego. Mercury's position reveals that his conscious thoughts were about being involved in seeing and causing death. It is notable that both the Sun and Mercury are in Gemini, one of the signature signs of serial killers.

Gemini is symbolized by twins, reflecting the dual personalities seen in many natives of this sign. Dahmer's ability to seem quiet, unassuming, and nonthreatening to neighbors and relatives is one side of his Gemini. These qualities allowed Dahmer to continue his grisly activities without raising suspicions. His Libra ascendant contributed to this attractive, innocuous, and pleasing facade. In Dahmer's role as the "good twin," he seemed completely harmless.

But inside Dahmer the "bad twin" was born and nurtured, and gradually took over his entire being. His evil side engaged in necrophilia, murder, cannibalism, and the severing of body parts.

Dahmer's metamorphosis from good twin to bad twin manifests itself at several sites in Dahmer's chart. Considerable influence is exerted by Pluto, the planet that deals in ghoulish evisceration and the eating of human flesh. Dahmer's eleventh house of friends is the residence of Pluto. Initially, Dahmer befriended his potential victims in order to lure them into his web, then used drugs to render them unconscious. Pluto extends its power by governing Scorpio, the sign encompassing Neptune, ruler of drugs. Neptune, occupying Dahmer's first house of temperament and moods, is the source of his bizarre fantasies and delusions, which sent his dreams and imagination plummeting into the depths of hell.

Pluto's negative alignment with two more planets, Sun and Mercury, both in the eighth house of death, sets up another problem for Dahmer. His thought processes and his ego were related to Sun and Mercury. Pluto has the power to inject the mind with compulsions and obsessions. So, Dahmer was unable to take his mind off the compulsive urge to destroy and mutilate his male sex partners.

Violent, destructive Mars affected Dahmer in two ways. He developed a drinking problem at an early age. The Army eventually booted him out due to his alcoholism. Mars is solidly entrenched in Dahmer's sixth house, which relates to military service. Weapons, including knives, are Martian gifts, explaining Dahmer's use of knives to stab, eviscerate, and mutilate the bodies of several victims.

The antagonistic and hostile conduct of Dahmer is attributable to his Moon in Aries, the sign that afflicted his emotions with aggressive discord.

In Dahmer's tenth house of reputation, Uranus spreads its eccentric influence with a broad brush dipped in black paint. Even as a youth, Dahmer sought the wrong type of attention through his quirky behavior around schoolmates. With Uranus in Leo, the sign of the exhibitionist, Dahmer's need for notoriety continued into his adult life. He succeeded beyond his wildest dreams, since his gruesome crimes are permanently etched in the public's mind.

If Dahmer thought his repulsive public image would fade away while he served the rest of his life in prison, he was wrong. Mercury, while ruling the twelfth house of prisons, occupies his eighth house of death, forming a precipitous link between loss of freedom and loss of life. While in prison, Dahmer exhibited the positive side of Gemini, the good twin, by adapting well to his surroundings and staying out of trouble. However, his incarceration terminated sooner than anyone expected when another inmate bludgeoned him to death. He died of massive head injuries. The manner of his death fits very neatly into his astrological chart, considering that Dahmer's Mars, ruler of beating, is in the sign of Aries. The part of the body ruled by Aries is the head.

Richard Trenton Chase

Tuesday, May 23, 1950, 1:28 A.M.
Sacramento, California • Time Zone: 07:00 (PDT)
Longitude 121° W 29' 36" • Latitude 38° N 34' 54"
Placidus Houses • Tropical Zodiac

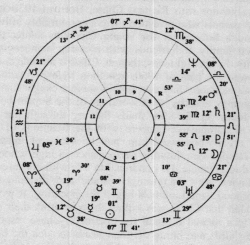

Heat waves rippled across Nevada's desert sands on August 3, 1977, but they didn't seem to bother Richard Chase, 27, as he trudged through scrub brush and cactus, completely naked and covered with blood. Agents from the Bureau of Indian Affairs, scouting the Walker River Reservation, spotted the tall, scrawny, nude hiker and arrested him.

With a blank stare, Chase complained that his car had mired down in the sand, and he'd left it to seek shelter. He didn't comment on the blood smears covering his skin. The officers placed him in the backseat of their desert cruiser and followed Chase's trail back to the stranded '66 Ford Ranchero. Inside it, they found a malodorous bucket of fetid, thick scarlet blood. Two rifles inside the car bore red smears on the stocks. The barrels looked as if they'd been used to stir the sickening pot. If the agents had known that Chase, in Dracula fashion, had collected the blood to drink, they might have sought psychiatric help for him. But, no matter how bizarre the incident, the agents found no reason to charge him with any crime. Tests on the red smears and the bucket's contents revealed that the blood originated from cows. Officials released Chase, who donned clothing he'd left in his Ranchero and drove back to his hometown, Sacramento.

In some cases, odd childhood behavior can give clues to future troubles, but not with Richard Chase. Born in 1950 in Sacramento to parents who provided love, a comfortably affluent lifestyle, and a little sister for young Chase to adore, the child impressed family and friends with pleasing manners and easy sociability. In his mid-teens, though, Chase's attitude changed as he followed the path of 1960s rebellion by experimenting with drugs and alcohol. Only one school subject caught his deep interest: biology and the inner workings of the human body, with special focus on the vital fluids flowing through the vascular system. A compulsive concern with the functions of his own internal organs possessed him, and he spoke of imagined illnesses. Despite deteriorating performance in high school, Chase managed to graduate. He continued to live with his parents while his behavior grew increasingly erratic and disjointed. In his neighborhood, small animals began disappearing. It would later be revealed that Chase was killing them to drink their blood.

Sent to a mental hospital for treatment, Chase responded by capturing birds and biting off their heads to suck the blood out. He also caught rabbits and used a hypodermic needle to inject himself with their blood. Chase stayed inside for a year, frightening other patients and staff, but earned a glowing diagnosis from one doctor, and was released to the custody of his recently divorced mother. Far from being mentally stable, Chase sank deeper into a world of delusions, hallucinations, and reclusiveness. He ventured out periodically to buy or adopt small pets, which promptly vanished. When investigators eventually found blood-covered blenders in Chase's residence, they realized that he had resumed quenching his vampiric thirst again.

Small prey no longer satisfied his twisted cravings. Soon after being rescued from the desert, Chase acquired a handgun and sought a human target. A middle-aged man, standing outside his own home, became the first of Chase's six victims.

Now that he'd experienced the thrill of murder, he wanted the taste of human blood. In January 1978, Chase barged into the Sacramento home of Teresa Wallin, 22, a new mother. Ignoring her pleas, Chase shot her to death. Dropping to his knees, he used a kitchen knife to invade her body, dipped a plastic cup into the blood, and lifted it to his mouth.

That same month, Chase raided another home, catching four people by surprise. He murdered three of them on the spot, and abducted the fourth. In his wake lay Evelyn Miroth, 36, her son Jason, 6, and a visiting friend, Daniel Meredith, 52. The woman had been mutilated with a knife. Chase took with him Miroth's nephew, little David Ferreira, not yet 2 years old. When police later found the child's body, they were horrified. His killer had severed the head, jammed the remains into a cardboard box, and dumped it amid other trash behind a church.

Chase fled the gory murder scene in Daniel Meredith's car. But while he'd loitered earlier near the victim's home, neighbors noticed him and were able to help a police artist prepare a sketch of the killer's face. Other witnesses recognized the published drawing, and led investigators to Chase.

A jury found him guilty of six murders. Sentenced to death, Richard Chase shook off his convoluted thinking process long enough to devise a method for cheating California's gas chamber. A doctor had diagnosed chronic depression in the condemned killer and prescribed powerful drugs to treat it. But instead of swallowing the capsules, Chase hoarded a handful, and ingested them all at once. He died in his cell on the day after Christmas, 1979.

Horoscope for Richard Trenton Chase
Born May 23, 1950, 1:28 A.M. PDT, Sacramento, California
Source: Birth certificate

Vampires are the stuff of legends and fright-night movies, but Richard Trenton Chase turned the mythical thirst for blood into reality. He murdered several people in order to quench his gory craving, rationalizing that he did it in order to save his own life. This morbid sense of entitlement comes from the placement of the Sun in his chart. Its dominance endowed him with the belief that he could do anything he wished with absolute impunity and no regard for anyone else. Vampires are associated with Pluto, the god of the underworld. Chase's Pluto is next to his Moon, the domain of women. Although Chase murdered several males, he drank blood only from his female victims. The placement of two planets, Pluto and Moon, in the fixed and determined sign of Leo in Chase's chart accounts for this behavior. Pluto in Leo adds the element of obsession/compulsion to his quest for the blood of women.

As a youngster, Chase exhibited extreme cruelty to pets, killing them to experiment with ingesting blood. The appearance of Pluto in his sixth house, associated with small animals, fed his obsession and sadistic cruelty.

Mars is a factor in the grisly murders of humans that followed, as it rules knives, stabbing, and evisceration. This violent planet is in Virgo, the analytical sign associated with health and biology, as reflected by Chase's early interest in the human body.

The dual nature of Gemini exhibited itself in Chase's life by the drastic and unpredictable metamorphosis that took place in his teen years, when he changed from a well-behaved youngster to an erratic user of alcohol and drugs. Neptune, the astrological domain of drugs, is one of the rulers of his first house, which involves personality and the physical body. Alcohol is represented by Mars, sitting in opposition to Jupiter, the planet bringing abundance to Chase's first house. A Mars/Jupiter opposition, the worst aspect in the chart, indicates a prolific and over-indulgent use of booze.

Another feature of Neptune, in addition to paving the way for drug usage, is the clouding of Chase's mind with hallucinations and delusions. Neptune is found in his eighth house of death, setting up potential for Chase to fill his fevered imagination with visions of murder. Deeper mental instability is suggested by the relationship of Mercury, planet of the conscious mind, and Moon, ruling the subconscious. In Case's chart, the placement of these two creates a negative aspect, setting up a precarious imbalance in his reasoning process. To add to this difficulty, both planets are in fixed signs: Mercury in Taurus and the Moon in Leo. Fixed signs are inflexible, so this configuration would make it nearly impossible for Chase to modify his thinking or behavior.

Chase's ascendant is Aquarius. This first-house ruler influenced his personal appearance as well as his temperament and disposition. As Chase sank into the abysmal role of killer-vampire, his physical appearance deteriorated. He went out in public appearing emaciated and covered with filth and blood. Aquarius is eccentric and strange, but Chase exceeded anything imaginable.

The tenth house, domain of mother, is ruled by Jupiter. As

Jupiter is the benefic planet, Chase's mother tended to protect him, insisting her son was innocent even after his convictions for multiple murders.

Sex is an issue of the fifth house, which is occupied by Uranus, the planet of eccentricity. This placement indicates that the murders Chase committed were at least partially motivated by sexual urges.

Chase was caught, convicted, and sentenced to death. Prison is a twelfth-house matter, and Saturn is the ruler. While in prison Chase suffered from depression, a Saturn affliction. When given drugs to help alleviate his problems, he chose to use the prescription for something far more sinister. Neptune, the planet of drugs, had already made inroads into Chase's early life. An even greater impact developed from Neptune's presence in his eighth house of death. He saved up his pills, a Saturn trait, and swallowed them all at once, putting his strange life to an end.

Danny Rolling

Wednesday, May 26, 1954, 12:50 A.M.
Shreveport, Louisiana • Time Zone: 06:00 (CST)
Longitude 093° W 45' • Latitude 32° N 31' 30"
Placidus Houses • Tropical Zodiac

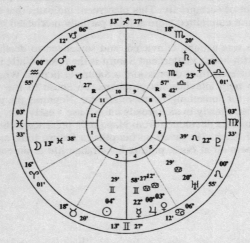

In late August 1990, within three consecutive days, five young people were savagely murdered near the campus of the University of Florida in Gainesville. Of the four female students, three were raped, one mutilated, and one decapitated. The killer left their violated bodies obscenely displayed. The only male victim was repeatedly stabbed until he died in a pool of blood. Panic spread through the city and the campus, causing hundreds of students to hurriedly leave the city and the state. Danny Rolling was arrested for armed robbery in early September, and ultimately pleaded guilty to the murders.

Rolling was born in Shreveport, Louisiana, on May 26, 1954. He and his brother learned early to avoid displeasing their father. A police officer, the humorless, short-fused Rolling patriarch dominated his family with an iron fist. A veteran of traumatic combat in Korea, he reportedly set hard, unreasonable rules for his wife and boys to strictly follow, and administered swift, harsh punishment for any deviation. According to Rolling's mother, her son was emotionally and physically abused from the time he was born. Rolling tried to love both of his parents, but felt that the affection was returned only by his mother. An aunt reported that Danny's father made it clear during his wife's pregnancy that he didn't want the child, and never changed his mind.

Extreme turmoil in the family drove young Rolling into retreat from normal feelings. But he still cowered in fear when he saw his father mistreat and even kill family pets. Rolling later admitted crying when his mother collapsed into a screaming nervous breakdown in response to her husband's alleged cruelty.

Repressed sexual urges possessed Rolling, who acted on them by becoming a nighttime voyeur in his neighborhood. He felt extreme excitement at being able to peek through partially open drapes or blinds and watch women undress or bathe. It became a habit, then a lifelong obsession.

To escape the turbulence in his home, Rolling joined the Air Force in June 1971, at 17. Despite his immaturity, he functioned well in basic training, and returned to Florida assigned to Homestead Air Force Base. With an opportunity to grow, learn, and establish a future, he chose instead to seek offbeat excitement, experiment with drugs, party every night, and live for concerts. He later acknowledged ingesting a wide variety of mind-bending hallucinogenic pills, smoking marijuana, and guzzling booze. His natural intelligence, good looks, and artistic skills were wasted in the hedonistic pursuit of pleasure.

The reckless indulgences caught up with him just as Rolling was on the verge of promotion. Found in possession of marijuana after a dealer had turned informant, Rolling was reduced in rank and sent to the stockade. The Air Force gave 19-year-old Danny Rolling a general discharge.

In September 1974, Rolling married a deeply religious woman, but was disappointed with her sexual response to his frequent needs. They separated several times and the troubled union finally ended in divorce. Rolling later said that during this period demons began visiting him and influencing his behavior. Reeling from what he perceived as rejection, he soon reverted back to his old Peeping Tom habits. The demonic force, whether drug induced or real, led him to the next step. After surreptitiously gazing at a young woman in her home, Rolling entered and raped her. From then on, his sexual fantasies centered on rape.

In the spring of 1979, Rolling's developing pattern of crime took form. Using a stolen handgun, he robbed convenience stores and supermarkets, roaming from Louisiana to Alabama to Georgia. Inevitably, he was caught and served his first prison term, nearly six years, in Alabama. The savagery, brutality, and death he saw among hardened convicts made its mark on Rolling's psyche.

When released in June 1984, Rolling waited only a short time before lust and greed drove him to rob and rape again. He roamed the nation from coast to coast, living as an outlaw. In 1986, he raided a grocery store in Mississippi, stole a car, and was apprehended. A short-lived escape gave him a few days of freedom before he landed back in the slammer. In one of the toughest of penitentiaries, Parchman, he endured two more years of hard time, which did nothing to stem his criminal urges.

Paroled in 1989, Rolling tried again to live with his parents, but more conflict with his father erupted. Shortly after he was fired from a menial restaurant job, a triple murder occurred in Shreveport, in which the raped female victim was left in a lewd pose. The crime was never solved. But Rolling later wrote of giving in to the demon that led him into yards at night to peer through windows.

Close contact between Rolling and his father predicably led to angry exchanges. Finally, the venom boiled over into an actual shootout between the two men. The furious cop missed several shots, but Rolling's aim proved more accurate. He dropped his father with a slug to the midsection and one to the forehead. Miraculously, the father survived.

Fearing another stretch in prison, Rolling fled to Kansas City, where he looted several more stores. In July 1990, he moved on to Sarasota, Florida, and used his accumulated cash to live like a vacationing yuppie, dating several young women. Still, he couldn't resist donning dark clothing at night to act as a voyeur, then entering the residence for the purpose of rape. In August, he took a bus to Gainesville, spent a short time in a hotel, used his remaining money for drugs, then camped in the woods.

At about 3:00 A.M. on August 24, Rolling entered the four-story Williamsburg apartment complex and sneaked into a unit occupied by two sleeping students, Christina Powell, 17, and Sonja Larson, 18. Using duct tape to prevent screams, he sealed Larson's mouth then stabbed her to death. In a separate bedroom, he raped Powell before making her lie facedown and plunging his knife into her back five times.

The next night, Rolling broke into another apartment and waited for Christa Hoyt, 18, to return home. As soon as she entered, he taped her mouth and cut away her clothing, then raped her. After stabbing her to death, he sliced open her abdomen, mutilated her breasts, and committed the gruesome act of removing her head, which he mounted on a shelf.

Two hours before dawn on August 27, Rolling forced his way into the Gatorwood Apartments, where he found Manuel Taboada, 23, asleep in his bed, faceup. Using the same razor-sharp knife, Rolling stabbed the victim so hard that the blade penetrated all the way to the victim's spine. The noise woke Tracy Paules, 18, who had been asleep in a second bedroom. When she appeared at Taboada's door, Rolling chased her, subdued her, and applied tape to her mouth. After ripping and cutting away the frightened girl's clothing, he raped her and used the knife to commit his final act of murder.

That same day, Rolling robbed a bank not far from Christa Hoyt's apartment. On September 2, after looting a market, police nearly cornered him, but in a wild shootout, he escaped to Ocala, Florida. His orgy of crime ended there on September 7, when he robbed a food store and was finally chased down by pursuing officers.

On February 13, 1994, Danny Rolling stood before a judge and pleaded guilty to five murders. Sentenced to death for each of the five counts, he now spends time in the state prison at Starke, Florida, drawing women and grotesque, demonic figures, writing, and waiting for his date with the electric chair.

Horoscope for Danny Rolling
Born May 26, 1954, 12:50 A.M. CST, Shreveport, Louisiana
Source: Letter from Rolling through Sondra London

According to Danny Rolling, demonic forces took control of his life and goaded him into first raping women, then savagely killing and mutilating them. Whether driven by demons or his own raging lust, Rolling's sadistic behavior is evident in his eighth house of death and his fifth house of sex.

Two planets, Neptune and Saturn, reside in the eighth house. Neptune supplies fantasies and delusions about death while Saturn adds cold, vicious cruelty. To make matters worse, Saturn is in Scorpio, the sign of sadism. With this dangerous blend of planets and signs, Rolling's path is full of deadly pitfalls.

The sexual problems began in Rolling's teen years with a compulsion to engage in voyeurism. Uranus, the planet of eccentricity, joins the Moon in co-ruling his fifth house of sex. The Peeping Tom fetish is a Uranian way of expressing sexuality. The Moon represents women, whose exposed bodies were the objects of his lustful night excursions.

Eventually, Rolling needed more than stolen glances at unclothed women, so he turned to rape. Rapists are generally known to have feelings of inadequacy. In Rolling's case, his Sun is the weakest planet in his chart, which results in low self-esteem and a virtually nonexistent ego. To intensify his feelings of inferiority, Pisces and the Moon help undermine his psyche. His ascendant, Pisces, rules the personality and temperament. The Moon, inhabiting his first house of personality, is in the sign of Pisces. This combination drains away any strength of character Rolling might have had. The urge to rape was further aggravated by violent Mars in opposition to Venus, the planet of women and love. Mars relates to sex, so this relationship to Venus creates in Rolling's mind an explosive inner conflict between love and sex.

The extreme depravity Rolling demonstrated in decapitating one of his rape victims is demonstrated by Pluto's opposition to his ascendant. Pluto's influence, in this configuration, is sadistic and controlling. Twisted acts of perversion involving dead bodies are Pluto associations as well. Displaying the dead woman's head on a bookshelf, making it instantly visible to anyone entering the room, is a reflection of his having Pluto in the sign of Leo. As Pluto is afflicted by this negative aspect, so is Leo. Therefore, Leo led to a flamboyant, demonstrative act of extreme perversity, in which Rolling flaunted his horrible crime and said, in effect, "Look what I can do."

Pluto not only brings sadism into Rolling's pattern of behavior, but this cruel planet also rules demonic possession. Asserting negativity by being opposite his Pisces ascendant, Pluto could cause Rolling to actually believe that demons possessed him. Or, since Pluto influences Rolling's ninth house of the courts, his assertion of demonic intrusion may have been nothing more than a defense ploy in his trial.

In Rolling's chart, the fourth house of home life and father bristles with negative energy. Jupiter and Venus team up there, sitting in direct opposition to Mars. This negative arrangement suggests pending turmoil in the home and points to trouble between Rolling and his father. Guns and violence are thrust into the picture by Mars, resulting in a shootout between Rolling and his overbearing father. The elder combatant was severely wounded, but survived, as portended by the intercession of Jupiter's benevolence.

Rolling served several years behind bars before he committed murder. The power of Mars ruling in his second house of money and sitting in opposition to Jupiter relates to the armed robberies Rolling committed. But being sent to prison twice taught him nothing. His twelfth house of prisons is governed by the sign of Aquarius, which is ruled by two planets, Uranus and Saturn. Uranus occupies his fifth house of sex. Rolling's sexual perversions, leading to rape and murder, finally put him on a path to Death Row. The second ruler of Aquarius, Saturn, looms in his eighth house of death. This solid, inflexible combination of astrological influence indicates that Rolling will remain incarcerated in Florida state prisons until he is put to death.

Wayne Bertram Williams

Tuesday, May 27, 1958, 1:31 A.M.
Atlanta, Georgia • Time Zone: 05:00 (EST)
Longitude 084° W 24' • Latitude 33° N 45'
Placidus Houses • Tropical Zodiac

With rare exception, searches for serial killers end with the arrests of suspects who are white males. Thus, it made sense that when bodies of young African American murder victims started turning up near Atlanta, Georgia, in 1979, investigators and the general public suspected racially motivated killings perpetrated by one or more Caucasian men. As the body count increased to more than 20, rumors circulated that the Ku Klux Klan must certainly be involved. That's why it stunned the community and the nation when Wayne Bertram Williams, 23, an intelligent freelance photographer from an affluent background was arrested in May 1981. Williams was the same race as all of the victims.

The chain of events started when a hiker stumbled upon the decomposed corpses of two youths, Ed Smith and Alfred Evans, near an Atlanta lake. One of the chief causes of death among young black men is murder, often gang related. So, there was little clamor for action at first, even though the victims were partially disrobed. Within a couple of months, more boys and teenagers vanished, generally from indigent families in Atlanta neighborhoods. Concern grew and the police intensified efforts to identify a suspect. As more bodies were discovered, investigators found few clues, but did notice tiny purple and yellow-green fibers clinging to the clothing of each victim. In addition, Georgia Bureau of Investigation forensic experts lifted hairs that appeared to be from a dog. Under electronic microscopes, specialists saw that the fibers all came from three common sources: an automobile floor mat, home carpeting, and some other ordinary household material.

When newspapers carried this information, the killer changed his modus operandi. The bodies, which included many young children, no longer were found in woods or fields. Instead, they were dumped into lakes and rivers. But if the killer hoped that water would flush away the incriminating evidence, he was wrong. Forensic experts continued to lift the tiny fibers and hairs from the victims.

The offer of a large reward failed to identify any suspects. Panic gripped the city and anger rippled through the nation. President Ronald Reagan held a press conference to inform television viewers that he'd made federal funds available to assist police. The murder count, averaging more than one each month, reached 26 by May 1981. Because bodies were being disposed of near bridges, the investigative task force decided on a new strategy. Using a group of volunteers called "trolls," they posted lookouts at every bridge within miles of Atlanta.

On the night of May 22, two of the trolls posted under a Chattahoochee River bridge heard a loud splash, but could see nothing. They radioed police at a nearby roadblock. Within a few minutes, the officers questioned a station wagon driver about his presence there. Wayne Williams, calm and collected, told them he was a music promoter returning from an appointment. They took his name and let him go.

Two days later, the bodies of Nathaniel Cater, 27, and Jimmy Payne, 21, were fished out of the Chattahoochee. A careful inspection revealed the same fibers clinging to their clothing. Investigators interviewed residents of the men's neighborhood and found witnesses who'd seen them with Wayne Williams.

A native of Atlanta, born in 1958, Williams grew up in the comfortable home of his schoolteacher parents. Extremely bright, but pampered and spoiled, the chubby youngster had demonstrated creative and entrepreneurial skills early in life, but grew lazy and dropped out of college at 19. He taught himself the expert use of cameras, and tried to organize a promotional agency for musicians.

Soon after he was arrested, Williams held a news conference to announce his complete innocence. But his alibis leaked badly. The noose grew tighter when experts matched the evidence fibers to a floor mat in the station wagon Williams drove, carpeting in his home, and a bedspread he used. They traced the manufacturer of all three, and astronomically narrowed the chances that any other individual would possess all of them. The dog hairs were also consistent with samples found in his home.

Residents of Atlanta noticed that immediately following Williams's arrest, the long string of murders came to an end.

At the 1982 trial, a parade of young African-American men told the jury that Williams had tried to lure them into his car for sexual purposes. Even though all of the evidence presented was circumstantial, the jury found Williams guilty of first-degree murder in two of the killings. He is serving two life sentences in prison.

Horoscope for Wayne Bertram Williams
Born May 27, 1958, 1:31 A.M. EST, Atlanta, Georgia
Source: Letter from Williams

Four signs of the zodiac can be called signatures of the serial killer. It is not surprising that all four of them hold prominent positions in Wayne Williams's chart. Even though he was convicted of killing only two young men, he was suspected of being involved in the serial murders at least 20 victims. Williams's Sun is in Gemini, his Moon is in Virgo, his ascendant is in Pisces, and his midheaven is in Sagittarius. Sagittarius is his strongest sign.

The Sun in Gemini describes a smooth talker and quick thinker. Williams used this talent to lure his victims into a false sense of security and to convincingly lie in response to questions from the police. Incidentally, the alibi he came up with, that he was a music promoter, is interesting since both music and promotion are related to Pisces, the ruler of his ascendant.

Williams's Moon in Virgo presages both his victims and the incriminating evidence which led to his conviction. With the Moon residing in his seventh house of partners, and ruling the fifth house of sex, it follows that Williams sought young men as his victims. Among the primary clues linking Williams to the crimes were minuscule fibers found on the bodies. These threads were so tiny that they required examination under a microscope. Virgo is the sign associated with small details as well as scientific investigation.

Williams's Pisces ascendant, ruler of his first house, describes a passive and sensitive person. Additionally, Pisces natives possess remarkable skills as successful liars and con artists. With Neptune as one of Pisces' rulers, these people usually have a talent for creating mass confusion. They also take great delight in casting a fog over events and situations for their own purposes. (*Note:* It is no coincidence that Neptune is prominent in the charts of defense lawyers). A career associated with Pisces/Neptune is photography. Williams taught himself how to use cameras and became quite adept with them.

The strong Sagittarius influence found in Williams's tenth house of reputation dictates how he is seen by the community at large. When Williams performed the extraordinary act of holding a news conference to protest his innocence, he displayed the flashy and flamboyant side of Sagittarius. The positive, upbeat, yet manipulative qualities of this sign led a number of people to believe him.

Murder is an eighth-house matter and is influenced in Williams's chart by the presence of Neptune. Since this planet is one ruler of his Pisces ascendant, the configuration reveals Williams's strong personal interest in, and hands-on involvement with, death. Neptune next to Jupiter, the planet associated with abundance. Jupiter, as the other ruler of Pisces, sets the stage for a large number of dead victims. Due to the uncertainty mapped by Neptune, as well as the lucky influence of Jupiter, Williams was charged with only two killings.

Mars, the planet of violence, occupies the first house and is in opposition to Williams's Moon, ruler of his victims. This Mars/Moon opposition, the most deadly aspect in his chart, points not only to the murders, but also warns of his ability to change his modus operandi for disposal of the bodies. Rather than leaving his victims in the woods as he did initially, Williams started dumping them in the river. His Moon is in Virgo, an earth sign, and Mars is in Pisces, a water sign. The nature of both Virgo and Pisces is adaptability, so Williams simply reacted to the threat of discovery by changing his methods and procedures.

Despite Williams's claim of innocence, the position of his planets paved a path to verdicts of guilt. Saturn, the planet of restrictions, is one ruler of his twelfth house of prisons. Uranus, the other ruler of the twelfth house, represents science and technology, and is found in the sixth house of the police. Scientific investigation by the police finally cornered Williams and led to his conviction, which sent him to prison to serve two life terms.

David Berkowitz

Monday, June 1, 1953, 4:52 P.M.
Brooklyn, New York • Time Zone: 04:00 (EDT)
Longitude 074° W 00' • Latitude 40° N 42'
Placidus Houses • Tropical Zodiac

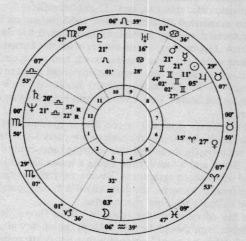

His chubby face, full womanly lips, and knitted eyebrows combined with his high-bridged nose, halo of dark frizzy hair, and vaguely mirthful stare chilled the nation when the image of David Berkowitz, the "Son of Sam," appeared in the news following his arrest.

New Yorkers had been hearing about the random murders for a full year, and the community was verging on panic as a task force of 300 investigators desperately searched for Son of Sam, whose crime spree had left six dead and nine wounded. News media had printed or broadcast a series of cryptic and deranged letters from the elusive killer.

When Berkowitz was captured on August 10, 1977, he complained to the police that he heard demons in his head commanding his every move. He spoke of the howling dogs that possessed him, craving blood. At first it was difficult for interrogators to comprehend what the suspect said in his whispery voice. They weren't sure they understood when he spoke of hearing a black Labrador retriever tell him that a demon named Sam, who had lived centuries before, had selected Berkowitz for a special mission. To obey the unearthly commands, Berkowitz had collected a small arsenal. From the trunk of his 1970 Ford Galaxy, officers snatched his .44-caliber revolver, .45-caliber semiautomatic rifle, shotgun, and .22-caliber rifle.

Born to unmarried parents in June 1953, when such a birth carried a societal stigma, Berkowitz had started life as Richard David Falco. His mother, an ex-dancer with the famed Ziegfeld Follies, had separated from her husband, and produced her son from an illicit romance. She gave the unwanted child to an adoption agency. A Jewish couple named Berkowitz took the boy into their loving home. They even let him keep his original middle name.

Social scientists generally agree that a combination of three particular behavioral traits in children are early signs of trouble: chronic enuresis (bedwetting), fire starting, and cruelty to small animals. Some add a fourth trait: being a loner. David Berkowitz displayed all of these symptoms. Reclusive, feeling rejected, and suffering mental torment, the boy killed a family parakeet, and would be called a budding pyromaniac.

When his adoptive mother died in 1967, David, at 14, was inconsolable even though he had seldom shown any affection for her. Much later, he would complain that her death resulted from an evil plot of nature against him. At 18, he joined the Army in hopes of achieving glory in Vietnam combat, but he wound up in a sedentary assignment. He did, however, learn the use of firearms, which he would later utilize in his death-dealing crime spree.

Near the end of his military service, Berkowitz, who had been raised in the Jewish faith, immersed himself in Baptist Christianity. After being baptized, he manifested his faith by acting as a street sermonizer, until his zeal faded. His old fascination with fire took hold again, and he claims to have set over 1,400 blazes in New York City.

Having been told his real mother was dead, Berkowitz formed doubts and set out to find her. He succeeded in 1975 and would continue to visit her periodically. But, he said, he never really forgave her for not keeping him as a baby.

Berkowitz held several jobs including cab driver, security guard, and postal worker. He lived alone in a drab apartment, never socializing and feeling completely rejected by everyone, especially women. He once wrote, "I walk down the street and they spit and kick at me. The girls call me ugly and they bother me the most. The guys just laugh." He began to hear voices of demons, sometimes from the mouths of dogs, screaming, demanding, calling for death. Trying to escape, he moved to another apartment, but a neighbor there, named Sam, owned a black Lab which, in Berkowitz's mind, howled the demands for death even louder.

On July 29, 1976, Berkowitz zeroed in on a pair of women sitting in a blue Oldsmobile. With his pistol concealed inside a paper sack he walked to the car, then raised the weapon and fired five shots through the glass, killing one and wounding the other. In October, he saw a man and woman sitting in a red Volkswagen and repeated his attack, seriously wounding the male. A month later, he varied the procedure, firing at two female pedestrians late at night. One of them recovered, but the wounds that the other woman sustained permanently paralyzed her.

The demonic voices left Berkowitz until the new year. At the end of January, he found a kissing couple parked after midnight, and blasted them with five shots from the same weapon he'd previously used, the .44-caliber pistol. The man escaped, but the woman died. In March, he confronted a college student, aimed the big handgun at her mouth, and killed her instantly.

While searching for another victim in April, Berkowitz received a citation for having no automobile insurance. Polite and compliant, he signed it, then drove away. Before dawn, he unleashed another hail of lead into a parked car, killing the young couple inside. From that double murder was born the "Son of Sam" legend. Berkowitz left an envelope in the victims' car containing a note he had scrawled. Addressed to a police captain, and containing several misspelled words, it said, "I am deeply hurt by your calling me a wemon [sic] hater. I am not. But I am a monster. I am the 'Son of Sam.' " It also made references to blood and rape, mentioned being programmed to kill, and begged the police to kill him or be killed. "I'll be back," the note warned.

The next intended victim was the black Lab owned by Berkowitz's neighbor Sam, but Berkowitz succeeded only in wounding the dog. After sending another bizarre letter to a newspaper columnist and similar raving notes to neighbors, he ventured out again on June 25 and wounded two more young people.

On the anniversary of his first kill, Berkowitz resigned from his post office job. Five nights later, he left his car parked too close to a fireplug, and set out on foot to search for prey. He watched from a distance as a cop ticketed his car. Undeterred, he spotted a couple who'd left their Buick to walk in the park at three o'clock in the morning. After they'd nearly brushed shoulders with Berkowitz, and returned to the Buick, the crazed gunman attacked. The woman would die from her wounds a day later, while the man lost one eye and suffered damage to the other. Another couple parked nearby witnessed the attack, and rushed away to hail the police. A local resident who'd been giving her dog a late walk got a good look at the heavyset man lurking in the park. Berkowitz escaped into the night.

The descriptions given by both witnesses were useful, but even more help came from the dog walker, who recalled seeing a cop putting a parking ticket on a car. A search of records nearly missed the crucial citation, but finally revealed that the vehicle belonged to David Berkowitz. On August 10, as Berkowitz reached his car to go on another blood hunt, police surrounded him. He smiled and said, "Well, you got me."

Months of legal battles ensued, in which the question of Berkowitz's sanity was repeatedly a factor. Finally declared legally sane, and convicted of a half-dozen murders, he was handed six sentences of 25 years to life.

Horoscope for David Berkowitz
Born June 1, 1953, 4:52 P.M. EDT, Brooklyn, New York
Source: Hospital records

Violence, murder, and twisted delusions are prominently displayed in the chart of David Berkowitz. A foreboding of death looms like a dark storm cloud over his key houses.

Berkowitz captured headlines not only for the serial murders, but also for his claim that a dog commanded him to kill. His notion that a neighbor's black Labrador retriever spoke to him stems from Venus and Neptune facing off in opposition to each other. Venus is found in his sixth house, the abode of domestic animals. Neptune, the planet of delusions, is situated in his twelfth house of secrets and isolation. With this combination, Berkowitz might truly believe that a dog had ordered him to commit murders.

A great deal of power can be seen in the placement of four

planets in Berkowitz's eighth house of death. This quartet of doom consists of Jupiter, the Sun, Mercury, and Mars, all four being in the sign of Gemini. Jupiter, equated with abundance, describes the significant number of his victims. The Sun, which represents his ego, takes a forceful position in the house of death, indicating that Berkowitz gained a sense of power and pride through committing his murders. Mercury, his strongest planet, rules communications and writings. Combined with the potent presence of Gemini, Mercury describes Berkowitz's need for public self-expression, which he gratified by writing to the newspapers to boast of his crimes.

The fourth, and perhaps most influential, planet in the house of death is Mars, which exerted violent and bloody control over Berkowitz. The red planet rules guns, his weapon of choice to carry out a reign of murderous terror. Mars also is associated with arson, which marked Berkowitz's early way of manifesting his twisted psyche. Another Mars effect is seen by its rulership of Scorpio, Berkowitz's ascendant. Since the ascendant rules his first house of personality, the presence of Mars inflamed Berkowitz with volatile traits and revealed his deep personal interest in death. The other ruler of his Scorpio ascendant is Pluto, which adds compulsion/obsession to the equation. Thus, Berkowitz felt compelled to obey orders issued by his mental demons, which he claimed took the form of a dog.

Berkowitz's desire for fame and public recognition is denoted by the presence of Pluto in his tenth house of reputation. This desire for attention is augmented by Pluto's placement in Leo, the sign most associated with grandiosity and pomposity.

In the rambling notes written by Berkowitz, he complained that women had shunned and mistreated him. This difficulty in relating to females is represented by the troublesome position of his Moon, the ruler of women, in Aquarius. With its square aspect to his ascendant, indicating conflicts, such a position accounts for his belief that women found him ugly. Saturn, the planet associated with insecurity, intensifies his sense of alienation by lodging in his twelfth house.

The rather peculiar procedure Berkowitz followed in killing his victims is related to his Mars, which rules shooting, and to his Moon's sign, Aquarius. Women, represented by the Moon, were his primary victims. He crept up on parked cars at night, an ability mapped by his sneaky Scorpio ascendant. In the incidents where he discovered that the targets were romantic couples, Berkowitz achieved his primary goal of killing the women, but also shot the men as a safeguard against being identified.

His success at escaping several crime scenes by sprinting away without being seen is a Gemini talent. The contradictory nature of getting close enough to his victims, all strangers, yet managing to remain unseen, is an Aquarian tendency.

In spite of his delusions, real or affected, Berkowitz was found legally sane and subsequently sentenced to a lifetime of imprisonment. This is to be expected since Berkowitz's twelfth house of confinement is occupied by both Neptune, which reflects the hallucinations that prompted him to kill, and Saturn, representing the law that finally ended the year of terror he inflicted on New York City.

Richard Allen Davis

Wednesday, June 2, 1954, 6:34 P.M.
San Francisco, California • Time Zone: 07:00 (PDT)
Longitude 122° W 25' 06" • Latitude 37° N 46' 30"
Placidus Houses • Tropical Zodiac

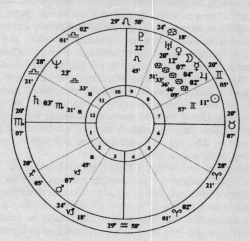

About 40 miles north of California's Golden Gate Bridge, surrounded by farms and wine country vineyards, sits the peaceful, safe town of Petaluma. Movie producer George Lucas, after seeing the community's Victorian homes and bucolic main street, which he thought symbolized wholesome values, selected it for the background of his classic film *American Graffiti*. Unfortunately, Petaluma later became known to the world for something entirely different. A blood-chilling murder committed there by a career felon named Richard Allen Davis would spotlight a justice system full of loopholes that placed dangerous felons back on the streets.

On the night of October 1, 1993, three residents spotted a husky, darkly clad man loitering in the neighborhood where 12-year-old Polly Klaas lived. At about ten that night, he was seen just outside her home, standing on the sidewalk, smoking a cigarette. Because an adjacent city park sometimes attracted homeless wanderers, the witnesses shrugged off their irritation and didn't bother reporting the transient. Had they known anything about his background, they would have immediately screamed an alert to the police.

Richard Allen Davis turned to crime before he became a teenager, committing burglaries, stealing from mailboxes, and lifting items from store counters. A native Californian, born June 2, 1954, he did not have a pleasant childhood. His parents reportedly moved from place to place, argued violently, and abused their son, the middle-born of five siblings. A psychiatrist told of an incident in which Davis's mother allegedly held his hand over an open flame as punishment. His anger at her grew deeper, according to a court document, when she entertained male guests in their home long before divorcing Davis's father. He grew up hating women. Davis tried to quench his anger by burglarizing homes. When that failed to satisfy him, he manifested a growing sadistic urge by dousing cats with gasoline and setting them afire, or torturing dogs with a knife.

School held no meaning for Davis, so he dropped out in 1971. Soon afterward, caught for yet another infraction of the law, he faced a tough choice offered by a judge: Go to a detention facility for juveniles, or join the Army. At 17, Davis became a soldier, but not a successful one. Shipped to Germany, he broke rules, fought, and plunged into drug usage. According to Davis, "I left here and hash was four dollars a gram. I get to Germany and it's sixty cents a gram. I go wild. . . . getting loaded on hash, coke, opium and shooting morphine. Then, I got kicked out." The Army discharged Davis in August 1972.

Back in California, drifting between minimum-wage jobs, Davis couldn't stay out of trouble. His girlfriend died of a gunshot wound to the head while in Davis's company, but it was ruled a suicide. Frequently arrested for various petty crimes and drug charges, he blamed his problems on alcohol abuse. Often the beneficiary of sympathetic judges, optimistic counselors, and generous public welfare, Davis usually received short or suspended sentences followed by probation for his crimes. He even lucked out when a fellow thug shot him in the back for cheating on a drug deal. The bullet drilled clean through his body, but missed all vital organs, allowing him to heal with no permanent damage.

Repeatedly caught for burglary, car theft, drug possession, and probation violations, Davis turned to more violent crimes in 1976. In the San Francisco Bay area, he kidnapped a woman, drove her Volkswagen to an isolated spot, and attempted to force her into oral sex at knifepoint. Terrified, she struggled, fled, and flagged down a passing car. Davis's luck ran out. The rescuer was an off-duty policeman who immediately arrested him.

Taken to a mental hospital, Davis soon escaped. A few days before Christmas, he broke into a home and woke the female occupant by beating her with a fireplace poker, but rushed out when she began screaming. Later, he carjacked a woman who had just left a bar, but she managed to grab a pistol from under the car seat and fired it to scare Davis off. The next night, he broke into a home to steal Christmas presents, then tried to hide in shrubbery outside, but was caught by police.

Still manipulating the system, Davis claimed that insanity drove him into a life of crime. A psychiatrist's report described him as extremely dangerous and concluded that, "If released, he would be certain to resume his pattern of criminal behavior: theft, burglary, and assaults against women." Given an indeterminate sentence of 1 to 25 years, a plea-bargained deal, Davis was out on the street in less than six years, paroled on March 4, 1982. He avoided trouble for a while, but with the help of a female accomplice, assaulted and robbed a woman in her apartment on November 30, 1984. Stopped by a traffic cop in Modesto six months later, Davis was cuffed, jailed, and sent to prison with a stiff sentence of sixteen years. He would serve only eight.

Released on July 27, 1993, Davis made his way to Petaluma. Just 65 days after leaving prison, he loitered outside the home of Polly Klaas on the first night of October. He could see through an open window the movement of Polly hosting two young girl-friends for a slumber party. Shortly after ten, the husky, grizzled stranger, reeking of beer, entered the house, slipped past a closed bedroom door where Polly's mother and little sister slept, and barged into the room where three girls chattered and giggled happily. When they saw the knife-wielding intruder looming over them, the gaiety ended. "Don't scream or I'll cut your throats," he growled. While he bound all three of them and slipped cloth hoods over their heads, Polly cried and asked him not to hurt her family. Ordering the two guests to count to one thousand, Davis picked up Polly and eased silently from the house. Placing his frightened captive in his beat-up old Pinto parked nearby, he drove off into the night.

On a hilly, rural road less than 30 miles from Petaluma, a

homeowner became concerned when she noticed a Pinto stuck in a ditch. She drove down the hill and heard the burly driver say he needed help to move his car. She sped away to notify police of the trespasser. Davis would later admit that in the woman's absence, he hid Polly Klaas, still alive, behind an adjoining embankment. When the woman returned, with two sheriff's deputies following, a sweating Davis claimed he had inadvertently turned on the private road en route to his relative's home. The officers patted him down, gave him a sobriety test, then towed his car out of the ditch. Polly Klaas had been kidnapped less than two hours earlier, and a police report had been made. But the deputies on patrol had not yet received it. Once again, Davis had caught a major break.

The next day, when newspapers and television announced the kidnapping, the story soon spread nationwide. It struck a visceral chord, outraging everyone. The kidnapper had not only committed a heinous crime, but he had blatantly violated the safety and sanctity of the victim's home. No one could feel safe anymore. Celebrities including Winona Ryder and Linda Ronstadt helped publicize the search.

The widespread hunt for Polly Klaas riveted the whole country. People prayed for her safe delivery, and came to know her family intimately. *America's Most Wanted* appealed for clues, but tips led nowhere. Finally, a discovery on November 27, nearly two months after the abduction, broke the case. Hikers on the rural road where Davis's car had been stuck found some of Polly's clothing, along with a black sweatshirt, cords that matched the ones used to bind Polly's guests, and an unrolled condom, all in a little pile. It didn't take long to link the discovery to the trespasser report two deputies had filed on Richard Allen Davis.

When investigators caught up with him 75 miles north of Petaluma, as the result of a drunk-driving arrest on October 19, Lady Luck finally deserted Davis. Realizing he faced serious consequences, he confessed to the kidnapping, but steadfastly denied killing little Polly. However, he led officers to the body, where it lay stuffed under a sheet of plywood near a long-deserted sawmill. She had probably died on the same night Davis abducted her.

In a prolonged trial, defense attorneys tried to blame Davis's criminal conduct on his childhood and his abuse of drugs and alcohol. His feigned pretense of remorse evaporated when he heard the jury pronounce him guilty of first-degree murder, with special circumstances that called for the death penalty. With television cameras focused on him, Davis grinned and flipped the universal one-finger gesture of angry defiance to the whole world.

At the sentencing on September 26, 1996, Davis, now 42, whined about his lawyers, criticized treatment from jail officials, and angrily denied sexually assaulting Polly Klaas. His next comment enraged everyone who heard it, including millions of television viewers. Davis said, "The main reason I know I did not attempt any lewd act that night was because of a statement the young girl made to me while walking up the embankment: 'Just don't do me like my dad.'" The thinly veiled suggestion of familial abuse sent Polly's father into a furious lunge at the killer. Deputies restrained the shouting father, while the heartbroken mother wept aloud. The judge later admitted that Davis's conduct made it easier to deliver a death sentence.

The horrific crime perpetrated by Davis was cited as a major factor in leading California to pass a stringent "three strikes" law aimed at keeping career felons in prison for life.

Davis occupies space on San Quentin's Death Row, along with more than 500 other condemned men, while waiting for the endless sequence of appeals to begin. Some of his cellmates have been on the row for more than 20 years.

Horoscope for Richard Allen Davis
Born June 2, 1954, 6:34 P.M. PDT, San Francisco, California
Source: San Francisco Chronicle. *December 10, 1993*

In Richard Allen Davis's chart, all signs point clearly to murder.

His eighth house of death is teeming with five powerful planets. They are the Moon, Jupiter, Mercury, Venus, and Uranus, all of which are in the sign of Cancer. The crab, which symbolizes Cancer, uses its claws to tenaciously grip and hold in place a massive shroud of death hovering over Davis's doomed eighth house.

The Moon, representing emotions and women, is the strongest of the group. It weaves hatred into the shroud. The hatred Davis felt for women started with his mother, who reportedly inflicted cruel punishment on him and hosted male guests in full view of her furious son.

Jupiter, the planet of good fortune, involved death in its bestowal of a thread of good luck for Davis by not allowing him to die when he was shot for cheating on a drug deal.

Mercury, which involves the conscious mind, embroidered the shroud with thoughts of death constantly festering in Davis's thoughts.

Venus, if unfettered by other planets, could have brought love to the tapestry. Unfortunately, in this case, Venus is next to Uranus, the planet of eccentricity. So, with this juxtaposition, the love turned to a morbid endearment for dealing a bizarre type of death, preferably to a female. Significantly, an interest of Cancer natives is children. Davis finally chose to murder a female child.

The crowded quintet of planets nestling in the eighth house might have remained benign, but Mars appeared in opposition to four of them, dyeing the shroud a bloody red. Taking up residence in the second house of money and material possessions, Mars first exerted influence on Davis by pointing the way to burglary, car theft, and robberies. Then, the red planet of violence, in its opposition to the Moon, heated up Davis's hatred of women to a lethal flash point. The Mars opposition to Jupiter, which rules abundance, relates to the long list of felonies committed by Davis. The Mars/Venus connection twisted even more tightly his emotional desire to kill. And the opposition between Mars and Mercury, which rules communication, opened the poisonous spigot that was Davis's mouth. His sarcastic manner of speaking and acerbic personality damaged relationships with his peers. It also infuriated a judge who admitted that Davis's behavior made it easier to hand out a death sentence.

As if that weren't enough, Mars is one ruler of Davis's first house of personality, and his fifth house of children and sex. Violence, mixed with lust and hatred, invaded Davis's already miserable personality. Ultimately, his morbid libido targeted an innocent female child.

Another factor in the makeup of Davis, as in most pedophiles, is low self-esteem. This stems from the weak Sun in Gemini, resulting in a minuscule ego. Davis utilized fast talking, lies, and manipulation, all Gemini traits, to compensate for his feelings of inadequacy.

Davis was in and out of prison most of his life. His luck in being released so many times, in spite of the seriousness of his crimes, is shown by the trine aspect, a favorable one, between Jupiter and Saturn, the latter residing in his twelfth house.

The final outrage he committed was the kidnapping, possible rape, and murder of little Polly Klaas. Pluto rules kidnapping and governs Davis's Scorpio ascendant. Murder is the final gruesome contribution from the presence of Mars throughout Davis's chart.

The dealings Davis had with the court system and the press are matters related to the ninth house, which hosts Pluto in Leo. This combination explains his outrageous behavior in flipping the world an obscene gesture while the television cameras focused on him, and especially when he implied that Polly's father had previously molested her.

Saturn sits in Davis's twelfth house, the ruler of prisons. Its placement in Scorpio describes the atmosphere of his confinement and his daily routine behind prison walls. Saturn is associated with dull, plodding monotony, which is all Davis can expect until his execution.

Peter Sutcliffe

Sunday, June 2, 1946, 8:30 P.M.
Bingley, England • Time Zone: -01:00 (BST)
Longitude 001° W 50' • Latitude 53° N 51'
Placidus Houses • Tropical Zodiac

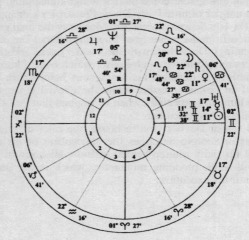

Perhaps the most recognizable sobriquet among serial killers is "Jack the Ripper," which was given to an unknown killer who stabbed and mutilated several women in nineteenth-century London. Because he was never identified, the mystery has fascinated crime readers for the last century.

In the years from October 1975 to January 1981, a series of similar murders in England caused news reporters to dub the killer "The Yorkshire Ripper." The name might bring to mind a large, powerful, brutish fiend who could easily overcome his smaller victims. That image did not fit the man eventually convicted of thirteen murders. Peter Sutcliffe, shy, introverted, soft-spoken, and small, led a quiet married life when he wasn't on the hunt for prostitutes to bludgeon and slash.

Yorkshire covers a portion of the northern half of England, and includes the cities of Manchester, Leeds, and Sheffield, which form a rough triangle in which Peter Sutcliffe roamed in search of women to kill. A native of the region, he was born in Bingley on June 2, 1946, the first child of parents who would produce six more siblings. Small and shy, he adored his mother and clung to her, while feeling alienated from his blustery, loud father. Sutcliffe heeded her deeply religious Catholic guidance. Pushed around at school by bullies who took advantage of his diminutive size, Sutcliffe dropped out at age 15.

The first young woman Sutcliffe dated would eventually become his wife, but not until he'd gone through a painful seven years of courtship. He felt miserable when, in 1969, he learned that his beloved was enjoying the company of someone else. Feeling betrayed, he sought solace in the arms of a prostitute, but found that he couldn't perform. When he asked her to return half the money he'd paid, she laughed, teased him about his impotence, and unleashed a burly bodyguard to send Sutcliffe packing. A seed of fury took hold in his mind.

A few weeks later, Sutcliffe returned to the hooker's haunts, wrapped a brick in a sock, and slugged her with it. Only he had the wrong woman. As he drove away, the confused victim regained consciousness long enough to note his vehicle license number. The local constabulary questioned Sutcliffe, but let him go when the injured woman failed to press charges. The close call would be the first of many extremely lucky breaks that would help Sutcliffe evade capture for five years.

Sutcliffe still loved his fiancée while healing from her betrayal, but felt that his mother was the only woman truly worthy of respect. For most females, he felt a seething hatred. In 1970, an event jolted him to the core. His father invited Peter, his fiancée, and one of his brothers to a mysterious meeting at a hotel. It turned out to be a devious trap to expose a longstanding sexual affair in which Sutcliffe's mother had been regularly meeting a lover. Mr. Sutcliffe even forced her to model, in front of Peter, some flimsy lingerie she had brought to dazzle her consort. Stunned and devastated, Peter Sutcliffe's internal anger flared.

He suppressed the fury long enough to marry his fiancée in 1974, but the cauldron continued to boil beneath the surface. More trips to the sleazy areas where prostitutes offered their services fueled Sutcliffe's rage. His job as a lorry (truck) driver made it easy for him to cruise the dark streets. He assaulted and carved up several more young women, seriously injuring them, before he finally unleashed all of his fury and killed one. In October 1975 he picked up Wilma McCann, 28, in Leeds, took her to a soccer field, bludgeoned her with a hammer, and then plunged a

knife into her chest and abdomen fourteen times. The next victim, Emily Jackson, 42, suffered even more violence in January
1976. Sutcliffe used a screwdriver to stab her 52 times and
smashed her skull with a hammer. A bruise on her leg appeared
to have been imprinted by someone stomping her with a size-
seven boot.

Increasing his tempo, Sutcliffe waited only a month before
leaving another battered and sliced victim in a soccer field. In
April, he left his bootprint again, in blood on a sheet. This murder took place in the victim's home, where she was found with
countless knife wounds in the stomach and four crushing hammer
injuries to her head. An outcry to capture the Yorkshire Ripper
grew louder when he attacked a 16-year-old schoolgirl in June,
and left her battered and punctured body in a playground.

Sutcliffe's luck at evasion held firm. In October, while trying
to stash the body of a hooker behind some rural shrubs, Sutcliffe
heard an approaching car and sprinted away. Later, he discovered
that he'd forgotten to retrieve some crisp, new paper money he'd
handed the woman for her services. After sweating it out for a
week, he returned, worried that the freshly printed notes might
be traceable to the cash paid him by his employer. Chilly weather
had limited the body's decomposition, so he searched her again,
but failed to find his money. His premonition turned out to be
accurate. The new bills, found by the police, led them to two
dozen firms that might have paid it out. Among several hundred
men questioned by investigators, Sutcliffe's innocent looks and
convincing alibis let him slip away again.

In the first few weeks of 1978, his brutality escalated. The
bodies of severely battered and mutilated streetwalkers shocked
even the police. Continuing Sutcliffe's remarkable luck, someone
else sent an audio tape to the police, falsely confessing to being
the Yorkshire Ripper. The deep voice couldn't have been Sutcliffe, so he skated through several more interviews conducted
by cops who picked him up when they noticed his car cruising
the known hooker hangouts.

Again, Sutcliffe mistakenly struck out at women who had
never considered selling their bodies. A 20-year-old university
student fell victim to him in September. In 1979 he killed a 47-
year-old civil service worker and another student, age 20. The
manhunt intensified, with every available police officer being
utilized. In January 1981, Sutcliffe was observed by police pick-

ing up a streetwalker in his car. When he gave false answers to questions, they decided to arrest him. Thinking fast, Sutcliffe asked for permission to relieve himself behind some brush, where he quickly ditched his weapons: a knife and hammer. At the station, investigators grew increasingly suspicious about this man who had been interviewed nine times previously, and the word circulated that Sutcliffe might be the Ripper. The arresting officer, his eyes wide, rushed back to the site where Sutcliffe had taken respite in the brush, and found the weapons.

For the first time, officers also noticed that Sutcliffe wore size-seven boots. Now the interrogator had what he needed, and fired a series of questions at Sutcliffe. "What about the Yorkshire Ripper?"

Sutcliffe heaved a big sigh and replied, "Well, it's me."

His luck nearly pulled him out again. The prosecutor announced a willingness to settle for a plea bargain in which Sutcliffe would acknowledge being guilty of manslaughter tempered by diminished capacity. A judge overruled the prosecutor and insisted Sutcliffe be tried for first-degree murder.

The jury found Sutcliffe guilty of thirteen killings and sent him to prison for life with a minimum of 30 years. After two years, another prisoner attacked the Ripper and slashed his face with broken glass. Sutcliffe was subsequently moved to a facility for the criminally insane.

Horoscope for Peter Sutcliffe
Born June 2, 1946, 8:30 P.M. British Summer Time, Bingley, England
Source: Somebody's Husband—Somebody's Son, *by Gordon Burn*

The stunning cruelty that marked Peter Sutcliffe's violent, ruthless execution of at least thirteen victims reveals a simmering hatred of women. In his chart, this overwhelming urge to kill can be seen in his crowded eighth house of death, which is jammed with no less than five planets.

Venus, the Moon, and Saturn, all in the sign of Cancer, reside in the turbulent eighth house. Venus denotes Sutcliffe's love of death. The Moon, nestling close to Saturn, illustrates Sutcliffe's loathing of women. All three planets are in Cancer, the emotional and tenacious sign that would not allow Sutcliffe's traumatized feelings to heal. This festering hatred of females turned to violence through the intrusion of Pluto, which governs obsession, and Mars, bringing in cruelty. The coupling of these two planets signified the probability that Sutcliffe would use extreme barbarity in taking the lives of his victims. Repeatedly plunging a knife into the flesh of a victim is a trait of Mars, while torture is related to Pluto. With both planets in Leo, this cruel, obsessive search for vengeance took root in his mind and grew to monstrous proportion. The entire combination of three planets in Cancer and two in Leo, jostling for position within the eighth house, set up the killing of women as an expected progression for Sutcliffe to take.

The seed of Sutcliffe's hatred was planted when he discovered that his girlfriend had been unfaithful. Mercury, ruling thought processes, and Uranus, governing the bizarre, occupy his seventh house of partners and marriage. So the devastating emotional trauma invaded Sutcliffe's mind and implanted irrationally bizarre notions about relationships with women. Trying to ignore the hurt, Sutcliffe married his girlfriend, but still reeled in emotional agony. His seventh house also contains the Sun, which rules his ego. Unable to stop thinking about the betrayal, Sutcliffe's self-esteem withered. When he sought solace in mother worship, his whole world crashed. Neptune in Libra appears in Sutcliffe's tenth house of mother, creating a tendency to idealize his mom beyond reality. When Sutcliffe discovered her infidelity, it completely crushed him and stripped him of all respect for women.

Many of his victims were prostitutes. Selling sex for money relates to the fifth house, where sex resides, while money is a second-house matter. These two houses fall under the rule of Mars and Saturn, which occupied the eighth house of death but radiated control well beyond that domain. Heavy-handed Mars influenced the sexual fifth house while materialistic Saturn controlled the second house. In this context, hookers, or women Sutcliffe thought were selling their bodies, became targets of his vengeful attacks.

Sutcliffe's chart holds two signatures typical of the serial killer: the Sun (in Gemini) and Sagittarius (ruling his ascendant). Gemini is his strongest sign. Its dual nature influences three planets: the Sun, governing Sutcliffe's ego; Mercury, guiding his thoughts; and Uranus, accounting for his eccentric behavior. It is notable that Gemini, the sign of the twins, makes a forceful presence in Sutcliffe's seventh house of marriage. Sutcliffe virtually led two lives, managing to maintain what appeared to be a stable, quiet marriage while secretly venturing out to murder and mutilate prostitutes. He so successfully played "the good twin" at home that his wife knew nothing about his evil exploits.

Sutcliffe's Sagittarius ascendant, ruler of his first house, governs his appearance, temperament, and calm, quiet disposition. Sagittarius is an adaptable, easygoing sign, but can be extremely manipulative. Another of its characteristics is the endowment on Sutcliffe of good luck. He successfully eluded capture for years even though he was questioned nine times. The glibness provided by Mercury in Gemini, together with his quiet personality, worked in his favor.

The dual nature of Gemini clearly demonstrated itself again when, this time to Sutcliffe's detriment, he was finally caught while attempting to pick up another victim. When questioned by police, he answered meekly, reverting to his soft-spoken other persona, and admitted he was the notorious Yorkshire Ripper. The "bad twin" finally showed his stripes.

While he was in court, his Jupiter/Sagittarius good luck almost triumphed again. Sutcliffe was nearly offered a plea bargain for manslaughter. However, sanity prevailed and he was sentenced to prison for life. His twelfth house, ruling prisons, is ruled by Scorpio, which is governed jointly by Mars and Pluto. The dangerous Mars/Pluto influence of this deadly sign finally turned against Sutcliffe. He was not in prison long before a fellow inmate slashed his face with broken glass. Both the act of slashing and broken glass are Mars ruled. Although no motive was given, the Scorpio influence here suggests it was probably an act of revenge. If so, it brings a note of irony into the tale of the Yorkshire Ripper. The man who brutally sought revenge finally became a victim of it.

Richard Eugene Hickock

Saturday, June 6, 1931, 1:06 A.M.
Kansas City, Kansas • Time Zone: 06:00 (CST)
Longitude 094° W 37' 38" • Latitude 39° N 06' 51"
Placidus Houses • Tropical Zodiac

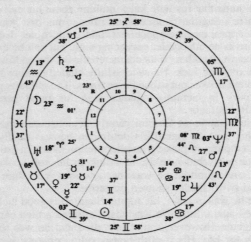

One of the most notorious crimes of the century, the subject of Truman Capote's classic book *In Cold Blood*, was perpetrated by Dick Hickock and his partner, Perry Smith (see separate profile), on a rural Kansas farm in November 1959. They raided the farmhouse in search of money and slaughtered all four members of the family: Herbert Clutter, 48; Bonnie Clutter, 45; Nancy, 16; and Kenyon, 15.

Hickock, a twice-divorced father of three boys, 28 years old at the time of the murders, had an IQ of 130 and the oily charm of Elmer Gantry. Despite his superior intellect, he wasted his life. As a teenager, he married a 16-year-old girl and plodded along in semi-skilled jobs painting cars, driving an ambulance, laboring for a railroad, and working as an auto mechanic. He tried to use his slick magnetism and loquacious personality to con his way into wealth. Flashing a quick grin and calling Smith "Honey," he seemed to exert powerful control over his cohort.

Long before the two men met in prison, a 1950 automobile accident injured Hickock and altered his physical appearance leaving his ruddy face asymmetrically proportioned. The wreck may have also been a factor in his lifelong attacks of migraine headaches. Still, with his blond hair, light blue eyes, and muscular body, standing about 5 feet, 10 inches, weighing 175 pounds, he could create a good impression on most people. Regarding religion, he declared himself an agnostic. One serious character flaw bothered those who knew him well—he had a sexual predilection for pubescent girls.

In sharp contrast to his partner, Perry Smith, a dreamer who fantasized about finding gold or sunken treasures, Hickock spoke of more typical pursuits such as the desire for owning a business, cars, horses, and women. "I want a slice of American success," he said. But he seemed unable to develop a realistic plan to reach his objectives. While Hickock did hold regular jobs much of the time, he relied too heavily on attempts at gambling or forgery, with very little success. He seldom accumulated any money, squandering it instead on hookers and booze. As soon as his first marriage fell apart, Hickock found another bride, also only 16. That union wouldn't last long either, because he made a serious mistake in 1956.

Being short of cash, Dick Hickock decided to supplement his income by committing a burglary. He was caught, tried, convicted, and sentenced to five years in Kansas State Penitentiary. Soon afterward, his young wife ended the marriage.

In prison, Hickock shared a cell with Perry Smith. To become accepted in the peculiar social hierarchy of convicts, both of them decided to decorate their bodies with tattoos. Dick sat still while a dragon was inked onto his skin, then later a cat, a skull, two nude women, and an assortment of names.

Dick and Perry parted company upon Smith's release by parole in July 1959. Hickock befriended another inmate who told him that he'd once worked for a wealthy farmer in Kansas named Herb Clutter. Inside Clutter's home office, the con said, a hidden wall safe contained at least $10,000 in cash. Within a few weeks, Perry Smith received a letter from Hickock suggesting a get-rich-quick plan. "After you left I met someone, you do not know him, but he put me on to something we could bring off beautiful. A cinch, the perfect score. . . ."

Hickock left prison on August 13, moved in with his parents in Olathe, Kansas, and worked in an auto body shop. In November, Perry Smith joined him, and the pair drove Hickock's '49

Chevy 400 miles to Holcomb, near the state's western border, stopping en route to buy clothesline cord, tape, and shotgun shells.

Late that night, they drove under a canopy of trees lining the long driveway to the isolated Clutter farm. Through unlocked doors, they entered the house and found Herb in his ground-floor office. His wife and two teenagers slept upstairs. When the intruders demanded money from the hidden wall safe, Clutter truthfully said he had no such safe nor much cash in the house. Furious, Hickock and Smith took him to the basement and trussed him like a pig ready for slaughter. Ransacking the house, they found Kenyon, forced him into the basement and bound him, too. The father insisted that he had no money and begged them not to harm his family. Leaving the pair tied, Smith and Hickock rushed upstairs and found Nancy, trembling, in the hallway. Smith entered Bonnie Clutter's bedroom and tied her up while she cried. Correctly figuring that Dick might try to sexually assault the teenage girl, he hurried into her room. He later said he probably saved her from being raped. Returning to the basement, they taped the mouths of Herb and Kenyon.

Frustrated, the intruders exchanged harsh words about what to do next. Smith, boiling inside with anger and frustration, exploded. He cut Herb Clutter's throat, then fired two shotgun blasts point-blank at the father and son, killing both of them. As he walked away, he left a bloody bootprint on a cardboard box. He repeated the slaughter upstairs with Bonnie and Nancy. The total loot the raiders took amounted to less than $50 in cash, a telescope, and Kenyon's portable radio.

Hickock and Smith drove back to Olathe. In his parents' home, Hickock dozed, ate dinner, and watched a basketball game on television. Within a few days, Smith and Hickock agreed to head south to Mexico, where they might strike it rich.

After fleeing to Kansas City, Hickock used his Svengali charm to swindle money from several stores. The pair drove to Mexico City, then to Acapulco, where they rented a boat in a ridiculous attempt to find sunken treasure, and wasted what little money they'd stolen. Arriving back in Texas on a bus, they hitchhiked through several states, finally landing in Las Vegas. There, the FBI caught up with the fugitives and arrested them. Hickock's prison pal, who had hatched the scheme against Herb Clutter, had heard of the murders and told police who the probable killers were. The bootprint left by Smith clinched the case against them.

On the rainy night of April 14, 1965, the State of Kansas ended the careers of Richard Hickock and Perry Smith. Both men, separately, mounted thirteen steps, had nooses cinched around their necks, plunged through a trap door, and died at the end of a hangman's rope.

Horoscope for Richard Eugene Hickock
Born June 6, 1931, 1:06 A.M CST, Kansas City, Kansas
Source: Birth certificate

On the surface, Richard Hickock's chart appears to describe an innocuous, hapless loser with no intense focus of energy in any one area of his life. However, closer examination of the underside is like turning over a rock. Unpleasant things appear.

It is interesting that the strongest house in Hickock's chart is his fifth, ruling sex and children, considering that he acknowledged interest in young girls. In fact, his involvement with youngsters was more than a passing interest; it was a sexual obsession. Pluto, which rules obsessions/compulsions, is found in Hickock's fifth house next to Jupiter. This configuration increases in Hickock the drive to express his devious lust. Pluto and Jupiter are both in Cancer, which causes the pedophilia gripping Hickock to be extremely acute. After he was captured, Hickock wrote a letter stating that he knew that a young girl would be at the Clutter farm even before he and Perry Smith made the trip. The main reason he chose the Clutter home as a target, he admitted, was not to rob them, but to rape the girl. His intent to sexually assault the teenager also explains his reluctance to leave the house, even when he realized the money-laden safe didn't exist.

The savage sign of Scorpio, governed by Mars and Pluto, rules Hickock's eighth house of death. Mars weaves shooting into the deadly tapestry, and Pluto threads it with ruthless obsession. Before Hickock's accomplice ended the lives of the Clutter family with a shotgun, Hickock attempted to rape the girl. He would probably have completed the act if Smith hadn't interceded. Hickock's desire to rape is indicated by Pluto's placement in his fifth house of sex.

Before the murders, Hickock's crimes were mostly con games and scams in which he utilized his glib tongue. His Sun is in

Gemini, the sign of a smooth talker and quick thinker. These abilities are reflected in his Pisces ascendant, which rules his first house of personality. Pisces is also governed by Neptune, the planet most associated with deception. Fast talking, a trait bestowed by his Gemini Sun, combined with his smarmy Pisces personality, creates the perfect picture of a successful con artist.

Hickock's first house also describes his physical appearance. With Uranus, the planet of eccentricity, residing in his first house, it follows that he might look odd. Due to an accident, Hickock ended up with an asymmetrical face, as if the two halves came from different people. It is rather intriguing that the results of his accident parallel the dual nature of his Sun sign, Gemini.

The cruelty shown by Hickock in his treatment of the Clutter family, even though he denied pulling the shotgun trigger, is clear by the position of his Mars. It is in opposition to his Moon, creating the worst possible aspect. With the Moon, which rules emotions, in the sign of Aquarius, this terribly negative configuration suggests a cold-blooded ruthlessness. Hickock exhibited no emotion of any kind after collaborating in the execution of four innocent people.

Most of Hickock's crimes, including the multiple murders, robberies, and fraud, were committed with a partner. The seventh house, ruling partners, is governed by Mercury, which resides in the second house of money. This quest for easy money provided the motive for their crime partnership. The fact that Mercury is in Taurus, a sign associated with money, augments this motivation.

Hickock and Smith were eventually caught, tried, convicted, and sentenced to death by hanging. The ninth house, ruled by Jupiter, relates to the court system. Jupiter is in opposition to Saturn, which rules hanging. An element of Jupiter's beneficence is shown by the sympathetic support Hickock received throughout the trial from his mother. Jupiter also rules his tenth house, which represents his mother.

Prison is a twelfth-house concern. Hickock's twelfth house is ruled by his Moon in Aquarius as well as Saturn and Uranus. Alienation and separation from his emotions, ruled by the Moon, are shown by the unhappy configuration in his twelfth house. He died by hanging, a reflection of Saturn, a loser to the end.

Arthur Shawcross

Wednesday, June 6, 1945, 4:14 A.M.
Kittery, Maine • Time Zone: 04:00 (Eastern War Time)
Longitude 070° W 45' • Latitude 43° N 05'
Placidus Houses • Tropical Zodiac

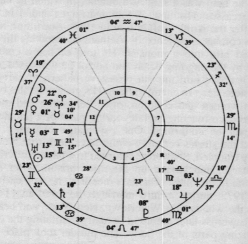

The hideously grotesque crimes committed by Arthur Shawcross are almost beyond the scope of imagination. In his own
written confessions, he admitted incidents of incest, bestiality,
necrophilia, pedophilia, and serial murder involving sexual mutilation and cannibalizing the genitals of his victims.

Acknowledging deep sentimentality regarding his mother, yet
profoundly hurt by her, Shawcross described how she dominated
him and his father. Years later, while hypnotized, he spoke of
alleged sexual abuse by his mother that left him bloody and
nearly paralyzed. Sex became a sick obsession with him during
his childhood, Shawcross said, when he was seduced by an aunt
and became incestuously involved with his younger sister. He
also tried homosexual contact with a playmate, was raped by an
adult male, and experimented carnally with several animals. As
a teenager, Shawcross recalled, he had sex with a teenage girl
and was caught by her older brother, who forced Shawcross to
fellate him.

A growing cauldron of anger at 19, Shawcross dropped out of

high school and became a solitary wandering loner, supporting himself by burglary. He sought solace for his inner fury by setting fires, a classic symptom of future serial killers. Among the few jobs he held was a stint as a butcher in which he carved up animal carcasses. His first of four marriages ended in divorce shortly after the Army drafted him in 1968. According to Shawcross, his combat experience in Vietnam changed his life forever and turned him into a monster. He told of being emotionally shattered by the ongoing death and horror he witnessed, explaining that it drove him into an obsessive pattern of carrying out solo missions deep in enemy terrain. His gory war tales of killing countless women and children, often beheading and mutilating them, and once roasting and devouring parts of a female victim, could never be confirmed. One psychiatric examiner, though, suggested the stories certainly could have been true.

Deeply troubled, Shawcross returned to a pattern of crime after his discharge, and wound up in Attica prison. After saving a guard's life in the midst of a mass rebellion, he won early parole. In June 1972, during a third marriage, he lured an 11-year-old boy into the woods near Watertown, New York, and beat him to death. Shawcross later admitted sexually mutilating the child and cannibalizing parts of the body. The murder took place just two days before he turned 27, consistent with a pattern seen in many serial killers of committing criminal acts close to their own birthdays.

Three months later, while fishing in a river, Shawcross spotted a little girl, age 8, playing nearby. He brutally raped the child; stuffed grass, leaves, and dirt into her mouth until she choked to death; then buried her under a bridge. A witness had seen the girl talking to Shawcross earlier that day. When confronted by police, he confessed. The uncontrollable urge to kill, he rationalized, came from his Vietnam experiences. Even though Shawcross was also linked to the boy's murder, the state tried him only for the girl's death. Finding him guilty of manslaughter, the court sentenced Shawcross to 25 years, as officials proclaimed that no parole board would ever release an admitted child rapist and killer.

Despite an early record of behavioral problems in prison, Shawcross learned to manipulate the system, and walked out with a parole in March 1987. The quiet, tough, short, muscular ex-con married his fourth wife; moved to Rochester, New York;

found a job making packaged salads; and promptly started an affair with another woman who frequently allowed him to borrow her car. Often preferring to be alone, he sought solitude by taking long walks, bicycling, and fishing.

Dark sexual urges had never left Shawcross. The next January, feeling spurned by his mother's refusal to be with him for Christmas, and twisted by his brooding, depraved sex drive, he picked up prostitute Dorothy Blackburn, 27. According to his own eventual confession, Shawcross strangled her to death inside the borrowed car after she'd drawn blood by violently biting him during oral sex. From a bridge, he dumped her body into freezing Salmon Creek.

The following spring and summer, several more Rochester-area women, mostly prostitutes, vanished. Decomposed and mutilated bodies began turning up along Genesee River banks and in wooded areas. Even though Arthur Shawcross, known as "Mitch" by local hookers, habitually cruised the streets and bought their services, he miraculously avoided becoming a suspect. No one remotely linked him to the crimes, not even when Dorothy Keller, a homeless part-time waitress whom Shawcross often dated, turned up dead. He seemed to have an uncanny blanket of invisibility.

The killing continued into 1989. In November, June Stotts, 30, who often visited Shawcross and his wife, accepted a ride from him to a beach along the river. Mildly retarded, the woman kissed her buddy and, as he later recalled, offered to give him her virginity. During the intercourse, though, he suspected she had lied about her virtue, so he accused her of misleading him. In his own recollection, she lost her temper and attacked him, screaming and clawing at his face. He had no choice but to protect himself, and "accidentally" suffocated her while trying to keep her quiet. After leaving her body in a grassy area, he revisited it a week later and couldn't resist having sex with it again. Later, using his experience as a meatcutter, he sliced the body open lengthwise, cut off portions of her genitals, and devoured them.

More prostitutes vanished, and officials finally accepted the possibility of one serial killer being responsible.

On January 3, 1990, a police helicopter passed over a car parked on a bridge where a female murder victim had been dropped into the icy waters the previous month. The aircraft followed as the driver hurried away. When the pursuers arrested Arthur Shawcross, 44, he claimed he stopped on the bridge simply to relieve his bladder. But under intense questioning, he gradually broke down and confessed to strangling eleven women. With sociopathic calm, though, he offered excuses for each killing. The prostitutes, he complained, had either tried to rob him or had cruelly teased him about impotence. He compliantly drew a map to indicate the locations where he'd left the bodies, and admitted making visits to them before the decomposing remains were discovered. He'd engaged in necrophilia and cannibalized more than one of them, he said. During his confession, Shawcross begged that no one tell his mother of his disgusting crimes, even though she hadn't spoken to him for seventeen years.

Convicted of ten murders, Arthur Shawcross escaped the death penalty since New York had not yet enacted such a law in 1990. A judge sentenced him to ten consecutive 25-year terms in prison.

Horoscope for Arthur Shawcross
Born June 6, 1945, 4:14 A.M. Eastern War Time, Kittery, Maine
Source: Misbegotten Son, by Jack Olsen, p. 165

The gruesome criminal record of Arthur Shawcross is almost beyond belief. From incest to cannibalizing the private parts of his female victims, his hideous acts suggest a grossly unnatural inward focus on his own fetid desires. This enormous selfishness becomes immediately evident in his chart.

Shawcross's Sun exerts massive power in his first house of personality and self. This placement represents the egotistical part of his personality. He thinks he is more important than anything else in the world and entitled to whatever he desires. His own activities, including what he says, does, and thinks, appear absolutely fascinating to him, and in his opinion, should be spellbinding to everyone else. With Mercury and Uranus also occupying the first house, it becomes the strongest in his chart. Uranus nestles solidly shoulder to shoulder with the Sun. This cozy aspect suggests that Shawcross wanted to be seen as eccentric and unusual, so he sought attention by saying outrageous things. His enormous ego expressed itself with grotesque stories and bizarre exaggerations. Since all of his first-house planets are in Gemini, the sign of communication, a great deal of his self-centered be-

havior is talk, talk, talk. Of course, his endless shocking solilo-
quies focused on himself. Many of them were later proven to be
untrue. Shawcross was absolutely mesmerized by his own unique
cleverness.

Of course, all this self-involvement in Shawcross's chart became incredibly dangerous when he began acting out his grotesque tales. His twelfth house is nearly as strong as the first
house. It is the domain of the Moon, Mars, and Venus. Shawcross's incredible acts of barbarous cruelty are indicated by Mars,
which accounts for the bloody violence he inflicted on little girls
and women. Mars is next to his Moon, ruler of women, who
became the primary targets of his savagery. Since both Mars and
the Moon are in Aries, a Mars-ruled sign, the savagery is intensified by the presence of Aries. With his Mars/Moon conjunction
hidden away in his twelfth house of secrets, Shawcross was able
to conceal any connection he had with the horribly mutilated
bodies he left unburied. The fact that his Gemini Sun is his
strongest also aided him in avoiding detection. The duality
brought by Gemini, the sign of the twins, successfully hid the
malignance underneath Shawcross's benign exterior. Gemini is
also a signature of a serial killer.

Shawcross's obsession with erotic lust is exposed by the presence of Jupiter and Neptune in his fifth house of sex. Jupiter
relates to his strong sex drive. Neptune rules Shawcross's fantasies, in which prurience dominated his fevered imagination.
With Mercury ruling his fifth house, he talked endlessly about
his sex life, either real or imagined.

Shawcross's dealings with the Army are quite interesting. Military service is a sixth-house matter, and in his chart it is governed by Venus. Since Venus is also the ruler of his ascendant,
all his trumped-up combat adventures, in Shawcross's version,
featured him as the hero. Many of his war stories concerned
killing women and children, not the enemy. It was later discovered that he never participated in combat, but was stationed in a
city with swimming pools, movies, and entertainment. These
pleasantries are all ruled by Venus, the influence of his sixth
house.

Death relates to the eighth house, which is co-ruled by Sagittarius and Jupiter. Jupiter also rules his fifth house of sex. This
placement shows a direct connection between sex and death in
his mind. Abundance is a Jupiter feature as well, which indicates

the long list of victims killed by Shawcross over a number of years. The fact that most of the women he killed were prostitutes is indicated by the influence of the fifth house.

The twelfth house, ruling prisons, is home to three planets, suggesting that prison plays an important role in the life of Shawcross. The years he spent locked up bears this out. The Moon and Mars in his twelfth house relate to the violent crimes against women that landed him in prison. Now incarcerated for life, it is a sure thing that Shawcross spends most of his time boring other inmates with his endless talk, bragging about himself and his crimes.

John Joseph Famalaro

Monday, June 10, 1957, 10:49 A.M.
Brookhaven, New York • Time Zone: 04:00 (EDT)
Longitude 073° W 23' • Latitude 40° N 52'
Placidus Houses • Tropical Zodiac

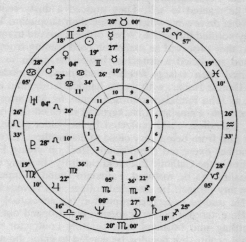

Newswatchers across the nation extended their sympathy to the family of beautiful Denise Huber when she mysteriously vanished in 1991. As the search for her stretched across an unendurable three years, public concern turned to heartfelt empathy. Anyone, especially parents of missing children, can understand the panic, fear, and desperate pain that occurs when a loved one disappears without a trace. When the police finally found Denise, the horror became incomprehensible. Her abductor and killer had kept the nude body in a deep freezer for the entire three years.

Denise had been on her way home from a Southern California concert in June 1991. Just a few miles from her destination, in the wee hours, a tire went flat on her Honda, and she pulled over to the side of the freeway. Nineteen hours later, her girlfriend, searching for Denise, spotted the abandoned car. A massive investigation and prolonged hunt ensued. Television programs featured the parents' tearful pleas for her abductor to please let them know what had happened to their beloved daughter. *America's Most Wanted*, the popular TV program that requests tips from

the viewing audience, profiled the case, and a national audience
gave their hearts to the Huber family.

In 1994, an Arizona couple met painting contractor John Famalaro near Prescott, and followed him to his home to inspect
supplies he wanted to sell. They noticed a dusty rental truck
sitting in his driveway, which aroused their suspicion. That evening, they notified the police. When officers arrived to investigate
the truck, they observed an extension cord leading from it to the
house, and suspected a drug lab. Inside the cargo section, the
police pried open a large freezer, and found the nude, frozen
body of Denise Huber, with wrists handcuffed behind her back.
As soon as John Famalaro returned home, he was arrested.

A check into Famalaro's background revealed that he'd been
a sickly, friendless child protected by his older sister. An age
gap kept him from being very close to his brother. His religious-
zealot mother exercised a profound effect on young Famalaro,
raising him in the Catholic faith and carefully shielding him from
any sexuality. As he matured, Famalaro found it impossible to
complete any project. He attended college, but never obtained a
degree. He studied to be a chiropractor, but never took the final
exams. He entered a police academy, but dropped out. Temporarily settling into business as a painting contractor, he made
substantial profits, but decided he wanted to enter the real estate
field.

Women became a major factor in Famalaro's life, starting with
the heavy-handed influence of his mother. It became all important for him to impress them. His first love, a college student,
became a grinding obsession for Famalaro, and when she became
pregnant and left him, he wrote a hundred-page journal bemoan-
ing the loss. Not a particularly handsome man, with his long nose
and weak, bearded chin, Famalaro used a glib tongue and extreme generosity to date other attractive, sophisticated women.
He treated one to a New York trip, taking her to Broadway plays
and lavish dinners, all first class. One morning, he inexplicably
removed her nightgown, quickly handcuffed her to a window
railing in their hotel room, and left her there for hours on full,
nude display. Another lover was stunned one day when Famalaro
handcuffed her to his bed and made her think he was going to
rape her.

Not long after Denise Huber disappeared, Famalaro moved his
painting business from Southern California to Prescott, Arizona.

In his home, he compulsively collected objects that would eventually lead to his downfall. Not only had he kept Denise Huber's
body, but he retained two cardboard boxes filled with her bloody
clothing, identification cards, her shoes, her car keys, and two
gruesome tools connected to her death.

The investigators' pulses raced when they found similar identification documents belonging to several other women. It appeared that a serial killer might have been apprehended.
Subsequent probing, though, located all of the women still alive
and wondering how Famalaro had come into possession of their
papers.

The suspect had also kept newspaper articles and video copies
of television programs in which Huber's parents had begged for
information about their missing daughter.

Under arrest for murder, Famalaro refused to speak about the
death of Denise Huber. Investigators finally traced the place of
the murder to a warehouse in Southern California where Famalaro had operated his house-painting business. A chemical test
revealed extensive blood stains on the concrete floor, and DNA
processing matched the blood to Denise Huber.

After Famalaro had abducted Huber in the vicinity of her dis-
abled car, he had transported her to the warehouse, fifteen miles
away. Inside the huge chamber, he had stripped her, sexually
assaulted her, and then bludgeoned her to death with a hammer
and a roofer's nail puller. Both tools wound up in the cardboard
box with Huber's personal possessions.

Whatever the fury was that drove Famalaro to extreme violence, it remained locked inside him. At the trial, in 1997, he
refused to testify. When a pathologist described the damage inflicted on Denise Huber, she referred to a photograph of the
victim's skull, graphically illustrating how the bones had been
pieced together like a jigsaw puzzle. It was estimated that Famalaro had struck her more than forty times.

As many serial killers do, John Famalaro had committed a
murder within a few days of his own birthday.

The prosecutor, working entirely with circumstantial evidence,
linked Famalaro to the use of handcuffs on Denise Huber's wrists
by eliciting testimony from the two lovers who had been subjected to Famalaro's odd habit of suddenly snapping cuffs on
them during sex play. Receipts for the freezer connected Famalaro to its purchase, within days after Denise vanished. A storage

facility manager told how Famalaro required 24-hour electricity to keep his freezer running. His odd possession of her shoes, clothing, and personal items, along with the murder weapons, sealed Famalaro's fate.

It all added up to a jury's verdict in June 1997 that Famalaro had kidnapped, sexually assaulted, and murdered Denise Huber. They deliberated a short time before recommending he pay for the crime with his own life.

John Joseph Famalaro, stubbornly refusing to reveal exactly what happened on the freeway when he encountered a helpless young woman, entered San Quentin's Death Row in September 1997, along with over 500 other men condemned to be executed for taking innocent lives.

Horoscope for John Joseph Famalaro
Born June 10, 1957, 10:49 A.M. EDT, Brookhaven, New York
Source: Birth certificate

The indescribable torture John Famalaro inflicted on both his victim, Denise Huber, and her family is shown by his dominant planet, the Moon in Scorpio, and its relationship to Saturn. His Moon, ruling women, is in Scorpio, the sign relating to torture and sadism. Kidnapping and murdering Denise, then keeping her body for three years while he let her family suffer, is sadism in its worst form.

Starting with his overpowering mother, women completely dominated his life. With the Moon next to Saturn, he also felt smothered by women and deeply resented it. Saturn, representing control, is evident in Famalaro's eventual habit of snapping handcuffs on his sexual partners, clearly reflecting his desire for full authority over his female companions.

Famalaro's mental condition is questionable, considering the Moon's opposition to Mercury. Both planets are associated with the mind, and are virtually butting heads within his chart. This strong negative aspect indicates probable mental imbalance. Another factor in his chart suggesting mental problems is the presence of Neptune in his third house of rational thinking. Neptune creates clouds of confusion, imaginary notions, and unreality in thought processes. Its position in the sign of Scorpio also lends suspicion and fear to his emotions.

The other important factors in Famalaro's chart are his dominant tenth house and his Leo ascendant. Both of these astrological configurations show an intense desire for recognition and admiration. He wanted desperately to impress people with his talents and to be envied for his success with women. But due to his erratic behavior, he never succeeded in anything. The nature of his Sun sign, Gemini, describes his interest in many different fields, but he never followed through on any of them. Gemini natives are interested in acquiring knowledge across a broad spectrum but are satisfied with a superficial overview rather than a complete understanding of any one subject.

Famalaro's eighth house of death is ruled by Pisces. Neptune, the ruler of Pisces, governs fantasies and delusions. His daydreams usually featured death in one form or another. Jupiter, the other ruler of Pisces, sits in negative relationship to the Sun, ruler of his ego. This terrifying aspect shows that murder was an ego trip for him. With Jupiter also influencing his fifth house of sex, there is a direct relationship in his life between sex and death.

Pluto, ruling kidnapping, resides in his first house, and sits in a negative juxtaposition to the Moon. This problematic aspect describes revenge against a woman, any woman, even a stranger. Famalaro sexually assaulted Denise Huber and, in a frenzied rage, bludgeoned her to death with metal tools. Mars, which rules beating, anger, and weapons, also creates a dangerous aspect by its orientation to the Moon. This positioning reveals Famalaro's desire to get even for the imagined slights he suffered from women. After the horrific murder, he kept his victim's body in a freezer for three years. This extraordinary act is explained by a combination of factors in his chart. Both his Mars and Venus are in Cancer. This is a grasping, controlling sign that does not let go. Another contributing factor is found in his twelfth house of secrets, which encompasses Uranus, the planet of eccentricity. Keeping a frozen body of a murder victim is certainly one of the most bizarre acts imaginable. The fact that only he knew of her whereabouts gave him a sense of great pride. This morbid behavior is induced by the presence of Uranus, the planet of eccentricity, in Leo, the sign associated with pride.

Famalaro's refusal to discuss his crime with anyone or to testify during his trial is a characteristic of secretive, mysterious Scorpio, his Moon sign. In addition, his Mercury, the planet of speech, opposes his Scorpio Moon. Adding to this complex configuration, Mercury is in Taurus, the sign of stubborn behavior. The bottom line is a reluctance to share information about himself.

The twelfth house rules prison, where Famalaro now resides. With unconventional Uranus still exerting itself, Famalaro's eccentricity will be observed by fellow inmates. It is likely that he will be considered a misfit on Death Row and subjected to abuse or ostracism. The other ruler of his twelfth house is Cancer, which is ruled by the Moon. The prevailing influence of women continues to haunt him and will not abate until his death.

CANCER

Under negative conditions, Cancer natives are exceptionally tenacious and emotionally manipulative. O. J. Simpson, who was acquitted in a murder trial, was born under the sign of Cancer, as was Kenneth Starr, the special prosecutor who investigated President Clinton. The claws of the crab, Cancer's symbol, can hold with a grip of death.

Patricia Ann Columbo

Thursday, June 21, 1956, 11:52 A.M.
Chicago, Illinois • Time Zone: 05:00 (CDT)
Longitude 087° W 39' • Latitude 41° N 51'
Placidus Houses • Tropical Zodiac

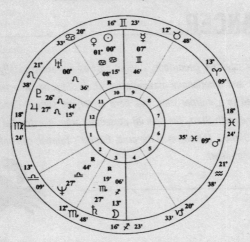

Love can drive people into extreme conduct previously unimaginable to them. Countless murders have been committed in jealous rage fueled by the passion of love. Love triangles also can lead to murder when the third party becomes consumed with an obsession to kill the spouse in order to eliminate the competition. Patricia Columbo and Frank DeLuca faced an entirely different obstacle to their love affair.

Patricia Columbo, at age 18, gave her heart to a man 20 years her senior, who also happened to be married. Frank DeLuca, 38, a pharmacist in Elk Grove, Illinois, was also the father of five children. It is often said that love is blind. Patty Columbo could see only that she wanted Frank no matter what happened. She didn't even care whether DeLuca obtained a divorce as long as he was willing to live with her. But, the problem was not DeLuca's wife; it was Patty's father.

Frank Columbo, 43, only five years older than Patty's paramour, could see no future in the relationship. His daughter, he figured, was too immature to be saddled with a man who had fathered five kids. The headstrong girl had been exerting more independence than she had yet earned, and Columbo had nearly reached the end of his paternal tether. Columbo decided to confront the situation and put it to an end. Armed with a rifle, he drove to DeLuca's pharmacy, called the proprietor outside, and stated his unequivocal opinion about the affair. When DeLuca protested, Columbo drove home his point by smashing the rifle butt into DeLuca's mouth. The force of the blow chipped several of DeLuca's teeth. He lifted both hands to stem the blood flow, but it leaked through, especially in the gap of his right hand, which had been left with only three fingers after an accident years earlier. Before stalking away, Columbo delivered a strong warning: "Stay away from my daughter."

At home, Columbo had a serious talk with Patty. He strongly expressed his opinion that she should see no more of the older man, and hinted that her continuance to do so would probably cause her to be written out of her parents' will. Her younger brother would inherit everything.

Stubborn and still in love, Patricia ran to DeLuca, who was having trouble smiling about anything. They spent the night together examining various options.

The plan they developed would solve everything, they hoped. Patricia asked among some acquaintances if they knew anyone who might be willing to make an offer Mr. Columbo couldn't refuse. She heard the name of an ex-cop who had once been a deputy sheriff in Cook County. Patty found him in October 1975, flirted until she felt confident that he wouldn't inform on her, and presented her plan. The hit man, along with an accomplice, agreed to eliminate Patricia's parents, in return for unlimited sex. The leggy brunette, with large liquid eyes and a gleaming smile, readily agreed. She even made several advance payments, over a period of weeks, taking on both men at the same time.

The ex-cop kept coming up with new requests. He needed pictures of Patricia's mother, father, and brother. After stalling another week, he told Patricia that the sex payments weren't quite enough. She would have to come up with some cash, too.

Patricia had no money, and her pharmacist lover couldn't come up with enough to satisfy the would-be hitmen. So, the desperate pair decided that the only way to get something done right was to do it yourself. On a warm spring evening, May 4, 1976, they paid a visit to the Columbo home. When they left,

Frank Columbo lay on the floor, his head bludgeoned to a pulpy mess and four bullets lodged in his body. The life of Mary Columbo, Patricia's mother, had been ended with a single shot in the center of her forehead. Patricia had concluded the blood orgy by plunging a knife into her kid brother's body more than 80 times.

During the massive police investigation, Patricia dreamed up a scenario similar to one presented by Dr. Jeffrey MacDonald in 1970 (see separate profile), in which drug-crazed hippies had invaded his home and killed his wife and two young daughters. Investigators were skeptical, and when they examined the crime scene for fingerprints, evidence turned up to solidify their doubts. They found prints from a three-fingered hand.

Boring in on friends of the two lovers, the sleuths found the pal who had suggested the hitmen. It didn't take long to track down the ex-cop, who corroborated the story of Patricia's desire to have her family murdered.

Attempting to slip away from responsibility again, Patricia tried to convince police that DeLuca had been the trigger man, and she been nothing but an innocent bystander. It didn't work. In July 1977, both DeLuca and Patricia Columbo were found guilty on three counts of first-degree murder. They slumped in their chairs when the judge ordered them to serve between two and three *centuries* in prison.

Resorting to the use of her body and looks, Patricia found a way to make life easier in prison. She organized sex parties for fellow inmates, joined by a few members of the prison staff. She reportedly acted not only as organizer, but also as an active participant in the revelry. When officials learned of the orgies, the sex ring was broken up, embarrassed staff members were disciplined, and Patricia was separated from fellow party animals.

She remains in prison, as does her lover. Murder seldom cements a love relationship or solves problems of the heart.

Horoscope for Patricia Ann Columbo
Born June 21, 1956, 11:52 A.M. CDT, Chicago, Illinois
Source: Clark Howard, author of Love's Blood, *in note to Dana Holliday*

This clinging, dependent, ultrafeminine woman is, in reality, a powerhouse who controlled and dominated the people around her. Financial gain was her primary goal in life.

Patricia Columbo's strongest planet, her Sun, rules her ego, and endows her with an attitude of arrogant superiority. The Sun is found in Columbo's forceful tenth house of social status and reputation. Her most powerful sign is Leo, which proffers leadership. All together, these configurations describe Columbo's demand for public acclaim and her need to be in charge. She is a person who absolutely must rule the roost (or the rooster).

Since her Sun is in Cancer, though, she adopted an appearance of feminine helplessness. Cancer is a controlling and manipulative sign, so these adorable attitudes were feigned for her personal gain.

Columbo's initial overtures to potential hitmen, requesting them to kill her family, were influenced by her fifth house of sex, which is ruled by materialistic Saturn. She readily gave sexual favors to men with the expectation they would help her eventually gain a sizable inheritance. With her Saturn in Scorpio, Columbo's sexual nature gained added manipulative and devious qualities.

Ultimately, she and her married boyfriend jointly killed her family. It is thought that the boyfriend bludgeoned her father and shot her mother, while Columbo stabbed her little brother to death. His body sustained numerous puncture wounds, indicating an emotional, rage-filled attack. This correlates perfectly with the fact that Mars, ruler of shooting, stabbing, and weapons, influenced Columbo's eighth house of death as well as the third house governing her brother. It appears to have no effect on either house related to her parents, the tenth and the fourth, which hints that her boyfriend probably murdered them. These astrological rulerships lend credence to the view that Columbo did stab her little brother to death, although she denied it.

Her younger brother is designated by the third house, which provides residence to a pair of planets, Saturn and the Moon. The Moon rules Columbo's emotions. Saturn is in Scorpio, an emotional sign, and blends resentment plus hatred into the mix. Violent Mars, an additional third-house ruler, is in Pisces, another emotional sign. With all of these feelings centered on Columbo's brother, together with her drive to dominate, it is not surprising that she murdered him without a qualm.

The eighth house of death also relates to inheritance since it involves money derived from the death of another. Mars makes a second entry into the picture by its role, as her eighth-house ruler, in Pisces, the sign of the dreamer. She killed in order to inherit money, but the idea was ridiculous, ill-conceived, ill-planned, and a failure. Pisces does not deal in reality.

Columbo's father is ruled by the fourth house, and her mother the tenth. Jupiter, the planet of generosity, is linked with her father by his indulgence during her childhood. But his disapproval of her lifestyle led to his death. Her mother is influenced by two planets, Columbo's Sun and Venus, both in Cancer. Columbo's desire to dominate her mother is made apparent by the strong presence of the Sun in the tenth house. The influence of Venus indicates affection and emotions, suggesting that Columbo may have felt affection for her mother during childhood. But Columbo's greedy desire for money and freedom overcame any love she may have harbored.

Columbo's life behind bars is apparently quite active. Pluto and Jupiter occupy her twelfth house of prisons, in close conjunction, both in Leo. Pluto gives Columbo the skill to exert influence over others, while Jupiter lends enormity to her power. Leo provides arrogant confidence. Unless she is kept under close scrutiny, she will continue to use her wiles to gain advantages during the decades of imprisonment she still faces.

Charles Joseph Whitman

Tuesday, June 24, 1941, 1:50 A.M.
Lake Worth, Florida • Time Zone: 05:00 (EST)
Longitude 080° W 03' 26" • Latitude 26° N 36' 56"
Placidus Houses • Tropical Zodiac

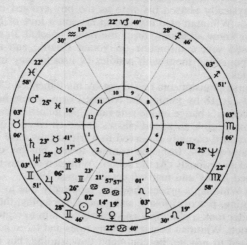

No one ever looked less like a killer than Charles Whitman. At age 25, his handsome face and athletic build suggested a quintessential all-American football player, with blond crewcut hair, blue eyes, fair skin, and a friendly grin that flashed glistening white teeth. It would have been impossible for any layperson to predict that on August 1, 1966, he would first murder his mother and his wife, then climb the 300-foot clock tower on the University of Texas campus, and methodically shoot at pedestrians in the square below, leaving 13 dead and 31 more wounded.

Ironically, though, he had secretly visited a psychiatrist shortly before the killings to discuss stress and mental turmoil, and had mentioned to the doctor some thoughts about "going up on the tower with a deer rifle and start shooting people." The psychiatrist, accustomed to ravings from troubled people, took no specific action.

No clue to Whitman's coming rampage could be found in his physical appearance, nor would his lifestyle tip off anyone in his social circle that Whitman would turn out to be a mass murderer.

As a child, he had served as an altar boy. He became an Eagle Scout at age 12 (at that time, the youngest ever to do so) and an accomplished musician, then later served as a scoutmaster. His ostensibly perfect young life did have flaws, though. Whitman's father physically abused his wife as the boy cringed in terror. The senior Whitman also instilled in his son a love of firearms. "My boys know all about guns," the father boasted. In addition, he imposed severe discipline on young Charlie and his little brother, punishing them with paddles or fists for any infraction of his rules.

The harsh punishments meted out by his father led Charles to escape at age 18 by joining the Marine Corps, where he earned a sharpshooter's badge on the rifle range. As an officer candidate, he became eligible to attend classes at the University of Texas. There, he once casually observed to a friend how easy it would be to shoot people from the campus tower, but his comment wasn't taken seriously. At the school, Whitman also met a pretty girl named Kathy and married her in August 1962.

When Whitman's grades dropped, reportedly due to focusing on gambling, practical jokes, and general horseplay, the Marine commander took a dim view and reassigned him to regular duty. Disgruntled, Whitman began breaking rules and faced court martial. Busted to private, he continued downsliding, but managed an honorable discharge at the end of 1964. Back at the university, partly supported by his father, he worked, took classes, and in his spare time became a scoutmaster once again. With this crammed schedule of activities, he felt intense pressure, and showed temperamental symptoms of it. To keep going at his high-speed pace, he began using Dexedrine (which contains amphetamine) "like popcorn." He complained to his wife and friends about terrible headaches.

After Whitman's parents split up, he brought his mother to Austin and expressed hatred for his father. He considered withdrawing from the self-imposed high-pressure schedule and leaving everything including classes, jobs, and his wife. But he changed his mind and worked even harder. Kathy worried that Charlie was near the breaking point.

Planning his assault about 36 hours before climbing the tower with an arsenal of weapons, Whitman wrote, "Lately I have been a victim of many unusual and irrational thoughts. . . . I've been having fears and violent impulses. . . ." His typed letter said, "It was after much thought that I decided to kill my wife, Kathy tonight. . . ." After describing his deep love for her, Whitman noted, "I intend to kill her as painlessly as possible." Writing about events that hadn't yet happened, Whitman typed, "Similar reasons provoked me to take my mother's life also. I don't think the poor woman has ever enjoyed life as she is entitled to. She is a simple young woman who married a very possessing and dominating man. . . ."

On Sunday, July 31, 1966, the temperature soared to triple digits and stayed unusually hot that night. After 10:30, Whitman spoke to his mother by telephone, and told her he was coming over to enjoy her air-conditioned apartment. Evidence would later show signs of an intense struggle while he stabbed her to death. He left another note complaining about his father's treatment of her: "She took enough of his beatings, humiliation, degradation. . . . He has chosen to treat her like a slut. . . . I have relieved her of her sufferings here on earth. . . . The intense hatred I feel for my father is beyond description. . . ."

Back at his own residence, Whitman walked into the bedroom where his nude wife slept, used a bayonet to inflict four deep stab wounds in her chest, and piously covered her corpse with a sheet. "I imagine that it appears that I brutally killed both my loved ones," he scribbled in a note. "I was only trying to do a quick, thorough job."

As the heat skyrocketed again on Monday, Whitman lugged a heavy military footlocker into the campus clock tower before noon. It contained enough provisions to camp out for a week: food, drugs, knives, rope, water, fuel, a staggering array of firearms—including a rifle scope—and ammunition. With the load on a dolly, he pushed it into an elevator, exited at the 27th floor, and wrestled it up cumbersome stairs toward the observation deck. En route, at a reception room, he met a diminutive woman, whom he instantly bludgeoned and shot. Moments later, a young couple exited the observation deck, and Whitman courteously allowed them to leave. But a vacationing family of six weren't so lucky. Whitman fired a shotgun and killed a teenage boy and his aunt, and severely wounded others in the group.

At last alone on the open-air deck, which provided a walkway around four huge clocks facing in each direction, Whitman blocked the door with the dolly. On the south side, he rested momentarily below the four-foot-high parapet, then opened his footlocker, extracted a scoped rifle, aimed carefully at a figure far below, and started firing.

Pedestrians 28 floors below began dropping to the hot pavement, some of them out of fright, some severely wounded, and some already dead. One pregnant woman would survive, but her stillborn baby's head had been smashed by a bullet. A teenager who stopped to help her keeled over, victim of a crack shot. The first police officer on the scene took a mortal wound.

As the body count mounted, police from several jurisdictions began arriving. Over 100 would be involved in trying to stop the massacre. They fired back, but Whitman had picked a perfect fortress and seemed immune to scores of slugs splatting into the concrete walls. An attempted attack from a small aircraft failed to pinpoint the gunman. Two officers finally managed to infiltrate the tower's lower entry and make their way to the upper floors, where they saw the bloody, lifeless bodies Whitman had left there.

Pushing open the door to the south side observation deck, the two nervous cops heard shots coming from the northwest corner. Slowly, handguns poised, heading in opposite directions to flank the gunman, they eased around the tower. Officer Ramiro Martinez caught sight of Whitman, who spun around to face him. A shootout ensued in which Martinez sent a slug into the white sweatband Whitman wore on his forehead.

One hour and 36 minutes after Charles Whitman's first tower victim fell, he lay dead on the narrow walkway.

A subsequent autopsy revealed a tumor in Whitman's brain. Specialists argued over the possible effect of the tumor. Had it contributed to the killer's outburst of random, callous murder? The issue would never be satisfactorily resolved.

Horoscope for Charles Joseph Whitman
Born June 24, 1941, 1:50 A.M. EST, Lake Worth, Florida
Source: Birth records

If Charles Whitman wanted attention, he picked a very original way to attain it. His relentless use of high-powered rifles to pick off 44 victims from atop the tower at the University of Texas gained a great deal of attention, and the case is still being discussed today. According to Whitman's astrological chart, attention is exactly what he sought.

It is interesting that Whitman's shooting spree gained him a place in the pantheon of notorious mass murderers, since the strongest point in his chart is his midheaven, which relates to his reputation. The midheaven, ruler of the tenth house of status and reputation, acts in this case as a broadcasting tower, shooting out information to the public. Whitman's cry for public attention is tied to his own personality, a first-house matter. Saturn, the planet of discontent and uncertainty, which rules his midheaven, is located in his all-important first house. To Whitman, making his name known to the public was the most important thing in his disturbed life.

Significantly, the other planet in his first house is Uranus, the planet of eccentricity, which sits arm-in-arm with Saturn, creating an aspect that foreshadows his deranged shooting spree. Both of these planets are in Taurus, his strongest sign. This combination encapsulates his personality with obsession, fixation, stubbornness, and obstinate behavior.

Whitman's father taught him to worship guns, and in the boy's mind, he would always associate the weapons with his dad. The Moon rules Whitman's fourth house of the father and sits in a discordant aspect relative to Mars, the planet of weapons. Mars also takes a negatively firm position in direct opposition to Neptune, the planet of confusion and delusion. So, in Whitman's muddled, stressed mind, he couldn't separate his feelings of anger toward his father from his fascination with weapons. This confusion probably caused in Whitman a need to defile the guns, which symbolized his father, by using them in a reprehensible deed. Whitman's relationship with his father, a fourth-house matter, had turned sour years earlier. Pluto, the planet of coercion, looms heavily in the fourth house and creates a negative aspect to Whitman's ascendant, which represents his own feelings. This arrangement is further aggravated by Pluto being in the overbearing sign of Leo. Thus, the father's stern domination of the boy and his mother damaged the child's feelings and left raw anger that lingered the rest of Whitman's life.

Whitman's Sun is weak; therefore he had difficulty asserting himself. With his Sun in Cancer, an emotional, impressionable sign, Whitman's sensitive nature went against the grain of his father's macho beliefs. If he had been allowed to follow his creative inclinations toward a career in the arts, such as music, his life and its tragic outcome probably would have been significantly different. Whitman's chart is an example of catastrophic misdirection.

Because Scorpio, the sign of emotional control, rules Whitman's seventh house of marriage, he fully expected to be in complete charge of his wife. As in most marriages, this did not work very well, and he wound up stabbing her to death. This tragic event is reflected in the co-rulership of Scorpio by Mars, the planet of weapons, including knives. Pluto, the other Scorpio ruler, governs senseless obsessions. As Whitman professed love for his wife, there was no rational reason for him to kill her.

Whitman also killed his own mother, his second victim of very personal, close-up murder, as contrasted with the impersonal homicides perpetrated from the tower. It is no coincidence that the two women Whitman loved were his first two victims, while he did not attack his father, whom he hated. The Moon rules women, and in Whitman's chart, the Moon occupies an inharmonious relationship with Mars, indicating a brooding hostility toward women. Whitman could find no other resolution to this love-hate conflict than to end the lives of his wife and his mother.

Whitman's eighth house of death is appropriately ruled by Jupiter, representing abundantly large quantities. This planet accounts for the magnitude of his rampage, which resulted in the death of fifteen people.

The explanation for his ultimate explosion of rage was complex. He planned several days ahead for his irrational killings, and prepared for it by stockpiling weapons and ammunition. Saturn, which rules planning and organization, also rules his midheaven, the strongest point in his chart. Whitman knew that his act was a suicide mission. The twelfth house, domain of suicide, is ruled by Jupiter, which also governs his eighth house of death. This planet serves a dual deadly purpose. In the eighth house, it reflects the enormous number of victims, while in the twelfth house, it represents his own suicidal intentions. Violent Mars, dwelling in Whitman's twelfth house, delivered the climactic effect he sought, when a fusillade of bullets ended the convoluted life of this mass killer.

Finally, it is notable that Jupiter, in addition to ruling his eighth house of death, also rules tumors, relating to the observation that Whitman's brain tumor may well have been the catalyst that led to the destruction of so many lives.

Gerald Armond Gallego

Wednesday, July 17, 1946, 9:00 A.M.
Sacramento, California • Time Zone: 08:00 (PST)
Longitude 121° W 29' 36" • Latitude 38° N 34' 54"
Placidus Houses • Tropical Zodiac

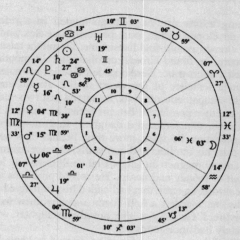

Gerald Armond Gallego is exceptionally rare in two categories associated with killers. First, he is one of the only known men whose wives joined them in capturing, raping, and murdering several young women. Second, he is a son of a killer, Gerald Albert Gallego, the first man to be executed in Mississippi's gas chamber in 1955. The senior Gallego had murdered a cop who tried to stop him after a theft of soft drinks from a store. Caught anyway, Gallego beat another officer to death during a jail break.

Gerald Armond, age 9 at the time of his father's death, didn't realize until years later that his dad had been executed. He did know, though, that several of his relatives had been sent to prison for murder.

Early in life, Gerald became a streetwise hustler and survivor. Before he turned 5, he had stolen candy from stores. Allowed undisciplined freedom by his mother, Gallego spent most of his time on the mean streets of Sacramento, California, running errands for prostitutes, pimps, and other hustlers. Seldom showing up at school, the skinny, ragged kid preferred to roll drunks in dark alleys, or pick locks to burglarize stores or hotel rooms. Alienated by human misery, he befriended a scruffy, stray dog and would long remain fond of small animals, unlike many sociopathic personalities who take pleasure in mistreating innocent creatures.

Following a few arrests, Gallego landed in a reformatory, where he developed a thick skin, powerful muscles, and a sexual aura that women would find irresistible. Despite a miserable behavior record, he found himself paroled after 33 months.

Free just a short time, Gerald raided a series of motels, which netted him a sentence of five years to life. Bright and able to manipulate sympathetic officials, he served just two years before wangling another parole. Still in his teens, he married a woman ten years older and fathered a daughter. Resuming a variety of criminal activities, he spent more time behind bars but utilized it to fine-tune his intellect and con skills. Outside again, Gallego used his animal magnetism and sexual abilities to bilk lovestruck women out of money and favors. He solved problems with them by physical force, a habit that had ended his short-lived marriage. Reportedly, he married a half-dozen more women without obtaining divorces. Gerald's mother raised his daughter, with whom he ultimately had incestuous sex.

In 1977, Gallego met a woman he wanted to keep. Charlene, diminutive at 5 feet, slim and gorgeous, caught his attention with her shimmering blond hair and moist blue eyes. Those attributes, along with a vivacious personality and limitless sexual appetite, caused Gerald to become a courtly, gallant gentleman, at least until he had married her. After that, he resorted to beating her when the mood struck him.

Gerald's appetite for young girls became an ongoing fantasy for both him and his accommodating wife. For his birthday on July 17, 1978, Charlene allegedly arranged for Gerald's 14-year-old daughter and her girlfriend to join the couple in a sexual tryst. Afterward, having enjoyed the session, she and Gallego decided they should repeat it with new girls. To make it more exciting, they would kidnap and rape "love slaves."

Two months later, Charlene emerged from their gold and white '73 Dodge van at a large shopping mall outside Sacramento. Dressed in tight cutoffs and a tank top, she looked no more than 16. Her part of the job, planned in every detail, involved luring a couple of girls to the van by offering drugs, where Gerald could

use a gun to force them inside. Within 30 minutes, Charlene
accomplished her mission, leading two casually dressed, gum-
chewing, tough-talking teenagers to the trap. After Gerald threatened the pair with a pistol, and Charlene bound them with duct
tape, he drove into the remote agricultural country surrounding
Sacramento. There, the frightened young women did as they
were told, performing forced and rough sex acts with both Gerald
and Charlene. Afterward, he led them to a ravine, and smashed
their skulls with a jack handle, then fired a bullet into each of
their brains.

The thrill of forced sex followed by the ultimate forbidden act,
murder, whetted the appetite of Gerald and Charlene Gallego for
more. They waited eleven months before trying again. Charlene
failed with her first couple of efforts to lure women, incurring
Gerald's hostility. Finally, she corralled a pair, age 13 and 14.
After a long drive to the Nevada desert and hours of forced sex,
Gerald used a shovel to bludgeon the pubescent girls to death,
then buried them in shallow graves.

Ten more months passed before the hunger sent the Gallegos
on another sex-death hunt in April 1980. They used a similar
ruse to capture Karen Chipman-Twiggs and Stacey Redican, both
17, at a Sacramento mall. Once again, they chose the Nevada
desert for the scene of rape and murder. This time, Gerald used
a hammer.

Each killing became less satisfying to the bloodthirsty couple.
It is alleged they killed two more women, one in Oregon. By
November 1980, the Gallegos needed another giant thrill. In Sacramento again, they changed the pattern by kidnapping a young
man and his date. In a rural area, Gerald executed the boy with
four bullets to the heart. They drove the captive girl to their home
and sexually violated her all night. Before dawn, they drove her
to the countryside where Gerald shot her to death.

Having grown more careless with each successful murder,
Gerald and Charlene believed they would never be caught. But
when they captured the young couple, a friend of the boy had
jotted down the license number of the car Gallego drove. It led
the police to the killer couple, who fled to another state. The
arrest came when, as fugitives, they stopped at an Omaha, Nebraska, Western Union office to pick up a money order from
Charlene's relatives.

Charlene eventually chose to avoid the death penalty by confessing the gruesome details of each crime. She received a sentence of sixteen years in prison, and was paroled in 1998. Gerald heard two judges, one in California and one in Nevada, sentence him to die.

In September 1998, though, the Federal Ninth Circuit Court of Appeals overturned Gallego's Nevada death sentence because the judge had instructed the jury that Gallego could possibly be paroled by executive clemency. Nevada officials must decide whether to conduct a new penalty trial, or sentence him to life imprisonment. Officially, he still faces execution in California.

Horoscope for Gerald Armond Gallego
Born July 17, 1946, 9:00 A.M. PST, Sacramento, California
Source: A Venom in the Blood, by Eric Von Hoffman, p. 54

Sexual obsession gripped every facet of Gerald Gallego's life. It even infected his marriage, in which his wife, Charlene, reportedly helped him lure teenage girls into his web of carnal desires. His lust drove him to commit incest, rape, and eventually several murders. Sex is in the sphere of the fifth house which, in Gallego's chart, is ruled by Saturn. Gallego's overpowering need for sexual activity might bring to mind a confident seducer of women in the mold of Don Juan. In reality, just the opposite is true. Saturn indicates the presence in his psychological makeup of uncertainty, discontent, and inadequacy. These self-doubts are exacerbated by Saturn's conjunction to Gallego's weak Sun, which reveals low self-esteem. As a result of this diminished ego, he developed a lascivious hunger for teenage girls, which ties in with that fact that the fifth house is also the domain of children. It is probable that Gallego's feelings of inadequacy made sex with gullible, pubescent girls enticing to him, since they would be easier to control. His seductions included his own daughter. Both his Saturn and his Sun are in Cancer, a configuration that undermines the qualities of home and family. These influences opened the way for Gallego to manifest his sick, perverted nature by indulging in incestuous sex.

Gallego's personality is a first-house matter. Mars resides there, providing him with a powerful sexual aura and animal magnetism that appealed to women in spite of his own self-doubts. But Gallego actually harbored a deep mistrust and hatred for women, as seen by an opposition between his ascendant and the Moon, the representative of women. Yet he married twice. His second wife found that Gallego's strange appetites paralleled her own, so they jointly abducted young women for the purpose of raping them.

The seventh house involves not only marriage, but also partnerships, so Gallego's wife became his partner in crime. Neptune, one of the rulers of the seventh house, is the planet associated with deception, conning, and being a hustler. Gallego and his wife/partner jointly employed these tactics not only to lure young girls as sexual prey, but also to pad a continually slim bankroll. Jupiter, residing in the second house of money, is the planet of self-indulgence and monetary matters, making it clear that Gallego and his wife were motivated not only by sexual lust, but by the greed for money as well.

Eventually, ordinary sex failed to satisfy Gallego, so the influence of Mars, ruling his eighth house of death, interceded. Since Mars is also in his first house and is next to his ascendant, his prurient desires became lethal. After raping the kidnapped women, Gallego beat and bludgeoned them. This violent action correlates to Mars occupying a negative position in relation to unstable Uranus, indicating a sudden, impulsive explosion of anger. The red planet also governs weapons, explaining Gallego's use of a gun to end his victims' lives.

Gallego's third house, associated with travel and transportation, is ruled by Scorpio. The elaborate ruse the couple concocted to satisfy their murderous natures involved an ornate van in which they sexually assaulted the girls before killing them. Scorpio, through its rulers, Mars and Pluto, is a sadistic sign associated with kidnapping and violence.

All of the crime forays carried out by Gallego and his wife were carefully planned in great detail. Saturn, which had so much effect on Gallego's psychological traits, also rules planning. Virgo, his ascendant and strongest sign, is associated with attention to detail.

Prison is in the domain of Gallego's strong twelfth house, reflecting his dismal record of serving time behind bars. Mercury, ruler of his ascendant, dwells in the twelfth house next to Pluto, ruler of kidnapping. When a kidnapped victim is murdered, the crime becomes a death penalty offense. Gerald Gallego was convicted of both and condemned to die, just as his father had been years earlier. Gallego's father, who was executed, is represented by the ruler of the son's fourth house, Jupiter. Significantly, Jupiter is square to the Sun, ruler of Gallego's twelfth house. This square aspect, a negative one, suggests that Gallego will suffer the same fate.

Myra Hindley

Thursday, July 23, 1942, 2:45 A.M.
Gorton, England • Time Zone: -02:00 (BDST)
Longitude 002° W 16' • Latitude 53° N 31'
Placidus Houses • Tropical Zodiac

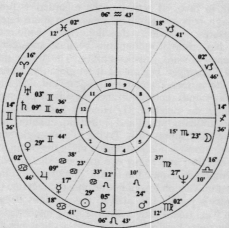

As Ian Brady's partner (see separate profile) in the diabolical "Moors Murders," which horrified the British population during the mid-1960s, Myra Hindley aided her lover in at least three sex-torture murders of pubescent children, and probably several more. During the trial, observers shuddered in shock as the prosecutor played a tape Brady and Hindley had made just prior to killing a young girl. The depraved couple had recorded 12-year-old Lesley Ann Downey pleading to be released so she could go home, then screaming in terror. While jurors heard the voice, they could refer to photographs Brady had taken after Hindley had completed stripping the girl of her clothing and lewdly posing her. The prosecutor's chilling words described what happened next. Hindley had gagged the child with a scarf and joined Brady in sexually violating Downey, after which they murdered her. At one point in the tape, Hindley's excited voice could be heard asking, "Do you see the terror in her eyes, Ian?"

Born during the midst of World War II, Myra Hindley spent her first three years without the presence of her father, who was in the British army. After Hindley's mother had a second baby, she decided two children were more than she could handle, so she sent Myra to live with her grandmother. In school, Myra seemed to have some ability at writing, but chose to ignore academic work in favor of activities she regarded as fun. As she passed through puberty, Hindley grew even more interested in social pleasures: movies, dancing, and hedonistic self-indulgence. No criminal inclinations became apparent, though; just a tendency toward irresponsibility. The tragic death of a friend in 1957 snapped her out of it temporarily, when she appeared to take a deep interest in religion, but that soon faded into the background, replaced by her pursuit of pleasure.

By the time she reached 21, Hindley had accepted enough responsibility to learn typing and shorthand, enabling her to land a job at a chemical supply firm. Trying to appear glamorous with hair bleached almost white and puffed up in the popular bouffant style, deep red lips, and heavy eye makeup, she flirted with another new employee named Ian Brady. She expressed fascination at his interest in Nazi philosophies, despite the fact that thousands of her country's people had died in the previous decade to rid the world of Nazi rule. Brady's other reading interest also excited her: his collection of sadistic erotica. She wrote in her diary, "He is cruel and selfish, and I love him." They drank heavily together, smoked dope, and indulged in offbeat sex play. At Brady's bidding, she bought several firearms for him. Finally, in 1965 he moved in with Myra and her grandmother.

Plunging deeper into the depths of sensual craving for depravity, Hindley and Brady decided to act out their fantasies. Hindley's younger sister had married a 17-year-old boy. During a visit one night by the new husband, Brady decided to impress him. He picked up a young homosexual, brought him home, took him into the kitchen with Myra, and began to beat him with an axe. Myra yelled for her brother-in-law to come in and help. He raced into the kitchen and nearly fainted while he watched Brady complete the job by strangling the youth. Horrified rather than impressed by Brady's brutality, the youth contacted police the next morning.

An investigation followed, which turned up evidence that Brady and Hindley had killed more than one victim. Searchers found the photos and tapes of Lesley Ann Downey, who had been missing for months, plus a trail to the grave of a 12-year-old boy who had vanished. Lesley Ann Downey and John Kilbride had been buried in the nearby rolling, featureless terrain called the Moors.

During the trial, which stunned England, Myra Hindley showed absolutely no emotion, even during the playing of the heartbreaking tapes. With her face blank, she sat still except to periodically write in her journal. Found guilty of three murders, Hindley and Brady received three concurrent life sentences. Eventually, Hindley confessed that she and Brady had also murdered Keith Bennett, 12, and Pauline Reade, 16, both of whom had vanished in the mid-1960s.

While sitting in prison, Myra Hindley returned to her writing. One of many entries she made in her journal said, "Curse all goddamned bad men . . . and curse the bad luck we women have . . . when we meet them and fall for them and lose our sense of perspective and just about everything else we have to lose."

Horoscope for Myra Hindley

Born July 23, 1942, 2:45 A.M. British Daylight Savings Time, Gorton, England*
Source: Inside the Mind of a Murderess, *by Jean Ritchie, p. 1–2*

Very few women have even been suspected of sexually torturing and murdering children. Even fewer have been convicted of such heinous crimes. The fact that Myra Hindley acted in concert with her male lover, Ian Brady, provides no justification. But her astrological chart does reveal certain predispositions for the outrageous behavior.

The strongest sign in her chart is Gemini, the sign of the twins, which happens to be one of the signatures of the serial killer. Hindley's dual personality is revealed by her Gemini ascendant plus three planets: Saturn, Uranus, and Venus, all nestling in the sign of Gemini.

The influence of Gemini on Hindley's ascendant, ruler of her personality, shows her interest in writing, reading, and intellectual pursuits.

---

*Hindley was born in the early-morning hours of July 23, but still fell within the range of Cancer according to astrological calculations that take into consideration the year of birth, 1942, and the latitude and longitude of her birthplace.

Saturn, in her twelfth house of secrets and hidden agendas, rests shoulder-to-shoulder with her ascendant, revealing her willingness to secretly plan the degenerate schemes she and her lover carried out. Hindley's selfishness and lack of empathy are also attributes of Saturn. These traits were evident in her unemotional reaction to the heartbreaking tapes played during the trial.

With the planet of eccentricity, Uranus, in her twelfth house of secrets, yet close to her ascendant, Hindley found quirky and kinky activities exciting. The secrecy of it all made them even more stimulating to her. The influence of Uranus gave her personality an erratic and bizarre twist.

Hindley's Venus in her first house, governing her appearance, indicates her love of beauty, makeup, hairdos, and fashion. As the first house also represents her personal desires, she indulged herself in any way she pleased and gave no thought to the possible consequences. Venus's negative aspect to Neptune illustrates her hedonistic and self-centered behavior.

During the cooling-off periods between at least five murders, she easily slipped into the role of her "good twin" side, exhibiting the home-loving qualities of her Sun sign, Cancer. These activities include cooking, housekeeping, and traditional homemaker functions. This same Sun sign, the "bad twin" of Gemini, turned evil when the killings were taking place. Hindley and her lover lived together in her grandmother's home. It was in this residence that they molested and killed their young victims.

The cruelty displayed in Hindley's chart is chilling. The Sun, representing her ego, is adjacent to Pluto, the planet of obsession. In addition, her Moon in Scorpio makes a negative aspect to Mars. Pluto and Scorpio create the condition that allows sadism and torture to flourish while Mars delivers the violence. The Moon represents children, who were kidnapped off the street by this killer couple. Since Pluto and Scorpio are also associated with kidnapping, coercion, and addiction, it is not surprising that murder and torture became addictive to Hindley and her lover. It was as if they were possessed and simply could not stop their repulsive acts.

Jupiter rules Hindley's seventh house of partners. With Jupiter close to Hindley's Mercury, which governs her mind, this alignment reveals that she was both mentally stimulated and deeply receptive to all of Brady's philosophies and ideas. His interests in Nazism and erotica made a deep impression on her both intellectually and emotionally. Hindley's Mercury is in Cancer, a receptive sign, which causes absorption of the influences surrounding it. The association of erotica and Nazi atrocities formed the foundation for their relationship.

Sex and children, both fifth-house matters, are ruled by Neptune. Since Neptune is the planet of delusions, and occupies a negative alignment to Venus, her notions of sex were not the positive traits of Venus, love and affection, but reflected the negative side, blind compliance and subjugation. These same deluded notions twisted her attitude about, and treatment of, children.

The eighth house of death in Hindley's chart is ruled by Saturn. This cold, cruel planet is close to her Gemini ascendant, which represents her personal interests. So this tie with her eighth house illustrates Hindley's very personal, morbid involvement with death.

Saturn, planet of law and restriction, rules Hindley's ninth house of courts. Thus, she was convicted and sentenced to serve the rest of her life in prison. She is still incarcerated. The long arm of the law as well as the public's hatred of Hindley both stem from the influence of Saturn.

In Hindley's chart, the twelfth house of prisons is under the control of Uranus and Saturn, both rulers of her midheaven. Since the midheaven represents her reputation, the English public sees her as an eccentric, cold-blooded killer, both negative Uranus and Saturn characteristics. Mars, another twelfth-house ruler, represents the violence and murders she helped commit. The least influential planet in Hindley's twelfth house is Venus, the ruler of affection and pleasure. One slight bit of Venusian good fortune for Hindley emanating from her twelfth house takes the form of a few sympathetic English citizens working to have her released. However, any sympathy shown for her is more than offset by the public's outrage over the terrible crimes she committed. Hindley and Brady's murders are so engraved in the public's mind that they will never be forgotten.

LEO

Relatively few killers are Leos, but those who were born under this sign tend to exclusively murder women. Notorious prostitute killer William Suff and Cape Cod slayer Tony Costa are Leos. This fixed and dominating sign also spawns dictators. Fidel Castro and Benito Mussolini were born under the sign of the lion. Leos want to be in charge and lead the way, and they can be very demanding and extremely self-centered in attaining their goals.

Tony Costa

Wednesday, August 2, 1944, 12:33 P.M.
Cambridge, Massachusetts • Time Zone: 04:00 (Eastern War Time)
Longitude 071° W 06' • Latitude 42° N 22'
Placidus Houses • Tropical Zodiac

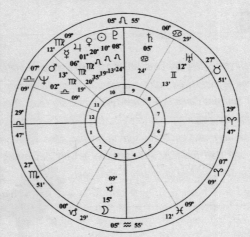

If Cape Cod, Massachusetts, is shaped like a scorpion's tail, then Provincetown sits near the stinger's tip. A half-dozen miles down the narrow, curving peninsula from the popular summer resort, Highway 6 divides thick piny woods that slope to Cape Cod Bay on the west side, and to the turbulent Atlantic ocean on the east.

On the biting cold morning of February 2, 1969, a motorist left the highway below Provincetown to meander along winding dirt roads through the South Truro woods. He spotted a blue Volkswagen that appeared to be abandoned. Intuition nudged his natural tendency not to touch or move anything, and he rushed back to town to notify the police.

The Volkswagen belonged to Pat Walsh, 24, a tall, dark-haired, attractive schoolteacher from Rhode Island. She had been visiting Cape Cod with her friend, Mary Anne Wysocki, 23. Both women had stayed overnight in late January at a Provincetown guesthouse. When police questioned the proprietor of the inn, she told of reading a note addressed to the women. A man named

Tony Costa, also a guest, had tacked a note on the women's door. Written on a brown paper bag, it asked for a ride to Truro, twelve miles southeast of Provincetown.

Antone "Tony" Costa, who worked sporadically as a carpenter, had taken up residency in the house on January 25 with an offer to help the owner do some repair work before the spring tourists arrived. Good looking, Costa wore gold-framed glasses over his brown eyes and kept his full mop of dark hair neatly styled, with long sideburns appropriate to the late 1960s. Beards were fashionable at the time, but Costa kept his dimpled chin cleanly shaved while cultivating a full, black mustache. Standing a little taller than average height, he kept his solid body in shape and wore turtleneck sweaters with tight white denims to accentuate it. He impressed acquaintances with his soft-spoken, articulate speech, which reflected intelligence noticeably above average. But people close to Costa had learned that he had a tendency to bend the facts to his own advantage.

In Costa's own recollections, as told to a social worker, his childhood had been relatively comfortable, but he'd felt withdrawn from society. He said he had bonded very closely with his mother but had endured a sense of emptiness because his father had died in World War II. Born in August 1944, Costa had never known his dad, and had grown up somewhat alienated from his stepfather and a half-brother. Sexual permissiveness existed in his household, and he'd experienced his first heterosexual contact at age 14. Raised as a Catholic, he had followed religious teaching until he became a teenager, at which time questions developed in his mind about literally believing the Bible. He always worried that he would die young.

At 17, Costa said, a girl three years his junior had seduced him. Then, he claimed, the girl accused him of forcing her into having sex. Her false testimony, Costa complained, had led to an unjust charge for assault and attempted rape. Although he was let off with a warning, he and his family were humiliated. To escape the stigma, he was sent to live with a relative in Provincetown, and attended high school there. A year later, he married a free-spirited girl after she became pregnant, and he fathered two more children with her. When she cheated on him, the marriage ended in divorce, but they remained friends. Costa worked much of the time as a carpenter but had problems keeping a steady income, and was arrested for failing to support his three kids.

Since he had been convicted in 1962 for breaking and entering, plus assault, and had served three years of probation, Costa faced being locked up for the first time in his life. The judge sentenced him to serve six months, which would have kept him behind bars until late March 1969. But a parole board let him out on November 8, 1968, after only a few weeks in the Barnstable House of Corrections. Free again, he returned to Provincetown and re-united with a young woman with whom he'd had a love affair. She lived in New York, but came to Cape Cod to be with Costa. When she returned to New York, Costa accompanied her, and left her in the city on November 23. A short time later, back in Provincetown, he heard that she had been found dead in her bathtub on November 24, apparently having committed suicide. Costa would later say that the sudden death sent him into a no-sedive of drug usage. It would be speculated that he knew more about the woman's death than he ever admitted.

A stash of drugs Costa kept would eventually be found in buried containers under a thin crust of frosty dirt in the Truro woods, near the abandoned Volkswagen site. According to Costa's ex-wife, he stole most of the drugs from a doctor's office. Costa also maintained a large garden in the woods, where he grew marijuana. The frozen ground of the Truro woods yielded even more. Over a period of several weeks in early 1969, investigators unearthed four bodies of young women who had been shot, then crudely dismembered. In addition to Pat Walsh, who had owned the Volkswagen, and Mary Ann Wysocki, officers disinterred Susan Perry and Sidney Monzon. All four had been seen at various times with Tony Costa.

When Costa was first questioned, he claimed that he'd bought the Volkswagen from Walsh, but allowed her to borrow it for a while. Later, he changed his story to say that the Walsh and Wysocki had purchased hashish from him and offered the car as payment. Gradually, his lies began to crumble. Additional probing of the frigid earth around Costa's "garden" turned up a hand-gun that was traced to him.

Prosecutors could find only enough evidence to charge Costa with two murders. A jury found him guilty in both indictments, and recommended imprisoning him for life without parole.

Until 1974, Costa spent most of his time in the Massachusetts

Correctional Institute at Walpole pursuing endless appeals and corresponding with his attorney about a novel he had written. The appeals reached the state supreme court, which affirmed the convictions in November 1971. Costa continued to compose letters suggesting new legal maneuvers.

It all came to an end on Sunday, May 12, 1974, when a guard at Walpole discovered Antone Costa's dead body, suspended from the top bars by a belt that also encircled his neck. He was 29 years old.

Horoscope for Tony Costa
Born August 2, 1944, 12:33 P.M. Eastern War Time, Cambridge, Massachusetts
Source: Birth certificate

Tony Costa's arrogance and egomania led him to believe that he could get away with murder.

It is most unusual to see, in any chart, the overwhelming concentration of planets that occupy Costa's tenth house of reputation and social status. Such an arrangement virtually screams of his bloated ego and strutting self-confidence. Pluto, the Sun, Venus, Jupiter, and Mercury are all jammed into the tenth house, signaling Costa's gigantic desire for public attention and acclaim. Three of the planets—the Sun, Venus, and Pluto—are in the sign of Leo. With this tight grouping, Leo clearly emerges as Costa's strongest sign. Such a dominant Leo infused Costa with the desire for power and influence over anyone with whom he came in contact. Pluto's presence in the mix lends a nearly obsessive willpower, made even stronger by the Sun. Sitting in close proximity to this potent trio, Mercury, as Costa's most powerful planet, offered skills in reading, writing, and communications. Since Mercury is next to Jupiter, the planet of abundance, Costa was excessively articulate and garrulous. With both Mercury and Jupiter in Virgo, these characteristics were amplified. Venus, the planet of personal charm, influenced Costa's desire to be recognized for his winning personality and good looks.

Most of these dominant traits were used by Costa to romance women or gain control over them. His Moon, which rules women, is in materialistic Capricorn. This practical sign is associated with the phrase "I use," and Costa used women for his own benefit. His Moon is also in opposition to Saturn. This difficult and dangerous aspect stresses the cold-blooded attitude he held toward women, as well as the heartless manner in which he disposed of their bodies.

Drugs were a major factor in Costa's life. He not only bought, sold, and stole them, but he also used them. Drugs are related to Neptune, which resides in his eleventh house of friends. This indicates that drugs were an important element in all of his friendships.

Neptune also rules Costa's fifth house of sex, making it clear that drugs were involved in his sexual relations with women. He lured them to their deaths by taking them to his "garden," a marijuana patch in the woods. Neptune is associated with deception and lies as well as drug use. Jupiter, the other ruler of Costa's fifth house, represents vast amounts, or overdosing. One of his girlfriends died mysteriously of an overdose. It was never determined whether Costa was involved, so the final Neptune influence, mysterious uncertainty, shows up only in his horoscope, not in his police records.

Costa's eighth house of death is influenced primarily by Uranus. Since Uranus is the planet of eccentricity, Costa had strange ideas about death. These quirky concepts, together with his dominating character, contributed to the deaths of several women. Uranus is in juxtaposition to violent Mars, making a square aspect, which creates negative energy. Mars rules both guns and knives. The women found in Costa's "garden" were shot and dismembered. This Mars/Uranus aspect is especially frightening since it is so unpredictable. The slightest provocation triggered Costa's Martian-driven anger, with disastrous, deadly results.

While Uranus exerts the strongest influence on Costa's eighth house of death, Venus takes the role of astrological ruler and also governs his ascendant. This association reveals Costa's personal interest and involvement in death. Mercury, the dominant planetary ruler of the eighth house, reinforces the extreme focus held by Costa on the subject of death in all of its ramifications.

Costa's Moon, sitting opposite Saturn in his third house of thinking, describes someone who suffers from deep depression. With the heavy influence of Saturn locked in an extremely negative aspect to the Moon, ruler of his emotions, it is quite likely that Costa was extremely melancholy.

The twelfth house of self-destruction is Venus ruled. Since Venus also governs Costa's Libra ascendant and his first house of personality, this tie indicates suicidal tendencies. His conviction for two murders put him in prison, another twelfth-house association. Costa's bursting, overwhelming ego would not allow him to adjust to the controls or indignities of confinement. With his attitude of superiority, he never would have made the difficult adjustment to a lifetime of incarceration. The influence of his Mercury, planet of communication, impelled him to spend a great deal of time preparing appeals and writing letters, all about himself. He also worked on a novel in which he devised several different scenarios about the murders he committed and named a friend as the killer. When Costa finally realized that his efforts to control the situation were hopeless, he sank into an even deeper depression. Saturn rules depression and failure as well as hanging. In the end, Costa exerted his desire for control by taking his own life.

William Lester Suff

Sunday, August 20, 1950, 6:12 A.M.
Torrance, California • Time Zone: 07:00 (PDT)
Longitude 118° W 20' 23" • Latitude 33° N 50' 09"
Placidus Houses • Tropical Zodiac

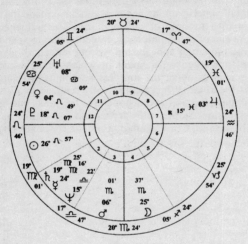

From January 1988 to January 1992, more than a dozen prostitutes in the dry, rolling terrain of Riverside County, California, were tortured, murdered, and mutilated. Police finally caught up with William Lester Suff, 41, and charged him with thirteen of the homicides. After the jury convicted him of twelve killings, they heard evidence in the trial's penalty phase to determine whether he should be executed for his misdeeds, or serve the rest of his life in prison. Ironically, their final decision may have been swayed by a brutal crime he committed almost two decades earlier.

Born on August 20, 1950, in Torrance, California, fifteen miles from downtown Los Angeles, Suff was the first of four sons and one daughter delivered to parents who battled constantly. For the first few years of his life, the family lived under adequate economic conditions, until they relocated to Riverside County. His father chose to sacrifice a well-paying job so that he could play drums in honky-tonk bars.

In the small, dusty town of Lake Elsinore, located on the

southeast end of a shallow lake, over a one-hour drive south of
Los Angeles, Suff existed in a social vacuum. Fringed by rugged
mountains on one side and dry brown desert on the other, the
community in those days attracted many people who were seeking refuge from the law: bikers, transients, and drug dealers. Bill
Suff plodded through high school with barely passable grades.
Conditions went from bad to worse when his father walked away
in 1967, leaving Suff, at age 16, and the family to survive on
public welfare. After graduation, Suff struggled with various jobs
until he joined the Air Force in 1969. As a military medic in
Texas, he returned to California to marry a pregnant teenager
he'd dated. He didn't want another man's baby, so Suff's mother
agreed to take the child.

Suff's Air Force career suddenly crashed in 1970 when he
was booted from the service with a less than honorable discharge.
The couple stayed in Texas, but Suff's developing pattern of
sullen behavior, laziness, violent temper, and inability to keep a
job continued through the next few years. His wife produced a
son in 1971 and a daughter in 1973. While the mother took
menial jobs, Suff stayed home with the kids. Bruises often appeared mysteriously on the little boy's body. Two months after
the daughter's birth, Suff called his wife at work, tearfully asking
her to come home. The daughter had died, he said.

Medical examination of the baby girl revealed deep bruises,
multiple fractures, human bite marks, a ruptured liver, and what
appeared to be a bone-deep cigarette burn on her foot.

Acquaintances of the Suffs described his unstable behavior to
investigators and spoke of loud arguments between Bill and his
wife. They told of Suff's split personality—an overly helpful,
talkative neighbor one time, and a belligerent tyrant the next.
Once he was charged with killing the baby, Suff's inconsistent
stories helped convict both parents of murder. A judge sentenced
each of them to serve 70 years in prison. They agreed to give
up their son for adoption. Before two years had passed, an appeals court overturned Mrs. Suff's conviction and freed her. She
soon obtained a divorce from her imprisoned husband.

Suff managed to turn incarceration into opportunity, and
earned a college degree during his almost ten years behind bars.
In 1984, Texas officials recognized his good behavior and paroled him to Riverside County, California.

After living with his family for a time, and sporadically working, Suff moved to a Lake Elsinore apartment with a new girl-friend who was several years older. While putting on the facade of a conservative but loquacious neighbor, Suff frequently found excuses to be away at night. He spent most of the absences buying the services of street hookers.

In October 1986, he landed a county job as a warehouse clerk, which frequently brought him in contact with sheriff's officers. Suff acquired secondhand uniforms and a highway patrolman's cap, which he used off the job to create the impression that he worked in law enforcement. A motorcycle accident the next year resulted in an insurance payment to Suff of $30,000, which eventually enabled him to dump the battered 1975 Dodge he drove and buy a new van.

The first prostitute murder, in what would be a four-year string, occurred in January 1988. A witness saw the hooker enter an older Dodge driven by an pudgy man with brown hair. A few days later, hikers found her body in the desert foothills. She had been repeatedly stabbed and her right breast had been sliced off.

A year passed before the next prostitute nearly died. Using his girlfriend's car, Suff picked the woman up in Lake Elsinore, took her to a vacant house, and physically attacked her. The hooker escaped his grasp, ran outside, and was rescued by friends who watched Suff speed away.

When the relationship with his older girlfriend ended Suff turned to a prostitute he often saw, suggesting they live together. She refused, and turned up dead in June 1989. In December, another of his "regulars" was found a few miles from the lake, beaten, strangled, and sexually mutilated. Twisted into a humiliating pose, she wore only a shirt bearing the words "Kings Canyon," a national park Suff had recently visited.

The frequency of prostitute murders increased an average of nearly one each month during 1991. All of the bodies were found near Lake Elsinore or in the general vicinity, and each had been strangled, beaten, and sexually savaged. The right breasts of several had been amputated and tossed on the ground within a short distance of the bodies.

Investigators noticed that the killer became more reckless with each new murder. He left identical tire tracks and shoeprints at several crime scenes, and lewdly posed the nude bodies so they would be discovered quickly. He seemed to be playing a game of taunting the police, daring them to find him. In his job at the warehouse, Suff often chatted with officers about the news reports of serial murder, and wished them luck in finding the killer.

A task force requested from known hookers any information about "johns" who behaved suspiciously. Gradually, the officers learned that the bespectacled killer probably drove a gray van, was pudgy in appearance, had brown hair, and wore Converse sports shoes.

Meanwhile, Suff met an 18-year-old convenience store clerk, and at age 39, married her. He often "found" women's clothing, and gave them to his young wife or to neighbors. Unaware of Suff's prison term in Texas, his wife bore him a baby daughter. In October 1991, the tiny girl was hospitalized with bruises, fractured bones, and brain-damaging blood clots. Suff denied any responsibility, but the child was permanently taken away.

The investigative web drew tighter, and finally, in January 1992, Suff was nabbed while trying to pick up a prostitute in Riverside. The interior of his gray van contained ample forensic evidence, and eyewitness testimony from hookers confirmed Suff as the suspected serial killer. He had known and socialized with several of his victims. A jury convicted Suff on twelve counts of first-degree murder and then heard the penalty-phase evidence. The account of his baby's death in Texas horrified them, and they recommended the death penalty. He arrived at San Quentin's Death Row on November 1, 1995, to begin the long wait for execution.

Horoscope for William Lester Suff
Born August 20, 1950, 6:12 A.M. PDT, Torrance, California,
Source: Birth certificate

The ruthless sadism and towering ego of William Suff, evident in his brutal murder-mutilation of a dozen prostitutes, spring from his chart like a coiled viper. Not only did these overbearing traits set the stage for his horrible crimes, but they also ironically helped police to capture him.

Egotistical self-confidence oozes through Suff's first house of personality, and overflows into the adjacent twelfth house of secrets and hidden agendas. The first house is occupied by the powerful Sun, domain of self-esteem, and surrounded by the influence of Pluto, Venus, and Suff's ascendant, Leo. Very disagreeable Leo characteristics of brash arrogance, pride, and boasting are further inflated by the alignments of these planets in negative aspects, and increased by the Sun's position in Suff's first house. Pluto is also a significant player on this strutting stage. Ruling torture, sadism, and coercion, Pluto is close to Suff's Leo ascendant, ruler of the first house. This close proximity allows Pluto's cruel qualities to darken Suff's temperament and disposition, making them a fundamental part of his personality. Venus, ruling affection and love, is hidden away next door in his twelfth house of secrets. Since Venus is quite weak, Suff's behavior exhibited virtually no fondness for anyone, other than himself.

When combined with Suff's uncontrolled ego, other factors in his chart are catastrophic. The Moon, in Scorpio, is Suff's strongest planet. With the Moon making square aspects to Suff's Sun, ascendant, and Pluto, the negative energy poses serious problems for him and especially for the prostitutes he knew. As the Moon rules women, it follows that his victims were all women. In spite of his powerful ego, shown by all the Leo influence, Suff didn't fight with or challenge men. Instead, he attacked and cruelly murdered unfortunate female prostitutes after superficially befriending and using them. The Moon's prominence makes women pivotal in his life. He deeply resented this feminine influence, as it impinged on his Leo bravado. Suff's solution to the problem, as he saw it, was to use women for his own purposes, then dispose of them.

The fifth house, ruling both children and sex, plays another meaningful part in Suff's unhappy life. Jupiter governs both his fifth house and his eighth house of death. When Suff was younger he was convicted of killing his own daughter, another female in his life, and was later accused of seriously injuring a second daughter. Jupiter sits in opposition to his Sun, creating a dangerously negative aspect that indicates open conflict between Suff and his children. His weak Venus allowed no love for anyone including his daughters. Because the Jupiter-ruled fifth house is also the domain of sex, Suff's prurient sexual nature comes into play, which accounts for his frequent interaction with hookers. Jupiter has power over Suff's eighth house of death, so sex and death are morbidly ingrained and inseparable in his psyche. Because Jupiter brings abundance into the equation, Suff's life was consumed with sexual activities while he dispensed a tragic multiplicity of death.

Neptune, as the other co-ruler of Suff's eighth house, is the planet of deception. The prostitutes he murdered were lured into his van ostensibly just for sex. However, Suff's real motive was sadistic murder. During the investigation into the homicides, Suff again used Neptunian deception in dealing with the police. His corpulent Leonine ego led him into the dangerous gamble of chatting with police about the murders, and probably into deliberately leaving clues at the crime scenes. Without a doubt, Suff believed he could outsmart any investigator. Interestingly, it was the rigid inflexibility of his nature, illustrated by all his Leo/Scorpio fixed signs, that caused him to be captured.

The negative Leo characteristics infecting Suff's behavior, especially the bloated sense of male pride, created in him the need to humiliate females by sexually displaying their mutilated bodies. This is a feature of violent Mars in Suff's Scorpio. Mutilation is a Mars feature, while Scorpio rules the sex organs.

Suff's twelfth house, ruler of prisons, is occupied by two planets, Venus and Pluto. Venus is so weak that it barely manages to express any of its influence, but the benefic quality of the planet seeped through with enough strength to allow Suff's early parole from prison after he served only a small portion of his sentence for killing his daughter. Pluto's residence is much stronger. Being in the sign of Leo, Pluto's merciless, unyielding nature will eventually avenge Suff's victims. Empowered by Leo's strength, Pluto's exerted influence will finally lead to Suff's death by execution.

VIRGO

Some exceptionally bizarre, yet quiet and unassuming killers show up in Virgo, including Ed Gein (role model for Psycho) and Andrew Cunanan, the killer of designer Gianni Versace. The quiet, seemingly passive characteristics of this sign make for a killer who is adept at avoiding detection. Negatively affected Virgo natives can be overly fastidious fault finders and hypochondriacs.

Edward Gein

Monday, August 27, 1906, 11:30 P.M.
North La Crosse, Wisconsin • Time Zone: 06:00 (CST)
Longitude 091° W 15' • Latitude 43° N 48'
Placidus Houses • Tropical Zodiac

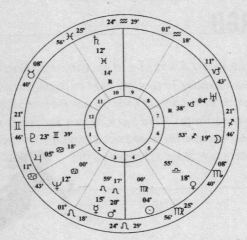

Reportedly the inspiration for several horror novels and movies, including *Psycho*, *The Texas Chainsaw Massacre*, and *The Silence of the Lambs*, Ed Gein committed ghoulish acts as repulsive as any attributed to the fictional killers.

Raised on a rural Wisconsin farm, Gein became reclusive early in life. After completing the eighth grade, he quit school and appeared to be content with working the land. When Gein's alcoholic father died in 1940, the family's 160 acres remained in the family to be tilled by Ed, his older brother Henry, and his domineering mother. Social life was virtually nonexistent, which pleased Mrs. Gein. She didn't want her sons contaminated by greedy, sexually devious, sinful women. Preaching to Ed and Henry about the purity of sexless lives, Ma Gein ruled her domain with a heavy hand.

Nothing mattered but the farm, so Ed and Henry put every ounce of energy into it. Distant neighbors seldom saw the three Geins, except when one of them appeared in Plainfield for supplies. When Henry died in 1944, they whispered some suspicions, but finally decided that he had succumbed to smoke and burns sustained during a marsh fire. When Ma Gein passed away after suffering a massive stroke in December 1945, they wondered whether Ed would stay on his beloved farm, all alone.

He did. But the townsfolk would have been shocked to know how he occupied himself in his solitude. Developing an obsessive interest in human anatomy, Gein devoured every book he could find on the subject, focusing special interest on the bodies of women. No longer having time to work the soil, keep farm animals, or bother with housekeeping chores, he relied on a government subsidy to survive, and sealed off every room of the two-story farmhouse except his small bedroom and the kitchen. Completely engrossed in fantasies about the female body, Gein decided to try some personal, hands-on exploration.

Making his first tentative probes at socializing, Gein shyly spoke to a few townspeople, and gradually began performing chores for them. Folks placed trust in the man they perceived as a lonesome, gentle soul, and even allowed him to earn a few dollars by babysitting. But no woman showed any personal interest in the small, unshaven, fortyish man. When Mary Hogan, the proprietor of a small bar, vanished, certainly no one linked the disappearance to good old Ed.

Unable to lure live women, Gein turned to the cemetery. No one knows exactly how many female bodies he lifted from graves. But what he did with them would horrify investigators who discovered the remains during a search of Gein's farmhouse. One officer said, "I had never seen anything like this. We found skulls and masks [made from facial skin]. We found a box that had a woman's organs in it . . . and chair seats made out of human skin. . . . There was the upper part of a woman's torso . . . with her breasts completely tanned." Gein later admitted that he would put these female parts on himself at night and go out in the yard and parade around in them.

Before the gruesome discovery, Gein had paid a visit to the hardware store in November 1957. The co-owner, Bernice Worden, who normally worked behind the counter, couldn't be found that evening. Her son discovered that the last transaction she'd made, as recorded on a receipt copy, had been a sale to Ed Gein. During the ensuing search, which lasted nearly a week, Gein's answers to investigators' questions finally tripped him up. Racing to the Gein farm, the police not only found multiple remains taken from burial sites, but they also discovered the headless, naked, butchered, disemboweled, sexually mutilated, and meticulously cleaned body of Bernice Worden. It was split lengthwise and suspended by the ankles in a woodshed.

While rain and sleet lashed the outside walls of the icy house, the officers continued to search the filthy, littered interior all night, turning up a mind-boggling array of grisly trophies. Among hundreds of Gein's morbid possessions, they found a soup bowl fashioned from a skull, bracelets formed from human flesh, a human-leather wastebasket, and organs kept in a refrigerator. It turned the searcher's stomachs when they located Mrs. Worden's heart in a saucepan on the kitchen stove. In the bedroom, they lifted the corner of a mattress and spotted a burlap sack that contained the woman's severed head. One of the masks made of human skin turned out to be the remains of Mary Hogan, who had vanished three years earlier. A final tally of the hideous collection counted body parts from fifteen different women.

Ed Gein spoke softly and courteously to the investigators, denying ever killing anyone, but admitting using the bodies for his personal pleasures. He acknowledged slicing genitalia from the corpses and sexually fondling them. He had devised masks by removing the facial flesh, and enjoyed placing them over his own face. The suspect's admission of necrophilia and cannibalism sent several residents rushing to doctors, concerned about "venison" Gein had generously given them.

Asked if Mrs. Worden looked like anyone he remembered, Gein said, "I did take her for resemblance of my mother; her height and everything was the same and she had resemblance in the cheekbones."

Suspected of killing a number of missing women from various parts of the state, Gein was charged with only one homicide, that of Bernice Worden. But the judge found him criminally insane in 1957 and committed him to a mental hospital. A few months later, the house and buildings on Gein's farm mysteriously burned to the ground.

In 1968, another judge, without a jury, heard extensive testimony in a new trial, after doctors had pronounced Gein mentally able to participate in his defense. His attorneys argued that the mortal gunshot inflicted on Mrs. Worden had been accidental. After hearing several witnesses, including the withered, harmless-looking defendant, the judge declared that Mrs. Worden's death was first-degree murder, but that Gein suffered from mental illness and was not guilty by reason of insanity. Sent back to the state hospital, Gein lived there peacefully until his death in 1984.

Horoscope for Edward Gein
Born August 27, 1906, 11:30 P.M. CST, North La Crosse, Wisconsin
Source: Birth certificate

The horrifying behavior of Ed Gein gives the word *grotesque* a whole new meaning. His treatment of female bodies, those he killed and those he dug up in a cemetery, is simply incomprehensible. In his chart, three particular planets, Saturn, Venus, and the Moon, provide the first glimpses into several factors that might have led to his gruesome behavior.

Gein's strange compulsions about women's bodies may have been rooted in his mother's resistance to allowing her son any normal contact with females. Saturn in his tenth house of mother hints at this. This planet's position, in direct opposition to the Sun, forms a negative aspect that filled Gein with a disturbing sense of being oppressed by his mother's firm control. The distress turned to hatred. Saturn rules the eighth house of death, so in Gein's mind, mother and death became irrevocably linked. It was no coincidence that one of Gein's victims closely resembled his mother.

Venus, the planet of love, co-rules his fifth house of sex. By forming a square aspect with Neptune, Venus issues negative energy, clouding Gein's understanding of love and affection, especially in relation to sex. The other ruler of the fifth house, Mercury, close to brutal Mars, signals that Gein's notions of sex were darkened with brutality and violence.

With Gein's thoughts of women already confused, his Moon made matters worse. The Moon, ruler of women, sits in direct opposition to both Gein's ascendant and to Pluto. The effect of this aspect on his ascendant suggests Gein would experience great difficulty in relating to the opposite sex. Pluto, ruling obsessions, sets up Gein's obsessive interest with the female anatomy. He plunged into the obsessive study of this subject by voraciously reading books and examining every illustration he could find. The study of biology is a sixth-house matter, which in Gein's chart is ruled by the feminine Moon. His sixth house is governed by the sign of investigative Scorpio, while planetary rule is provided by violent Mars and obsessive Pluto. Gein's interest in women's bodies clearly became obsessive, compulsively morbid, and finally lethally violent.

Plagued by a need to satisfy his carnal lust through contact with women, Gein's fragile ego ruled out any chance of normal relations with them. His Sun, ruling his ego, is precariously weak; therefore, Gein's self-esteem and self-confidence were low. The Sun's position in Virgo, a quiet, passive sign, made it difficult for him to assert himself in the outside world. Gein's Sun resides in his fourth house, ruling the home. His home became his entire world when he retreated into it following his mother's death.

The townspeople saw Ed Gein so infrequently that they had no suspicion that he might be dangerous. The first house in his chart, ruling Gein's appearance, contains Jupiter in Cancer, a kindly and caring sign, so Gein's eccentricities were seen by others as harmless. The people who assumed this were in for a sickening surprise. The two faces of Gemini, sign of the twins, and ruler of his ascendant, certainly applied to the duality of Gein. The community saw him as a benign recluse, in direct opposition to the real Gein, a festering mass of confusion ready to commit murder in order to satisfy his carnal lust.

As with most killers, the violent planet, Mars, lurks in Gein's picture. In his chart, Mars occupies the third house of brothers and mental processes. It was rumored that Gein had caused his brother's death, but no evidentiary support ever turned up. Mars, affecting his mental processes, rules knives and surgical procedures. At first, Gein sliced up female bodies he stole from a cemetery. Then, he killed at least one woman, probably two, eviscerated them, and used the body parts to make gruesome keepsakes. He also cannibalized them. His Moon, representing both food and women, sits in a negative aspect to Saturn, which rules Gein's eighth house of death. The implications of this arrangement are so mind-boggling, they are beyond the scope of conventional astrology.

The ninth house rules the courts. Aquarian influence on Gein's ninth house shows that his eccentricity had escalated into legal madness.

His twelfth house rules places of confinement, including mental hospitals and prisons. With Venus as the ruler of his twelfth house, Gein adapted relatively well to confinement. Virgo, Sagittarius, and Gemini are all adaptable signs, giving him the ability to make the necessary adjustments. He was already reclusive, so being behind walls represented little change for Gein. He lived quietly in mental institutions until his death.

Andrew Cunanan

Sunday, August 31, 1969, 9:41 P.M.
National City, California • Time Zone: 07:00 (PDT)
Longitude 117° W 05' 54" • Latitude 32° N 40' 41"
Placidus Houses • Tropical Zodiac

The fashion world was plunged into mourning on July 15, 1997, when legendary designer Gianni Versace was killed by two bullets shot into the back of his head at point-blank range. Within hours, police suspected that gay gigolo Andrew Cunanan had pulled the trigger. They launched a manhunt that spread across the nation as celebrities who had known Versace expressed shock and sadness at his death, and worry that he might be seeking more victims.

The search for Cunanan had already been ongoing for nearly three months before the cold-blooded execution of the fashion king. The FBI had included Cunanan on its "Ten Most Wanted" list a full month earlier for the murders of four other men in three states. Versace's death in Miami only intensified the manhunt and made it a cause célèbre as the result of news media clamor. Singer-actress Madonna, who had worn a Versace creation at the premiere of her movie *Evita,* and who had been entertained in Versace's home along with actor Robert DeNiro, publicly mourned her friend. She said, "What has happened to

Gianni is a tragedy. My thoughts and prayers are with him and his family." Other celebrities openly cried in speaking of his untimely death at age 50.

The suspected killer, Andrew Cunanan, 27, who stood 5 feet, 10 inches and weighed about 160 pounds, attracted many gay men with his solid physique, mysterious dark brown eyes, and neatly trimmed brown hair. His exotic appearance stemmed from his mix of Filipino and Caucasian heritage. Raised in San Diego, Cunanan had once served as an altar boy. Attending high school in the affluent coastal resort of La Jolla, he frequently faced criticism from fellow students for being insincere and manipulative. With remarkable prescience, they voted him "least likely to be forgotten." In 1988, Cunanan's father, a Filipino native, fled San Diego, where he had been a successful stockbroker, to avoid accusations of financial chicanery. The teenage boy stayed with his mother temporarily, then enrolled at the University of Southern California in Los Angeles. But he soon dropped out and devoted his time to various romantic relationships, preferably with wealthy men.

Extremely glib and not very concerned with telling the truth, Cunanan ingratiated himself with affluent men by weaving stories about his family's status and wealth. But not all of his alleged victims were necessarily rich, famous, or influential.

While socializing in San Diego, Cunanan met and struck up a friendship with David Madsen. Although Madsen told a female pal that he thought Cunanan was "secretive and elusive" and might be into something "shady," Madsen invited the handsome new acquaintance to his home in Minneapolis, Minnesota. Cunanan accepted and used his charisma to become involved in Madsen's circle of intimates, which included a 28-year-old man named Jeffrey Trail. In late April 1997, a Saturday night, Madsen and Cunanan were seen dining together, then later dancing at a night spot called the Gay 90s. Cunanan reportedly spent that night with Trail.

On Tuesday, April 29, one of Madsen's co-workers became worried because David hadn't shown up at his job for two days. He called the caretaker at the apartment where Madsen lived and asked for a check of the residence. The caretaker used a passkey to enter the apartment, and found a dead body rolled up in a bloodstained carpet. Nearby lay a bloody claw hammer. When the police arrived they expected to identify the body as David

Madsen, but were startled to discover the victim to be Jeffrey
Trail. In a nylon gym bag bearing the name Andrew Cunanan,
they discovered an empty handgun holster and fifteen rounds of
.40-caliber ammunition.

An acquaintance of Jeffrey Trail told police that Jeff had
planned to meet "Andrew" on the evening of April 27. The dead
man's watch had stopped at 9:55 on that date.

Six days later, two fishermen discovered Madsen's body along
the shoreline of East Rush Lake, northeast of Minneapolis. He
had been shot in the head with two .40-caliber slugs. The victim's red 1995 Jeep Cherokee was missing.

In May, Cunanan became a suspect in two more murders. Police linked him to the death of a respected and wealthy Chicago
real estate developer, Lee Miglin, 72. On May 4, Miglin's wife
found his bruised body, with the throat slashed, inside their garage. David Madsen's red jeep stood parked at the curb, but
Miglin's 1994 Lexus had been stolen. The trail led next to New
Jersey and the murder of William Reese, 45, a cemetery caretaker. His red Chevrolet pickup had vanished. As the nationwide
dragnet spread, it spawned rumors that Cunanan had AIDS and
may have been committing murders out of revenge. No substan-
tiating evidence of these allegations ever surfaced. But Cunanan's mother would announce to the world that she thought her
son was a "high-class homosexual prostitute."

In the South Beach section of Miami, Florida, homosexual
residents made no secret of their lifestyle. Nearby, famed designer Gianni Versace, who was allegedly gay, lived in a palatial
home remodeled from two Art Deco hotels. The designer had
reportedly met Andrew Cunanan on previous occasions. On July
15, Versace took a short walk to buy an Italian newspaper. As
he reached the marble steps to the gated entry of his home, someone raised a .40-caliber handgun and shot Versace twice in the
head. In a parking garage not far away, police located the red
Chevrolet pickup stolen from the New Jersey victim, William
Reese, along with clothing belonging to Cunanan. Investigators
soon discovered that he'd been staying in a local hotel for nearly
two months.

The search for Andrew Cunanan filled headlines and television
news reports. For more than a week the story made headlines,
with everyone wildly speculating about Cunanan's hiding place.
Had he escaped to another country? Was he in plain view dressed

as a woman? Would he kill again? An alleged hit list of celebrities frightened well-known entertainers.

It turned out that Andrew Cunanan hadn't put much distance between himself and his final crime. He'd been hiding on a luxurious houseboat, unused by its owner, less than three miles from Versace's home. On July 23, police found him there. Bloated from too much drinking, Cunanan had stuck the barrel of his .40-caliber handgun in his mouth and pulled the trigger one final time.

With his death, the answers to endless questions also evaporated forever.

Horoscope for Andrew Cunanan
Born August 31, 1969, 9:41 P.M. PDT, National City, California
Source: Birth certificate

The quest for easy money and luxury, in return for little effort, pulled Andrew Cunanan into male prostitution, murder, and finally suicide.

Cunanan's first house of the physical body, appearance, and personality is dominant in his chart. It is inhabited by the Moon and Saturn, both in Taurus. The conjunction of these two planets indicates a materialistic person actively concerned with status and security. Taurus signifies the desire for beauty and value, suggesting that Cunanan yearned to possess flashy jewelry, expensive cars, and valuable paintings, and wished to live in a luxury home. Unfortunately, the Saturn influence brings a scarcity of success, and a restriction from gaining what is desired. Failure plunged Cunanan into a deep depression.

Saturn continued to exert control in Cunanan's chart by ruling both his tenth and eleventh houses. The tenth house involves reputation, while the eleventh house governs friends. This double dominance illustrates the need for Cunanan to associate with influential people and make wealthy friends. His unrealistic notion that rubbing elbows with the rich and famous would somehow induce them to share their wealth doomed him to disappointment, one of the negative blows Saturn can deliver. So, seeking his elusive dream, Cunanan found himself frequently on the move, which required him to adapt to different people and various situations. Such activity demonstrates the influence of his mutable Virgo Sun sign. But since his personality is ruled by Taurus, a stubbornly fixed sign associated with money, Cunanan deliberately gravitated primarily toward rich surroundings. By doing so, he limited his opportunities and chances for success.

Seekers of wealth who refuse to work, both men and women, sometimes turn to prostitution. The fifth house rules sex. The Sun, planet of ego and self-esteem, occupies Cunanan's fifth house, so Cunanan chose to boost his self-esteem through his sexuality. Since the Sun, planet of the male sex, is the only ruler of his fifth house, Cunanan's sexual partners were men. As previously mentioned, Cunanan's Moon is in Taurus, occupying the first house. A favorable aspect shows up in the Sun's position relative to the Moon, reinforcing the association between sex and money in Cunanan's life. It is not surprising then, that he enjoyed occasional success as a prostitute.

Cunanan's sixth house, which relates to services, is quite strong. Uranus, Mercury, and Jupiter, all in Libra, are residents of the sixth house, along with Pluto. Libra, ruled by Venus, is also associated with beauty and luxury. The influence of Libra only increased Cunanan's desire for an expensive lifestyle. He chased it by offering his services as a prostitute. Pluto is in Virgo, the sign associated with service. Even though Cunanan wanted to be a person of influence, and hoped for money and power, he ended up as nothing more than an employee hired to deliver sexual services.

Mars, occupying Cunanan's eighth house of death, rules guns. Cunanan's victims were all shot to death. It is uncertain what motivated five murders, but robbery can't be ruled out since Cunanan always needed money. The murder of Gianni Versace, a celebrity, led to Cunanan's ultimate demise. Pluto, in a negative aspect to Mars, represents revenge. Cunanan was obsessed with money and glamour. Apparently, the killing of Versace was revenge motivated. Frustration, a Saturn trait, is powerful in Cunanan's chart. His resentment of Versace, a millionaire at the peak of his career, may have been too much for Cunanan to bear.

Jupiter rules Cunanan's eighth house of death as well as his twelfth house of self-destruction. Killing the prominent celebrity, a Jupiter characteristic, was undoubtedly a suicidal act. Neptune, influencing Cunanan's twelfth house of secrets and self-destruction, lends mystery and speculation to his motives. The final ruler of the twelfth house is Mars, the planet of violence and of guns, located in the eighth house of death. Cunanan was found a few days after murdering Versace, having shot himself to death.

LIBRA

One of the most notorious Libras is mass murderer James Huberty, who invaded a McDonald's restaurant and slaughtered 21 people. Remarkably, his birthday is separated by only four days from that of George Hennard, who in 1991 invaded a Texas Luby's cafeteria and slaughtered 22 people, in an eerily similar set of circumstances. Libra is symbolized by the scales of justice. When their sense of balance is disturbed, negatively affected Libras can erupt in murderous rage.

Angelo Buono

Friday, October 5, 1934, 4:09 A.M.
Rochester, New York • Time Zone: 05:00 (EST)
Longitude 077° W 36' 57" • Latitude 43° N 09' 17"
Placidus Houses • Tropical Zodiac

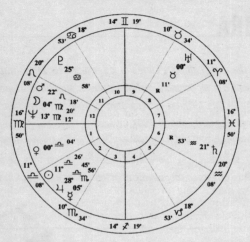

In October 1977, the first nude, raped, strangled female victim of California's notorious "Hillside Strangler" was discovered next to a Los Angeles freeway. The body of prostitute Yolanda Washington, 19, had been posed in a spread-eagled, face-up position that appeared to be deliberately provocative. Her killer had not attempted to hide the body. On the contrary, the circumstances indicated that he intentionally wanted early discovery.

Over the next four months, nine more young female victims appeared on Los Angeles hillsides, nude and obscenely posed. Some had been tortured. Because the first few had records of prostitution, early speculation centered on the possibility that a serial killer of streetwalkers roamed the city. But later victims included two schoolgirls, whose bodies were tauntingly placed close to the L.A. police academy. Several more murdered women had held ordinary jobs, nullifying the theory of a predator who delighted in killing hookers. Crime scene evidence also suggested that two men were probably involved, and at least one of them knew the inner workings of police procedures.

As suddenly as the killings had started, they came to a mysterious halt in February 1978. All of the trails grew cold. Public pressure to solve the case, though, remained as hot as L.A.'s Santa Ana winds.

The string of murders may have remained unsolved if a Washington security guard named Kenneth Bianchi, 27, hadn't made some crucial errors. When two young Bellingham women were found strangled, homicide detectives discovered links to Kenneth Bianchi. The city's police chief recalled the Hillside Strangler case from his previous job in Southern California, and recognized similarities in the crimes. He telephoned the L.A. task force. They learned that Bianchi had lived in close proximity to several of the California victims, had once been rejected as a candidate for the L.A. police academy, and had been known to flash handcuffs and police badges. Ironically, Bianchi had twice been questioned by the L.A. cops in connection with the murders, but hadn't been arrested.

The Washington investigators cinched the link when they found a woman's ring in Bianchi's possession. It belonged to Yolanda Washington, the first Hillside Strangler victim. Faced with a possible death penalty, Kenneth Bianchi cut a deal. He agreed to tell all in exchange for life. In his confession, which he later recanted, Bianchi named his cousin Angelo Buono as his partner in the Los Angeles murders.

Angelo Buono, 44, a dark, muscular, curly-haired son of Sicilian parents, owned and operated an automobile upholstery shop in Glendale. Two inches short of 6 feet, he was known for his long hairy arms, large powerful hands, prominently long nose under close-set eyes, and a low forehead. He owned an extensive collection of guns, and had a reputation for seducing a string of young women. He and his cousin liked using Buono's house, next to the upholstering business, to host girls who preferred parties, drugs, and sex over work or school.

The investigation revealed that Bianchi and Buono started "arresting" girls by flashing phony badges and placing them in Buono's car, which resembled an unmarked police vehicle. They sexually assaulted some of the victims during the ensuing rides, but chose to take most of them to Buono's home. There, they would bind the frightened young women with white cord and force them into perverted, injurious sex acts. Afterwards, one or both men would strangle the victims, then place the posed nude bodies where they would be easily found close to freeways. The cousins reportedly experimented with execution methods. One girl, said Bianchi, endured injections of air into her veins, which failed to cause intended death by embolism. She also survived injection of caustic cleanser into her blood vessels and a bungled attempt at suffocation with a plastic bag over her head. Finally, she succumbed to strangulation.

Another targeted victim, Catherine Lorre, 27, averted disaster when the pair of "vice cops" tried to arrest her in Hollywood. While complying with their demand for identification, she flashed a photo she always carried with her. Examining it closer, the ersatz officers saw young Catherine sitting on the lap of her father, famed movie actor Peter Lorre. Certainly, they reasoned, if the daughter of someone so well known became a murder victim, the case would be treated with much greater intensity than the death of a prostitute or runaway. They immediately released the lucky Ms. Lorre.

Searching for hard evidence to corroborate Bianchi's stories, detectives put Angelo Buono under months of surveillance, but found very little that would conclusively tie him to the murders. After officers tentatively arrested Buono, the district attorney worried that Bianchi's wavering and changing testimony wouldn't hold up in court. The few threads and fibers found on victims that seemed to match material used in Buono's upholstery work provided dangerously slim connection. Rather than risk a trial that might result in finding Buono not guilty, which would exonerate him forever, the D.A. asked judge Ronald George to drop the murder charges against Buono. Controversy raged. Judge George harshly criticized the decision and recommended to California Attorney General George Deukmejian that his state prosecutors present the case to a jury.

During a prolonged trial that lasted an astounding two years, the press happily reported details of the extraordinary sexual tastes attributed to Buono. Witness testimony told of his preferences for sodomy, use of various sex toys, his habit of biting or beating women while raping them, and other aberrations. Jurors listened attentively for 24 months, and finally, after nineteen days of deliberations, convicted Buono of nine murders. Perhaps persuaded by Kenneth Bianchi's escape from the death penalty, the jury recommended life in prison without parole for Angelo Buono.

The successful prosecutor, George Deukmejian, became governor of California; the judge who persuaded him to take the case, and who sentenced Buono to spend the rest of his life in prison, became chief justice of the California supreme court.

Horoscope for Angelo Buono
Born October 5, 1934, 4:09 A.M. EST, Rochester, New York
Source: Birth certificate

This man whose name means "good angel" proved to be extremely devilish, indulging in torture, rape, sodomy, and serial murder.

The sign of Virgo, Buono's ascendant, appears prominently in his chart with its powerful influence over the Moon and Neptune. As one of the signatures of serial killers, Virgo exudes the negative characteristics of furtive adaptability and trickery. The makeup of Virgo encompasses the Moon, planet of women and emotions, so a picture emerges in which Buono secretly hated females. However, he felt no reluctance to use them for his personal sexual pleasure, or for profit by forcing them into prostitution, and finally for the thrill of murdering them. Neptune, planet of deception and fraud, also asserts negativity by its relative position in the chart, nestling close to Buono's Virgo ascendant. This alignment shades his personality with a sense of unreality, and the inability to understand the ramifications of the insidious cruelty he inflicted on young women. The fraud that stems from Neptune inclined Buono to become a deceitful liar and con man.

The role of sexual predator emerges in Buono's chart by the influence of several planets, especially in Buono's twelfth house, which involves behind-the-scenes activities. Buono, with the help of his cousin, Kenneth Bianchi, lured young women to his home, offering drugs, then using the girls for perverted sexual trysts. Neptune, residing in the twelfth house, comes into play again as the planet of drugs and deception. Buono and Bianchi often pretended to be undercover cops in order to deceive their intended prey. Also lurking in the twelfth house are Mars, planet of force and perversion, along with the Moon, domain of women. Buono's residence became the lurid playground of orgiastic excesses, as seen by the fourth house, involving the home, being ruled by Jupiter, the planet of excessiveness. After the two men used the girls for their own perverse pleasures, their activities took a grim, evil turn. Saturn, planet of selfish hatred and greedy materialism, rules Buono's fifth house of sex. In addition to governing the fifth house, Saturn occupies the sixth house of service. It follows that Buono, after satisfying his own sexual needs, forcibly persuaded his women to become prostitutes. This enabled him to sell sex, turning it into a materialistic, profitable service. With the Neptunian influence over Buono's perceptions, it came easy for him to think of sex as a business transaction.

Remarkably, in spite of Buono's simmering dislike of women, he was reportedly married seven times. The explanation for this probably relates to the placement of his Sun, ruler of the ego, in Libra, the sign of marriage and partnership. The Sun's position is extremely weak, suggesting a vulnerable ego that constantly needed reinforcement. The ability to attract seven women into marriage could certainly have been fodder for his self-esteem.

Buono's eighth house of death is co-ruled by Uranus, the planet of unpredictability and cold-bloodedness. An opposition between Uranus and Mercury, a dangerously negative configuration, sets the stage for Buono's unspeakable torture of his victims, in which he and Bianchi experimented with intravenous injections of air and a caustic cleanser. They also attempted to electrocute one girl, which is another reflection of Uranus, the ruler of electricity. Mars, the other planet ruling Buono's eighth house, is positioned in an exceptionally cruel aspect to Saturn. Saturn influences their methods of sexually using women, then disposing of their nude bodies, cruelly displayed as if they were trash.

Courts are in the domain of the ninth house. In Buono's chart, Taurus, the sign of determination, rules his ninth house. The determination of a judge doomed Buono, when the magistrate insisted that the suspect face murder charges. Venus, lodged in his first house, interceded to save Buono's skin. He received a sentence of life in prison rather than the death penalty, a positive influence of Venus.

Buono's midheaven, the strongest point in his chart, rules fame, or notoriety.

Certainly one of the most notorious of serial killers, as half of the infamous "Hillside Strangler" team, Angelo Buono's name remains well known in the annals of cruel serial murderer.

James Oliver Huberty

Sunday, October 11, 1942, 12:11 A.M.
Canton, Ohio • Time Zone: 04:00 (Eastern War Time)
Longitude 081° W 22' 43" • Latitude 40° N 47' 56"
Placidus Houses • Tropical Zodiac

McDonald's fast-food restaurants usually are associated with pleasure; hungry people chewing Big Macs, children eating Happy Meals, everyone washing down tasty french fries with oversized soft drinks. But on July 18, 1984, a man simmering with rage turned the San Ysidro, California, McDonald's into a bloody execution chamber. Using a 9-mm semiautomatic pistol, a 9-mm Uzi assault rifle, and a 12-gauge pump-action shotgun, he indiscriminately fired into the crowd for over an hour, killing 21 and wounding 19 men, women, and children.

James Huberty, originally from Canton, Ohio, contracted polio in his childhood, leaving him with an odd walk that made him the butt of jokes from schoolmates. His mother, saying she heard a religious calling, deserted the family when Huberty was seven. As he grew into a tall, awkward, and bespectacled loner, Huberty took solace in guns, practicing obsessively with them.

While his absent mother devoted her life to religious fervor, Huberty declared himself an atheist. Remarkably, while attending college in Ohio, he found a woman who overlooked his tense reclusiveness, married her in 1965, and fathered two daughters. He chose a profession that would not require much social interaction: mortician. But his boss expected Huberty to mix with the grieving families, and he couldn't do it. He left to become a welder. Wherever he worked, he gained a reputation for his nasty temper and negative attitude. He complained about social ills and seemed happy only when talking about guns or practicing with them. Another rejection angered him when he tried unsuccessfully to volunteer for military duty to fight in Vietnam.

Home life for Huberty seemed to hold little happiness. He tolerated nothing from his wife and daughters, often punishing them with physical violence. As his inner turmoil grew, he began hearing clamoring, demonic voices. Just as Son of Sam, David Berkowitz, had claimed, Huberty heard a dog speak evil thoughts to him. Ongoing conflict with neighbors caused them to fear him. He spoke of a massive conspiracy against him, which he blamed for the loss of a job he'd held for thirteen years. In reality, the public utility simply went out of business.

Life in Ohio for Huberty fell into a continual pattern of conflict with neighbors, business operators, civil servants, and everyone around him. Seeking escape in 1983, he moved his wife and daughters to Tijuana, the Mexican city just below California's southern border. Uncomfortable there, he moved them again to San Ysidro, just north of the border. Still miserable, and unable to find work as a welder, he completed training as a security guard and obtained a license in April 1994. It allowed him to carry a visible firearm, and to utilize his love for guns. After one job application resulted in an insulting rejection, he landed night employment guarding a condominium complex.

The pay provided enough money to move his family to a better apartment in San Ysidro, from which Huberty could see a McDonald's restaurant just down the street. But within weeks, his boss fired him. Now he became more tense, seldom smiling, summer sweat popping out on his balding head. A traffic citation he received didn't help. (Such a ticket caused Son of Sam to be apprehended.) On a warm Wednesday afternoon, shortly before 4 P.M., July 18, 1984, he dressed in his favorite outfit, camouflage pants with a short-sleeved dark red shirt, and walked out of the apartment carrying a heavy blanket-wrapped bundle.

In the McDonald's parking lot, Huberty stepped out of his car. He entered the restaurant carrying a holstered pistol, his Uzi, a shotgun, now unwrapped from the blanket, and a heavy bag of ammunition. After firing the shotgun into the ceiling, Huberty aimed the Uzi at a woman who managed the eatery, and squeezed off a lethal round that hit her in the face. He shouted orders for everyone in the crowded room not to move or they would die. Some tried to obey while others scrambled in panic. More gunfire erupted. The father of a family group begged Huberty not to continue shooting, but collapsed to the floor with fourteen bullet holes in him. Another woman fell mortally wounded. It made no difference to Huberty that many of his targets were helpless women and children. His intent to kill became obvious as he fired multiple rounds into victims already wounded. He carefully aimed a 9-mm round into the back of a crying infant's head.

One of the employees, huddling behind a stove, managed to grab a phone, dial O, and whisper that someone was shooting up the place. At first the operator insisted he dial 911, but at his begging, made the connection for the frightened caller. Meanwhile, three young boys who'd just arrived became the targets of Huberty's shotgun. Two of them died, crumpled outside on their bicycles. A photo of one dead boy would later horrify TV audiences and newspaper readers.

The staccato belching of Huberty's guns continued. An elderly husband tried to comfort his mortally wounded spouse, wiping the blood from her face. Huberty yelled at him, then shot him point-blank. Witnesses later said that in between shootings, Huberty appeared to be grotesquely dancing to the beat of music from someone's radio.

In the noisy pandemonium, screams and gunshots echoed inside the building. Several people escaped, some bleeding from various injuries. When the first police car screeched to a halt in the parking lot, Huberty peppered it with lead. More officers arrived, and Huberty took aim at the uniformed men who systematically moved into sheltered, strategic positions. The wild gunman vaulted over a counter inside, and found cowering employees in the kitchen. Some of them leaped in all directions trying to move out of harm's way, but Huberty carefully aimed at the heads of three young women who kneeled in paralyzed fear, and killed each of them. Those few who made it to a small storeroom safely locked themselves inside.

The slaughter continued, seemingly without end. For more than an hour, Huberty fired, reloaded, and fired again. He used more than 150 rounds of ammunition. At last, a SWAT team arrived and surrounded the restaurant. A marksman using a telescopic sight aimed from the roof of an adjacent post office, waiting for a good shot. It came at 5:17 P.M. The officer carefully squeezed the trigger and sent a .308-caliber slug into James Huberty's chest. He died instantly. The gory carnage had ended with 21 fatalities, 22 counting Huberty, and 19 wounded.

A subsequent autopsy examined Huberty's brain for abnormalities that might explain his cruel, murderous behavior, but found nothing unusual about it.

The McDonald's restaurant would never again open for business. Grieving officials of the company had it torn down and donated the vacant site for a memorial to the victims.

Horoscope for James Oliver Huberty
Born October 11, 1942, 12:11 A.M. Eastern War Time, Canton, Ohio
Source: Birth certificate

Does the horrifying act of slaughtering 21 innocent men, women, and children, plus wounding 19 more, involve colossal self-esteem in the shooter, or does it relate to a withered ego needing to be fed by notoriety? In the case of James Huberty, a swollen ego existed, as seen by the Sun being the strongest planet in his chart. At the same time, his Cancer ascendant suggests a moody, supersensitive person whose feelings were easily hurt and who deeply felt the sting of any criticism. Other segments of his chart reveal a vortex of turmoil and conflict within the life and mind of this troubled killer.

Ego is a province of the Sun. The powerful position of this fiery ball in Huberty's chart magnifies his ego, even while sharing crowded space in his fourth house of home and father with four other jostling, busy planets. Mars, Venus, Mercury, and the Sun are all in the sign of Libra, whose positive characteristics include peace and harmony, but on the negative side can render laziness and self-indulgence. The fifth planet residing in Huberty's fourth house is the Moon, which brings moodiness and instability. Moon is in Scorpio, the emotional and highly secretive sign that signals revenge. Huberty's Cancer ascendant, and his Moon in Scorpio, indicate that his brooding, intense emotions were precariously balanced, ready to erupt.

In the center of Huberty's five Libra planets lies violent Mars, which infused him with antagonism. He fought with employers, friends, his own children, and his neighbors. Mars is the ruler of two other houses in which people involved in Huberty's life can be seen; the tenth house of career and the fifth house of children. Huberty's neighbors are represented by the third house, which is ruled by Mercury, the planet of unrest. His antagonistic nature even affected his second house of money, through the conjunction of Mars and the Sun. Huberty lost jobs and income as a result of his anger and hostility. Mars also illustrates his obsession with guns.

Huberty's first house of personality and temperament is occupied by Jupiter and Pluto. Jupiter's position in Cancer aggravates Huberty's moodiness and sensitivity, which are attributes of his ascendant. Pluto, the planet associated with revenge, adds the potentially dangerous element of obsession and compulsion to Huberty's temperament. Leo, the sign in which Pluto appears, creates a volatile potential for Huberty to take dramatic revenge against the world. Huberty's strongest sign, Libra, is symbolized by balanced scales, indicating that his emotional nature was constantly in danger of losing its balance and tipping over into violence.

The third house, governing Huberty's mind, is occupied by Neptune, the planet associated with clouded thinking. It is in a negative position related to Pluto. This aspect ushers in the irrational thoughts of conspiracies and delusions that swept through Huberty's brain like a twisting tornado prior to the mass murder.

Troubled men often cannot stand the constraints of marriage. Huberty, though, remained married to the same woman throughout his abbreviated life, taking his family with him even though they moved around the country and to Mexico. The seventh house of marriage is ruled by Saturn, which sits next to Uranus, an aspect suggesting an unusual marriage. But the relationship gave Huberty an element of stability, one of the positive qualities of Saturn. By forming several harmonious aspects to the planets in Huberty's fourth house, Saturn's calming influence partly mitigated the strife in his home life.

Huberty's eighth house of death is ruled by Aquarius, the sign of instability. Since Aquarius's rulers, Uranus and Saturn, are next to each other, this aspect gives added power to both planets.

They are in Gemini, a sign associated with mental activity. This placement explains Huberty's bizarre ideas and haunting thoughts about death, reflecting Uranus's eccentric influence. The unpredictability brought by Uranus suggests that Huberty's decision to commit mass murder was unplanned and unexpected. But Saturn's influence reveals that this idea had been building for some time. Huberty stockpiled weapons and dressed in camouflage before committing his carnage. Planning and organization are Saturn characteristics.

There is no evidence that Huberty had any previous connection with the family-oriented fast-food restaurant he chose as his killing ground. But his chart foreshadows the odd choice. Huberty's Cancer ascendant rules family as well as food. In addition, the sixth house rules restaurants and is occupied by Huberty's Jupiter in Cancer next to his ascendant.

The twelfth house of self-destruction and suicide is governed by Mercury, which rules the rational mind. The implication is that Huberty realized in advance that the mass murder he planned would lead to his own death. Although his thinking was clouded by the influence of Neptune, Mercurial rationality gave his vision enough clarity to understand what he was doing.

Huberty's midheaven rules his reputation. Significantly it is in Aries, which is governed by violent, bloody Mars. The mass murder he committed ensures enduring notoriety for the tragic legacy he left behind.

Jeremy Strohmeyer

Wednesday, October 11, 1978, 2:10 A.M.
Los Angeles, California • Time Zone: 07:00 (PDT)
Longitude 118° W 14' 34" • Latitude 34° N 03' 08"
Placidus Houses • Tropical Zodiac

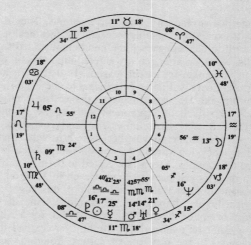

At age 18, Jeremy Strohmeyer had everything going for him. Good looking, bright, popular at school, and living comfortably with his affluent family in Long Beach, California, he planned to apply for acceptance at West Point or the Air Force Academy. In his senior year at Wilson High school, he earned high marks with little effort, and played on the volleyball team. With nothing but a bright future ahead of him, Strohmeyer chose instead to turn his back on golden opportunity in favor of hedonistic excitement, drugs, parties, dark sexual urges, and ultimately murder.

Life didn't start so optimistically for Strohmeyer. He was born on October 11, 1978, in a hospital for mental patients, to a teenage girl who already had one son by another man and would have a third son after Jeremy. The young mother had a long history of drug abuse and serious psychological disorders. The father spent more time in than out of prison. While little Jeremy waited for adoption, a foster family cared for him.

In 1980, a couple in their mid-thirties who already had a preschool daughter, couldn't resist the beautiful little blue-eyed 18-month-old boy, and adopted him. They gave Jeremy love and all the advantages of wealth. Choosing not to keep the adoption a secret, they told him as soon as he could understand what it meant.

Fortune had smiled on the adoptive parents. They'd picked a child with exceptional intelligence and perfect health. He performed well in elementary school, and demonstrated smooth social skills. Not long after Jeremy entered high school, the family moved to Singapore for career reasons. In that city-state, where laws are extremely restrictive (it's illegal to chew gum), Jeremy's behavior slipped. He started hanging out with a band of American kids who liked to experiment with booze. At the special school for U.S. citizens, Jeremy was nearly expelled. His protective parents wondered whether their boy was simply being railroaded. They felt certain he couldn't have been intoxicated while on the campus, as was suggested to them.

When they moved back to Long Beach in 1996 and enrolled Jeremy as a junior at Wilson High School, the parents, now living in near-luxury, hoped that he would resume the previous exemplary behavior they'd seen. Jeremy did, for a while. Then as senior, after he'd turned 18, Strohmeyer learned the use of amphetamines in the fast lane of parties, drinking, and staying up all night with his circle of buddies. Ignoring the advice of his parents and teachers, Jeremy let his grades fall. An arrest for drunk driving failed to enlighten him but did cost him his driver's license.

Love bit Strohmeyer hard during that period when he met a 17-year-old senior from another school. He spent every spare minute with her and wrote long, poetic love letters to her. The girl, seeming to care for him but not in the way Strohmeyer wanted, couldn't cope with the smothering attention. When she left and moved to another state to live with a man, Strohmeyer continued to declare his love in letters.

As a substitute, Strohmeyer found sexual excitement on the Internet. He spent endless hours visiting pornographic Web sites, especially those portraying men having sex with girls no more than five or six years old. He would one day say that he had "accidentally" stumbled on child-porn material, but that thin rationalization didn't account for the hundreds of files he stored in his personal computer.

As a lark, Strohmeyer had his tongue and nipples pierced, and wore decorative baubles in them. Disagreements with his parents led to his temporarily moving out of the home, but as many young people discover, it is difficult to survive without an income. He asked them to subsidize an apartment, but they wisely resisted and allowed him to move back into his bedroom.

In May 1997, the father of Strohmeyer's best buddy invited the two teenagers to join him for a Memorial Day trip to Las Vegas. The trio stopped just across the Nevada border at a casino. While the adult gambled, the pair of youths spent hours in a video game arcade.

At about 3:35 A.M., May 25, Strohmeyer, dressed in his usual droopy walking shorts, a baggy dark blue T-shirt, and a baseball cap turned backward, felt a ball of wet paper strike him. He whirled to see a little African-American girl and another child hurling the wadded paper towels at one another. He would later learn the girl's name: Sherrice Iverson, age 7. Grinning, Strohmeyer retrieved the missile that had hit him, hurled it at Sherrice, and gave chase. Sherrice, wearing a blue sailor-style dress and black cowboy boots, sprinted away with Strohmeyer in pursuit. They raced in circles for several minutes before she escaped into the ladies restroom. The sanctuary she sought was short-lived, because in Strohmeyer's value system he could go wherever he wanted. The little girl's brother, who had been left to watch her while their father gambled, was nowhere in sight.

Inside the restroom, Sherrice grabbed a Wet Floor sign and swung it at Strohmeyer, grazing his arm. He would later say that something went "haywire" in his mind. He grabbed the girl and carried her into a stall for the handicapped. Strohmeyer's buddy had followed him, and stood on the toilet seat of the adjacent stall, where he witnessed the child struggle and heard Strohmeyer threaten to kill her. In the observer's subsequent statement, he claimed that he walked out, feeling that something bad might happen.

Strohmeyer held Sherrice, removed her boots, and sexually assaulted her. When he heard two other women enter the room, he held his hand over the child's air passages and stifled her with the weight of his own body. He later said that he thought he had damaged her so badly that she wouldn't be normal. So when the women left, he jerked Sherrice's head to break her neck. Leaving her dead body in the stall, Strohmeyer casually walked out.

He and his buddy worried during the remainder of the weekend in Las Vegas and the trip home. Their concern was not for the dead child, but for themselves. They had very good reason to be concerned. A security camera had recorded Strohmeyer and his buddy following the little girl into the restroom.

During the next few days, Strohmeyer sought counsel from his school buddies, all of whom promised not to inform. The security camera tape appeared on multiple television news reports, and Wilson High students recognized the image. Many of them also felt it would be wrong to inform on their acquaintance. Eventually, three female students accepted the importance of bringing a killer to justice, and told the school principal that the mystery man in the videotape was Jeremy Strohmeyer. Also, the young woman he had loved so deeply, who had returned to Southern California, told her father, who in turn contacted the police. They grabbed Strohmeyer at his home as he was packing his belongings to flee.

Instead of facing a possible death sentence, Strohmeyer finally agreed to plead guilty and accept a sentence of life in prison. His buddy, according to officials, had committed no crime, so faced no charges. At the sentencing hearing on October 14, 1998, three days after his 20th birthday, Strohmeyer claimed he had minimal recollection of the killing, and blamed drugs, his early infancy, the casino, his buddy, his ex-girlfriend, and the Internet for his troubles. He repeated much of the litany when interviewed by Barbara Walters for the television program *20/20* that was shown to the nation on October 30, 1998, adding that he was not the monster that existed in popular perception.

Strohmeyer's sentence allows no possibility for parole. At age 20, he faced a literal lifetime behind bars.

A corollary issue, perhaps as important as meting out justice for murder, emerged from the Strohmeyer case. His buddy had witnessed part of the crime, and several pals and many classmates back in Long Beach recognized him when television news played the videotapes taken by security cameras. Yet most of them admitted reluctance to step forward and share that vital information with authorities. You can't "narc" on a pal. I'm no "snitch." There's nothing lower than an informer who would "rat" on his friend.

That attitude raises a serious question. Why does society adopt the code of hardened criminals, in which informants are hated more than the lawbreakers? What is wrong with helping the police solve a crime? A person who provides information to authorities is made to feel guilty, probably because that is how lawbreakers want them to feel, and society has gullibly accepted the rule. "Tattletales" are shunned among children, "squealers" are punished, and "snitches" are treated like lepers. All of these negative synonyms carry a dark stigma. Where did this attitude originate? Maybe from entertainment media in which audiences root for the villians who are portrayed sympathetically, and hiss at the informer who is invariably characterized as a spineless coward.

In the last decade of the 20th century, it has become fashionable among youth to emulate the appearance and behavior of convicts or outlaw gangs, with garish tattoos, shaved heads, baggy clothing, and obscene language. The unwritten law among prison inmates absolutely prohibits snitching, so the gullible imitators inexplicably adopt this code, shrugging off the notion that it would be far more responsible to assist law enforcement agencies whose main goal is to protect society.

Fortunately, in the Strohmeyer case, a small trickle of responsible students and adults who recognized his image in the security videos bravely stepped forward and helped solve the crime. They should be applauded for having the courage, intelligence, and responsibility to reject the ridiculous, mindless condemnation of informants.

Horoscope for Jeremy Strohmeyer
Born October 11, 1978, 2:10 A.M. PDT, Los Angeles, California
Source: Birth certificate

In Jeremy Strohmeyer's mind, his interest in child pornography, which led him to murder, was not his fault. The Internet made him do it.

Serious psychological disorders are indicated in Strohmeyer's chart. Scorpio, his strongest sign, is associated with obsessions and compulsions. Mars, Uranus, and Venus are all found in Scorpio. In Strohmeyer's fourth house, Mars is next to Uranus, indicating a highly volatile and unpredictable nature. His Venus in Scorpio makes a negative aspect to the Moon, ruler of women and children. This alignment indicates problems in his relationships with women. Any attempts he made at expressing affection, an action ruled by Venus, turned out to be controlling, possessive, and smothering.

Strohmeyer's ascendant is Leo, the dominant point in his chart. The ascendant, ruler of the first house, represents his personality, temperament, and disposition. Since the ascendant takes a negative position in respect to all of his Scorpio planets, the egotistical and arrogant qualities of Leo appear. Violent Mars and unstable Uranus are two of the planets in Scorpio, so when thwarted, Strohmeyer could explode in violence. Saturn, residing in Strohmeyer's first house, is in a negative aspect to Neptune, which lodges in his fifth house of sex and children. This orientation suggests that Strohmeyer possibly entertained fears about sexual inadequacy, although they may have had no basis in reality. Saturn rules fears and Neptune introduces unreality. The combination provides the first inklings of his interest in sex with children.

Strohmeyer's third house contains three planets: Pluto, the Sun, and Mercury, all in Libra. As his Libra Sun also rules his Leo ascendant, ruler of his appearance, he is quite good looking. The conjunction of Sun and Pluto augments his obsessive-compulsive traits. With three planets in Libra, the sign associated with beauty, a luxurious lifestyle was important to Strohmeyer.

His interest in computers in shown by the Moon in Aquarius, the sign ruling electronics. With the combination of his Moon opposing his ascendant, and his obsessive personality, represented by the Pluto alignment with Scorpio, this interest became an addiction.

The fifth house of sex and children is occupied and co-ruled by Neptune, the planet of confusion. Neptune's square relationship to Saturn illustrates Strohmeyer's strong, personal involvement with, and possible fear of, sex. Jupiter, the other fifth-house ruler, is in his twelfth house of secrets. Strohmeyer kept secret much of his interest in sex and children, carefully hiding it from adults and many of his friends. Jupiter's abundance also reflects the enormous number of pornographic files he kept in his computer.

In addition to ruling Strohmeyer's fifth house of sex and children, Jupiter and Neptune flex their muscles again by governing Pisces. The eighth house of death is reigned over by Pisces, so the combination establishes a deadly chain linking sex, children, and death in Strohmeyer's destiny.

Drugs in general are ruled by Neptune, the planet associated with escape from reality. Strohmeyer used amphetamines, stimulants that produce hyperactivity and nervousness, the feelings associated with Uranus. The conjunction of Uranus and Venus in Strohmeyer's chart indicates his fondness for the drugs. His Moon in Aquarius, a Uranus-ruled sign, augments this attraction. With the Pluto-Scorpio alignment exercising strong influence in his chart by pointing to an addictive personality, Strohmeyer should have avoided drugs completely. He reputedly was high on amphetamines when he committed the molestation and murder.

The ninth house of legal matters and courts is ruled by Mars, which governs Scorpio. One of the dominions of Scorpio is pornography. The Mars influence suggests that Strohmeyer would have faced the death penalty if convicted. When the discovery of Strohmeyer's computerized child pornography collection was allowed into evidence, he pleaded guilty in exchange for a life term. His refusal to accept responsibility for his acts is partly a legal defense, but also reflects his dominant Leo ascendant. The insolence of afflicted Leo gives him a sense of entitlement and the arrogance to blame everything in his life for his problems, except himself.

Jeffrey MacDonald, M.D.

Tuesday, October 12, 1943, 5:53 P.M.
Jamaica, New York • Time Zone: 05:00 (Eastern War Time)
Longitude 073° W 51' • Latitude 40° N 36'
Placidus Houses • Tropical Zodiac

With his green beret tilted at a rakish angle, a pin of silver wings gleaming on the chest of his crisp uniform, and his trouser cuffs bloused inside mirror-polished combat boots, Dr. Jeffrey MacDonald beamed with pride at his perfect military image. He'd successfully completed the tough airborne training, including parachute jumps, that ranked him among the elite in the U.S. Army. And he'd accepted an assignment in the medical service at Fort Bragg, North Carolina, which kept him from the rigorous hell of Vietnam combat.

A cursory glance at Dr. MacDonald's life would have made most other soldiers envious. The 26-year-old doctor had a beautiful pregnant wife, two charming young daughters, good looks, and the brightest future possible. But that future exploded like a napalm bomb in the predawn hours of February 17, 1970.

On that cold, drizzly morning, the military police (MP) headquarters received a call and heard a male voice whisper, "Five forty-four Castle Drive . . . help . . . stabbing . . . hurry!" The caller weakly repeated the plea, then fell silent. Jeeps and an ambulance raced to the address, within Fort Bragg, and officers rushed inside where they found a bloody scene of death. Mac-Donald's wife, Colette, 26, lay face up on the bedroom floor with her pink pajama top wide open, blood pooling around multiple stab wounds in her torso. Someone had placed a blue pajama top over her exposed chest. Medical examiners would later discover that she had endured a savage assault which also fractured both of her arms. The word *PIG* was painted in blood on the bed's headboard in letters eight inches high.

In another bedroom, an MP aimed a flashlight at a tiny lifeless form huddled on the bed. Kimberly MacDonald, 5, had been attacked with a sharp knife that left slash wounds on her neck and face. Across the hall, the horrified soldier spotted yet a third victim. Kristen MacDonald, only 2, had suffered countless stab wounds in her back and neck through which nearly all of her blood had leaked onto the covers and floor. Both of the children had also been cruelly beaten.

Dr. Jeffrey MacDonald, who had made the emergency call, dressed in blue pajama bottoms, lay still next to his wife. He, too, had been wounded, but compared with the three dead victims, his injuries appeared superficial. One blood-bubbling stab wound in his chest had punctured his lung.

When MacDonald was able to speak coherently, he told of falling asleep on the living room couch and being awakened during the night by his wife's screams for help. Leaping up, he'd been attacked by one of the four intruders who had entered his home—three men and a woman who wore a floppy hat over her long blond hair. They looked like hippies, and the woman carried a lit candle. He'd heard her chant, "Acid is groovy—kill the pigs." Struggling to rise, he was stabbed with an icepick and struck with a baseball bat. As he attempted to run toward his wife's screams, another blow knocked him unconscious. Upon wakening later, he found the bodies of his family and telephoned for help.

The whole scene echoed the horrifying attack on Sharon Tate and her guests just six months earlier by a group of "hippies" that turned out to be the Manson family. A magazine containing a description of those murders was found near MacDonald's sofa. But a noticeable difference struck investigators. While the interior of the Tate home resembled a gory battlefield, MacDonald's furniture was relatively undisturbed. Other evidence looked suspicious, but not enough to bring charges against the surviving husband and father. Four months after the tragedy, following several hearings, the Army dropped legal action against him. MacDonald's widowed mother had paid his legal fees. Following his honorable discharge, he entered private medical practice and was able to repay her generosity.

In July 1971, MacDonald moved to Long Beach, California, to take charge of emergency services at St. Mary's Hospital. He spoke freely about the murder of his family on television, once as a guest on Dick Cavett's show.

One viewer felt troubled over what MacDonald was saying. Freddie Kassab, Colette MacDonald's father, had grown increasingly convinced that his son-in-law might have played a part in the murders and had self-inflicted the minor wounds to his own body. Over a long period of time, Kassab obtained transcripts of the hearings and examined them in minute detail. Discovering what he regarded as misleading and inconsistent comments by MacDonald, Kassab initiated pressure to bring him to trial.

After a series of legal battles, a grand jury heard testimony in 1975 and issued an indictment, but the trial was repeatedly delayed. In 1979, nearly a decade after the murders, MacDonald was pulled from the affluent playboy lifestyle he'd built in California to face charges in Raleigh, North Carolina. The prosecution presented circumstantial evidence, including an account alleging that holes in the blue pajama top found on Colette's body lined up with wounds in her chest. MacDonald had admitted placing the garment on her. The jury found him guilty of first-degree murder for the death of little Kristen, on the basis that he killed her to cover up the other two killings. The deaths of Colette and Kimberly, the jury said, were second-degree murder. MacDonald was sentenced to three life terms in federal prison.

The legal battles weren't yet completed, though. An appeals court overturned the convictions in 1980, freeing MacDonald to return to his comfortable life on the California coast. His freedom lasted nearly three years before the U.S. Supreme Court reversed the decision and sent MacDonald back to prison. The case remains controversial, largely because a woman named Helen Stoeckley claimed that she had participated in the massacre. Officials regarded her confession as unreliable due to her known heavy usage of drugs. She died in January 1983. Other arguments pointed out that a strand of hair from a blond wig had been found at the crime scene, and never admitted as evidence, but the prosecution said that tests revealed the source of the hair was one of the children's dolls.

Certainly, MacDonald's early life gave no hint that he might turn into a killer. He met his future wife, Colette, in junior high school. Later, at his Long Island, New York, high school, MacDonald was the popular student council president, king of the senior prom, football quarterback, and voted most likely to succeed. That prediction came true as he sailed through prestigious Princeton University and obtained his medical degree at Northwestern University. Following his internship of one year, he enlisted in the Army and earned his place with the Green Berets.

Two books take opposing viewpoints on the issues. *Fatal Vision* by Joe McGinniss suggests that MacDonald is guilty, while *Fatal Justice* by Jerry Potter, insists that MacDonald is innocent. MacDonald himself has steadfastly maintained his innocence, and continues to wage legal battles from his cells in various federal prisons.

Horoscope for Jeffrey MacDonald, M.D.
Born October 12, 1943, 5:53 P.M. Eastern War Time, Jamaica, New York
Source: Birth Certificate

One of the most publicized and controversial murder convictions in the second half of the 20th century, the case of Dr. Jeffrey MacDonald is still argued today. Did he kill his wife and two young daughters, or did a group of "hippies" do it, as MacDonald claims? His astrological chart contains several strong hints on the subject.

McDonald's most powerful planet, his Moon, inhabits his first house of personality and temperament. Both the Moon and his ascendant, ruler of his first house, are in Aries, MacDonald's most influential sign. Aries points to a competitive, energetic, physically active person. The Moon, ruling women, sits in direct opposition to his Sun in the seventh house of marriage. This negative aspect might allude to the possibility that there were severe conflicts between MacDonald and his wife. McDonald's Sun is in Libra, the marriage sign. The Sun's presence in his seventh house of marriage implies that he probably dominated his wife.

Mars, the planet of violence and cruelty, extends a long shadow over MacDonald's life. The red planet rules Aries, McDonald's ascendant, thus affecting his personality by attributing positive characteristics of energy and initiative, while also suggesting that he could be antagonistic. Residing in the third house, Mars is next to Saturn, the planet that can instill negative traits of selfishness and hatred. McDonald's wife and two children were beaten and stabbed to death. Both of these methods are ruled by Mars. His own slight wound was caused by a scalpel, another Mars-associated weapon. All of this first-house emphasis indicates self-involvement to an extreme degree. McDonald's personal interests, likes, and dislikes are the most important matters in his life. He is the center of his own universe.

MacDonald's children are a fifth-house matter. Pluto, planet of coercion and control, dwells in the fifth house, but cannot escape the far-reaching effect of Mars. The two planets are in a negative aspect to one another, which unlocks the door to Pluto's darker traits of manipulation, obsession, and even torture, to run amok in the house of children. The Moon acts as ruler of the fifth house. Since the Moon is the dominant planet over MacDonald's personality characteristics, the relationship between him and his children was one of the most important controlling factors in his life.

His sixth house is made strong by the occupancy of three planets: Venus, Mercury, and Neptune. This house is associated with the military service as well as medical issues, clearly relating to MacDonald's chosen profession as a Green Beret and military Army doctor. The Army is ruled by both Mars and Saturn, with Mars indicating energy and competition, plus war and weapons, while Saturn brings organization and responsibility, along with possible depression and hatred. Mars also rules the surgical profession. The role of Venus in the sixth house is a plus for MacDonald. During his tenure as an emergency doctor, while awaiting an appeal ruling, patients and colleagues alike described MacDonald as caring and sympathetic. These are Venusian qualities. Mercury and Neptune are closely conjunct and opposing his ascendant, creating a negative aspect. Mercury rules communications in general, such as talking and writing, while Neptune is the planet of deception and creative lies. This configuration supports those who disbelieve MacDonald's account of the events on the night his wife and daughters died.

Death, which significantly entered the destiny of MacDonald, is connected with the eighth house, ruled by Scorpio. The Manson/Tate murder association he made is interesting, as Manson is a Scorpio. Pluto, from its residency in the fifth house of children, reaches out as a co-ruler of the eighth house, along with Mars. Notably, Pluto rules conspiracies and groups. The group of hippies described by MacDonald may have really existed. Drugs were another factor in the murders. Neptune, ruler of drugs, appears in MacDonald's sixth house of work and police. McDonald maintained that the killers were apparently high on drugs when they raided his residence on the military reservation. One report, though, suggested that MacDonald used drugs to maintain his high energy level, and may have been under the influence on the murder night.

The fourth house, ruling his home, is governed by the Moon. The negative aspect of the Moon's opposition to the Sun, which affected MacDonald's marriage, also spills discord over into his home life.

Prison is a twelfth-house association and is ruled by Saturn, Uranus, Jupiter, and Neptune. Saturn relates to the law as well as restrictions and confinements. Uranus's erratic quality describes the unusual situations MacDonald has faced during his extended imprisonment, such as being released by the Army, retried, convicted, released again, then re-imprisoned, followed by a roller coaster of appeals. Jupiter, planet of plenty, represents the many years he has been behind bars. And finally, Neptune reveals the presence of deception and lies. Questions about MacDonald's guilt or innocence are part and parcel of Neptune's nature. Speculation and mystery, Neptune qualities, fostered by MacDonald for his own benefit, show the power of his dominant first house. The remarkable presence of his personality and enduring persistence will keep this case alive and in the public eye into a new millennium.

Lee Harvey Oswald

Wednesday, October 18, 1939, 9:55 P.M.
New Orleans, Louisiana • Time Zone: 06:00 (CST)
Longitude 090° W 04' 30" • Latitude 29° N 57' 16"
Placidus Houses • Tropical Zodiac

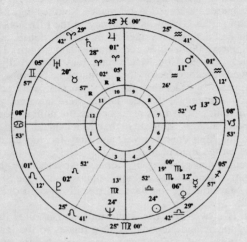

Forever linked with the November 22, 1963, assassination of President John Fitzgerald Kennedy in Dallas, Texas, Lee Harvey Oswald's name and reputation is still a battleground for vociferous disagreements about his involvement in the crime. Conspiracy theorists argue that Oswald was nothing more than a patsy duped by the real killers into taking the blame. Opponents point to the government investigation described in the Warren Commission report, which unequivocally stated that Oswald, acting alone, fired the deadly shots.

A native of New Orleans, Louisiana, Oswald was born in October 1939, just two months before his father died of a heart attack. His mother, struggling under the responsibility of raising three young sons, sent them to a Catholic boarding school, then later to a Lutheran orphanage. She rescued them in 1945 after entering into a second marriage, which became turbulent. As a child, Oswald frequently spent time in New Orleans with an uncle allegedly tied to Carlos Marcello, the regional mob boss. The unrest in Oswald's home resulted in a series of moves around the Dallas–Fort Worth area, forcing the youngster to constantly change schools. Despite this, he functioned well both academically and socially.

After the marriage ended, cramped housing caused Oswald to sleep with his mother until he reached puberty. In his teens, he changed. His grades dropped and he turned antisocial. Both his brother and his half-brother escaped the unhappy home life by joining the military, but their mother, dragging Lee along, followed the half-brother to New York. Forced to repeat the pattern of moving from school to school, Lee resisted by becoming a chronic truant. By 1953, exhibiting symptoms of a bitter loner, he landed in a New York facility for troubled boys.

Returning to school after a few weeks, Oswald performed marginally. On the streets, he heard of Communist efforts to free convicted spies Ethel and Julius Rosenberg, and rallied to the cause. Reportedly, this activity planted a seed for his eventual interest in Marxism. But before it could bloom, his mother moved him back to New Orleans.

Oswald is often described as a wimp or nerd, physically timid. But eyewitness accounts of his time in New York and New Orleans portray him as a scrappy fighter, unafraid of anyone. To utilize his excess energy, Oswald joined a student group attached to the Civil Air Patrol (CAP) in 1955. The unit commander was a strange, politically active homosexual, David Ferrie, a pilot who had connections to the underworld.

A few days after Oswald turned 17, in 1956, he dropped out of high school to join the Marine Corps. The controversy that muddles Oswald's history heats up regarding his military service. Ostensibly just an ordinary kid who wanted to escape an unsatisfactory life, it is strange that during his three-year tour, Oswald learned to speak the Russian language, could recite from Marx's *Das Kapital,* and worked in a highly confidential security area in Japan, near a CIA installation. Although he was later accused of shooting Kennedy by snapping off three difficult, long-distance rifle shots, Oswald's performance on military rifle ranges was mediocre at best. Two courts-martial that Oswald faced, for carrying an unauthorized gun and for fighting, landed him in the brig for nearly a month. In September 1959, the corps granted Oswald's request for a hardship discharge to help his "sick" mother.

Oswald had a considerably different agenda in mind when he

left the military. He promptly obtained a passport and set sail for France, then to London, Stockholm, and Helsinki, where he received a visa for travel to the Soviet Union. He arrived in Moscow on October 15 and immediately set in motion procedures for defecting from his U.S. citizenship and swearing allegiance to the Soviet Union.

The Communists put Oswald to work in a factory, during which he grew increasingly disillusioned. In February 1961 he met Marina Prusakova, and married her in April. One month later, he and his new bride departed and made their way back to Texas, where Oswald worked at a welding shop, then for a photo printer in Dallas.

In January 1963, according to available evidence, he purchased by mail order an Italian rifle equipped with a telescopic sight. Soon after, someone attempted to assassinate an ex-Army general living in Dallas, and Oswald would later become a suspect in the case.

Having lost his job with the photo printer, Oswald left Marina in Dallas with a friend and took a bus to New Orleans. That spring, he joined a group called the Fair Play for Cuba Committee, which supported Fidel Castro and participated actively by handing out leaflets to pedestrians. Of the mysterious figures loosely connected to the FPCC, one was David Ferrie, who had been Oswald's commander during his brief stint with the CAP youth group in 1955. Ferrie was also a known associate of mob boss Carlos Marcello, the man conspiracy theorists believe orchestrated the assassination.

A trip to Mexico City followed in September, allegedly an effort to reach Cuba. But Oswald soon returned by bus to Dallas and took a job in the Texas School Book Depository building. Three shots were fired from a sixth-floor window of the building on November 22, 1963, and President John Fitzgerald Kennedy slumped over in his limousine below, fatally wounded. The rifle Oswald had apparently purchased by mail order was found on the sixth floor.

Less than an hour after the shooting, several miles away, Dallas police officer J. D. Tippit stopped a pedestrian, thought to be Oswald. After a brief confrontation, Tippit fell dead from four gunshot wounds. A short time later, officers arrested Oswald in a nearby theater.

A shocked and grieving nation watched the aftermath on television that weekend as the incredible events were pieced together by news reporters. Then, on Sunday, November 24, one of the most stunning events ever shown on national television unfolded. As officers led Oswald to a waiting car in the basement of the police station, a local underworld character and strip club owner, Jack Ruby, stepped out of the surrounding crowd of reporters. Ruby, who reportedly had ties to Carlos Marcello, fired a single .38-caliber shot into Oswald's chest, silencing him forever.

Surrounded in mystery and controversy, Oswald may always remain one of the largest enigmas in American history.

Horoscope for Lee Harvey Oswald
Born October 18, 1939, 9:55 P.M. CST, New Orleans, Louisiana
Source: Birth certificate

Enormous speculation surrounds Lee Harvey Oswald and the assassination of President Kennedy. To this day there is still fervid debate on the subject of whether he acted alone. His astrological chart provides some interesting insights.

Oswald's burning desire to be important virtually bubbles from the top of his chart, where his powerful tenth house of reputation lies. The two planets dwelling in the tenth house, Jupiter and Saturn, shout of Oswald's determination to gain status and to become a person of substance. His midheaven, ruler of the tenth house, is in Pisces, governed in turn by Neptune, the planet of myths, legends, lies, and mysteries. Jupiter, the domain of exaggeration, and one of the tenth-house occupants, faces off with Neptune. This negative aspect sets off an eruption that clouds the sky with even more confusion regarding Oswald's reputation. Saturn, the second occupant, brings a driving ambition for status, but sits in a boiling negative aspect to the Sun. This reveals Oswald's feelings of inadequacy and frustration. Unfortunately for Oswald, his Sun, planet of ego, turns out to be quite weak, indicating withered self-confidence. So within Oswald's psyche, an internal conflict raged between his ambition to become famous and his lack of self-esteem.

Both Jupiter and Saturn are in Aries, a Mars-ruled sign. One motive of political assassins is to gain public recognition, which relates to the Jupiter/Saturn configuration. As assassins historically have been people with low self-esteem who have accomplished little or nothing in their lives. Killing powerful men, an

Aries trait, is a twisted way of gaining personal power.

Oswald's Moon, in Capricorn, steps into the mix with ruler-ship of his emotions. Capricorn pours in another dose of driving ambition. Cancer, governed by the Moon, rules his ascendant. The influence of Oswald's strong emotions on his temperament and disposition is significant, since Moon/Cancer personalities are capricious and unstable. He was a creature of his moods, as seen in his trip to Russia, and the quick return after getting married. The Moon, ruling his emotions, is in his seventh house of marriage.

Scorpio, which encompasses the planets of Venus and Mercury, rules Russia. It is not surprising that with Venus, the planet of love, in this sign, Oswald found his love while living in Russia. Mercury rules speech and mental activities. This configuration explains his interest in and ability to learn the Russian language.

Oswald's eighth house of death is ruled by Mars, the planet of guns and shooting. Mars sits in opposition to Pluto, indicating an obsession with guns and violence. It is often found that killers with weak egos overcompensate by using violence. But there is another even more interesting revelation in the Mars-Pluto configuration. Pluto occupies the second house of money, while Mars, with its relation to guns, resides in the eighth house of death. This might confirm the suspicion that Oswald was paid money for bringing about a death with the use of a gun! The other rulers of his eighth house are Uranus and Saturn. Uranus, the planet of eccentricity, opposes Mercury. This aspect shows strange, irrational, and obsessed thoughts about death. Ambitious Saturn's influence on Oswald's eighth house of death is shown by its placement in his tenth house of public recognition. He knew that death in some form would bring him recognition. Ironically, both the death of President Kennedy and his own contributed to his place in history.

Secrets pop up in Oswald's chart through the twelfth house of hidden agendas, ruled by Mercury. Information is the domain of Mercury, and that planet opposes Uranus, which is associated with irrationality. This aspect relates to Oswald's disturbed thinking, and as Uranus rules his eighth house of death, these confused thoughts concerned death. Mercury is in a negative aspect to Mars, the ruler of his house of death, indicating serious discord involving violence and guns.

Did Oswald have friends linked to organized crime? His eleventh house of friends is occupied by Uranus, the planet of eccentricity. Violent Mars leers pompously from its seat in the eighth house of death, and rules the house of friends. More important, Pluto dwells in Oswald's second house of money. Pluto, planet of control, manipulation, and crime, which could certainly refer to the Mafia, sits in opposition to Mars and the eighth house of death, creating a dangerously negative aspect. These alignments may very well hint of connections between Oswald, money, organized crime, and death.

When Oswald was shot to death, he took his secrets to the grave. His reputation, represented by his Pisces midheaven, leaves only mystery and intrigue.

SCORPIO

Scorpio is the sign of obsession and compulsion. Stalkers and cult leaders such as Charles Manson turn up here. Revenge killers and sadistic murderers such as Gary Heidnik and Perry Smith are also typically Scorpio. Misaligned planets can cause Scorpio natives to be secretive and obsessed, and to use sadistic methods to seek revenge.

Perry Edward Smith

Saturday, October 27, 1928, 9:30 A.M.
Huntington, Nevada • Time Zone: 08:00 (PST)
Longitude 115° W 41' • Latitude 40° N 18'
Placidus Houses • Tropical Zodiac

Aficionados of true-crime books and movies first heard of Perry Smith in Truman Capote's classic book *In Cold Blood* and in the 1967 semidocumentary motion picture of the same title. The bloodbath execution that Smith and his partner, Richard Hickock (see separate profile), perpetrated in 1959 on a rural Kansas family of four horrified the nation.

Doom stalked Smith from the beginning of his life. His mother, Flo, a full-blooded Cherokee, entertained audiences by trick riding in a traveling rodeo. She met a fellow performer, a tough Irish horseman called Tex John Smith, and entered into a marriage as turbulent as ten minutes astride a wild bronco. Perry later recalled that, as an infant, constantly on the move, he lived on chocolate and condensed milk, a diet he claimed wrecked his kidneys and caused enuresis (bedwetting), which plagued him his whole life. When injuries forced the parents to leave the rodeo circuit, Flo became an alcoholic, and eventually a prostitute. She left Tex, taking Perry, age 6, and three younger siblings to San Francisco. As she descended deeper into the gutter, where she would eventually drown in her own vomit, Flo decided to put Perry in a Catholic orphanage. He later reported that his stay there turned him against religion, God, and especially nuns. Smith spoke of mistreatment by the nuns, of them beating him mercilessly for wetting the bed, dunking him in ice-cold water for punishment, and calling him a half-breed "nigger." In later years, Smith made dark allusions to sexual abuse as well.

Before Perry entered the third grade, his father took him from the orphanage. Tex and his son lived a nomadic life roaming the nation in a homemade trailer house, finally settling in Alaska. There, the boy learned wilderness survival, ate wild game, and hunted for gold. Striking it rich would become an enduring fantasy for him, a dream in which he would dive in a warm, crystal-clear ocean to discover ancient sunken treasures. He collected books and maps on the subject. Smith also taught himself music on a harmonica and guitar that he carried everywhere he went.

Life with his father turned sour, though, with verbal and physical confrontations. Tex evicted his teenage son. The youth hitchhiked to Seattle and joined the Merchant Marine, then later the Army during the Korean conflict, where he was decorated with a Bronze Star. Mustered out in 1952, he left Fort Lewis, Washington, on a motorcycle, planning to rejoin his father at a rustic Alaska hunting lodge hand-built by the senior Smith. But a devastating wreck on a rain-slicked highway delayed the reunion. Perry spent six hospitalized months enduring repeated surgeries on his shattered legs, which would remain stunted and forever a constant source of pain. From then on, he always kept a large supply of aspirin that he chewed and downed with root beer, seeking relief from the suffering. The short legs and tiny feet, under a thick, muscular body just 4 feet, 8 inches tall, gave Smith a disproportionate appearance, causing him to shy away from women. He became prudish about sexual matters, condemning any overt display of prurient behavior.

Tex Smith's Alaska wilderness lodge never attracted customers. He took out his frustration on Perry, and they parted company again. Hitchhiking across the Midwest, Perry caught a ride with a con artist who suggested they finance their journey by burglarizing a business. Their success lasted a very short time, ended by a traffic cop who pulled them over for running a red light in Missouri and wondered where the scruffy pair had obtained a load of typewriters. Jailed, Smith and his pal escaped, and wound up on an FBI wanted list. The feds caught up with Smith in a sleazy section off New York's Broadway, where he'd spent the winter. On May 14, 1956, he landed in prison at Lansing, Kansas, with a five- to ten-year sentence.

From his cell, Perry Smith corresponded with his remaining sister. The other sister and his brother had both committed suicide. Convinced that he had psychic ability, Smith claimed that he had mentally seen his brother's death a week before it happened. In his letters, he blamed his parents for the shattered childhood that put him on a pathway to doom. His sister rejected what she called self-pity and told him he was responsible for his own troubles, an opinion that caused Smith to loathe her. A pent-up cauldron of simmering hate and anger already existed inside Smith, and the criticism only added to it. His external behavior, though, fooled most people. Outwardly he appeared calm, talking in a quiet whisper, using a remarkable vocabulary belying his limited education. He kept his black hair well groomed. The deep brown eyes, always moist, appeared sleepy, soft, and introspective, and he sometimes recited poetry from a collection he kept.

Smith confided his sisterly hate to cellmate Richard Hickock, and also tried to impress Dick with a story about once using a bike chain to beat a man to death in Las Vegas. Perry would later admit he'd made it up. While entertaining one another, both men also sat for tattoos. Smith's arms and torso were decorated with a tiger, snakes, skulls, a tombstone, and various names. Perry and Dick formed a strong friendship, despite conflicting personality characteristics. Smith deplored cruelty to animals, while Hickock bragged of deliberately running over stray dogs. Hickock talked endlessly of his sexual conquests, especially of young girls, which offended Smith's prudishness. Hickock laughed at Smith's narcissistic inability to pass a mirror without looking at his reflection. When the two men crawled into their bunks after lights out, Smith often tried to stay awake to avoid wetting the bed and to forestall recurrent nightmares.

Parole came for Perry Smith on July 6, 1959. He promised to keep in touch with Hickock, who would remain behind bars three more months. Smith set out to find an ex-Army buddy he admired, but failed, so wandered aimlessly, breaking parole. At a general-delivery address, he received a letter from Hickock in which his pal described a plan to steal a fortune from a wealthy Kansas farmer. Another inmate had told Dick that he'd worked for the intended victim and "knew" that farmer Herbert Clutter kept at least $10,000 in a wall safe.

Destitute, homeless, and friendless, Smith made his way to Kansas to team up with his old cellmate.

They drove to tiny Holcomb and arrived at the isolated Clutter farm late on a chilly night, under a full moon. When the hell-bent duo entered the house, everything went wrong. Clutter, 48, calmly (and truthfully) told the intruders that he had no hidden wall safe nor any money in the house. Enraged, they tied him up in the basement, then forced the son, Kenyon, 15, from his upstairs bedroom into the basement, and trussed him with lengths of clothesline. Hunting for plunder, the pair ascended the stairs, where they found Clutter's wife, Bonnie, 45, and daughter, Nancy, 16, in separate bedrooms.

The next morning, a beautiful autumn Sunday, November 15, 1959, all four members of the Clutter family were found dead in their home, victims of shotgun blasts. Herb's throat had also been slit. The only clues left behind were bloody prints from the sole of a boot.

Perry Smith and Richard Hickock escaped with a telescope, a portable radio, and less than $50 in cash. After stealing a car, they used Hickock's con skills to bilk several Kansas City stores for a few hundred dollars. Chasing Smith's dream of hunting sunken gold, they traveled to Acapulco, Mexico. The fantasy quickly evaporated, as did their money. In Mexico City, they sold the car, but Dick used most of the money to pay for prostitutes. Perry bundled up his few possessions and mailed them to general delivery, Las Vegas. They bought bus tickets to the U.S. border, then hitchhiked through the desert, planning to kill any Samaritan who picked them up, then steal his money and car. The first few drivers who gave them rides, Smith later said, were not "suitable targets." The man they finally chose as a victim, fortuitously made a last second decision that saved his life. Just as Hickock signaled Smith to slug him, the driver pulled over to pick up another hitchhiker. Several potential victims never knew how close they came to disaster as the two fugitives made their way to Las Vegas.

In the Lansing prison, the inmate who'd told Hickock about Herb Clutter and the nonexistent wall safe heard about the crime and instantly knew who the killers were. He contacted the police and gave the information needed. A nationwide manhunt sought Hickock and Smith.

Fate stepped in to help. On December 30, 1959, just minutes after Smith collected his bundle of possessions from the Las Vegas post office, police recognized him and Hickock from wanted posters and made the arrest. In the bundle he had picked up were a pair of boots that matched the bloody footprints in the Clutter home. If the police had seen him five minutes earlier, they would never have found the boots, which provided the only forensic evidence.

The police kept the two captives separated. Hickock insisted that Smith had fired all four lethal blasts that slaughtered the family, and had cut Herb Clutter's throat. Smith eventually admitted it, saying that a sudden, compelling rage just blew up inside him, and he blindly started pulling the shotgun trigger.

Tried and convicted, Hickock and Smith were sentenced to die on the gallows. On the rainy night of April 14, 1965, they individually climbed the thirteen steps at the Kansas State Penitentiary in Lansing. Hickock went first and dropped into hell. Before Smith mounted the scaffold, he said, "It would be meaningless to apologize for what I did. Even inappropriate. But I do. I apologize." He spat out the gum he had been furiously chewing, stood still for the hood to be fitted on, plunged through the trap door, and died instantly from a broken neck.

Horoscope for Perry Edward Smith
Born October 27, 1928, 9:30 A.M. PST, Huntington, Nevada
Source: Birth certificate

When Perry Smith heartlessly pulled the shotgun trigger, again and again, to slaughter a family of four, he seemed to be pointing the weapon at a mirror of himself and the unhappy circumstances of his own family life. A look at the simmering resentment that consumed him begins in the fourth house of his chart, which is associated with home and father. Uranus and the Moon, both in Aries, reside there in a chaotic and violent atmosphere.

Uranus represents the erratic, unpredictability of the nomadic life Smith and his father lived, constantly traveling from one place to another. The Moon, ruler of emotions, is Smith's strongest planet; it reflects the emotional stress he suffered as a result of this troubling upheaval. Aries is ruled by violent Mars, bringing aggressive discord into the home life, which is seen in the fights between Smith and his father, causing even more emotional strain.

Smith restlessly roamed the country, both before and after the murders, in a futile quest for riches. The sign of Sagittarius, associated with travel and adventure, rules Smith's ascendant. Venus, planet of love and beauty, in Sagittarius, pops up in his twelfth house of self-delusion. Smith's idealized love for new places and fresh adventures were not grounded in harsh reality, just in his utopian fantasies. His map collection became part of Smith's romantic notion of finding buried treasure, another reflection of his Sagittarius personality. Saturn in Sagittarius, looms heavily in Smith's first house of the physical body, slamming the brakes on his goals of finding his paradise or hidden treasures; Smith's legs were permanently disfigured in a serious accident.

The physical disability and pain from his stunted legs opened a door to allow the dark side of Smith to emerge. This dark side makes several appearances, starting in his Sun sign, Scorpio. Scorpio is associated with compulsions and addictions, coercion, and brooding intensity. It is extremely secretive. Smith's Sun in Scorpio opposes his Jupiter, a clash leading to magnification of these negative Scorpio traits. Smith's low self-esteem, created by the Sun's weak position, made it difficult for him to cope with his inner demons, so he overcompensated with a tough, macho facade. Underneath lay the sensitive man who worked to increase his vocabulary, as seen by Mercury, planet of mental pursuits smiling down from his tenth house of reputation.

Partners belong to the seventh house which, in Smith's chart, is ruled by Gemini. Richard Hickock, his partner, was a Sun sign Gemini. The other planet in Smith's seventh house, Mars, ruler of guns, aligns negatively with Uranus. This juxtaposition gives rise to the negative traits of instability and violence radiating from both planets and infecting the behavior of these two partners.

Pluto, taking its name from the mythological god of the underworld, leers from Smith's eighth house of death. The name proves apt in the destiny of Smith, because the influence of Pluto helped paved his path to the underworld. Pluto's square aspect to his Moon in the fourth house indicates severe emotional problems. A psychologist suggested that Smith murdered the Clutter family as an act of revenge against the misfortunes relating to his own broken family life. Pluto rules revenge. The festering issue of family also emerges with the placement of two planets in Smith's fourth house of home and family. The Moon, ruler of emotions, occupies a square aspect to caustic Mars, an arrangement that tore his family apart with antagonism and violence. Adjacent to the Moon, Uranus is in the same negative alignment with Mars. In this aspect, the Martian influence delivers guns and knives into the mix. When the sudden explosion of rage coursed through Smith, he cut Herb Clutter's throat and shot all four family members.

Smith's second house of money, or absence of it, is ruled by Saturn, planet of depression and hatred. The botched robbery that turned to murder started with the intent to steal money. But the failure to find riches depressed Smith and Hickock, so they flared into hatred, then murder.

Love didn't play a big part in Perry Smith's life. As mentioned, Venus, the planet of love, can be found in his twelfth house of secrets, in a tenuous role. If he held much affection for anyone, Smith kept it hidden from view. Venus also exerts meager influence over his sixth house of small animals, reflecting the affection he gave to innocent creatures.

Few people would have heard of Perry Smith and Dick Hickock if not for Truman Capote's book *In Cold Blood*. The author developed a great fondness for Smith when he researched the book. It has even been said that Capote fell in love with him. There are many astrological similarities between Smith's and Capote's charts, indicating a strong symbiotic relationship. Capote seemed truly mournful when Smith's life ended on the gallows.

Charles Milles Manson

Monday, November 12, 1934, 4:40 P.M.
Cincinnati, Ohio • Time Zone: 05:00 (EST)
Longitude 084° W 27' 25" • Latitude 39° N 09' 43"
Placidus Houses • Tropical Zodiac

A small-time thief and drifter who spent half of his first 30 years in prison, Charles Manson went on to orchestrate one of the most high-profile crimes of all time, and to catapult himself on a hell-bent trip into legendary status among criminals. Members of the public who cannot identify photos of their U.S. senators, the Chief Justice of the Supreme Court, or even their local mayors can instantly recognize the wide-eyed, hypnotic, evil image of Manson.

Born to a 16-year-old prostitute in 1934, the child couldn't have a surname because his mother had no idea who had impregnated her. When she married, her son became Charlie Manson. Frequent exposure to all varieties of sex, extreme permissiveness, and a sleazy lifestyle influenced his first ten years. At 12, his unruly behavior landed him in reform school, from which he twice escaped. A concerned aunt tried to put him on the right path, but failed. Burglaries, car theft, and armed robberies earned Manson increasingly longer sentences in youth facilities, then jail, and finally prison.

Paroles for Manson meant opportunities to commit more crimes. In 1954, while temporarily on the outside, he married a teenager, stole cars, and drove them across state lines, which put the FBI on his trail. The short marriage ended in divorce.

Inside state and federal prisons, the short, wiry con learned manipulation and survival techniques. According to a fellow inmate at Washington's McNeil Island, Charlie performed homosexual favors for more powerful convicts in exchange for protection. Aided by his above-average intelligence, Manson became a wily trader and master of verbal exploitation. When prison officials blessed him with parole in 1967, the timing couldn't have been better. The world of free youth had entered a sexual revolution of flower power, hippies, drugs, and rejection of social traditions. Manson, 33, with long hair and beard, looked much younger than his years and blended perfectly into the mass of migratory youth. In the wide-open Haight-Ashbury district of San Francisco, where LSD was as common as candy, Charlie found his niche in life.

By using lessons learned in prison, and aided by generous doses of "acid," he mesmerized runaway girls with his Svengali personality and mediocre guitar skills. Charlie became a sort of messiah for promiscuous, love-starved teenagers. Using them first for his own sexual pleasures, Manson learned to treat his harem as bait to lure young men into the fold. His followers became his "Family."

Drifting from the Bay Area to Hollywood, Manson and his Family took up residence in an old motion picture location ranch where countless westerns had been filmed. The 40 to 50 members lived by scrounging, begging, borrowing, selling whatever they could, and stealing. With a Christ-like position in the group, Charlie preached universal love to the accompaniment of Beatles music, followed by drug-induced nude dancing and sex orgies around campfires.

Regarding himself as a professional musician, Manson visited the son of actress Doris Day to pitch the idea of forming a band. The meeting took place at a secluded home, 10050 Cielo Drive, but did not go well, and Manson suffered a blow that fueled the explosive mixture of anger already inside him.

The drug trade often results in casualties. An African-American dealer whom Charlie disliked died from a gunshot wound. Gary Hinman, a hopeful entertainer, nearly lost an ear to sword-wielding Manson before being stabbed to death by Family members. A movie stuntman know as Shorty Shea vanished. Meanwhile Manson's devoted followers wallowed in his mantra of "Helter Skelter," in which he predicted a race war that would elevate him and his tribe to become social leaders. The first blow to Manson's plans came when police picked up three members of the Family on suspicion of killing Hinman.

Furious, Manson's Family struck back on August 9, 1969. Without their leader's presence, Charles "Tex" Watson, Patricia Krenwinkel, Susan Atkins, and Linda Kasabian drove that night into the elite residential hills overlooking Hollywood, and stopped at 10050 Cielo Drive. Inside the home, actress Sharon Tate, more than eight months pregnant, hosted a gathering of friends: coffee heiress Abigail Folger, famed hair stylist Jay Sebring, and writer-producer Voytek Frykowski.

The intruders encountered a young man, Steven Parent, on his way out after visiting a friend who occupied a guest house, and killed him. During the next hour, they committed one of the bloodiest massacres in Los Angeles crime history, beating, stabbing, shooting, butchering, hanging, and mutilating the four people in the house and the unborn baby. They dipped fingers in blood to scrawl words on the bodies and on walls.

Within a couple of days, elated by the headlines, Manson led the same group, plus Leslie Van Houten, in raiding the hillside home of Leno and Rosemary LaBianca. After Manson allegedly walked out and left with Kasabian, three of his disciples, Krenwinkel, Watson, and Van Houten attacked again, carrying out another bloody slaughter on the middle-aged couple. To complete the job, they scrawled the words *Healter Skelter* [sic] in blood on a refrigerator door.

Panic struck in Southern California as the news of the carnage spread, and no one felt safe from a possible repeat attack. Meanwhile, the Family had retreated to remote mountains above Death Valley. They reveled in more sex, running stolen dune buggies over the terrain and laughing at the law. When Manson saw that a road on lower slopes was being repaired, he organized a raiding party and burned a road-grading vehicle. In October, county officers moved in and arrested several key members of the group, including Manson for the arson. Jailed in the rural town of Independence, east of the towering Sierra Nevada mountains, Charlie acted as if he expected an early release. It probably would have happened if Susan Atkins, one of his most loyal subjects, hadn't also been arrested elsewhere and talked to a cellmate.

Atkins, an ex–topless dancer and known member of the Family, had been charged in Los Angeles with being involved in Gary Hinman's murder. She whispered to another inmate that she was innocent of that crime, but had participated in the Tate and LaBianca murders. The information found its way to investigators, galvanizing the task force into quick action. Now the ragged hippies in the Independence jail became murder suspects under a nationwide spotlight.

The spectacular trial lasted for months, while Manson enjoyed playing the role of evil incarnate. When he shaved his head and carved a swastika between his eyebrows, so did fellow defendants Patricia Krenwinkel, Susan Atkins, and Leslie Van Houten. Young women outside the court, sitting cross-legged on the lawn, imitated the gesture in support of their Family leader. One of them, Lynette "Squeaky" Fromme, would be arrested in 1975 for attempting to assassinate President Gerald Ford. Linda Kasabian testified for the prosecution, and left the courtroom as a free woman.

Prosecutor (and later author) Vincent Bugliosi, one of the finest trial lawyers in the nation, realized he faced an uphill battle in trying to convict Manson, who may not have actually helped kill the victims. With masterful strategy, he presented his theory of Manson's control, along with the evidence, and wound up by saying that the victims ". . . from their graves, cry out for justice." On January 25, 1971, a jury found all four defendants guilty of first-degree murder. Charles "Tex" Watson, tried separately, faced the same verdict. All five were sentenced to death, but a Supreme Court ruling in 1972 overturning the death penalty caused Manson and his Family to be resentenced to life imprisonment. All five are eligible for regular parole hearings, but to date, none have been released.

Horoscope for Charles Milles Manson
Born November 12, 1934, 4:40 P.M. EST, Cincinnati, Ohio
Source: Birth certificate

The dominance Charles Manson held over his "Family" of misfit runaways was awesome—and yet his dependence on them turned out to be his Achilles heel. Manson had a certain vulnerability in his failure to understand the nature of his women, especially when they left his sphere of control. His seventh house of relationships and partners is a particularly significant hotbed of negative aspects.

Three planets, all in the controlling, manipulative sign of Scorpio, reside in Manson's seventh house: Jupiter, the Sun, and Venus. Jupiter's contribution of excesses is evident in the scope of Manson's influence and the large number of followers he accumulated. Venus, ruler of his Taurus ascendant, reveals Manson's need for control. He gained his power and dominance through Taurus, which glowed from the horizon at the moment of Manson's birth. Young women seemed particularly enchanted by his hypnotic wizardry, and usually outnumbered the men among his band of misfits. This is attributable to the presence of Venus, the planet of promiscuity, in this active seventh house. Manson's Sun rules his ego. Even though he appears to be the walking manifestation of an inflated ego, the weak aspect of his Sun suggests the contrary. It is more likely that he overcompensates for very low self-esteem. This is significant, as it reveals Manson's desperate need for admiration and respect. In spite of his controlling demeanor, Manson is a dependent person.

Mercury, the planet of rational thinking, is also in Scorpio. The negative traits of Mercury come into play due to the planet's alignment with Manson's Moon, the ruler of his emotions. This aspect reveals a tendency for him to suffer mental problems, since his thoughts and conscious thinking are constantly at war with his emotions.

The Moon, ruler of women, is his strongest planet. This fact, if he knew it, would be quite demeaning to him, as its strength shows that women are the most important people in his life. Aquarius, the Moon's sign, represents eccentricity, explaining the bizarre behavior Manson seemed to inspire among his female idolizers. The Moon opposes Pluto, the planet of coercion, exhibiting Manson's eagerness to control these women. He carefully picked girls, usually ones who had deserted conventional home life and would readily subjugate themselves to him. But the Aquarian connection betrayed him when a female member of his Family leaked evidence that found its way to the police, causing the killers to be charged with murder. Manson's Moon is positioned in a negative aspect to Uranus, the planet of erratic behavior. The negative influence of both Aquarius and Uranus on Manson is described by the erratic, irrational, and unpredictable nature of each of the women in his flock.

Pluto and the Moon also exercise influence over the fourth house, which represents the home and family. Manson's notion of domestic life is not exactly traditional, so it is interesting that he selected the word *Family* to describe his group. Pluto in Cancer, the sign associated with family, rules groups, cults, and sects, all descriptions of Manson's group of followers.

Drugs fueled every activity of Manson's Family, including parties, sex, and murder, and were an essential element in his control. Neptune, ruling drugs, dwells solidly in Manson's fifth house of sex. It nestles in close alliance to Mars, the planet of knives and violence. Manson used drugs to incite his mob into violence, to bend their minds to his way of thinking. Also ruling the fifth house of sex is his Sun, relating to Manson's egotistical need to oversee his family's sexual activities. He manipulated the women with music and drugs, and made available their sexual favors to motivate his male disciples. Manson seldom participated in group sex, but supervised the activity. This way, he was above the crowd, playing the role of leader, exhibiting his Scorpio ego.

His eighth house of death is ruled by Jupiter, from its seat in the seventh house. This planet of magnitude represents the excessive carnage and the number of victims Manson's gang slaughtered. Revenge was Manson's motive for the Tate killings. Jupiter is in Scorpio, the sign associated with revenge. Manson, who was not present during the bloodshed, was charged with and convicted of conspiracy to murder—an interesting charge, as conspiracy is a characteristic of his strongest sign, Scorpio.

Uranus, planet of eccentricity, occupies Manson's twelfth house of prisons. Every time he is seen on television, he takes pleasure in displaying eccentric behavior. Neptune and Mars also hold positions of influence over this house of confinement. He is kept away from the general population, to shield him from Martian violence, but he still manages to practice the deceitful characteristics of Neptune. The irrational posturing that stems from Uranus has also damaged any chance for Manson's parole. Uranus is in Aries, the sign of discord, an alignment that indicates mental instability with potential of expression through aggressive and combative behavior. Thus, Manson chooses to sabotage himself, virtually assuring that he will never be released from prison.

William Heirens

Thursday, November 15, 1928, 8:30 P.M.
Chicago, Illinois • Time Zone: 06:00 (CST)
Longitude 087° W 39' • Latitude 41° N 51'
Placidus Houses • Tropical Zodiac

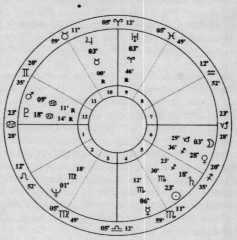

"**F**or heaven's sake catch me before I kill more . . . I cannot control myself," William Heirens scrawled in scarlet lipstick on the living room wall of his second female murder victim. A compulsion to kill had seized the Chicago teenager, sending him on murderous missions that inspired news media to label him the "Lipstick Killer."

In 1940, at the age of 11, Heirens became sexually confused after stumbling upon a couple locked in a passionate embrace. Seeking counsel from his strictly religious mother, he heard only reactions of disgust and warnings that sex is filthy and that just touching another person intimately can cause disease. In his attempt to repress natural urges, he took to entering homes and stealing women's underwear. Gradually, the act of burglary gave him erotic release.

Other than the twisted sexual confusion, Heirens seemed normal in his formative years. The son of a business executive and a strict but generous, loving mother, he attended a parochial school. But, just prior to his scheduled graduation from the eighth grade, Heirens was arrested for possession of a loaded handgun. Follow-up investigation revealed that he had burglarized nearly a dozen homes and torched six more. A search of his home produced several revolvers, pistols, and rifles. The stunned parents accepted a recommendation to enroll the boy in a private institution similar to a military prep school for a year. His exemplary behavior and extraordinary IQ allowed him to transfer to college, and eventually to enter the University of Chicago at age 16.

An initial attempt at intimacy with a teenage date reportedly sent Heirens into convulsive vomiting. He once again sought sexual fulfillment by burglarizing homes and bringing a wide assortment of loot to his college dormitory room. It would be estimated that he committed close to 500 burglaries. But as the thrill of surreptitiously entering a residence tapered off, Heirens needed a new source of erotic pleasure. He found it in June 1945. In the apartment of a 43-year-old divorcée, Alice Ross, he woke her while fumbling around. When she challenged him, he stabbed her repeatedly and ended her life by slashing her throat. The gaping wound troubled Heirens, so he grabbed a dress from the victim's closet and used it to bandage her neck. The rush of excitement caused him to ejaculate.

No one knows exactly how many homes Heirens raided during the next four months. In October, a nurse caught him ransacking her apartment. The intruder hit her with enough force to knock her out, tied her up, and fled. Two months later, he murdered again.

Frances Brown, in her early thirties, stepped out of the bathtub and started to towel herself when a noise startled her. She spotted Heirens, who had sneaked into her apartment by climbing a fire escape. As the woman started screaming, Heirens aimed a pistol at her head and fired two rounds at point-blank range. Unsatisfied, he attacked her dead body with a knife. She had been clean, and now Heirens had messed her up with blood, so he put her back into the bathtub, carefully washed the body, and covered her nudity with a robe. Deeply distressed over his actions, Heirens withdrew a tube of lipstick from the victim's purse, and printed on the living room wall his desperate plea to be caught.

If he had been captured, 6-year-old Susan Degnan would not have died on January 7, 1946. The little girl woke up as Heirens entered the apartment through her bedroom. Instead of immediately ending the child's life, as he had the two women who interrupted his sexual pursuits, Heirens kidnapped Susan. The note he left demanded $20,000 in small bills and ordered the parents to wait for instructions. But Heirens had no intention of returning the youngster alive. In a nearby basement, he murdered her, dismembered her body, sliced it into multiple pieces, wrapped the remains in her pajamas, and calmly strolled through the early-morning mists of Chicago dropping grisly body parts into sewer openings. Two witnesses observed him making strange stops as he walked. Police were summoned, and they found the horrifying deposits Heirens had made.

Despite abundant fingerprints Heirens had left at the crime scenes, and the discovery of the child's remains, another five months passed before Heirans was captured. In June, a maintenance man heard someone entering the apartments where he worked, and called the police. A detective arrived just in time to stop another tragedy. He found Heirens pointing a pistol at the janitor and a woman. After the gunman pulled the trigger twice, only to have his weapon misfire, the detective struggled with the college sophomore, only 17. An off-duty officer who lived in the apartment rushed to his colleague's aid by slamming three flowerpots against Heirens's head to knock him unconscious.

In jail, Heirens refused to talk at first, but with his tongue loosened by sodium pentothal (in the days before stringent civil rights rules) he spoke of the murders being committed by someone named George Murman. Heirens admitted illegal entry of homes to seek sexual thrills, but denied any murders. George Murman, officers found, did not exist except in Heirens's fantasies. Psychiatric examination concluded that Heirens was "a sexual psychopath with maniacal tendencies," but met the legal standards for sanity, so could stand trial for the three murders.

Convicted, Heirens was sentenced, on September 5, 1946, to three consecutive terms of life in prison. His mental state grew worse behind bars, and he was temporarily confined in a facility for the criminally insane, but eventually returned to prison. After 30 years, still incarcerated, he resumed his college education through correspondence courses, and earned a degree. Now over 70, Heirens holds the distinction of occupying space in Illinois prisons longer than anyone else in the state's history.

Horoscope for William Heirens
Born November 15, 1928, 8:30 P.M. CST, Chicago, Illinois
Source: Birth certificate

Heirens's fifth house of sex trembles as if struck by an earthquake, wreaking havoc on his destiny. The Sun, ruler of his ego, is firmly rooted in the fifth house, in Scorpio. This sign is ruled by Pluto, which infuses Heirens with compulsiveness, obsession, and thoughts of torture. The mix becomes dangerous with the influence of Mars, which brings in violence, guns, and knives. The Sun's companion resident of the fifth house is Saturn. This planet offers Heirens skills in planning and organization. So the stage was set for well-planned entries into homes, at first to burglarize them, then later to act out sexual obsessions, and to use weapons on the objects of his lust.

These objects of lust, of course, were women, who are dominions of the Moon. Perhaps Heirens could have fought off the compulsion to kill women, if the Moon hadn't been negatively aligned in direct opposition to bloody and violent Mars. Such a configuration loads the picture with the negative aspects of both the Moon and Mars. Aggressive hostility is dumped in by Mars, while the Moon pushes Heirens to the precipice with moody instability.

Heirens's Sun, or ego, is the weakest planet in his chart. He needed a boost to his feeble self-esteem, and found it through forced sexual relations. At first, while entering homes to steal women's underwear, Heirens only fantasized about actual sexual contact with the female residents. Theft relates to the second house in his chart, which is the domain of Neptune, planet of confusion and delusions. Eventually, this confusion changed his thoughts, centering them on lethal contact with the women in the homes he entered. Mars represents his obsession with guns as well as dismemberment and mutilation. Pluto, lodged adjacent to Mars, makes terrible contributions to this deadly brew, pouring in the ingredients of obsession and compulsion. His Moon/Mars opposition paved the way for the stabbing and shooting of two adult women. His final ruthless killing involved the kidnapping and mutilation of a young girl. Children are also fifth-house concerns, along with sex. All of his violent, compulsive, yet organized methods were used in her case. He kidnapped the child from her bedroom in the middle of the night. Pluto, lurking in his twelfth house next to his ascendant and influencing his fifth house of sex and children, rules kidnapping. After murdering the child, he dismembered her, and placed different parts of her body around the city.

Heirens's ascendant is ruled by Cancer, an emotional, moody, and unpredictable sign, and the strongest in his chart. These characteristics of Cancer describe his personality, temperament, and disposition. Pluto's alignment next to Heirens's Cancer ascendant curses him with a compulsive and addictive personality. This aspect also describes his famous statement, "For heaven's sake catch me before I kill more . . . I cannot control myself." The obsessive nature of Pluto, in the emotional grip of Cancer's crab claws, indicates that Heirens felt possessed by a force he was unable to control.

The eighth house of death is governed by Uranus and Saturn. Uranus rules eccentricity. Mars and Pluto, both in Cancer, reside in his twelfth house of prisons. The violence and cruelty he inflicted on his female victims are shown by Mars in Cancer. This combination of planets and signs doomed Heirens to spend more than half of the century in confinement, where he remains today.

Gary Michael Heidnik

Monday, November 22, 1943, 3:40 A.M.
Eastlake, Ohio • Time Zone: 05:00 (Central War Time)
Longitude 081° W 27' 02" • Latitude 41° N 39' 14"
Placidus Houses • Tropical Zodiac

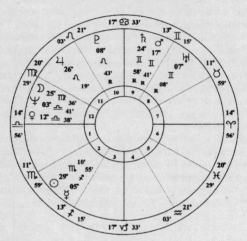

Even hardened cops couldn't believe what they found after arresting Gary Heidnik in March 1987. Led to the putrid basement of his Philadelphia house by a woman who had escaped, they rescued from captivity three other nude, chained, and shackled women, emaciated, ravaged, and in need of immediate hospitalization. A search of the house, located in a seedy residential area, turned up stacks of pornography. The kitchen's contents made officers retch and gag when they found human body parts stored in cooking pots and in the freezer.

An acquaintance of Heidnik told police that he had seen the maniac pick up prostitutes, usually African-American women, bring them home, and chain them in the basement. The first victim, he said, was killed, dismembered, and buried. But extensive digging in Heidnik's yard turned up nothing.

In the lockup, another inmate attacked Heidnik and beat him severely. Afterward, police isolated him from other prisoners. Heidnik attempted suicide by hanging himself with a T-shirt in the shower, but a guard rescued him just in time to save his life.

Some wished the guard had not bothered, or that Heidnik had never been born.

In 1946, nearly three years after Gary Heidnik's birth in Ohio, his father and mother divorced. He and his little brother stayed four years with their alcoholic Creole mom, who stumbled through three more marriages before she eventually took her own life. Returning in 1950 to the custody of their remarried father, who, according to Heidnik, ran the household with a Gestapo grip, the two children suffered stringent punishment for any infraction of the rules. The father, questioned years later, denied such allegations, and said his sons were raised just like any other kids.

At school, Heidnik earned passable grades, but didn't mix well with classmates. Membership in the Boy Scouts planted the seed for his desire to attend a military school, and he achieved it by enrolling at Staunton Military Academy in Virginia, where his performance garnered praise from officials. He scored well in subjects such as economics and finance. Inexplicably, though, he made a sudden decision to drop out and return to his father's home in Ohio to resume public high school. Still restless, he quit again at age 18 and joined the U.S. Army in 1961. Trained as a medic, he landed in Germany as a hospital orderly. Soon afterward headaches and nausea plagued him. Army doctors treated him with powerful drugs. The condition became so serious that Heidnik was shipped back to a stateside hospital, where he began hallucinating. Military psychiatrists decided he was suffering from a schizoid personality, and honorably discharged him in January 1963 with a disability pension.

Despite the diagnosis, Heidnik found employment in Philadelphia as a licensed practical nurse and attended college part time. But continued hallucinations, headaches, and confusion increasingly put him in the center of a mental tornado. In and out of hospitals, he was wracked by depression and tried to commit suicide several times. During questioning by doctors, he would become mute, or use sign language he invented, and engage in extremely eccentric behavior. At times, he collapsed into a catatonic state. It didn't help when his African American girlfriend deserted him.

Attempts to identify the root of his problems failed, and Heidnik plunged into a downward spiral. He rejected social standards and customs, including bodily hygiene. The rules he lived by came from his own warped sense of morality. And he stopped seeking treatment in 1972. During the next few years, he fathered four children in various temporary relationships, but would never have anything to do with his offspring.

In Heidnik's mind, religion called. He founded his own church and appointed himself bishop. Before long, he attracted a sizable congregation, more than a few members from a list of outpatients at a nearby mental institution. Observers who might have scoffed would soon take serious notice as Heidnik used his early interest in finances to invest church "income" and eventually converted a modest sum into a bankroll of over $500,000. As bishop, he possessed full authority to use the money as he saw fit. Expenditures covered the cost of his Rolls-Royce, two Cadillacs, a Rolex watch, and Heidnik's garish gold cross hanging from a gold chain around his neck.

In 1978, Heidnik took his mentally retarded girlfriend to visit her severely handicapped sister in the institution. They arranged for the sister, age 34, to leave with them on an overnight pass, but failed to return her the next day. After officials came to Heidnik's residence to recover the missing patient, they discovered that she'd been sexually abused. Heidnik faced charges that sent him to jail, then to a series of hospitals for the criminally insane until March 1983, when he won a parole. His retarded girlfriend vanished and was never found.

Deciding to get married, Heidnik heard from a young woman in the Philippines who answered his personal ad in a magazine, and through correspondence, agreed to travel to the United States and marry him. Shortly after the simple wedding, she was disillusioned to find him in bed with three black women. He answered her complaints with physical and sexual abuse over several months. Pregnant and heartbroken, the unhappy wife fled back to her homeland.

Considering his role as a bishop, no one understood why Heidnik chose to occupy a battered old house in a tough neighborhood. He took an attractive black prostitute there in late November 1986, four days after his 43rd birthday. After sex, he allowed her to don only a blouse, then forced her downstairs and chained her in the cold, musty basement.

Three days later Heidnik dragged a second black woman, clad only in a blouse, into the frigid, filthy chamber. She couldn't have been more shocked, since she had known Heidnik for four years. The fear in both captives increased dramatically when Heidnik carried a pick and shovel into a hole in the concrete floor, and worked as if digging a grave. Over the next three weeks, the women endured daily mandatory sex with him, a starvation diet that barely sustained them, and beatings if they made any noise. Near Christmas, Heidnik picked up a pretty African American shopper, age 19, by offering to take her out to dinner. She accepted, but after being drugged she wound up as a nude prisoner in his basement. He fed the trio of captives thin sandwiches only after the new arrival satisfied him sexually.

The fourth woman, captured in January, didn't settle into slavery so readily. Trouble brewed between her, the other three, and Heidnik. To punish their misbehavior, he suspended them by their wrists from the ceiling, or would force one woman to beat the others with a club. The sexual enslavement extended not only to his using them daily, but to demanding they have sex with one another. He allowed infrequent bathing, and provided only a portable toilet in the basement for them. They were constantly hungry, and even consumed dog food at his orders. In mid-January, he added a fifth prisoner, an 18-year-old prostitute.

When the second woman Heidnik had captured became ill, he punished her by dumping her into the dirt hole and covering it with plywood. Sicker than he had imagined, she lay there until she died. To dispose of the body, Heidnik cut it into countless pieces and tried to reduce the head and limbs by boiling them, permeating the whole house with a putrid odor. As the remaining captives became more desperate, Heidnik resorted to extreme measures, using electric shock, cutting food rations, and even showing one the boiled head of the deceased victim. It would be alleged that he even fed them cooked human flesh. In February, he put three of them in the dirt pit, filled it with cold water, and touched the electric wire to their handcuffs. One of the women keeled over, face down in the water, dead. He shoved the corpse into a freezer and later buried it in rural woods. In mid-March, he picked up another prostitute as a replacement for the dead woman.

After four months of captivity, Heidnik's first prisoner, always his favorite, had gradually persuaded him of her willingness to comply with his wishes, so he began favoring her with special privileges, even taking her on rides. In late March, she saw her opportunity, escaped, and called the police. They caught Heidnik parked nearby in his Cadillac and jailed him.

Rushing to the house, officers found the three survivors chained in the basement, one of them shivering in the dirt hole under a sheet of plywood. Upstairs, they discovered frozen and partially cooked human body parts.

Over the next year, Heidnik paled in his cell, and grew a long beard to enhance his countenance of insanity. In June 1988, a jury heard ghastly testimony from the ex-prisoners and rejected the plea of insanity. They found Heidnik guilty of murdering two women and committing a long list of crimes against the survivors. One of his victims had been electrocuted; fittingly, a judge sentenced Gary Heidnik to die in Pennsylvania's electric chair. He was executed, however, by lethal injection in July 1999.

Horoscope for Gary Michael Heidnik
Born November 22, 1943, 3:40 A.M. Central War Time, Eastlake, Ohio
Source: Birth certificate

The hideous behavior of Gary Heidnik, enslaving and torturing six women, weighs heavily for a verdict of insanity. Yet his ability to function normally in other walks of life, such as making sound financial investments, appears to counterbalance the scales in favor of legal sanity, as found by a jury. Was Heidnik mentally deranged? The strong presence of Neptune, joined by two other revealing planets in his twelfth house of secrets and hidden agendas, makes a convincing argument that delusions and hallucinations tormented his mind. But it takes several looks at his chart to see the whole story.

Appropriately, Heidnik's strongest house is his twelfth, the domain associated not only with secrets, but also with places of confinement, self-delusion, and hidden agendas. Neptune, the planet of delusions, sets up the potential for Heidnik to be plagued by warped impressions of reality. The Moon and Venus join Neptune in this all-important abode where dark traits loom. Heidnik's bizarre plan revolved around captive female slaves, as reflected by the Moon's presence and its rulership of women. Venus, in the sign of Libra, is the planet of dissipation and promiscuity. With the Venusian connection to Libra, marriage became part of Heidnik's strange scheme. One of his loonier notions was that his captive victims would consent to marry him, or be forced to, and produce his children.

More mental instability pours into Heidnik's chart through the position of Mercury in direct opposition to Uranus. Mercury, as one of the twelfth house's rulers, is the domain of conscious thoughts. Uranus, occupying the eighth house of death, is the planet of eccentricity. The energy radiating from this configuration sets up the irrational conduct of Heidnik in shackling women with chains, confining them in a damp dungeon, and allowing two prisoners to die.

The handling of finances and money were significant parts of Heidnik's life, even in his youth. Money falls under rulership of the second house, in which Heidnik's Sun and Mercury dwell. The Sun, ruling his ego, is not particularly strong. Therefore, he desperately needed the feelings of self-esteem and accomplishment, represented by his Sun in Scorpio, that accompanied the accumulation of money. The presence of Scorpio signifies the importance of monetary matters. Mercury, as his strongest planet, reflects Heidnik's keen intelligence in understanding finances and investments.

Most of his wealth came from his dabbling in religion: establishing a church and appointing himself as bishop. The ninth house rules religion and is the abode of two planets, Mars and Saturn. Mars, in a positive mode, endows initiative, drive, and energy. Saturn governs structure and organization, qualities essential to the success of his religious endeavor. Both of these planets are in Gemini, Heidnik's strongest sign. The influence of Gemini gave him the persuasive abilities he used on his congregation in order to control it and to make the enterprise profitable.

With success came an overwhelming desire in Heidnik to perpetuate himself by producing children. But his unorthodox plan mirrored bizarre thinking. His tenth house of status and reputation is occupied by Pluto, the planet of manipulation, torture, and kidnapping. That same house is influenced by Cancer, which is ruled by the Moon, planet of women. Thus, Heidnik felt compelled to kidnap women for the purpose of producing his offspring. The Scorpio-Sun connection played a second role in Heidnik's chart to influence his skewed intentions. Scorpio, a sexual sign, is controlling and sadistic, explaining Heidnik's demands for sexual debauchery. With his Moon ruling emotions as well as women, imprisonment of his chattels for sexual and reproductive reasons seemed, to Heidnik, a logical means to accomplish his deranged goals.

This extraordinary saga reached a finale when Heidnik was arrested, convicted, and sentenced to die. Heidnik was executed by lethal injection in 1999. Neptune, ruling drugs, in his twelfth house of prison, described his demise.

SAGITTARIUS

An unusually large number of serial killers fall under the Sagittarius sign. Three of them—Richard Speck, was a mass murderer, while Charles Starkweather and Erik Menendez would more accurately be called a "spree killer," having murdered several people in a short time. Interestingly, Ted Bundy and Charles Starkweather share the same birthday, eight years apart. Negative afflictions of Sagittarian natives include unreliability and indiscriminate behavior.

Dennis Nilsen

Friday, November 23, 1945, 4:00 A.M.
Fraserburgh, Scotland • Time Zone: 00:00 (Universal Time)
Longitude 002° W 00' • Latitude 57° N 42'
Placidus Houses • Tropical Zodiac

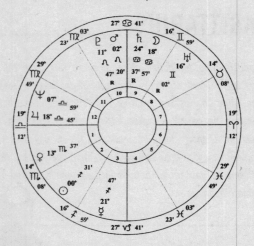

Not all gruesome serial murders are perpetrated in the United States. One of the most loathsome killers in history killed fifteen young men in London, England.

A native of a small town on the chilly North Sea coast of Scotland, Dennis Nilsen was the offspring of a Norwegian soldier who resettled in Fraserburgh. The emigrant married, sired a son, then deserted his young wife and child, never to be seen by them again. Baby Dennis and his mother moved into a comfortable brick home with her fisherman father, who would be a powerful influence on the boy. Scots are known for stubborn independence, and the lad's adventurous grandfather instilled plenty of it in his adoring grandson. His death in 1951 left the boy devastated.

While he was devoted to his mother, young Nilsen seemed to crave the companionship of males. Even as a young child, Nilsen felt a disturbing sexual interest in other boys. He redirected his love to a pair of adopted pet birds until a cruel neighbor killed them, once more robbing Nilsen of a placement for his affection.

He developed a fear of ever loving anything or anyone again.

Young Nilsen escaped the chill climate of home by joining the army at age 15, and thrived among the all-male ambience. Despite his internal attempts at resistance, the magnetism that drew him to other men continued to grow during his time in service. Like another serial killer, Arthur Shawcross (see separate profile), Nilsen learned meat-cutting skills in his job as a cook. At various posts, he attempted heterosexual contacts with prostitutes but felt nothing for females. He also experienced sex with men, but wrestled with overwhelming guilt each time. The depression that followed planted in Nilsen an obsession with death.

Among the few productive or wholesome interests in which Nilsen became interested was movie making. He bought a motion picture camera and shot endless rolls of film in amateur productions.

In his eleven years of army service, Nilsen proved an exemplary soldier, but with the inherited contrariness of his grandfather, started resisting military policies. That, combined with the growing guilt over his sexual preference, led him to drown his pain in booze. He left the army in 1972.

Back in Scotland, a rift grew between Nilsen and his family. He moved to London and joined the police constabulary. The camaraderie he sought never materialized, and he found himself spending evenings alone with a bottle. Turning inward, Nilsen became narcissistic and self-absorbed. He hunted for companionship in gay bars, but none of the encounters provided emotional satisfaction. Frustrated and directionless, he left the police force in 1973.

Indigent, Nilsen took menial jobs, then finally landed in civil service, where he spent the next eight years. Still driven by homosexual urges, he made clumsy attempts at liaisons, but they generally fizzled like wet firecrackers. He withdrew further into himself.

Hope flared when Nilsen met a young man who seemed a potential soul mate. They moved into a flat together on Melrose Avenue. But the roommate turned fickle and continued to see other men. Nilsen, trying to make his mate jealous, brought a woman to their residence and made an awkward attempt at sex. It failed, as did the relationship with his roommate, who soon moved out. On Christmas 1978, Nilsen spent the day alone, posing in the mirror as a corpse.

A week later, he picked up a teenager and brought him home to spend the night in a drunken orgy. Nilsen later said, "I remember thinking that I wanted him to stay with me over the New Year whether he wanted to or not." With that in mind, Nilsen made an attempt at strangling the lad with a necktie but couldn't complete it, so had to finish the job by dunking his victim's head in a bucket of water. He then bathed the corpse, put it in bed, toyed with the body a few times, and eventually hid it under the floorboards. It stayed there over seven months. Finally, in August, he cremated the withered corpse in his backyard and scattered the ashes.

Now committed to a bizarre method of finding lasting companionship, Nilsen waited six weeks before inviting a young Canadian tourist to his home. After strangling his guest, Nilsen slept with the body, hid it, and retrieved it for sex four times over the next month. He made photographic records before decomposition ruined the beauty of his dead companion.

A third body soon joined the Canadian under Nilsen's floorboards. As the corpses putrefied, Nilsen found a way to more efficiently rid himself of the remains. He cut the bodies into small pieces and stuffed them into two suitcases. The pair of charnel containers rested in an outdoor storage shed all summer, with Nilsen attempting periodically to neutralize the stench by using disinfectant.

As the list of victims grew to six, Nilsen became an expert in his knowledge of rigor mortis and anatomical surgery. His mind became more detached and his recollection of the events grew hazy.

The growing number of victims taxed Nilsen's creativity for disposal. As he carved the bodies, he stored various parts in separate containers, while drinking growing quantities of rum to fortify himself. He still gagged, though, while slicing through the putrid flesh. Once again, he resorted to cremation to rid himself of old remains. He noted, "The large bonfire is blazing fiercely while I stand near in a nervous sweat."

After two more funeral blazes, Nilsen moved from the house on Melrose Avenue to a smaller flat at 23 Cranley Gardens. The new quarters, more cramped with less storage space and no yard for burning, presented new problems. He dismembered the next two victims and boiled the pieces in a large pot all night, then flushed chunks of gray flesh and shattered bones down the loo.

Keeping the naked skulls, he stored them in various hiding places.

Dennis Nilsen's macabre social life finally came to an end by one of the most common problems in the world: clogged plumbing. His landlady called a service to clear the drains, and they found fetid chunks of rotting tissue and bone in the sewer. Before the police arrived, Nilsen attempted to remove the sickening remains, but didn't find them all. After brief questioning, he caved in and confessed to fifteen murders. Forensic scientists found countless bits of bone and layers of human ash at Nilsen's previous address, and body parts in his newer residence.

Neighbors and investigators couldn't have been more surprised at the admissions. The reclusive, bespectacled, well-dressed civil servant had fooled everyone. At the highly publicized trial, several surviving guests of Nilsen came forward to testify. The court found him guilty of six murders and sentenced him to life in prison, since there is no death penalty in England. He will actually become eligible for parole in 2008, but no one expects it to happen. Nilsen spends his time in prison writing journals about himself and his crimes.

Horoscope for Dennis Nilsen
Born November 23, 1945, 4:00 A.M. Universal Time, Fraserburgh, Scotland
Source: Birth certificate

"Killing for company." Dennis Nilsen used that phrase in describing his motives for murdering at least fifteen homosexual partners. Cancer, Nilsen's strongest sign, includes traits that perfectly support his rationale. Nilsen picked up men, brought them home for sex, and when they wanted to leave, he killed them. Characteristics of Cancer include supersensitivity and strong emotions, together with a clinging, smothering nature. Expressions of caring and concern by a Cancer native can be suffocating to friends or associates.

Nilsen's severe mental disorders are also influenced by Cancer. The Moon, Cancer's ruler, beams from the ninth house in diametrical opposition to Mercury. This unfortunate aspect unleashes negative mental traits from both planets. Nilsen's subconscious mind is ruled by the Moon, while his conscious mind is governed by Mercury. Both levels of thinking were ravaged by emotional disturbances, resulting in his inability to process thoughts in any rational way. To add to this unfortunate configuration, his Moon is adjacent to Saturn, also in Cancer, an alignment suggesting acute depression.

Mars, ruling knives, stabbing, and dismemberment, occupies the high ground in Nilsen's tenth house of reputation and nudges against his Cancer midheaven. Being in the dramatic sign of Leo, Mars not only influences Nilsen's grotesque behavior, but also assures that the English public would be suitably shocked about the horrifying butchery that made stunning headlines. Pluto, another ominous occupant of his tenth house, represents compulsions and obsessions. This manipulative planet, in conjunction with Mars, sets the stage for Nilsen's compelling need to murder and dismember his homosexual lovers.

By using his various homes as storage places for his victims' bodies, Nilsen created the most bizarre environment possible in his charnel dwellings. One ruler of his fourth house of home life is Uranus, the planet of eccentricity, which appropriately resides in his eighth house of death.

Uranus sits in opposition to Nilsen's Sun, which occupies his second house of material possessions. This negative juxtaposition, combined with Uranus in the eighth house of death, sets the stage for his ghastly need to keep the corpses as his possessions. The Sun's involvement, bringing in the negative characteristic of domination, points the way to the only method Nilsen could find to dominate and keep his boyfriends: to kill them and store their bodies. The eccentric influence of Uranus reveals Nilsen's preoccupation with necrology. This obsessive study of death preoccupied him, as seen by the affiliation between Nilsen's first house, ruling himself, and the eighth house, ruling death. Venus, the planet governing both houses, is in Scorpio, the sign of obsession and compulsion.

Nilsen's gruesome death game took an even more hideous turn when he engaged in necrophilia, the sexual use of dead bodies. His fifth house of sex is ruled by Jupiter and Neptune. Jupiter, planet of excesses, represents the numerous homosexual partners he brought home and killed. Neptune rules delusions, which possessed Nilsen's mind and pushed him into his strange perversity. Both of these planets are hidden away in his twelfth house of secrets and hidden activities. He certainly had good reason to hide his activities from the world, and managed to do so for an astonishing length of time.

Nilsen's remarkable ability to avoid detection for so long is understandable, considering his appearance and outward demeanor. His Sun sign is Sagittarius, which bestows positive traits of adaptability, a pleasant appearance, and a facade of dignity. In addition, Nilsen's first house of appearance and personality is governed by Libra. This Venus-ruled sign is placid, friendly, and likable. Jupiter, the planet of good luck, is also found in Libra next to his ascendant. These influences confer on Nilsen the inclination to be a well-dressed, quiet, and unassuming person. With so many aspects in his favor, he easily avoided any suspicion.

The twelfth house, ruling prisons, is occupied by Neptune and Jupiter, both in Libra. This combination made Nilsen's adaptation to confinement remarkably easy. Mercury, the planet of mental pursuits and writing, resides in his third house of communications, giving him the ability to pen his journals, while his life sentence provides all the time he will ever need.

Charles Raymond Starkweather

Thursday, November 24, 1938, 8:10 P.M.
Lincoln, Nebraska • Time Zone: 06:00 (CST)
Longitude 096° W 40' • Latitude 40° N 48'
Placidus Houses • Tropical Zodiac

Most people called him "Little Red," referring to his short, bow-legged stature and the greasy red hair he combed into a ducktail. But Charles Starkweather resented the nickname and the disrespectful slurs about his appearance, especially when people referred to him as a "redheaded peckerwood." He thought of himself more in the image of movie icon James Dean, who had died in an auto wreck in 1955. The role of a sensitive teenager played by Dean in *Rebel without a Cause* appealed to Starkweather so much that he tried to imitate Dean's speech, clothing, and hairstyle and even his gestures. He empathized with the internal anger he saw in the actor's personality.

At age 18, in 1957, Charlie didn't care much for his job as a garbage truck driver because he thought it caused people to feel superior to him. Nearly illiterate, he had dropped out of school at 16 to make his own living. Having grown up in poor circumstances with six siblings, Starkweather coveted wealth and success. Rejected by most female peers, he found his lovemate in precocious, tiny Caril Ann Fugate, 14. Starkweather thought she shared his rebellious attitude toward society.

His discontent flared when the garbage disposal company fired him. Worried that he wouldn't be able to finance dates with his girlfriend, Starkweather decided to rob a service station in his hometown, Lincoln, Nebraska. On the bitterly cold night of December 1, 1957, just five days after his 19th birthday, Starkweather drove his old Ford into the Crest gas station and held a shotgun to the chest of attendant Bob Colvert, 21. After collecting about $100, he drove Colvert out of town, shot him in the back of the head, and left the body facedown on a frozen country road. Serial killers often kill near their own birthdays.

The loot didn't last long, so Starkweather couldn't pay his rent and was evicted from his apartment. On January 21, 1958, he drove to the rural home of Caril Fugate and immediately got into an argument with her mother and stepfather, both of whom had tried to discourage the relationship. It has never been firmly established whether Caril Ann was present then or showed up later. Charlie had carried a .22 rifle in with him, saying he and Caril were going hunting. As Charlie later recalled it, "I told [her mother] off and she got so mad that she slapped me. When I hit her back, her husband started to come at me, so I had to let both of them have it with my rifle." He didn't explain that he also bludgeoned the 2-year-old daughter, Betty Jean, with the rifle butt, then strangled her by jamming the barrel tip down her throat.

Following the slaughter, Starkweather hid the father's body in a chicken coop, dragged the mother into an old outhouse toilet, and stuffed the child into a cardboard box, which he also stowed in the outdoor privy. In some accounts of the murders, Caril Ann helped him. In others, she arrived home later to find Charlie there alone, and Starkweather told her that the missing trio had been kidnapped. In either case, Charlie and Caril Ann occupied the house for nearly a week, watching television, having sex, eating all of the food supplies, and enjoying complete independence. To keep relatives and visitors away, they posted a note on the door announcing that the whole family was ill with the flu.

Suspicious relatives called the police, who arrived to investigate. Caril Ann reportedly turned them away. On January 27, the police returned, searched the premises, and discovered the dead bodies. By that time, though, Charlie and Caril Ann had left.

Two days later, sheriff's deputies were summoned to the farm of August Meyer, 70, because someone had spotted Charlie's old

Ford parked on the property. Even though the Ford was gone by the time officers arrived they surrounded the farmhouse and called out for Starkweather to surrender. Silence. They lobbed teargas bombs. No response. Finally, they invaded the home, only to find the body of farmer Meyer, nearly beheaded from a shotgun blast.

Charlie and Caril Ann had made good their escape, but the Ford had mired down on a rural muddy road. In Nebraska, people are always willing to lend a hand. Robert Jensen, 17, and his girlfriend Carole King, 16, happened to drive by, saw the stranded couple, and offered them a ride. At gunpoint, Charlie ordered Jensen to drive them to an abandoned schoolyard. After robbing Jensen of all the money he had—four dollars—Starkweather marched him down the steps of an old storm cellar and executed him. With Caril Ann waiting in Jensen's car, Starkweather led Carol King into the cellar, forced her to strip, and tried to rape her, but became impotent. Embarrassed and angry, he shot her in the head and sexually ravaged her with a hunting knife.

With every cop in the county on the alert, it didn't take long to find the young murdered couple. But the fugitives had slipped away again, in Jensen's car.

Cruising through the suburbs of Lincoln, Starkweather recognized an upscale home he'd served on his garbage collecting route. He and Fugate barged in, found the wife of a steel company executive and her maid, and held them captive. The ragged, filthy couple raided the refrigerator, ate their fill, and when one of the victims tried to protest, Starkweather stabbed both women to death. A short time later the executive arrived home. Starkweather shot him, hid Jensen's car in the garage, and drove away with Fugate beside him in the victim's late-model Packard.

Nebraska's governor declared a state of emergency and authorized roadblocks by National Guard troops. Over 1,200 searchers scanned the towns and countryside in a massive dragnet.

Starkweather and Fugate had already crossed the border into Wyoming, but Charlie realized he needed to switch cars again. He spotted an Oldsmobile parked alongside the road, pulled over, and saw a man sleeping inside. Merle Collison, a shoe salesman, had stopped for a short nap. Starkweather pumped two bullets through the driver's side window. Collison, trembling with fright, emerged with his hands up, but Starkweather pulled the trigger nine times, blasting the dead victim back into the driver's seat. After Charlie had pushed the body onto the floor, and Caril Ann had crawled in, he attempted to drive away but lurched to a halt in just a few yards. He didn't know how to release the emergency brake.

Another Midwestern Good Samaritan noticed the lurching car, and offered to help. When he leaned inside to release the brake, he saw the body at the same moment Starkweather raised the rifle. Instead of capitulating, the new arrival grabbed the barrel and pulled at the weapon. While Charlie screamed curses, Caril Ann leaped out.

At last, the killer's timing turned sour. As the two men struggled over the rifle, a highway patrolman coasted to a halt to see what was wrong. Caril Ann, evidently tired of the killing game, ran screaming to the police cruiser. "It's Starkweather," she shouted. "He's going to kill me. He's crazy."

Charlie let go of the gun, jammed the accelerator to the floor, and peeled out onto the highway. The patrolman called for backup and rocketed after Starkweather in hot pursuit. Careening along in a high-speed chase, officers fired a couple of shots into the Packard's rear window. Glass exploded and a shard barely winged Starkweather. He skidded the car to a halt, jumped out with his hands up, and bellowed, "You shot me! I'm bleeding to death." Although the wounds proved to be superficial, he flopped down on the pavement.

Extradited from Wyoming, Charlie gave a full confession en route to Nebraska. He rationalized that he'd killed people "because I wanted to be somebody." Admitting that he had been responsible for the death of all eleven victims, Starkweather asked officials to "go easy on Caril Ann." But he soon changed his mind when he learned that she planned to testify against him.

Since Caril Ann was charged with only one murder, in the death of Robert Jensen, Starkweather and Fugate faced separate trials. Prosecutors chose that one because Fugate had admitted holding a rifle on Jensen and King while Charlie robbed them of four dollars. That made her equally culpable in the eyes of the law. In Starkweather's trial, he testified, incredibly, that each of the killings had been in self-defense. The jury found him guilty of first-degree murder and the judge sentenced him to die in the electric chair.

In Fugate's trial, she insisted that she was innocent of any crime. Charlie had held her hostage, she said, and she had no control over the events. Jurors didn't believe her and found her guilty. She was sentenced to serve the rest of her life in prison.

On June 25, 1959, Starkweather smirked at witnesses as guards strapped him in the electric chair. He even suggested they adjust one of the straps more tightly. At midnight a massive surge of electric power ended his life.

Caril Ann Fugate was the youngest woman in the United States to enter prison with a life term. After she'd served 18 years, in June 1976, a merciful parole board released her back into society.

Horoscope For Charles Raymond Starkweather
Born November 24, 1938, 8:10 P.M. CST, Lincoln, Nebraska
Source: Birth certificate

Most of the publicity surrounding the 1958 killing spree perpetrated by Charles Starkweather suggested that he sought revenge against society for imagined slights. Behavioral scientists, for the most part, agree. But his astrological chart suggests a corollary motive that may have been equally important in precipitating the violent murders.

The fifth house of sex in Starkweather's chart points an accusing finger at sexual compulsion as a major motivational culprit. Venus in Scorpio and the Sun in Sagittarius are both solidly rooted in Starkweather's fifth house of sex. Scorpio introduces sexual obsession into the picture, while Sagittarius offers self-gratification. The sultry atmosphere is charged even further by Venus, the planet of pleasure, posing in lascivious opposition to Uranus, the planet of eccentricity. Starkweather's ideas of pleasure centered around compulsive, bizarre sex with his 14-year-old adolescent girlfriend. The carnal pleasure turned lethal through the Uranus connection, by that planet's rulership over the eighth house of death. With this negative and dangerous configuration, Starkweather's lust for unusual sex eventually became intertwined with death and destruction. In addition, Starkweather's Sun, ruling his ego, is pallid and weak. Its position in the fifth house of sex means that Starkweather would probably seek prurient activities as a means of boosting his shrunken ego. Finally, Mars, as the ruler of Scorpio, enters the stage like a jackbooted stormtrooper, bringing weapons and violence. Thus, Starkweather's sexual needs turned from hedonism to homicide.

Starkweather's first house, governing his appearance, temperament, and disposition, is ruled by his Cancer ascendant. This Moon-ruled sign is moody and emotional. As Cancer's ruler, the Moon looms on the other side of Starkweather's chart, in opposition to his ascendant. Such an alignment indicates the strong potential for Starkweather's mind to be fevered with emotional distress. Women are ruled by the Moon, so they are at the core of Starkweather's mental turmoil. The fact that he chose such a young girl to be his lovemate hints at feelings of sexual inadequacy. His Moon in Capricorn, in a negative alignment with Saturn, reveals that he was uncertain about his own sexuality when relating to women his own age. Capricorn, a Saturn-ruled sign, reflects feelings of inadequacy or ineptitude.

The planetary ruler of Starkweather's first house of personality is Pluto, from which compulsions and kidnapping are generated. Starkweather and his accomplice kidnapped a young couple. Since Pluto, ruler of kidnapping, also reigns over forced sex, and is one of the governors of Starkweather's fifth house of sex, the kidnapping ended by Starkweather attempting to rape the young woman before murdering her.

As usual, in the charts of killers, the violent planet Mars makes an unwelcome intrusion. Starkweather's eighth house of death is heavily influenced by two planets: Uranus, contributing erratic behavior, and Saturn, mixing in depression and selfish hatred. Saturn's alignment with Mars, a negative opposition, blights the configuration with the worst traits of both planets. Further complications result from Saturn being in the sign of Aries, which is ruled by Mars. Among the negative traits associated with Mars are guns, violence, and rape, while Saturn chills the scene with cold-bloodedness. Starkweather actually relished being known as a cold-blooded, cruel killer.

Starkweather's young girlfriend, after being captured, claimed that her participation in the killing spree was involuntary. The seventh house of partners is ruled by Saturn, domain of hatred and restraint. Considering Saturn's negative relationship to the Moon in Starkweather's chart, it is possible she told the truth. The position of Moon, ruler of women, relative to Saturn indicates that he was the dominating influence in their relationship. Starkweather later asserted that she was a willing participant. But

Neptune's weight in the matter may indicate that Starkweather might well have been a liar.

Starkweather's dream of wanting "to be somebody" is also a Neptune trait. This planet of dreams and delusions floats in the clouds of his third house of mental processes. Neptune finds itself in conflict with Mercury, the planet of rational thinking. This aspect blurred Starkweather's ability to understand the real world. He wanted to be actor James Dean, an extremely far-fetched delusion.

Today, it is not uncommon for condemned inmates to spend from 12 to 20 years on Death Row awaiting execution. Starkweather died in the electric chair just eighteen months after the murders he committed. The planet Uranus, which shows up frequently in his chart, stepped in once more. After playing an important role in Starkweather's life, Uranus, as the ruler of electricity, played an even bigger part in his death.

Ted Bundy

Sunday, November 24, 1946, 10:35 P.M.
Burlington, Vermont • Time Zone: 05:00 (EST)
Longitude 073° W 12' 45" • Latitude 44° N 28' 33"
Placidus Houses • Tropical Zodiac

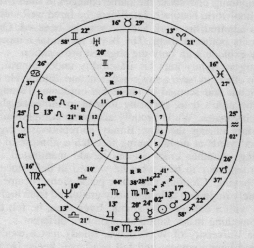

Several books and movies have made Ted Bundy and his crimes infamous. His name is now synonymous with the term *serial killer*. No one is absolutely certain how many young women he murdered, but he confessed to ending 30 lives. More than a few of his victims were similar in age and appearance: late teens or early twenties; long, straight dark hair parted in the middle; oval faces with full lips; and arched eyebrows. Each of them bore a remarkable resemblance to a woman who had once made Bundy painfully aware of his shortcomings.

Born in a home for unwed mothers on November 24, 1946, Theodore Robert Cowell never knew his real father. His mother would only admit that she had been impregnated by a military man and refused to ever name him. Her conservative Philadelphia parents, unable to bear the stigma then associated with illegitimate birth, let everyone think they had adopted the child. So Ted's early childhood was tainted with a lie, that his mother was his sister.

In 1950, to escape whispered rumors about the family relationships, Ted's mother took him to live with distant relatives in Tacoma, Washington. She also assumed a phony surname until the spring of 1951, when she married John Bundy. If young Ted sensed anything odd about the name changes, it didn't show up in his schoolwork. Naturally intelligent, he fared well with teachers, who admired his work and the way he behaved. Only one of his traits bothered them. The boy's mercurial temper could violently explode with only the slightest provocation.

As long as Bundy kept his irascibility under control, he appeared to others to have a shy grace, wit, and dignity. He became a Boy Scout and seemed to enjoy the outdoors. Through high school, he didn't date, choosing instead to fantasize about his female classmates. While proudly accepting compliments about his conduct during the day, Bundy surreptitiously crept into neighbors' yards at night, hoping to catch a glimpse of women undressing. Another crack in his facade manifested itself in Bundy's tendency to take what he wanted in department stores without paying. Clothing and other possessions became disproportionately important to him. Bundy graduated from high school in 1965 with a college scholarship. Even then, he felt troubled about something inside him that made him different.

At the University of Washington, Bundy met a wealthy, sophisticated young student and fell head over heels. He realized that she came from a social level far above his own, but hoped to bridge the difference with charm and good grades. He gazed like a lovesick puppy at her long dark hair, parted in the middle, and her perfect oval face. They dated frequently and Bundy did his best to meet her standards. But he felt like a mongrel from the dog pound trying to keep up with a thoroughbred poodle. When his dream girl transferred to Stanford University in 1967, Bundy followed. She grew bored with him, and let him know it that summer. Crushed, Bundy returned to Washington. Determined to win her back, he reached for higher status through political activism, and achieved considerable success. Working for the election of the state's governor, Bundy associated with influential representatives of the political hierarchy. Simultaneously, he polished his charm by courting beautiful women. Having earned a diploma in psychology, Bundy decided to pursue a career in law.

Wearing his accomplishments like a new silk suit, Bundy, now 26, again sought out his first love, who seemed impressed with the changes in Ted. Romance bloomed in 1973 and she accepted his proposal of marriage.

The evil in Bundy's mind was not satisfied. In early 1974, several beautiful young women vanished from the Seattle area. On January 31, police were summoned to the rented bedroom of college student Lynda Ann Healy, 21, to investigate a bloody bed and a ripped, bloodstained nightgown in her closet. She would never be found alive. Within a few weeks, students Donna Manson, 19; Susan Rancourt, 18; Kathleen Parks, 22; Brenda Ball, 22; and Georgann Hawkins, 18, all vanished.

With no warning or explanation, Ted Bundy walked away from his socialite fiancée, and ignored her requests for an explanation. He spent a great deal of time with another woman who hoped to marry him, even though she worried about his moodiness, temper, and long periods of absence.

One of his favorite hangouts was Lake Sammamish, a few miles east of Seattle, which attracts thousands of sunbathers during the sparkling Washington summers. On July 14, 1974, Bundy approached a bathing suit–clad young woman, introduced himself as "Ted," and asked if she would help him load a small sailboat on his car. Seeing a heavy cast on his left arm, and lulled by his smile and polite charm, she agreed to help, and accompanied him to his Volkswagen. There, Bundy told her the boat was at a house up the hill, and invited her to ride there with him. She politely declined, and returned to her beach towel. A few minutes later, she smiled when she saw another young woman walking with "Ted" toward the parking lot.

On that day, Janice Ott, 23, and Denise Naslund, 18, disappeared from the Lake Sammamish beach, and would never be seen alive again.

Two months later, a grouse hunter climbed a hill four miles from the lake, and stumbled upon a skeleton. Investigators swarmed over the wooded terrain, and found scattered bones that turned out to be the remains of Janice Ott, Denise Naslund, and possibly Georgann Hawkins. In March 1975, in remote foothills, hikers unearthed more bones. A battalion of searchers combed the area and found what was left of Lynda Healy, Kathy Parks, Brenda Ball, and Susan Rancourt. A massive manhunt ensued, with every cop in the state looking for "Ted," who drove a Volkswagen Beetle.

But Ted Bundy had left the state the previous September and

had moved to Salt Lake City to attend the University of Utah. Within weeks after his arrival, three teenage girls disappeared from the area. Before the first snowfall, two of the bodies were located where they'd been dumped in the high country. The killer had bludgeoned and strangled them to death.

The next intended victim, Carol DaRonch, 18, was approached on November 8 by a handsome, well-dressed man who identified himself as a cop. He said he'd seen someone trying to break into her car in the mall parking lot. She reluctantly agreed to go with him in his Volkswagen to make a report. Her suspicion turned to terror when he sped away in the wrong direction. When he snapped handcuffs on one of her wrists, she struggled, even though he pointed a gun at her. Her chance came when the passenger door flew open, allowing her to tumble from the moving car as he sped away. Crying and trembling, she gave police a full description of Ted Bundy.

That same night, a pretty young high school student vanished and would never be found. Nearly a dozen Utah girls would fall victim to a cruel predator. In neighboring Colorado, the marauding stranger killed three more young women.

· In August, a highway patrol officer stopped Bundy after a high-speed chase and searched his VW. Finding a ski mask, a tire iron, a pantyhose mask, and handcuffs, the officer arrested him. A meticulous search of the car produced hairs that matched the missing women. In a subsequent lineup, Carol DaRonch picked Bundy as the man who had abducted her. Convicted of kidnapping, and facing a sentence of up to fifteen years in prison, Bundy didn't resist when officials sent him to Colorado to face murder charges. On June 7, 1977, allowed to use the courthouse law library, he leaped from the second-story window and escaped. He hid in mountains around Aspen for a few days, then was recaptured trying to flee in a stolen car. Legal motions and courthouse appearances occupied him for nearly six months. Then, on December 30, he cut a hole in the ceiling of his cell, wormed through a crawlspace, and escaped again. Using stolen cars, plane rides, and buses, he made his way to the welcome warmth of Tallahassee, Florida.

Late Saturday night, January 14, 1978, a darkly clad man entered the Chi Omega sorority house where University of Florida students slept. He used a fireplace log to savagely bludgeon Margaret Bowman and Lisa Levy. During the lethal assault, he sexually ravaged and mutilated them with his teeth. Two more young women escaped with serious injuries, and another caught a good look at the assailant as he sprinted out of the building. A few blocks away, he attacked another young woman who survived, but sustained injuries that would never completely heal.

Within three weeks, Bundy struck again. Now, instead of seeking college women who fit certain physical characteristics, he abducted a 12-year-old named Kimberly Leach. Driving a stolen van, Bundy took her to a remote location where he sexually assaulted the little girl before slitting her throat and dumping her in an abandoned pigsty. He was nearly captured that night, but with his usual luck, slipped away. Finally, on February 15, his luck ran out in Pensacola when an officer chased Bundy's stolen Volkswagen and arrested the fugitive after a physical struggle.

In a long complicated trial for killing the two Chi Omega women, Bundy played the lawyer and fought hard to avoid being condemned to death. Prosecutors presented evidence matching Bundy's teeth to bite marks left in the victims' flesh. The killer's charming magnetism failed to work on the jurors. In July 1979, they convicted him and recommended a death sentence.

In the midst of a separate trial for killing little Kimberly Leach, Bundy called to the witness chair a woman who had declared love for him. "Will you marry me?" Bundy suddenly asked. She replied in the affirmative. "Then I do hereby marry you," declared Bundy. The surprising nuptials turned out to be legal.

His cavalier treatment of courtroom procedure backfired on him when the jury turned in a guilty verdict and recommended the death penalty.

During protracted appeals, Bundy blamed pornography for making him a killer. As his date with execution grew closer, he tried to bargain for his life by offering information about 30 murders he'd committed across the country. Most analysts think the number of victims was probably far greater. His last gambit failed.

On January 24, 1989, guards strapped Bundy into the three-legged oak chair referred to as "Old Sparky." All of Bundy's victim's were women. The executioner—who wore a hood, and was reportedly a woman—threw the switch that sent a lethal surge of electricity through Bundy's body. At 7:06 that morning, his murderous life came to an end.

Horoscope For Ted Bundy
Born November 24, 1946, 10:35 P.M. EST, Burlington, Vermont
Source: Birth certificate

The name Ted Bundy still raises goose bumps, even though he's been dead more than a decade. The mere mention of his crimes brings to mind images of a bright, good-looking young man using his charm to lure young women, then savagely murdering them. Women, the obsessive focus of Bundy's life, are represented by the Moon. In his chart, the Moon is locked in a death struggle with eccentric Uranus, agitated by the two planets' ominous alignment in direct opposition to each other. The negative aspect activates Uranus's erratic, strange, and unpredictable behavior. The most frightening part of this conflict is the entry of Mars, bringing violence into the struggle. By lodging at the Moon's side, Mars is also in opposition to Uranus, which causes both planets to curse Bundy with their most unpleasant traits. The entire effect tended to warp his behavior and darken his outlook on life, with specific anger toward women.

The Moon and Mars are squeezed together by the presence of three other planets, putting all five within the tight borders, or cusps, of the fourth house. Venus, Mercury, and the Sun join Mars and the Moon in this cramped space. In symbolizing women, the Moon is corrupted by the presence of violent Mars, so it would be expected that Bundy's aggressive fury and use of weapons might lead to beating and stabbing his female victims. Venus and Mercury, along with the Moon, are in the sadistic and controlling sign of Scorpio. Bundy is blessed by Venus with smooth charm, and gifted by Mercury, the planet of speech, with the ability to sweet-talk women.

Remarkably, despite Bundy's handsome features, intelligence, and glib tongue, his chart reveals a shrunken ego. The Sun's position in the fourth house is weak, suggesting low self-esteem. Bundy's Leo ascendant, though, in control of his first house of appearance and personality, turns away from the Sun's impotent rulership. So, Bundy overcompensated for the weak ego by adopting a facade of confidence. In his later court appearances, Bundy jousted with judges, performed for the public, preened for the cameras, and gave garrulous press conferences, gloating in his fame. All of these actions are symptoms of the swaggering sign of Leo. His proud Leo ascendant also mirrors his interest in associating with rich and influential people, hoping to have their status rub off on him.

Underneath this blustering facade, Bundy grappled with strange obsessions. Taurus, his midheaven, is a sign associated with compulsions and obsessions. The two planets opposing it, Mercury and Venus, are both in Scorpio, another compulsive, obsessive sign. This probably accounted for his driving urge to kill women who resembled an aristocratic lover who had once rejected him.

Bundy's eighth house of death is ruled by Pisces, which falls under the reign of Jupiter and Neptune. Jupiter, in Scorpio, dispenses enormity, relating to the long list of women who died at Bundy's hands. Scorpio infects the eighth house with sadistic treatment. The presence of Neptune brings mystery, indicating the unknown number of murders and the myriad unlocated bodies.

The ninth house of courts is ruled by Mars, which brought upheaval to his trials. His violent crimes and volcanic temper were also within the fiery swath of Mars. Eventually, he was convicted in Florida of three murders, including the brutal sex slaying of a 12-year-old girl. This was the first known child among Bundy's long list of victims. Children and sex are matters of the fifth house, which, like the eighth house of death, is ruled by Bundy's Jupiter in Scorpio. Jupiter's negative alignment with Pluto and Saturn virtually places a ticking time bomb in the house of children and sex. Jupiter fills it with obsession, Scorpio tosses in sadism, Pluto adds perversion, and Saturn lights the fuse with hatred.

For the murders of two college students and a little girl, Bundy was sentenced to die in Florida's electric chair. The twelfth house, ruling prisons, is the abode of Pluto and Saturn, both in the arrogant sign of Leo. Saturn rules the law, along with restrictions and confinements. Pluto, planet of compulsions and obsessions, influenced Bundy's determined efforts to have his sentence overturned. The Leo factor caused him to use manipulative and controlling techniques, such as offering information about missing victims and unsolved murders, in trade for delays. But it didn't work. The final ruler of his twelfth house of prisons is Cancer, governed by the Moon. The Moon is aligned negatively to Mars, and both planets are in opposition to Uranus, the planet of electricity. So, in this sense, his female victims found retribution. The Martian violence Bundy used to kill women, symbolized by the Moon, sent him to prison. And the Moon-Mars opposition to Uranus sealed his fate, a violent death in the electric chair.

Erik Menendez

Friday, November 27, 1970, 11:23 P.M.
Livingston, New Jersey • Time Zone: 05:00 (EST)
Longitude 074° W 18' 55" • Latitude 40° N 47' 45"
Placidus Houses • Tropical Zodiac

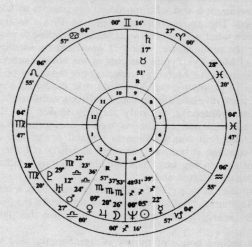

For profile, see Lyle Menendez.
Horoscope for Erik Menendez
Born November 27, 1970, 11:23 P.M. EST, Livingston, New Jersey
Source: Birth certificate

The life of young Erik Menendez revolved around his home and his father, according to his bottom-heavy chart. Nine planets are crowded into the second house of money, the third house of brothers, and the fourth house of home and father. This entire complex occupies the lower one-fourth of the charted circle.

Erik's strongest house is his fourth, associated with the home and father. It contains three planets: the Sun, Neptune, and Mercury, all in Sagittarius, his most influential sign.

The Sun is next to Neptune, declaring in unequivocal terms that Erik is a confused individual.

Neptune's influence might have raised some eyebrows if it had been allowed as evidence in the murder trial. Since Neptune rules deceit, it signifies an adept liar. The same planet also happens to be one of the rulers of his eighth house of death.

Mercury, the planet of speech and writing, resides in the fourth house and governs his Virgo ascendant, a sign that also relates to written communications. While in high school, Erik wrote a screenplay about a son who murdered his parents to hasten his inheritance. The manuscript was typed by Erik's mother, who had no idea what it foreshadowed. Matters relative to mother are found in the tenth house, which is governed by Gemini under the rule of Mercury. Typing, as part of the writing process, falls within the realm of Mercury, underscoring the irony of her participation in preparing the document that predicted her doom. Another stark revelation is mirrored in Erik's accusations that his father, Jose Menendez, not only sexually abused him, but psychologically traumatized him as well. Considering that Erik's Neptune and Sun configuration is aligned negatively with his Virgo ascendant, it becomes apparent that Erik is quite capable of telling convincing lies, thus shedding serious doubts on the allegations of paternal abuse.

The strong influence of Sagittarius reflects Erik's interest in sports. Sagittarius relates to the love of travel and the need to be physically energetic and independent. It is also the sign of the playboy.

Erik's second house of money is significantly, and symbolically, full. Money was extremely important to Erik, and his parents generously supplied whatever he needed. Three planets—Mars, Pluto, and Uranus—occupy the second house, giving the matter of finances even greater weight.

Mars, which influences his ninth house of foreign travel, points to the high cost of jet-setting around the globe. The red planet also happens to be associated with competitive sports, highlighting Erik's interest in tennis and the worldwide travel required to participate in tournaments.

Uranus, the planet of eccentricity, describes Erik's impulsive, extravagant, and irresponsible spending habits.

Pluto, the ruler of compulsive greed, points to the primary motive of the slayings. This small planet exerts additional importance as governor of Erik's third house of brothers.

The third house is extremely influential in its rule of Erik's brother, Lyle. Venus, Jupiter, and the Moon, all of which are in the secretive, dangerous sign of Scorpio, reside in the third house. Venus represents sibling love between the two brothers.

Jupiter rules Erik's eighth house of death, and by its very presence in the house of brothers, adds another strand linking Erik and Lyle together. The Moon is the third and last planet in this house. It rules the emotions. Since Jupiter is closely conjunct with the Moon, its position intensifies Erik's emotional feelings and reactions. He was known to cry whenever he felt stress. He sobbed when his brother testified at the first trial and wept aloud when Lyle called the emergency number to report the murder of their parents. Erik's Moon is aligned in opposition to Saturn. This negative aspect indicates feelings of inadequacy and depression. With the Moon's presence in Scorpio, Erik's mental state is infected with obsessive and compulsive overtones.

Mars and Pluto also exert power over Erik's volatile third house. These two potentially violent planets reside in the second house of money. Mars rules guns and shooting, while Pluto governs plotting and conspiring. This dangerous configuration sets up the plot hatched by the brothers to kill their parents for money.

After the murders and the wild spending sprees, investigators began suspecting the brothers. Eric's Mercury-governed Virgo ascendant, ruling communications, reappeared. Having already spawned Eric's screenplay, this planet-sign complex set the stage for another dramatic episode of communications. Mercury rules speech. On Halloween, Erik spoke to his psychiatrist and confessed to the murders. The taped session helped seal the brothers' doom.

Saturn, in the ninth house of courts, governs the law. This time the ninth house did not mean foreign travel for Erik. Instead, it gave him many short trips to court, where Mars and Venus exerted legal powers. Mars represents the acrimony and sexual accusations hurled by defense attorneys at the dead parents. Venus's more benefic influence appeared when jurors at the first trial couldn't reach a verdict. The next trial resulted in conviction of both brothers. Saturn's influence of law and order is reflected in the length of time the system took to complete judicial proceedings. Both brothers were finally sentenced to serve life in prison without parole.

Gary Gilmore

Wednesday, December 4, 1940, 6:30 A.M.
McCamey, Texas • Time Zone: 06:00 (CST)
Longitude 102° W 14' • Latitude 31° N 08'
Placidus Houses • Tropical Zodiac

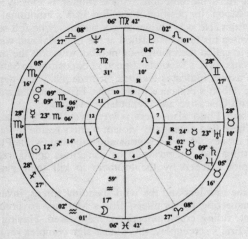

Seldom do brutal killers reach the legendary status of a Jesse James or John Dillinger. If any contemporary murderer came close, it was Gary Gilmore, whose story gained national interest not because he lost a legal fight against execution, but because he insisted the state make good its imposition of the death penalty. While attorneys struggled to win delays or commutation for him, Gilmore declared that he had taken it seriously when a judge sentenced him to death, and that he expected Utah to keep its word. The public was suddenly torn between loathing for Gilmore's heartless murder of two innocent Mormon men and admiration for his willingness to accept the ultimate punishment: execution by firing squad.

Two best-selling books, one of them a Pulitzer prizewinner by Norman Mailer and the other by Gilmore's younger brother Mikal, plus a popular motion picture, added to the dark fame of Gary Gilmore.

Some people say that Gilmore never had a chance. Before his birth, the shady activities of Gilmore's father kept him from staying in any one location very long. The elder Gilmore and his pregnant wife were driving from Alabama to California when it became necessary to make an unscheduled stop in McCamey, Texas, three weeks before Christmas in 1940, for their second child to be born. According to Gary's birth certificate, he was called Faye Robert Coffman, a false name chosen by parents who couldn't let their real identity be known. They conveniently changed it to Gary Gilmore, but didn't bother to formalize the conversion. In Gilmore's formative years, constantly on the move, he often saw his prison-hardened, alcoholic father batter his tormented, embittered mother. Even as Gary approached puberty and his father gave up booze, the ongoing family conflict tarnished his life and that of his two brothers. The addition of a fourth son in 1951 didn't ease the tension.

As a rowdy youth, Gary fought, shoplifted, endured beatings from his father, and served time in reform school. Migrating between Utah, California, and Oregon, Gilmore failed to take advantage of his natural intelligence, choosing instead to be disruptive and belligerent. Away from the classroom, he was a reckless daredevil, engaging in dangerous, almost suicidal stunts. At 13, he began burglarizing homes. By the time he turned 15, Gilmore had set a lifelong pattern. He escaped twice from an Oregon detention facility, and endured extra punishment when recaptured. He came out in 1956 emotionally scarred from the brutal experiences in the institution.

Once again locked in conflict with his father, Gilmore spent less time with his family and more time with street hoodlums and easy women. Within a few months, he landed back in jail for a burglary. After being released, he couldn't stay away from trouble, and escaped from pursuing police by fleeing to Southern California, then to Texas. Caught and extradited back to Oregon, he served two more terms marked by rebelliousness, fights, and violence. Gilmore was behind bars when his father died. He came out bitter, coiled like a viper, ready to strike out at anything in his way.

While rifling through his mother's private papers one day, he found his birth certificate. Gilmore confronted his mother with his suspicion that he'd been conceived during an illicit relationship. She explained the circumstances, but Gilmore refused to believe it. In his fury, he committed another robbery, which sent him back to prison in 1964. This time, in Gary's absence, one of his two younger brothers underwent surgery to repair old stab wounds he'd suffered in an attack by a jealous husband. He died on the operating table. When Gilmore learned of it, his tough outer shell cracked, and he sobbed like a child. But the emotional blow appeared to change Gilmore, at least to Oregon prison officials, who took mercy and granted him an opportunity to attend art school away from prison. He double-crossed them, and was soon caught in an armed robbery. While waiting for trial, he attempted suicide by slashing his wrists with a broken light bulb, but failed at that, too. In a sentence hearing he asked for leniency, pointing out that from age 14, he'd spent over nine years in prison and had lived fewer than three years on the outside. The judge sentenced him to serve nearly another decade, but the system would smile on him again with another early release.

On April 9, 1976, Gilmore was paroled to the custody of relatives in Salt Lake City. He worked temporarily for an uncle in a shoe store, and fell in love with a beautiful young mother of two. He jeopardized his last chance to live a straight life by turning again to booze and drugs. He lost the job and began to support himself through theft. One day, in a temperamental rage, he struck his new love, and she moved away.

Having put himself on the precipice of a self-destructive vortex again, he jumped into dead center. Riding around on a warm night in late July with his lover's younger sister, Gilmore parked his pickup truck near a gas station in Orem, Utah. While she waited, he walked inside to the pay counter, and ordered the attendant, Max Jensen, 26, to give him all the cash. He then forced Jensen, a faithful Mormom, into the restroom and commanded him to lie facedown on the floor. For no apparent reason, other than cold malice, Gilmore fired two bullets into the back of Jensen's head.

As if nothing had happened, Gilmore and the girl went to a movie at a drive-in theater. That night in a motel, his attempt at sex with her failed.

Just 24 hours later, Gilmore entered the office of a different motel and ordered the night manager, Ben Bushnell, 25, to lie face down. With a single shot to the head, Gilmore murdered another young believer in the Mormon faith. Both of his victims were hardworking fathers and graduates of Brigham Young University. As Gilmore exited, with a cashbox under his arm, he stopped to ditch the handgun under some bushes and accidently discharged the weapon, injuring his thumb.

A witness saw the second crime, recognized Gilmore, and called the police. They captured him near the airport. He'd been out of prison less than four months.

On October 7, having been found guilty of two murders, Gary Gilmore was sentenced to die for his crimes. There hadn't been an execution in the United States for ten years, so few people expected him to ever pay the supreme penalty.

Gary Gilmore decided to test the state's willpower. If they could so easily hand out a death sentence, would they really have the courage to put a man to death? He refused all appeals, and demanded that the penalty be carried out. News media, enraptured with the remarkable stand, headlined the Gilmore story for months. As the date drew closer, Americans curiously read and watched each new development. As with all pending executions, vocal activist groups demonstrated to put an end to the death penalty, while others loudly called for bringing the matter to a swift conclusion by giving Gilmore what he demanded, and deserved.

Just after dawn on January 17, 1977, guards marched Gary Gilmore to a warehouse on prison grounds. They strapped him into a wooden chair in front of a mattress and a bulwark of sandbags. To the very end, Gilmore remained calm, speaking casually to several officials and witnesses. When the warden finally asked him for any last comments, Gilmore reportedly said, "Let's do it." Following administration of last rites, attendants placed a black hood over his head. From behind a temporary screen, five sharpshooters fired rifles, all but one loaded with lethal bullets, and Gary Gilmore's life came to an end. Certainly no mythical hero, he died as he had lived, a career criminal and a cold-blooded killer.

Horoscope for Gary Gilmore
Born December 4, 1940, 6:30 A.M. CST, McCamey, Texas
Source: Birth certificate

Like a comet hurtling toward earth on a path of fiery self-destruction, Gary Gilmore was consumed with a compelling death wish. His life's highway, full of ruts and potholes, is well marked with astrological signals of doom, especially in the sixth house of law enforcement and the twelfth house of prison and suicidal tendencies.

The tortuous journey starts, though, with the relationship between Gilmore and his father. Friction between them generated emotional sparks that crackle through the fourth house, domain of the father. Jupiter, ruler of the fourth house, is aligned in a negative aspect with Saturn, the planet of hatred and bitterness, and both planets are in Taurus, the sign of festering obsession. So, under these grinding influences, the raw feelings that developed between father and son during Gilmore's childhood never healed.

Saturn and Jupiter, while inflicting negativity on the agitated fourth house, cast long shadows in the sixth house where they dwell. The sixth house is the domain of police and law enforcement. Rulership of law, as well as depression and futility, are within Saturn's scope of power. But Saturn's negative alignment with Pluto, planet of obsession, compulsion, and torture, creates an environment that turned Gilmore's bitterness against his father into hatred for the law, and filled him with compulsive desires to break all the rules. Jupiter, planet of expansiveness, magnifies Gilmore's despair and disrespect for the law. To make matters even worse, one more planet stakes out residency in the agitated sixth house. Uranus, known for dispensing eccentricity, sits in glaring opposition to Gilmore's Scorpio ascendant, generating fierce negative energy. This dangerously unstable aspect opens the gate for Gilmore's irrational behavior and inability to stay out of trouble with the law. All of his sixth-house planets are in the fixed and determined sign of Taurus. So Gilmore's attitudes and actions regarding law enforcement were shackled to him like a massive ball and chain.

The twelfth house of prisons also holds three planets: Mars, Venus, and Mercury. Mars and Venus are close together and sitting in stark opposition to Jupiter and Saturn, the two destructive planets ravaging Gilmore's sixth house. This powerful conflict illustrates the discord in his life, which led to repeated incarcerations. Mars is the planet of violence. Its close association with Venus explains Gilmore's rash, hedonistic and headlong dive into self-destruction.

Mercury, ruling speech and communication, also opposes Uranus, which radiates eccentricity and erratic behavior. This aspect explains Gilmore's argumentative nature and his tendency to verbally abuse anyone who crossed him.

Gilmore's weak Sun, in Sagittarius, rules his ego, indicating low self-esteem. Sagittarius is the sign of the playboy. The flaccid Sun's placement in the first house of personality gives rise to Gilmore's facade of phony self-confidence and pretense of being a devil-may-care libertine. Sagittarius natives, if influenced by the sign's negative aspects, are indiscriminate, careless, and too trusting. As a result, Sagittarius natives tend to associate with the wrong people, and make disastrous decisions, as Gilmore certainly did.

Gilmore's Moon, ruling his emotions and women, is in Aquarius. His final romantic involvement was deeply emotional and very important to him, but the negative aspects of his Moon impaired the couple's relationship. Gilmore's eighth house of death is co-ruled by the Moon. The affair became so painful that they attempted to carry out a dual suicide pact.

The eighth house's other ruler is Mercury, in Scorpio. This combination's influence is shown by Gilmore's obsessive focus on death and self-destruction. His mental attitude, ruled by Mercury, literally aimed bullets at his own heart.

Obsessive Pluto occupies Gilmore's ninth house, which encompasses the justice system. Because Pluto is aligned negatively with Mars, violence and guns became part of Gilmore's destiny. The compulsiveness infused by Pluto activated the Martian influence, setting the stage for Gilmore to commit two senseless, compulsive murders. Pluto wasn't yet finished, though. By its negative alignment with Saturn in his sixth house of the police, Gilmore was soon arrested.

After Gilmore's conviction and death sentence, the obsessive traits previously described took control of him. His Sun, the other ruler of his ninth house, reflects another partial motive for his desire to be executed. Since the Sun rules ego and self-esteem, Gilmore's insistence on facing the firing squad, which was highly publicized, boosted his ego immensely.

However, most of the motivation for Gilmore's demand to die lies in the strong oppositions between his sixth and twelfth houses. The twelfth house rules suicide and self-undoing. The powerful negative energy in this house, mixed with the dominant forces of fatalistic Saturn and Jupiter in the sixth house, sealed his fate. Everything Gilmore did in his life pointed in this self-destructive direction. He took control of his life only at the very last, by commanding the justice system to deliver its lethal fusillade of bullets and bring his troubled existence to a violent end.

Richard Speck

Saturday, December 6, 1941, 1:00 A.M.
Kirkwood, Illinois • Time Zone: 06:00 (CST)
Longitude 090° W 41' • Latitude 40° N 52'
Placidus Houses • Tropical Zodiac

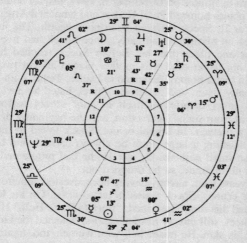

In 1988, a cellmate focused a video camera on Richard Franklin Speck as he preened and leered at the camera. To the embarrassment of Illinois state officials, Speck was caught on film grotesquely prancing around in blue panties and showing off his female hormone–enhanced breasts. To add to the stunning display, he engaged in sex play with a fellow inmate. With an evil grin, he drawled, "If they only knew how much fun I'm having in here, they would turn me loose."

If national television audiences could have seen the tape at that time, they would have angrily demanded to know what was happening in the nation's prisons. Richard Speck was supposed to be serving hard time for the mass murder of eight nurses in 1966. Turning him loose would be the last thing most Americans would want. After all, Speck had been sentenced to die for his crimes, but survived due to the 1972 hiatus on capital punishment imposed by the U.S. Supreme Court. So, there stood Speck in front of a camera, over 6 feet tall, paunchy, pale, and wearing heavy eye makeup. He blatantly gloated about the women he'd killed, laughed at the courts that had imposed the death penalty, taunted his jailers, and defied his fate.

From the beginning, it seemed that Richard Speck was ill-fated. Born in Illinois on December 6, 1941, just 24 hours before Japanese planes bombed Pearl Harbor and launched America into World War II, Speck suffered from poor health. The influence of females on his life began early, since Speck had five sisters, all except one older than he. Before Speck reached his sixth birthday, his father died. His mother placed all but two of her children in foster homes, relocated to Dallas, Texas, with Richard and his baby sister, and remarried. Speck hated his new stepfather. His anger manifested itself in poor school performance, withdrawal from social interaction, and the beginning of alcohol abuse as a preteen. In school or out, Speck loved to intimidate peers by flashing a large knife he always carried, and by using it to abuse small animals. By age 16, he had progressed no further than ninth grade, so he dropped out.

Three years later, already having been arrested numerous times for minor crimes, Speck visited a tattoo artist. On his left forearm, he had this motto inscribed: "Born to Raise Hell." His growing rap sheet, still mostly misdemeanors, reflected the blue-inked creed on his skin. He raised hell with women, too, treating most of them with harsh cruelty. But in 1962, he found a lovemate, age 15, and married her. Speck was a poor provider, spending whatever money he could find on drugs and being fired from job after job. When a daughter was born, he added her name to the various tattoos decorating his arms. Police hauled him in on suspicion of burglary and forgery and sent him to prison for 14 months. During his time behind bars, he stewed in fury, convinced that his young wife was having sexual affairs. All women were sluts in his mind.

Soon after his release, Speck assaulted a woman in Dallas, threatening her with a carving knife. After serving another short prison term, he attempted to reunite with his wife, but she filed for divorce and remarried as soon as it was final.

By 1966, Speck had been arrested 37 times. Working sporadically on cargo ships, he gradually made his way back to Illinois. Any money he earned, or stole during burglaries, Speck squandered on drugs or in bars. In Monmouth, he flirted with a barmaid who found him repulsive and openly rejected his advances. Her body was found a few days later near the tavern where she worked, her underclothing ripped to shreds. Within a few days, someone who fitted Speck's description raped a Monmouth woman and threatened her with a oversized knife. Neither the murder nor the rape was ever solved.

Speck found work aboard a Lake Superior ore barge in early 1966, but his poor health cost him the job within a week. An appendectomy landed him in a hospital, where he met a nurse who seemed to sympathize with him. Speck's Hyde personality remained hidden while his "gentle and quiet" Jekyll behavior, as the nurse recalled, persuaded her to accept dancing and swimming dates with Speck. To impress her, he even landed another assignment aboard a freighter in late June. Once again, booze and drugs inflamed his uncontrollable temper, and he lost the job after fighting with a ship's officer.

Hoping to pry some money from a sister who lived in Chicago, Speck turned up in the Windy City in early July. His sister loaned him a few dollars, while he tried to land a berth on merchant ships. Waiting for a promised job, he drank, played cards at a union hiring hall on the south side of Chicago, drank, and popped pills. He slept in cheap flophouses. On July 12, Speck played pool with a group of sailors, joined them in injecting drugs, then decided to take a walk that night. His route took him one block past the hiring hall to a two-story townhouse where student nurses lived. Leaving the sidewalk, Speck slipped into the shadows at the rear of the building an hour before midnight.

Eight nurses occupied the rooms inside: five American senior students and three from the Philippine Islands. Corazon Amurao shared an upstairs room with her friend, Merlitta Gargullo. Preparing for bed, Corazon heard someone knock on the locked bedroom door, and sleepily answered. Richard Speck pushed the tiny nurse backward. Wielding a knife and a handgun, he corralled four other nurses from across the hall, and forced all six women into the tiny bedroom. While he told them he wanted money, Speck cut and ripped a sheet into strips to use in binding the frightened young women. At 11:20, nurse Gloria Davey arrived home from a date, and Speck immediately herded her into the bedroom prison. It would later be observed that Davey resembled Speck's ex-wife, whom he suspected of cheating on him. "Don't be afraid," he reassured them. "I'm not going to kill you."

When he led Pamela Wilkening into the hallway, the others

heard a plaintive sigh, but did not attempt to escape. Perhaps comforted by his promise, or paralyzed with fright, they remained in the bedroom.

At 20 minutes after midnight, Suzanne Farris and Mary Ann Jordan arrived home, only to be led at gunpoint into the crowded upstairs bedroom. But instead of binding them, he forced the new arrivals into another bedroom. Muffled screams, then dead silence, reached the captives. Speck returned, and led trembling Nina Schmale out.

Now, as nervousness turned to terror among the five bound women, they made pitifully inadequate attempts to hide. Speck returned and forced Valentina Pasion out. Within minutes, Merlita Gargullo became victim number six. Her voice came through the wall crying, "It hurts." Corazon Amurao managed to squeeze her diminutive body, facedown, under a bunk. She heard Speck lift Pat Matusek up as the young woman begged to be untied, and carry her out. When he entered the bedroom again, he didn't bother to take his last victim elsewhere. Corazon, from her narrow viewpoint, saw him brutally rape Gloria Davey for more than 20 minutes before he killed her. Under the bunk, Corazon closed her eyes, concentrated on remaining motionless, and held her breath. When she opened them again, Speck had left.

Corazon waited, praying that the intruder had lost count and forgotten her. Finally, at 6 A.M., she worked up enough courage to crawl outside and scream for help. Police found the eight bodies scattered throughout the townhouse, beaten, strangled, and stabbed. Gloria Davey, who resembled Speck's ex-wife, had been raped and mutilated.

From Corazon Amurao's description, which included the "Born to Raise Hell" tattoo, investigators put out a poster with a sketched likeness of the mass killer. They posted it at the nearby hiring hall. Probing the U.S. Coast Guard files, the police discovered a seaman's identity card bearing a photo that resembled the drawing and the name Richard Speck. The single survivor knew that face, and police put out a dragnet for Speck. He narrowly missed being apprehended when a hotel manager called police to complain that a guest had held a gun on a prostitute. The responding cops hadn't yet heard of the manhunt, and released Speck with a warning.

On July 16, in another flophouse, Speck began yelling for help. He'd slashed his wrists. But police again failed to connect the self-destructive tramp to the headlined crimes, since Speck had used a false name to check in. The injured transient was taken to an emergency medical facility where a doctor who'd read news accounts saw the distinctive tattoo. Minutes later, when police arrested Speck, he claimed he couldn't remember anything he'd done on the night of the murders.

Psychiatrists stated that Speck's low IQ, frequent head injuries, and drug use had driven him into a vortex of uncontrollable hate for women. In the eyes of the law, though, he was capable of standing trial. With Corazon Amurao's unequivocal identification of Speck, and bloody fingerprints he'd left at the crime scene, no doubt ever existed about his guilt. The jury deliberated less than an hour and recommended the death penalty. The judge agreed, but the Supreme Court eventually saved Speck's life.

In 1988, he obscenely strutted in front of a video camera. Three years later, on the day before his 50th birthday, Richard Speck died in his prison cell of a massive heart attack. Afterward, the shocking tape was shown on national television and to a U.S. congressional committee, who then called for tighter controls in penitentiaries.

Horoscope for Richard Speck
Born December 6, 1941, 1:00 A.M. CST, Kirkwood, Illinois
Source: Birth certificate

To Richard Speck, all women were sluts and liars. Where did this hatred come from, and how did it lead him to commit one of the most heinous mass murders in the public's memory? Speck's negative attitude toward women is painfully evident in his chart.

Speck's eighth house of death is occupied by Saturn and ruled by Mars. Saturn, planet of selfish hatred, infused Speck with a detached cold-bloodedness. Mars brought cruelty and violence. A chilling factor was introduced by the alignment of Mars to the Moon, which represents women. This negative aspect allowed the full weight of brutal, pitiless force to run rampant during the hours Speck spent with the female nurses he chose to kill. Beating, stabbing, and rape are also associated with Mars. In order to control the frightened victims, Speck threatened them with a gun, another Mars influence. Mars occupies the seventh house, in Aries, a sign that agitates and increases the red planet's violent nature.

Saturn not only infused Speck with hatred, but also linked sex and death in his mind. This came about due to Saturn's rulership of his fifth house of sex, while residing in his eighth house of death. The ominous link reached its pinnacle when he raped one of the nurses before ending her life.

Simmering hatred for women festered in Speck's psyche. His first house, the domain of personality, appearance, and temperament, provides residence for only one planet—Neptune in the sign of Virgo. Neptune sits in a negative alignment with the Moon, signaling more difficulties and confusion between Speck and women. This unfortunate aspect activates Neptune's unpleasant trait of deception. The tendency to lie and deceive, in Speck's distorted view, worked both ways. He never trusted or believed any female, so he felt no compunction about being unscrupulous with them. Virgo's involvement creates a predisposition for Speck to find fault with women, deserved or not.

Neptune's negative influence reached even further in Speck's destiny. Drugs, one of Neptune's associations, were a continual problem for him. His thought processes fell under Neptune's forked trident as well. The close proximity of Neptune to Speck's Virgo ascendant endows it with additional power and influence, thereby making delusions and misperceptions an intrinsic part of his personality. Neptune is a strange planet, and its influence in his first house defined Speck's peculiar appearance, which was an important factor in identifying him after his murder spree.

Speck's ninth house, ruling publicity, is the abode of Uranus and Jupiter. Uranus, the planet of eccentricity, is next to Saturn, the evil resident of his eighth house of death. The hatred Speck showered on women is represented by Saturn. The other occupant of Speck's ninth house, Jupiter, reflects not only the enormity of the slaughter, but also the massive news media coverage his crime and his life generated.

The Moon, ruler of women, is in Speck's tenth house of reputation. One of the survivors of his massacre identified him and testified against him in court. The courage she showed in doing so brought widespread admiration for her and universal loathing for Speck.

Speck's twelfth house of prisons is ruled by Mercury. Sagittarius, Mercury's sign, representing good luck, showed up when he escaped the death penalty.

Uranus, planet of eccentricity, exerts a bizarre influence on Speck's fifth house of sex. He apparently became a transsexual, at least in some respects, before he posed in front of a video camera. The fact that he was allowed to get away with this incredible behavior, and be taped in the process, is a Sagittarian influence. No one but a Sagittarius could get away with such flouting of prison procedures.

Any good fortune Sagittarius may have brought finally failed Speck when he died of a massive heart attack.

Edmund Emil Kemper III

Saturday, December 18, 1948, 11:04 P.M.
Burbank, California • Time Zone: 07:00 (PDT)
Longitude 118° W 18' 29" • Latitude 34° N 10' 51"
Placidus Houses • Tropical Zodiac

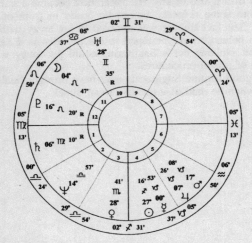

A giant among serial killers, Ed Kemper stands 6 feet, 9 inches, and weighs in the neighborhood of 300 pounds. Since his whole family towered above other people, he never felt out of place as a child. The hatred that constantly flared between his parents often resulted in physical fights. Kemper's reaction was to retreat into odd games in which he pretended to be a convicted killer sitting in the gas chamber. Whenever an urge to murder took root in his mind, small animals suffered torture, death, and beheading at his hands. Strange sexual urges possessed him. Sometimes, he would hover over his sleeping mother and fantasize about killing her.

In 1957, when his father left the family, his mother, Clarnell, moved him and his two siblings to Montana. A stepfather tried to cope with the boy's brooding by teaching him about guns and hunting, but without much success. Kemper ran away to join his real father in California, only to find himself dumped in a rural home with his strict grandparents. Miserable, he returned to his mother in 1964, but she promptly sent him back.

Kemper's grandmother kept a tight rein on him, instilling in the 15-year-old a boiling hatred. In August, he stood on the porch of her home, aimed his .22-caliber rifle at the back of her head, and fired. Just to be certain she was dead, he pumped two more slugs into her and then dragged her body onto a bed and repeatedly stabbed her with a butcher knife. His grandfather drove into the yard a short time later, and Kemper sent a .22-caliber round into his brain. Reeling in confusion, the young killer telephoned his mother in Montana to announce the "accidental" shooting of his grandparents. Upon her urging, he called the sheriff and meekly surrendered.

During a psychiatric examination, Kemper explained that he had simply wondered what it would be like to shoot his grandparents. The doctor's report labeled Kemper dangerously psychotic, suggesting that killing his grandparents had been a substitute for a desire to kill his mother. Officials confined him in Atascadero State Hospital, where Kemper received therapy for his concealed aggressions. While there, he held a job, buffed his body, and appeared to be responding well to treatment. Out of his keepers' sight, however, Kemper spent time with sexual deviants discussing every perversion imaginable. Administrators, impressed with Kemper's intelligence and apparent responsiveness to therapy, released him to the California Youth Authority in 1969, noting that he should never be near his mother. Shortly after Kemper's 21st birthday, the parole board released him to the custody of his mother. They lived together near the coastal resort town of Santa Cruz.

During eighteen months spent with his mother, Kemper worked various jobs, hung out at a bar frequented by cops whom he befriended, sustained serious injuries in a motorcycle crash, and kept his eyes on the mini-skirted college girls at University of California, Santa Cruz. Even though he moved out of Clarnell's apartment in July 1971, Kemper visited her frequently. His mother belittled his lifestyle, criticized him, and suggested that no woman would be interested in the lumbering hulk.

To test women's reaction to his appearance and personality, Kemper began picking up female hitchhikers. He found plenty of them among the free-spirited UCSC students and their counterparts at Stanford University or across the bay at University of California, Berkeley. He later estimated that more than 100 trusting young women were passengers in his car before he began planning to kidnap, mutilate, and murder them.

On May 7, 1992, he offered a ride to Anita Luchessa and Mary Ann Pesce, both 18, and drove them to an isolated orchard. After forcing Luchessa into the luggage compartment, he stabbed Pesce repeatedly with a small knife before cutting her throat. Using a larger knife, he tortured Luchessa to death. Moving the bodies into his apartment after dark, he beheaded both of them, thinking of them as trophy kills. Eventually, Kemper would admit necrophilic sexual acts and cannibalism. He buried the remains in the Santa Cruz hills, where they would remain until they were discovered by hikers in August.

Four months after the first two murders, Kemper picked up Aido Koo, 15. In the hills above Santa Cruz, he asphyxiated her by shutting off her air supply with his huge hands. Thinking the tiny girl dead, he raped her, during which she revived. This time, he used a scarf to strangle her. After carving the body to small pieces the next day, he buried the remains but kept the head.

Perversely, despite a love-hate relationship, Kemper moved back in with his mother. Within a few days, he picked up Cynthia Schall, 18, rescuing her from a hard rain. Parked out of sight of passersby, he shot her as she huddled in the car's trunk. After hiding her corpse in his mother's home all night, then using it for sex, he dismembered it. Again keeping the head, he tossed the bagged body parts down steep cliffs into the ocean.

On another rainy day, February 5, following a violent argument with his mother, Kemper picked up two more young hitchhikers: Rosalind Thorpe, 23, and Alice Liu, 20. Without warning, he raised a pistol and shot both of them, killing Thorpe instantly but wounding Liu. Stopping near a beach, he fired a final lethal shot, ending Liu's life. That evening, he beheaded both of them as they lay in the car trunk. Following the usual sexual play, he butchered the torsos and scattered body parts in different areas of the woods and sea cliffs. The inept disposal allowed the remains to be discovered within a few days.

Panic struck the region as news of the killings spread. Kemper grew nervous, and gave reprieves to several young women who rode with him, temporarily suppressing the urge to kill. On April 20, 1973, he said goodnight to his mother and retired to his bedroom. An hour before dawn, he entered her bedroom carrying a hammer and knife. After delivering a crushing blow to her head, he used the knife to cut her throat, then sliced all the way through her neck to lift the head away. Driven by his lifelong fury at Clarnell, he slashed off limbs and battered the head. He would later say, "I humiliated her corpse."

Worried that Clarnell's best friend, Sally Hallet, would realize something was wrong, he called to invite the woman to dinner. As soon as she walked into the residence, he slugged, her then lifted her by gripping her throat in the crook of his arm. She died within moments. Kemper stripped the body and sexually abused it. Exhausted, he slept for hours.

Possessed now by an empty feeling, Kemper loaded several guns into his car and headed aimlessly along highways. He drove in a mindless stupor, losing track of time. Coming to a stop in Pueblo, Colorado, he realized that the killing must end. "The original purpose was gone," Kemper later said, referring to the murder of his mother. He telephoned the Santa Cruz police, who arranged for his arrest in Pueblo.

In a trial lasting three weeks, jurors heard stomach-turning evidence including Kemper's confession. Experts presented endless psychiatric testimony attempting to explain the ghastly behavior, but the jurors were skeptical. They found him sane and guilty of eight first-degree murders. One year earlier, the U.S. Supreme Court had decreed existing death penalty laws unconstitutional. At the time of Kemper's sentencing, California had not yet enacted new provisions for capital punishment. By law, he received a sentence of life in prison. Every two years, he comes up for parole hearings, but in all likelihood, will die in prison.

Horoscope for Edmund Emil Kemper III
Born December 18, 1948, 11:04 P.M. PDT, Burbank, California
Source: Birth certificate

Two signs that are common to many serial killers, Sagittarius and Virgo, appear prominently in Edmund Kemper's chart. It can be said they are signatures of the serial killer. The Sun, ruling his ego, is in Sagittarius while his ascendant, ruling his personality, is in Virgo. Sagittarius is a friendly, outgoing, optimistic sign, reflecting how Kemper probably appeared to his potential victims. Virgo's qualities are passive, quiet, and articulate. These two signs, operating in tandem, endowed Kemper with personality traits he needed to become one of California's most notorious killers. He used this adaptability, showing his seemingly nonthreatening side to scores of female hitchhikers who accepted rides from him. He chose from among them the victims he would stab, shoot, mutilate, decapitate, and use as his objects of necrophilia.

The first house in Kemper's chart, ruling physical appearance, temperament, and disposition, holds an ominous clue to his criminal activities. Saturn, the planet of limitations, fear, repression, and hatred, resides in his first house. Kemper's huge size was an emotional disability for him. He felt self-conscious, which negatively affected his relations with women. His fear of rejection, another trait imposed by Saturn, led him to fantasize about sex with unconscious or dead women. Kemper stated that he was "disappointed" in not achieving sexual fulfillment with his victims. He continued the gruesome acts, still seeking satisfaction. Kemper explained, "That is why [I attempt] sex after death sometimes, because it's through frustration." Both disappointment and frustration are negative traits of Saturn.

Kemper's Moon, ruling women, dwells in his eleventh house of friends. He befriended the hitchhikers when they accepted rides, to establish his trustworthiness. When asked by a psychiatrist about the murders, Kemper said, "When I was psychologically in the mood for [killing], the person didn't have a chance." Moods are also attributes of the Moon. When Kemper picked up a hitchhiker, and was not "in the mood," he deposited her at her destination. However, when the mood struck him, he lashed out in lethal violence. Kemper's Moon is aligned negatively to Pluto, planet of obsessions and compulsions. In addition, both planets are in the fixed, dominating, and controlling sign of Leo. The destructive and coercive natures of Pluto and Leo on Kemper's emotions were so powerful that he felt a driving compulsion to commit his perverted, sadistic acts. Nothing could stop him.

Much of Kemper's life was centered on his mother, represented by the tenth house. Uranus, planet of eccentricity and contradictions, looms in the tenth house, setting the stage for the tumultuous relationship between son and mother. Uranus is in Gemini, the sign associated with communications. Initially, the problems stemmed from verbal abuse, which led to arguments. The powerful Sun, planet of the ego, occupies Kemper's fourth house of the home, and is positioned in direct opposition to Uranus and Mercury. While the Sun rules Kemper's ego, Mercury influences his speech and thoughts. Thus, in his mother's home, the conflict between Kemper and his mother soared like a thermometer in July. But it was restricted to verbal bickering and shouting, with no physical violence.

The contradictory side of Uranus is indicated by the continuation of the pair living together even after Kemper reached adulthood. At last, Mars tossed gunpowder into the emotional fires. The violent planet is negatively aligned with Uranus, an aspect fraught with danger. Kemper ended up bludgeoning his mother, decapitating her, and dismembering the rest of the body. Mars rules such unmitigated, gory violence. Uranus, so instrumental in the gradual buildup to this lethal explosion, also sits in a negative configuration with the Sun, fueling the irrationality that clouded his mind. It formed a powder keg in Kemper with the potential for unimaginable cruelty. He even described himself as "a walking time bomb."

Behavioral scientists might argue that sex with a corpse is not really sex. Whether this is true or not, Kemper's fifth house of sex is filled with energy, providing an abode for two planets. Jupiter, planet of excesses, represents the multiple number of bodies he sexually defiled. Mars, ruling guns, knives, and decapitation, is significant in view of Kemper's admission that removing a woman's head was a sexual thrill for him. He described killing an innocent victim as a "triumph . . . an exultation over death." The sense of triumph and exultation is attributable to the Sun's negative aspect to Mars. Kemper also claimed that the act of decapitation originated in his childhood fantasies. Fantasy is ruled by Neptune, which finds itself in a negative relation with Mars. Thus, Kemper's imagination leaned toward barbarity and cruelty. Another twist appears in regard to Kemper's compulsion to decapitate the women. Mars controls the eighth house of death and governs the sign of Aries. The part of the body ruled by Aries is the head.

Both Mars and Saturn are in Capricorn, a calculating and cunning sign. Kemper stated that he had "rules of operation" while searching for potential victims. When cruising the highways on days he felt compelled to kill, he carefully watched for the police or possible witnesses.

The twelfth house of prisons provides furtive lodging for Pluto, the ruler of kidnapping, depravity, and perversion. Obsessions and compulsion are also Pluto traits. Kemper has stated that if he were released, he would be compelled to kill again. By his own admission, Kemper has permanently sealed the prison doors that will keep him confined for the remainder of his life.

CAPRICORN

Capricorns are generally practical and materialistic. As a result, Capricorn murderers are often motivated by large of amounts of money, such as from an insurance settlement or an inheritance. Lyle Menendez is an excellent example. Oddly, several Capricorn killers have taken as their victims children or young people; Ian Brady and Dean Corll are two such Capricorn natives. When the surrounding planets become capricious, Capricorn people can be strict, humorless misers—and sometimes they can be murderers as well.

Ian Brady

Sunday, January 2, 1938, 12:40 P.M.
Glasgow, Scotland • Time Zone: 00:00 (Universal Time)
Longitude 004° W 15' • Latitude 55° N 53'
Placidus Houses • Tropical Zodiac

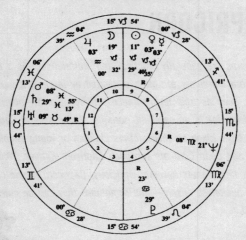

"**I**'ve got to get home," cried the nervous 12-year-old girl. "I'll get killed if I don't." Young Lesley Ann Downey had no idea how prophetic her words were.

With a tape recording capturing every pitiful word, Ian Brady, 28, tried to calm her. "No, no, not yet. . . . You are such a beautiful little girl," he said. Then he nodded toward his lover, Myra Hindley, 24 (see separate profile). She led Lesley Ann into a bedroom, stripped her nude except for shoes and socks, and invited Brady to join them. Hindley gagged the terrified victim, and for the next hour the perverted couple abused her, and photographed their crime so they could continue to enjoy it even after they had killed and buried the little girl.

It wasn't the only murder committed by the hellish pair. Brady and Hindley would be labeled in England as perpetrators of the infamous "Moors Murders" during the mid-1960s.

Typical of many serial killers, Ian Brady demonstrated extreme cruelty early in his life. He took every opportunity to inflict pain on helpless pets—beating or stoning dogs, burying cats alive, and decapitating several rabbits. Among playmates, he was recognized as a terroristic bully. The illegitimate offspring of a waitress in Glasgow, Scotland, Brady launched his criminal career while still in his adolescence. He built a rap sheet from age 13 that included theft, housebreaking, and burglary. In his teen years, grown to 6 feet and with ash-blond hair, Brady adopted Nazism and the theory of Aryan racial superiority.

After several clashes with the law, Brady seemed to settle down. He took a job as a stock clerk and met a bleached blond named Myra Hindley, who worked as a typist in the firm. The blending of Brady and Hindley was like mixing gasoline and fire. He impressed her with his collection of books about Hitler, Eichmann, and Nazi atrocities. Pleased with her response, Brady displayed his special private library of erotic literature about sadism, which seemed to bond the pair even more tightly. While most lovers dream of romantic dates or exotic trips together, Brady and Hindley fantasized about pornography, robberies, and murder.

Soon afterwards, several young people vanished, and no traces of them could be found despite widespread publicity and intensive searches. In November 1963, John Kilbride, 12, disappeared. Lesley Ann Downey dropped out of sight in December 1964, and so did Pauline Reade, 16, and 12-year-old Keith Bennett.

Brady and Hindley moved in together with her grandmother in 1964, and at Brady's urging, she bought two pistols and a rifle for him. The couple became cozy with Hindley's sister and her husband. Trying to impress the new friends, Brady boasted that he could easily commit murder. To prove it, he picked up a homosexual youth, Edward Evans, 17, in October 1965, and invited Hindley's brother-in-law to watch. In full view of the horrified observer, Brady bludgeoned Evans with an axe, then strangled him to death.

The witness, sick about the event, notified police the next day. A search of Brady's residence turned up the victim's body, plus claim tickets for two suitcases stored at a railroad station. Recovery and opening of the luggage turned up stomach-churning photos of a naked, frightened little girl, Lesley Ann Downey, along with tape recordings of her pleading to go home. Police also found notes written by Brady linking him to the murder of John Kilbride. Other photos contained in the suitcase were of Brady and Hindley in the lonely, heath-covered wastelands outside Manchester, called the Moors. Using landmarks in the pictures, investigators located the graves of Downey and Kilbride.

At the trial, in which Brady and Hindley stood accused of three murders, jurors heard the heartbreaking tapes of Lesley Ann Downey pleading to go home, and saw the lewd photos of her. Found guilty on all counts, Brady and Hindley were sentenced on May 6, 1966, to life imprisonment.

While Hindley expressed love and loyalty to Brady during decades of incarceration, she ultimately changed and condemned him. She also confessed that they had murdered Keith Bennett and Pauline Reade and led investigators to Reade's grave in 1987. Representatives of the Crown, though, chose not to open new trials, assuming that the Moors Murderers would never be released from prison.

Horoscope for Ian Brady
Born January 2, 1938, 12:40 P.M. Universal Time, Glasgow, Scotland
Source: Birth certificate

Ian Brady, the dominant half of the notorious Moors Murders team, is a Sun sign Capricorn, the exact opposite of the sign of Cancer, under which his lover and co-killer, Myra Hindley, was born. Opposite signs, though, can become highly complementary partners. Each one contributes qualities the other lacks. Hindley utilized her Cancer traits to take care of Brady and assume the role of his mother in many ways. He, in turn, made most of the decisions, including when, where, and how they would kidnap, sexually abuse, and murder young children.

Several elements of Ian Brady's chart suggest he was the instigator of the murders. His Sun, realm of the ego, in its alignment with reputation-ruler midheaven, hints that Brady had the self-esteem of a whale in a school of sardines. He clearly dominated his partner, although she became a willing acolyte. Ominously, the Sun also rules Brady's fifth house of sex and children. The sexual abusing of pubescent boys and girls was initiated by Brady, but he soon drew Hindley in as a full participant.

Brady's strongest sign is Capricorn, the makeup of which includes Mercury, the Sun, midheaven, and the Moon. Such a combination magnifies the traits of this practical, cold-blooded, materialistic sign. The natural element related to Capricorn is earth. In Brady's childhood, he was taken on a trip to the country and allowed to roam among the heath-covered wastelands called the Moors. He sat for hours, staring into space, and developed a mystical relationship with the terrain. Brady later used the area to bury his small victims.

Mercury in Capricorn relates to his interest in reading and studying about Nazis. Brady's affinity for Hitler extended to similarities in their charts. Hitler was a Sun sign Taurus with his Moon in Capricorn. Brady is a Sun sign Capricorn with his ascendant in Taurus.

Venus, the ruler of Brady's Taurus ascendant, is also in Capricorn. With Mercury, planet of mental pursuits, nudging very close to Venus in the ninth house of education, Brady loved exposure to learning and to new ideas.

The Moon rules emotions. But Brady's Moon in Capricorn indicates an emotionless, cold, and unfeeling personality. With all this Capricorn influence bearing down on Brady's midheaven, ruler of his reputation, this autocratic dictator wanted everyone to recognize his supreme power and authority.

Brady's eighth house of death is ruled by Jupiter, planet of excess and waste, including the waste of young lives. Pluto glowers across the chart in direct opposition to Jupiter, setting up a menacing potential, since Pluto reigns over kidnapping and torture. The situation is aggravated by Pluto's threatening occupancy of the fourth house, which rules Brady's home. It was in this residence, shared with his lover Hindley, that the cruel couple sexually ravaged and murdered children.

Pluto assaults Brady's destiny again by taking a position opposite the Moon. This alignment reveals the sadistic cruelty he exhibited in the commission of the ghastly crimes. Pluto also rules Brady's seventh house of partners, influencing the kind of relationship he sought and found in Myra Hindley and corrupting it with the negative activities. Sadism and torture are Pluto characteristics, and Hindley adapted quite well to them in the name of love for her man. One more influence of Brady's chart, Mars, the bloody planet of violence, casts a shadow over his partner. Mars occupies the twelfth house of secrets, relating to the surreptitious night probes the couple made to kidnap, rape, and murder children.

Two other planets join Mars in Brady's twelfth house of secrets, crowding it with potential for danger and violence. Saturn, planet of selfish hatred, locks horns in opposition to Neptune, which rules imagination. This negative aspect inflates Brady's merciless aptitude for cruel violence, which he used on his victims. Uranus, planet of eccentricity, sits almost in contact with his ascendant, Taurus. This infects Brady's Taurus personality with abnormal irrationality.

Prison is also a twelfth-house matter. The negative aspects of its three resident planets indicate that he will remain in captivity forever.

Lyle Menendez

Wednesday, January 10, 1968, 12:10 P.M.
Queens, New York • Time Zone: 05:00 (EST)
Longitude 073° W 52' • Latitude 40° N 43' 05"
Placidus Houses • Tropical Zodiac

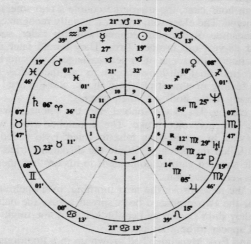

On Sunday evening, August 20, 1989, entertainment executive Jose Menendez and his wife, Kitty, lounged on a plush couch in the family room of their multimillion-dollar Beverly Hills mansion, watching a James Bond movie on television. They both dozed off before the clocks chimed the hour of ten.

Two young men carrying shotguns quietly eased into the front entrance and tiptoed through a lavish hallway. They heard the television blaring, and moved toward the sound. One of the gunmen raised his weapon, aimed it at Jose's head, and pulled the trigger. A thunderous blast echoed through the home, waking both sleepers. The shooter had barely winged Jose, who yelled in alarm. A second shot destroyed the back of his head.

Kitty Menendez, horrified at the sight of her husband's exploding flesh, bone, and brain tissue, sprang upright. The lethal weapons barked again, sending pellets into her legs and arm. Collapsing on the floor, she crawled, then made it to her feet again. Two more shots toppled her to the floor, but miraculously, she still had the strength and will to live. As she struggled, the inept gunmen sprinted to a car parked outside, reloaded, and raced back to the severely wounded woman. With the barrel tip touching Kitty's face, one of the killers delivered a shot that finally ended her life.

Over an hour later, the murdered couple's two sons returned to their home. The elder son, Lyle, 22, usually recognized as the more handsome of the pair, entered with his taller, somewhat awkward 18-year-old brother, Erik. They would later describe their reaction to the scene of violent carnage. Lyle said he overcame the emotional jolt long enough to call the police. Erik reported a feeling of almost paralytic shock, and the need to look more closely at the bodies of their parents.

After calling 911, Lyle sobbed into the phone, "We're the sons, . . ." but his voice broke. The dispatcher asked what the problem was. In a quavering falsetto voice, Lyle yelled, "They shot and killed my parents." While the dispatcher tried to calm him, Lyle shouted garbled commands to his brother, then falteringly answered questions.

When the news broke the next morning, overwhelming sympathy for the two orphaned boys spread across the nation. Although they didn't seem as heartbroken as some might expect, they did appear to be grieving.

Lyle and Erik Menendez had grown up in a luxurious though highly controlled environment. Their father strongly expressed his expectations for his sons' success. He also made it clear that he would be in complete charge of the planning and implementation of their goals. Some insiders thought that the two boys were never allowed to be normal children. Education at the right schools was a must, so Lyle attended Princeton University, but struggled and was suspended a year for cheating. Erik settled for UCLA.

In the relationship between the two brothers, Lyle had shown considerable dominance, while Erik seemed less aggressive, perhaps more sensitive. But they appeared to have a tight bond, despite the difference in self-confidence. Lyle showed an almost arrogant ability to control events and people, while Erik was sometimes judged as insecure. Both boys were competitive. In 1985, Lyle won a regional tennis championship in his age class, and Erik responded with a similar win for younger players. Lyle later angered his father when he mentioned he'd like to quit school to become a professional tennis player.

Prior to the killings, in the summer of 1989, there were whispers among people close to the Menendez family that some dark problems existed. Lyle's reckless behavior had upset his father repeatedly, and Erik seemed to be brooding. Even their mother appeared to sense that something was wrong.

A massive investigation of the murders dealt with rumors of a drug hit, jealous business dealings, and other wild speculations. Some observers expressed quiet concern about the two boys going on extravagant spending sprees: buying an expensive new sports car, making impulsive investments, and traveling worldwide. Their remarkably quick recovery from grieving was puzzling to many of their acquaintances.

Homicide investigators had been wondering about the same things and were becoming increasingly suspicious that Lyle and Erik were the mysterious killers of their own parents. The theory grew when a screenplay co-written by Erik Menendez and one of his close friends turned up. It told the story of wealthy family in which the egotistical 18-year-old son kills his parents, inherits a vast fortune, and later dies with a complacent smile on his face.

But the sleuths needed more than a fictitious script. Then, in early March 1990, a female friend of a psychologist whose clients included the Menendez brothers contacted investigators with a stunning development. She said she had overheard the boys, in a private session with her friend, yelling about killing someone. Erik, she said, had sobbed, "I can't kill anymore." The psychologist, she thought, had taped the the confession.

On March 8, a swarm of detectives arrested Lyle Menendez at the mansion. Erik, playing tennis in Israel, flew home to voluntarily surrender. The defense wanted separate trials for each of the brothers, but the judge compromised by conducting one trial with two juries.

The prosecution presented the theory that the greedy, spoiled brothers committed murder to inherit the $14 million dollar family fortune. In the highly publicized proceedings, the brothers admitted shooting their parents, but tearfully claimed they did so out of fear that Jose Menendez was going to kill them to prevent the boys from revealing that he had sexually molested them for years. The D.A. countered by suggesting that the boys, 18 and 22 at the time of the murders, were certainly capable of getting away from any parental abuse. After weeks of emotional testimony, one jury and then the other failed to reach a verdict. A second trial, jointly prosecuting both defendants with one jury, became necessary in early 1996.

As in the earlier trials, the controversial confession taped by the psychologist played a pivotal role. The prosecution pointed out that not once in the revealing tape could anything be heard about sexual abuse being inflicted on either of the brothers.

Ruling on the hotly disputed issue of self-defense, the judge stated that evidence did not show the boys to be in imminent danger on the night of the shootings. Lawyers for Lyle and Erik, he said, might assert that Jose Menendez had been killed in the heat of passion, but no evidence existed regarding any threat of death from Kitty Menendez.

In the summation, the prosecutor argued that the brothers clearly premeditated the murder as shown by their carrying loaded shotguns into the house that night, then stepping outside to reload. "How could they shoot their mother like this?" he asked.

Their defense acknowledged that the boys fired the lethal shots, but asked the jury to find them guilty of manslaughter instead of murder.

On March 20, the jurors returned with verdicts that both brothers had committed first-degree murder with special circumstances. The judge sent them both to prison for life without the possibility of parole.

Horoscope for Lyle Menendez
Born January 10, 1968, 12:10 P.M., EST, Queens, New York
Source: Family birth announcement

An obsession with money and status consumed Lyle Menendez and eventually led him to conspire with his brother to kill their parents. Capricorn, Lyle's strongest sign, is associated with status, money, power, and influence. His Sun, midheaven, and Mercury are all intertwined together within this materialistic sign. The Sun rules his ego and is next to his midheaven. This configuration shouts of someone who craves public acclaim and insists on being envied for his wealth and affluence. The midheaven acts as the broadcast beacon to tell the world about the mighty Menendez, thus inflating his Sun-ruled ego. Mercury, ruling his speech and communications, is ensconced in his tenth house of reputation and social status. Doing double duty, Mercury also influences Lyle's second house of money, which serves to solidly link his overwhelming need for riches to his driving demand for prestige.

Lyle's first house of appearance, temperament, and disposition is occupied by the Moon. This is his strongest planet and, significantly, rules not only the third house of brothers, but also the fourth house, representing the father. Good looks are within the province of Taurus, explaining the importance of personal appearance to Lyle. The Moon and his ascendant are both in Taurus, a sign associated with money. Unfortunately, his Moon beams across the chart in direct opposition to Neptune. This negative aspect illustrates Lyle's inability to effectively handle money. Neptune is the planet of deception, and Lyle was conned out of a considerable sum as a direct result of his failure to understand anything about finances. Venus, the occupant and ruler of Lyle's Taurus ascendant, lurks in his eighth house of death.

The eighth house rules not only death but money gained from death, such as insurance or inheritance. The inheritance waiting for Lyle gradually dominated his thoughts. Venus is aligned negatively to Jupiter, the ruler of abundance, or vast quantities. In this context, the love endowed by Venus became an unhealthy desire for extravagance.

From its abode in the fifth house of pleasure and hobbies, Jupiter magnifies Lyle's lust for expensive toys. Lyle's hobbies required only the very best of equipment. His father had already invested a great deal of money in Lyle's tennis activities. The other ruler of his fifth house is the Sun. This representation of ego indicates that Lyle wanted nothing but the best. Even the gifts from his generous father were not good enough for him.

Lyle's mother, who also spoiled him, is represented by his tenth house. With the strong Capricorn influence, meaning "I use," abounding from his tenth house, he used her for his own purposes, treating her like a servant. Another strong influence of the tenth house of mother comes from Saturn, which hides away in Lyle's twelfth house of secrets and hidden agendas. The secret plans he made with his brother to murder both parents stem for Saturn's position in Aries. This is significant since Aries is ruled by violent Mars, the planet of guns. Lyle shot his mother several times, then went outside to reload, returned, and fired the final shot into her face. Aries is not only the ruler of both guns and shooting, but also rules the human head.

The fourth house of home and father is governed by the Moon. Lyle accused his father of sexual and psychological abuse. The Moon's opposite alignment to Neptune, the planet of lies, creates a telling negative aspect, and reveals the use of deceit. The entire configuration reduces the credence of Lyle's excuse that his father had abused him. The chart suggests the alibi was untrue.

Erik, Lyle's brother, is represented by the Moon, ruler of the third house of siblings. Lyle dominated his younger brother and was the primary architect of the whole scheme. Lyle's Sun/Moon alignment, a positive aspect, illustrates the closeness between the brothers throughout their lives. Without this emotional attachment it is unlikely they would have conspired to murder their parents.

Conspiracy is a Pluto-ruled matter. Pluto is found next to Uranus, planet of eccentricity. Erik was not only Lyle's brother but also his partner, and Pluto rules the seventh house of partners. Uranus, by locking arms with Pluto, shadows this plot with overtones of eccentric, irrational conspiracy.

The ninth house, ruling the courts, provides exclusive residence to the Sun, and is influenced by Saturn. The Sun illustrates the large amount of publicity this case engendered, while Saturn rules both the law and, in Lyle's case, prison.

The twelfth house rules prison. Saturn occupies the house, so it shackles Lyle with restraint and confinement. Neptune exerts influence through a negative alignment, indicating that brother Erik was the cause of Lyle's imprisonment, as seen by Neptune also making a negative aspect to the ruler of Lyle's third house of brothers. Lyle's greed, shown by Jupiter in his fifth house, was of course the fundamental reason for his incarceration. Lyle Menendez and his brother will spend the rest of their lives in prison. The long arm of the law, represented by Saturn, finally won.

Dean Arnold Corll

Sunday, December 24, 1939, 8:45 P.M.
Fort Wayne, Indiana • Time Zone: 06:00 (CST)
Longitude 085° W 07' 44" • Latitude 41° N 07' 50"
Placidus Houses • Tropical Zodiac

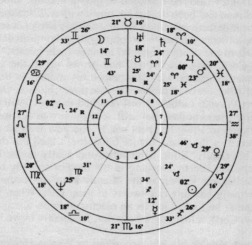

In most cases involving serial killers, the public breathes a sigh of relief when the accused murderer simply dies before taxpayers spend millions on incarceration, defense attorneys, and a prolonged trial. All the better if the death is violent. In the case of Dean Corll, though, too many questions remained unanswered.

When Elmer Wayne Henley, 18, telephoned the Pasadena, Texas, police on the morning of August 8, 1973, he stated he wanted to reveal some important news. He had shot and killed the man he lived with, an electrician named Dean Corll, 33. According to Henley, Corll had threatened his life, so the teenager reacted in self-defense. His blood-curdling explanation of the details regarding homosexual sex slaves and multiple torture-murders made the killing of Corll insignificant by comparison.

When police vehicles screamed to a halt at Corll's neat, white frame home, three shaken teenagers greeted them. According to Henley, another youth, and a 15-year-old girl, Corll had lured them to a party with promises of drugs. Instead, he gave them paint or glue to sniff, after which they passed out. Henley claimed that he regained consciousness just as Corll handcuffed him. The other two teenagers had been bound with chains, nude and spread-eagled, to heavy sheets of plywood. Recognizing the danger, Henley said, he managed to grab a gun and shoot Corll. The dead man had been drilled six times with a .22-caliber pistol.

Skeptical detectives grilled Henley and his two cohorts. Gradually, the officers learned of mind-boggling homosexual parties that ended in the death of several teenage male guests.

Dean Corll, they discovered, had grown up in the area and was a quiet, respected kid who helped his mother in her candy store, her sole source of income to raise three children. Originally from Fort Wayne, Indiana, Corll returned there in 1960 to assist his elderly grandmother, but still sent money to his mother as well. Drafted in 1964, he spent nearly one year with an unblemished record in the Army before obtaining a hardship discharge to help his family. Slim, handsome, and neatly dressed, he resumed civilian life by working in his mother's candy business, where he became known as the "Candy Man" in recognition of his generously handing out sweets to local kids. When she sold the business, he took a job as an electrician with a major utility company. Corll, remaining a bachelor, frequently moved his residence.

The dark side of his life, according to Wayne Henley, began in 1970, when Corll started a pattern of luring boys from 13 to 19 into his home for the purpose of homosexual rape, torture, and murder. He reportedly gave them airplane glue to sniff, then shackled the victims while they were unconscious. Wayne Henley met him in 1971, and moved in. Thereafter, Henley said, Corll paid him to lure teenagers with promises of drugs.

According to Henley, after the victims had been chained to specially designed plywood boards, Corll would sodomize and torture them, sometimes sexually mutilating them. Afterward, Corll would strangle the boys or shoot them.

As the ghastly tale unfolded, police asked where the bodies were. Henley led investigators to a boat shed in the southwest sector of Houston. Records revealed that Corll had leased the structure since November 1970. A crew of jail trustees, wielding spades, probed the dirt floor and began turning up the decomposing remains of young bodies wrapped in sheets of plastic.

Henley acknowledged witnessing the victims' murders, but vehemently denied participating in the killings. He named several of the boys, some of whom he'd known since high school. Another alleged accomplice, named by Henley, came under police scrutiny. When they found him, he and Henley led the searchers to more burial sites, some of them on beaches of Sam Rayburn Lake and High Island.

Over the next few days, the police uncovered the remains of 27 adolescent boys, all strangled or shot to death. In Henley's initial statement, he said, "In all, I guess there were between 25 and 30 boys killed and they were buried in three different places."

As the police inquiry intensified, Wayne Henley's role slowly changed from innocent bystander, to a witness of serial murder, to procurer, and finally to a reluctant helper in the killings. At last he confessed that he had participated in several of the murders, but continued to insist that Dean Corll tortured, sexually abused, and killed most of the victims.

Corll's death at the hands of Wayne Henley left a plethora of unanswered questions. Corll's mother defended his reputation, and thought the two young henchmen played a much larger part in the murders than was ever revealed. In July 1974, a jury found Henley guilty of multiple murders and a judge sentenced him to serve six 99-year terms in prison.

Horoscope for Dean Arnold Corll
Born December 24, 1939, 8:45 P.M. CST, Fort Wayne, Indiana
Source: The Man with the Candy, by Jack Olsen, p. 278

The "Candy Man" started by giving treats to toddlers and wound up luring teenage boys with the promise of drugs. His eighth house of death signals the violence and excessiveness that characterized Dean Corll's cruel sexual bondage, torture, and murder of no fewer than 27 adolescent boys.

Bloody Mars occupies Corll's eighth house, turning it into a gruesome fortress of violence. Jupiter, the planet of excesses, sits shoulder to shoulder with Mars in the same house. In its usual role of advocating violence, the Mars influence encouraged Corll to chain his captives to plywood sheets for the purpose of sexually abusing them. Jupiter gratuitously opened the floodgates to assure plenty of victims. Corll's birth sign, Capricorn, is associated with the slogan "I use." Those two words became grimly appropriate in view of Corll's use of a young henchman to help locate and persuade teenage boys to enter his lethal web. "I use" takes an even darker meaning in view of Corll's subsequent exploitation of the victims for hideous sexual purposes.

As bait, the accomplice promised that Corll would provide plenty of drugs. Drugs are associated with Neptune, which also rules money, deception, and liars. The pledge of free-flowing cocaine and marijuana was never kept. Instead, Corll offered cheap airplane glue to be sniffed. These disagreeable traits of Neptune were activated in Corll's life as a result of that planet's negative alignment in opposition to Mars and Jupiter. So Corll's promises to pay the accomplice were lies as well, since Neptune resides in the second house of money. Corll's employment of the youthful helper is seen by Venus's placement in the selfish and predatory sign of Capricorn. Venus occupies the sixth house of employees, in a negative aspect to Saturn, the planet of schemes and plots.

Corll's residence became a prison, a place of torture, and an execution chamber for his captives. The fourth house of his chart, which rules the home, is jointly governed by Mars and Pluto. Mars, as mentioned earlier, occupies Corll's eighth house of death. At the same time, the red planet's influence over his residence fills it with gory violence. Pluto brings compulsive sex and torture into the equation. The planet actually occupying the fourth house is Mercury, which governs Corll's conscious mind. Aligned in direct opposition to Mercury is the Moon. This worst possible aspect sets up affliction of Corll's thinking process, undermining it with dangerous instability. Two mental planets opposing each other suggests the possibility of insanity. Since the Moon also rules Corll's twelfth house of self-destruction, his twisted thinking set him on the path to his own death.

In his youth, Corll was close to his mother. The tenth house, ruling mother, is ruled by Taurus, his midheaven. Since Taurus is governed by Venus, the planet of love and affection, a close bond existed between mother and son. When Corll finally left her and the candy store, he became an electrician. His Taurus midheaven, representing his career, is abutted by Uranus, the ruler of electricity.

The Sun, Corll's strongest planet, represents his ego and resides in the fifth house of sex. He expressed his domination and control through sexual manipulation for his own twisted pleasure. His Sun also rules his Leo ascendant. This close connection between Corll's personality and sexuality is significant as his sexual interests turned into torture and murder. Jupiter is the other ruler of his fifth house of sex and resides in his eighth house of death. This relationship ties sex and death together in his mind.

Mars, ruler of guns, reared its violent head again from the occupancy of Corll's eighth house of death. Corll's own death came from a handgun wielded by his young accomplice, who used it to end his crime partner's life.

AQUARIUS

Contradictions abound in the Aquarius makeup. One of the first spree killers in contemporary American history, Howard Unruh, was born an Aquarius. When dealing with Aquarians born under negatively aligned planets, a good rule of thumb is to expect the unexpected.

Howard Unruh

Thursday, January 20, 1921, 11:00 P.M.
Camden, New Jersey • Time Zone: 05:00 (EST)
Longitude 075° W 07' 12" • Latitude 39° N 55' 33"
Placidus Houses • Tropical Zodiac

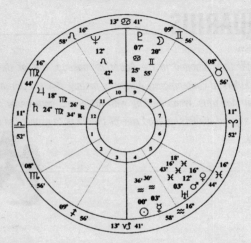

"**M**ass murderer" has become a standard category in describing various types of homicides. This brand of murder is often associated with the names Charles Whitman, James Huberty, and George Hennard (who killed 22 victims and wounded 23 at a Texas Luby's Cafeteria in 1991.) The bloody outbursts of sudden violence in which numerous innocent victims die has been attributed to the increasing societal pressures that seem to have compounded since the revolutionary decade of the 1960s. However, one of the first major mass murders in the United States took place in 1949, perpetrated by a man who had witnessed mindless killing as a combat soldier in World War II. Four years after that conflagration ended, Howard Unruh conducted his own private war by coldly shooting thirteen men, women, and children to death.

Unruh was born in Camden, New Jersey, in 1921. The quiet, introspective boy grew up in the Lutheran faith and spent a great deal of time studying the Bible. As he physically matured to a slender 6 feet, 2 inches, with blue eyes and brown hair, he re-

mained shy and incommunicative, especially with girls. Some
regarded his full lips, upturned nose, high cheekbones, and
slightly tilted eyes as handsome, but his colorless personality
kept him from bonding to anyone.

Not long after completing high school, Unruh faced the same
quandary encountered by every healthy young man in America:
enlist or wait for the military draft. World War II loomed on the
horizon, and all branches of the service were recruiting heavily.
Unruh went into the Army, and while other young men sought
pleasure in off-duty hours, he stayed in the barracks to read his
Bible. Introduced to guns, he became fascinated with them, and
dedicated an extraordinary amount of time practicing, polishing,
and worshiping firearms with the same zeal he'd applied to scrip-
ture study. Trained as a machine gunner, Unruh fought with a
tank battalion through the Italian campaign and in France. During
the Battle of the Bulge, he was with General George S. Patton's
armored division when they broke through just after Christmas
1944 to relieve encircled troops at Bastogne, Belgium. Destroying the enemy became routine for Howard Unruh, and he seemed
to adapt well to the task—so well that he kept meticulous records
of each German soldier he killed, including the exact date and
time. When he could, he noted the fallen man's description. Unruh's skills as a warrior earned him several decorations.

At the war's end, Unruh returned home and used the G.I. bill
to attend Temple University in Philadelphia. His goal, he said,
was to become a pharmacist. During a separate Bible study class,
he met a young woman and started dating for the first time in
his life. Both the romance and the college pursuits soon ended,
after which Unruh moved back into his parents' Camden home.
Bitter, tortured by internalized anger, and growing more paranoid
about the way acquaintances treated him, Unruh became even
more reclusive. In the same manner that he had kept personal
written records of his combat kills, he began entering in a private
journal his grievances against neighbors. Anyone who dared vi-
olate Unruh's code of insult or mistreatment that inflamed his
hypersensitive mind became a diary entry, no matter how minor
the infraction. When not scribbling his list of offenses, Unruh
practiced target skills with his beloved collection of guns. In the
basement of his parents' home, he honed an already high level
of marksmanship.

To keep his growing need for privacy intact, Unruh, now 28,

built a high fence around the tiny backyard and installed a tall gate he designed and crafted himself. That gate became the catalyst that changed his life forever and drove him to end thirteen other lives. When he came home in the early morning of September 5, 1949, Unruh glared in angry disbelief at the open gap in the fence where his gate had been. Someone had stolen it. It was the final straw in the huge volume of insults Unruh thought he had endured from people in the vicinity. Now, it was time to seek retribution.

Unruh dressed up in his best suit, complete with bow tie, then stuffed two handguns in his waistband, one of them being a 9-mm German Luger left over from the war. As soon as he sat down opposite his mother at the breakfast table, she sensed from his expression that something was wrong and felt a cold rush of fear. When Unruh rose and lifted his fist high, grasping some metal object she couldn't identify, the woman realized he meant to hurt or kill her, and fled screaming to a neighbor's home.

Having failed to dispatch his first planned victim, Unruh rushed outside and headed for a shoe repair shop down the block. He stepped inside where cobbler John Pilarchik, whom Unruh had known for years, labored over his workbench. The angry gunman fired his Luger twice, instantly killing Pilarchik, then stalked outside again. Just a few steps away, Unruh entered a barber shop where another lifelong acquaintance, Clark Hoover, snipped away at the hair of 6-year-old Orris Smith. In a calm voice, Unruh addressed the barber. "I've got something for you, Clarkie," he said and aimed the Luger. Smith lunged in front of the child in a protective stance, but too late. Unruh squeezed off a shot that drilled into the boy's head. Without hesitating, the gunman pumped two more fatal slugs into Hoover. Unruh walked out, oblivious to horrified screams from the boy's mother and sister.

The owner of a corner drugstore, Maurice Cohen, topped Unruh's list of hated enemies. Mr. Cohen's wife, Rose, had recently yelled at Unruh for taking a shortcut across her backyard, near the Unruh home. In Unruh's fevered mind, that insult could be avenged only by killing the transgressor.

At the entrance to the drugstore, Unruh's insurance agent, James Hutton, just happened to be exiting as Unruh arrived. The friendly agent nodded at his longtime client and uttered a courteous greeting. Unruh returned it with a pair of blasts from his pistol. Hutton dropped to the sidewalk, mortally wounded. From inside the store, Maurice Cohen had seen everything. He raced upstairs to the residential apartment hoping to protect his mother, wife, and son.

In hot pursuit, Unruh loped up the stairs and heard noises from inside a closet. The pistol belched twice, sending lead through the closet door. Unruh opened it and watched Rose Cohen slump to the floor. Pressing the weapon close, he ended her groaning with a bullet to the brain. In an adjacent room, Unruh found the Cohen matriarch, Minnie, desperately trying to telephone for help. Another lethal slug put an end to her pleas.

Still searching for his original target, Maurice Cohen, Unruh glanced through a window and saw his prey scrambling across a neighboring roof. Holding his pistol in a military grip, Unruh aimed, fired, and caught Cohen in the back. Wounded but still breathing, Cohen lost his grip, slid down the slope, and plunged to the sidewalk. Unruh's next shot hit Cohen in the head. The body count reached seven. The only survivor in the drugstore massacre was the 13-year-old son, Charles Cohen.

Outside again, Unruh spotted a man leaning over the body of the insurance agent, and executed him as well. Continuing his deadly stroll, Unruh reached an intersection where three occupants of a car waited at a traffic signal. Unruh approached, pointed his pistol into the open window, and killed the female driver; her son, age 10, and her elderly mother, who sat in the backseat. Within ten minutes, Unruh had killed eleven people.

He walked another block, and fired at a truck driver climbing down from his cab. This time, the shot just wounded the victim's leg, and Unruh didn't follow up. Instead, he circled back toward his home, but stopped and attempted to enter a grocery market next to the cobbler's shop. But the grocer had locked up in panic. In movies, one gunshot always disables locks, but Unruh's bullets had no effect, so he moved on to a tailor's shop. The proprietor's wife, who had heard the earlier explosions, dropped to her knees and begged, "Oh my God, don't." Without hesitation, Unruh killed her.

A few doors away, Unruh caught sight of some motion out of the corner of his eye, and turned toward it. Two-year-old Tommy Hamilton stood in the safety of his home, looking out a window. Unruh casually lifted the pistol again. Amid the sounds of a popping handgun and shattering glass, the toddler fell dead. Victim number thirteen ended the incredible slaughter.

En route home, Unruh wounded a mother and her boy, but took no more lives. Inside his house, Unruh realized that a battalion of police busily surrounded the property. The phone rang. Expecting to hear an officer demand surrender, Unruh listened as a local newspaper editor said, "I'm a friend. I want to know what they're doing to you."

"Well, they haven't done much to me yet," Unruh replied, his voice remarkably calm. "But I'm doing plenty to them."

"How many have you killed?"

"I don't know yet. I haven't counted 'em, but it looks like a pretty good score."

"Why are you killing people, Howard?"

Unruh paused a few moments before answering. "I don't know. I can't answer that yet. I'm too busy. I'll have to talk to you later." Unruh carefully recradled the phone.

When a tear gas bomb smashed through Unruh's window and bullets smacked into the walls, he decided to surrender. With hands raised, he marched outside and faced 50 gun-wielding cops. One of the uniformed officers snapped cuffs on the placid killer and barked, "What's the matter with you? Are you a psycho?"

In the same calm voice he'd used during his twelve-minute killing spree, Unruh thoughtfully replied, "I'm no psycho. I have a good mind."

Psychiatric experts disagreed. During a battery of tests administered on Unruh, in which he said he would have killed many more if he'd had enough ammunition, the doctors found that Unruh was suffering from dementia praecox aggravated by catatonic paranoia. According to the 1949 understanding of mental instability, Howard Unruh fit the definition of incurable insanity. No trial was necessary. He was committed to the New Jersey State Mental Hospital for the remainder of his life.

Horoscope for Howard Unruh
Born January 20, 1921, 11:00 P.M. EST, Camden, New Jersey
Source: Birth certificate

Without a doubt, Howard Unruh suffered crippling delusions and a host of mental disorders that drove him to the cold-blooded slaughter of thirteen innocent victims. This dementia is insinuated by the powerful presence of the Sun and its juxtaposition with other planets in Unruh's chart. Unfortunately for the combat veteran, his Sun is aligned directly opposite Neptune, resulting in the worst possible positioning of these two planets in relation to one another. Since the Sun represents the ego and ability to function as a mature individual, while Neptune rules delusions and unreality, this dangerous arrangement created in Unruh the potential for serious behavioral problems. It not only indicated that he would be frustrated by failure to reach illusive goals, but also signaled an alarming probability of mental confusion. The residence of Unruh's Sun in Aquarius, the sign of eccentricity, created an additional powder keg of danger. Combined, these forces clearly suggested that this troubled individual might explode in reaction to societal impositions or restrictions.

More fuel was added to this volatile mix by Mercury, the planet of habitual thinking, which appeared in Aquarius next to the Sun. Strong negative influences created by the Sun and Mercury opposing Neptune made Unruh's habitual thinking process bizarre and quirky while leading to his obsessive need to be a recluse.

The Sun also rules Unruh's eleventh house of friends and acquaintances through Leo on the cusp. Thus, people he knew in his neighborhood became the focal point in Unruh's delusions of victimization, then later became his targets for vengeance.

Mars, planet of war, soldiers, violence, and guns, next came into play in Unruh's destiny. His Mars in Pisces belligerently holds its position in close proximity to Uranus, planet of the unexpected. This conjunction explains Unruh's sudden, unanticipated binge of violent murder with the use of his precious firearms. He collected guns and became an expert in their use, a pattern that can be seen by the appearance of Mars and Pisces in Unruh's fifth house of hobbies and pursuits of pleasure. Unruh's fascination with weapons began during his military experiences as a World War II soldier, which certainly involved Martian war and violence. Three planets in the sign of Pisces indicate a deep need for solitude. Unruh demonstrated this by his reclusiveness during the war, avoiding socialization in order to read his Bible. Later, in combat, he also worked alone.

Another influence over Unruh's military service, which is ruled by the sixth house, was Jupiter in Virgo. A characteristic of this configuration is the tendency for petty details to become extremely important to the individual, thus explaining Unruh's odd habit of taking meticulous notes about each enemy soldier he killed. Back in civilian life, he manifested this urge by keeping a journal in which he detailed neighbors' transgressions against his privacy and dignity. Recording these imagined slights, and keeping them secret, is also reflective of Unruh's twelfth house of secrets and undoing. Saturn rules depression and restrictions, both of which were integral parts of Unruh's personality.

World War II may have provided the seed for Unruh's fascination with death. Even so, another explanation exists in the control of Venus over his eighth house of death through Taurus on the cusp. Venus sets up the deep interest while Taurus provides the intensity, which eventually led to Unruh dealing out death with a stunning lack of remorse.

Unruh's home life after the war came under the influence of Saturn, through Capricorn on the cusp, governing his fourth house of home and family. Saturn's power points to a strict, inflexible domestic environment. Unruh is a classic example of a reclusive personality who saw his home as a fortress against outside intrusion, which he reinforced by building a high fence to prevent intruders from invading his privacy. When someone violated his territory by removing the gate, the power of Mars and Uranus took over, and he erupted into a lethal orgy of revenge.

Finally, Mercury made another entry into Unruh's life with its rulership of his twelfth house of prisons and confinement. Mercury controls the individual's mental state. Experts declared Unruh to be legally insane, which kept him from being tried for mass murder. Saturn, the planet of long-range restrictions, also governs Unruh's twelfth house. In view of this combination, it makes sense that Howard Unruh was placed in an institution for the criminally insane to be permanently restricted from re-entering society.

Warren James Bland

Thursday, January 21, 1937, 11:40 A.M.
Los Angeles, California • Time Zone: 08:00 (PST)
Longitude 118° W 14' 34" • Latitude 34° N 03' 08"
Placidus Houses • Tropical Zodiac

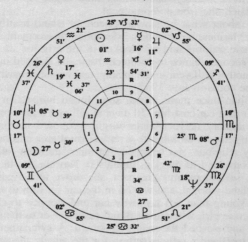

Most killers do not significantly change their pattern of crime over the years, but Warren Bland, in his depraved lifetime, graduated from raping women to sexually assaulting a boy, age 11, and finally to molesting, torturing, and murdering a 7-year-old girl. Long prison sentences and extensive psychological treatment abjectly failed to modify his behavior. By the time Bland, at age 54, faced charges for murdering little Phoebe Ho, he had been convicted thirteen times and spent 30 of the previous 33 years behind bars. His is the story of a revolving-door prison system in which a manipulative convict repeatedly convinced officials that he deserved another chance at freedom.

Born in Los Angeles on January 21, 1937, Bland grew up in a normal, reasonably affluent household. His father passed away suddenly when Bland was 12, leaving him with no male role model. Already 6 feet tall by that age, the youth lost an already mild interest in school, preferring to tinker with anything mechanical. Hot rods and motorcycles fascinated him, and his first tattoo inked the word *Gearbox* on his right shoulder. Girls grabbed his attention at 17, and he started dating a 15-year-old classmate. He dropped out of school in his senior year, and married his reluctant young sweetheart in July 1955. On their wedding night, he brutally raped the terrified virgin. Less than three months later, she won an annulment.

Angry about what he saw as rejection, Bland hastily joined the U.S. Marines, but found the discipline unacceptable. He deserted basic training and was locked in the brig for six months. Given a second chance to complete basic, he skipped out again, served another half year in the lockup, and was summarily kicked out of the corps in July 1957.

A civilian once more, Bland soon found himself in trouble. The theft of a car cost him 30 days in jail and a long probation. He met another naive teenage virgin, proposed marriage, and when she refused, took her to a remote rural area and raped her. Devoutly religious, she believed that marriage must follow sex, so she consented to quickie nuptials in Nevada. In the autumn of 1958, several months pregnant, she drove into a gas station where Bland worked, and waited in the car for him to finish his shift. A young man left a nearby bar and stopped to chat with the attractive girl, whereupon Bland rushed over to them, pulled a knife, and slashed the man's abdomen. A sympathetic judge listened to Bland's rationalization for the attack, then foolishly allowed him to remain out of jail.

Bland's wife tolerated his savage treatment of her, but when she saw him mistreating their baby daughter, she fled with the child and filed for divorce. In December 1958 and January 1959, a series of similar rapes took place in the Long Beach area, and eyewitness accounts linked them to Warren Bland, who lived nearby. He pleaded not guilty by reason of insanity, which led to extensive psychiatric examinations ordered by liberal courts. Bland learned the right things to say, even though some of his inconsistent stories sounded preposterous. He lied, twisted facts, and successfully manipulated the shrinks, who recommended hospitalization for treatment. Instead of hard prison time, Bland spent several years in Atascadero State Hospital, and was granted freedom in September 1967.

Within a year, another string of rapes in Long Beach included a ruthless attack on a girl, age 15, who nearly bled to death from having her throat slit. Another potential victim escaped, called the police, and gave a detailed description of her assailant and his car. Patrol officers pulled Warren Bland over a short time afterward. All of the violated women attended lineups and identified the 6-foot man, about 20, with receding hair. In April 1969, a judge handed Bland concurrent indeterminate sentences, which would allow parole within a few years. The jailwise con put on his best behavior again, impressing officials with his rehabilitation, and marched out of Folsom Prison in August 1975.

This time, Bland gave a ride to a young mother who carried an infant and was accompanied by her daughter, age 11. After sexually fondling the woman at knifepoint, he pushed her and the baby out of his car, and drove off with the young girl. Parked inside a garage, and threatening to cut her throat, Bland forced the child to perform oral sex, tried to rape her, then tortured her by clipping clothespins and a medical hemostat on her private parts. He later dumped her, alone and frightened, on a city street.

The horrified mother and her traumatized daughter, reunited in a hospital, were able to pick out Bland's photo from an album of sexual predators. Suspected in other rapes as well, Bland was convicted and imprisoned once again. Resorting to his exemplary conduct, he talked officials into allowing him conjugal visits with a woman he called his wife. Using prison-learned skill with a typewriter, Bland wormed his way into a clerk-typist job working for a top official. In the spring of 1980, he tasted freedom again.

It lasted six months. Five days after Christmas, Bland courteously offered a ride to a young pedestrian. The boy, only 11, made the mistake of accepting. It cost the child a horrifying session of forced sex and torture. But he kept his wits about him enough to memorize details about his captor and the interior of the van in which he endured the most degrading moments of his life. Police watched for the vehicle, and found it four weeks later. Warren Bland faced a sentence of nine more years. Child molesters rank low in the esteem of fellow convicts, and Bland suffered a gaping wound to his neck when a prisoner slashed him. By January 1986, the purple scar had healed, and Bland left prison under parole.

Earning his living as a house painter, Bland seemed to have finally found the road to a decent life. But when Phoebe Ho, the 7-year-old daughter of Chinese immigrants, vanished on her way to school in South Pasadena a week before Christmas, investigators soon zeroed in on the man with an appalling record of sexual crimes. Residents of Southern California reeled in shock when a transient, hunting for aluminum cans, stumbled on the child's body in rural Riverside County. A pathologist concluded that little Phoebe had been tightly bound with wrist and ankle restraints that dug into the flesh, then had been starved, tortured, and repeatedly injured by sexual penetration for nearly a week before finally being killed. The hideous brutality even stunned investigators, who promised themselves that this crime would not go unpunished.

Hair and fibers on the pitifully ravaged child's body gradually pointed to Warren Bland. He felt the heat, stole a car, and fled 100 miles south to San Diego, where he dyed his thinning hair and worked in a fast-food restaurant. Bland also came into possession of valuables taken from an elderly woman he'd visited a few days before she was found murdered in her apartment. He made the mistake of writing to an ex-cellmate, who was arrested a short time later. The letter led authorities directly to Bland. A San Diego officer staked out the mail drop, saw Bland, and dropped him with single shot when the fugitive tried to run. Near death, Bland recuperated in a hospital jail ward.

A federal court stepped in and convicted Bland of carrying a gun while on parole, and sentenced him to life. But the Riverside police weren't satisfied. The county tried him for the kidnap-rape-murder of Phoebe Ho in January 1993. Bland presented a story in which an ex-prison buddy and his girlfriend captured the child and later picked up Bland. He claimed he was nothing but a passenger when the couple took Phoebe to a remote empty building. Bland said he watched but never participated in the torture and murder. A skeptical jury, recognizing Bland's long history of lies, convicted him and recommended the death penalty. A judge concurred, and sentenced the career criminal to die at San Quentin.

California legislators, sickened by Warren Bland's frequent return to freedom after repetitive acts of violent rape, enacted a law that provides for notifying local law enforcement when repeat sex offenders are released into a community. As Bland sits on Death Row, he is hated by other sexual predators who can never again anonymously blend into neighborhoods to search for more victims.

Horoscope for Warren James Bland
Born January 21, 1937, 11:40 A.M. PST, Los Angeles, California
Source: Birth certificate

The cruelty and cold detachment of Warren Bland, in his commission of a long series of rapes and finally at least one brutal murder, infuriated the general public and galvanized police with pledges to put him behind bars. One investigator described him as "disturbingly icy." Bland's chart offers ominous warnings of his dangerous potential, particularly by the frightening alignment of Mars. Not only is this violent planet found in the sadistic sign of Scorpio, but it also sounds a chilling alarm by sitting in direct opposition to Bland's Taurus ascendant. The fiery mix of savage sexuality from Scorpio, cruel violence from Mars, and the Taurus trait of stubborn refusal to change sets up disastrous possibilities. Mars threatens potential rape, shooting, stabbing, and beating, all of which Bland actually did inflict on various victims. Uranus, occupying the twelfth house of secrets, and lodged in close proximity to the ascendant, adds unpredictability. So Bland's astrological influences paved the way for an unexpected eruption of cruelty, assaults, rape, and murder.

Even though the signs pointed to such possibilities, a big question remained. Would Bland's psyche push him over the precipice into a vortex of rape and murder, or would it demand that he control himself and reject criminal impulses, as most people do?

The answer lay in the placement of Bland's Sun. If ego is an important element in the psyche, trouble looms on the horizon. Bland's Sun, ruler of his ego, is the strongest planet in his chart. Its placement in Aquarius, which contributes eccentricity, suggests an ego the size of a ship, with a loose cannon rolling around on the deck. Not only would he be a dominating and controlling individual, but his sadistic obsessions would be uncontrollable, since his Sun opposes Pluto, the ruler of obsessions and compulsions. The Sun's occupation of the tenth house, residence of status and reputation, creates in Bland the self-important sense that he is superior to everyone around him in intelligence, skill, power, and even sex.

Bland's fifth house of sex is occupied by Neptune, which sits in dangerous opposition to Saturn. This juxtaposition indicates that obsessive fantasies of hate and resentment festered deep inside him. Initially, his compulsive sexual needs, laced with sadistic urges, focused on young women. Unfortunately, the fifth house is also the domain of children, as well as sex. Bland's raging lust eventually focused on helpless youngsters.

The Moon, representing women, resides in his first house of personality, temperament, and disposition. So, when his Martian cruelty and Scorpio lust demanded satisfaction, Bland hunted women to rape. But when the Neptune-Saturn influence on his house of sex and children took control, Bland targeted little girls, and even a male child. At last, his inner demons drove him to the ultimate crime—murder—and little Phoebe Ho suffered horribly before her life ended.

Death is an eighth-house matter. Jupiter in Capricorn rules Bland's eighth house, indicating the cold-blooded nature of his crimes, the volume of rapes he committed, and the merciless killing for which he faced murder charges.

The ninth house, ruling courts and the justice system, is occupied by Jupiter and Mercury. Jupiter brought an element of luck in Bland's early dealings with the courts, as reflected by short sentences and early releases. Mercury, ruler of speech, indicates his ability to verbally manipulate officials and psychiatrists. Both planets are in Capricorn, a sign that involves craftiness and the law. Bland's knowledge of the law and justice system, as it related to him, was exceptional. As Capricorn's phrase is "I use," he often used his knowledge to circumvent justice. But his luck and cunning finally evaporated when a jury convicted him.

His twelfth house, ruler of prisons, is the abode of Uranus, which is aligned negatively with Mars. The red planet's involvement with guns and violence influenced Bland's capture, in view of the nearly fatal gunshot wound he received. He survived only to receive the death penalty. All together, the influence of three planets casts menacing shadows over the twelfth house. Neptune relates to sex and children. Mars introduces rape and cruelty. And Jupiter is the planet of death. The combination spells doom for Warren Bland.

PISCES

Pisces' criminals can be as slippery as their namesake, the fish, wriggling away from the grasp of justice with frightening ease. Ironically, Pisces natives Randy Kraft, Mike DeBardeleben, and Sirhan Sirhan share birthdates of March 19, all within five years. The shy, sensitive personalities seen in many of these killers mask the violence hidden underneath.

Richard Ramirez

Sunday, February 28, 1960, 2:07 A.M.
El Paso, Texas • Time Zone: 07:00 (MST)
Longitude 106° W 29' 11" • Latitude 31° N 45' 31"
Placidus Houses • Tropical Zodiac

T he "Night Stalker" sent waves of terror across Los Angeles
County during the hot summer of 1985. Media coverage of
his cruel and bizarre treatment of his victims, performed upon
them inside their own homes, resulted in skyrocketing sales of
locks, burglar alarms, and guns. In every neighborhood of southern California, eyes were riveted to television news reports describing the horror of his crimes, and people prayed for the killer
to be apprehended. Meanwhile, Richard Ramirez, 25, gloated as
he lay in a filthy skid row flophouse bed, certain that his belief
in devil worship protected him. The fame he had always craved
was his at last, and he hoped that it pleased his master, Satan.

Born in El Paso, Texas, on February 28, 1960, the last of five
children, Ramirez had black curly hair, slightly tilted dark eyes,
prominently high cheekbones, and a wide mouth with full lips.
His temperamental father and gentle mother worked long, back-
breaking hours to support the large family. But the boy cringed
whenever his father mercilessly beat one of his children. In a
household of four boys and one girl, Richard learned quickly to

defend himself, and was not afraid of anyone or anything—except his father.

Diagnosed with epilepsy at age 5, Richard suffered several seizures as a child. He performed satisfactorily in school until he reached grade seven; then his marks took a nosedive. He preferred to play alone and avoid social contact with everyone except an adult cousin who had returned from combat in Vietnam. The veteran entertained young Richard with stories of raping Vietcong women, and showed him what appeared to be shrunken heads he'd brought home. The grotesque tales, accompanied by chilling photographs, became a source of sexual excitement for Ramirez.

In the spring of 1973, Richard visited his veteran cousin to hear more wild tales and smoke some pot. The man's wife, unhappy with the ex-soldier's chronic unemployment, began nagging him. In full view of young Ramirez, the hotheaded cousin raised a .38-caliber handgun and shot his wife to death. Stunned, Ramirez could only nod when the killer ordered him never to snitch about what he had witnessed. After that episode, Ramirez began fantasizing about death and giving thought to Satanism. A few months later, he visited an older brother in Los Angeles. Fast life in the city fascinated the young teenager, especially the access to pornography and prostitutes that it afforded, and he longed to return as soon as possible.

Back in El Paso, ongoing conflict with his father led Ramirez to live with his sister and her husband. The brother-in-law reportedly introduced Ramirez to the excitement of slipping into backyards at night to peep at women. Having graduated from marijuana to LSD and heroin, Ramirez needed money to buy drugs. He followed the path of least resistance—theft and burglary—and became an expert at it.

In his first job at a large motel, Ramirez began using a passkey to enter rooms and take valuables. He also indulged in peeping at female guests. He finally worked up enough nerve to enter a room when he knew the woman was showering, and grabbed her as she stepped out of the bathroom. As he prepared to rape her, Ramirez's plans were suddenly interrupted when the woman's husband barged in. The furious spouse beat Ramirez soundly and called the police. At 15, he faced serious charges, but the couple chose not to press charges, so Ramirez emerged with nothing but a few scars.

Shortly after his eighteenth birthday, Ramirez returned to Los Angeles on a bus. Now over 6 feet tall, sinewy, and streetwise, he made a profession out of stealing cars, committing burglary, and selling dope. He acquired a copy of *The Satanic Bible,* listened incessantly to loud heavy metal music, and became a devoted servant of Satan. On the mean streets of L.A.'s skid row, he evolved into a mean, tough loner with the instability of nitro-glycerin.

The Night Stalker committed his first known murder on June 27, 1984, when he sneaked into the home of Jennie Vincow, 79, and decided not only to rob her, but to commit murder as well. While the woman still slept, he plunged a knife into her chest repeatedly, then slashed her throat with such rage that he nearly severed her head. Routine crimes followed for several months until he reached flash point again in March 1985. In Rosemead, he followed a young woman into her garage, demanded money, and fired a pistol at her. Miraculously, her upheld keys deflected the bullet. Thinking he had killed her, Ramirez entered the residence, found the woman's female roommate, and shot her to death. Still unsatisfied as he drove away, Ramirez followed a car driven by a young woman. When she stopped, demanding to know what he wanted, he fired two rounds, killing her instantly.

Within nine days, Ramirez attacked again. After creeping into the home of a middle-aged couple, he aimed a bullet at the forehead of the sleeping man. The victim's startled wife attempted to protect herself with a shotgun, but found it unloaded. Furious, Ramirez shot her, raped her, and gouged her eyes out. When he left, he took the gruesome trophies with him.

Over the next six months, Ramirez repeated the pattern, entering homes, killing the male residents, and raping the females. In some cases, he allowed the women to live. Several times, he deliberately left his trademark, a pentagram drawn with lipstick on the victim's body or on a wall. His weapons varied from handguns to knives, hammers, a machete, or any other instrument available to bludgeon, stab, or garrote the victims. In one case, while raping the mother of an infant, he forced her to let him drink milk from her breasts.

Ramirez usually gained entry through a window or sliding glass door, which were often left open by the occupants due to the sweltering hot summer. Investigators soon realized the killings fit a pattern. They found identical shoeprints at many of the ·

crime scenes. Surviving witnesses described the intruder, pointing out his large, cruel dark eyes, bad teeth, height, and protruding cheekbones. Composite drawings appeared frequently on the news.

Feeling the heat, Ramirez temporarily moved his base of operations to San Francisco, where he killed a middle-aged Chinese couple. They mayor of that city angered investigators by holding a press conference and revealing information about the common thread of shoeprints. Ramirez hadn't known of the prints he'd left, and he promptly walked onto the Golden Gate Bridge, dropped the incriminating shoes in the bay, then returned to Southern California.

While Ramirez raided a Mission Viejo home, deep in Orange County, an observant youth outside noted the license number of the killer's orange Toyota. Ramirez had felt confident that Satan protected him, but his extraordinary luck at evading capture began crumbling. An informant told police about the strange behavior of a tall Hispanic named "Rick," and identified the fence to whom Rick sold the loot from victims' homes. When police found the Toyota in a parking lot, they lifted a fingerprint. The brand-new state computer, called Cal ID, processed the fingerprint and regurgitated information about Richard Ramirez, along with a photo taken in a previous arrest.

The picture of a gaunt young man staring angrily at the camera hit the news waves immediately. On August 30, 1985, Ramirez walked out of a bus station and noticed that people seemed to be staring at him. A stack of newspapers caught his eye, and he quickly understood why. His face occupied several front pages. At that moment, a responsible citizen observed Ramirez and called the police.

Thinking he might be safe in a Mexican-American neighborhood, Ramirez ran as police sirens screamed nearby. Panicky, he tried to carjack an auto, but when the female driver screamed, several men wrestled Ramirez to the ground. Within moments, police arrived and snapped handcuffs on the Night Stalker.

In September 1988, a jury found Ramirez guilty of killing thirteen people: nine women and four men. Various police agencies suspected double that number of victims. The judge sentenced him to die at San Quentin. Ramirez hadn't helped his cause by flashing devil worship signs during the trial.

News watchers were puzzled over the next few years when

they heard that numerous attractive young women wrote to Ramirez to confess how they were attracted to him. One of the jurors in his trial even visited him and declared her love. Another love-smitten young woman, who spent as many hours as possible with Ramirez, finally married him.

Richard Ramirez arrived at San Quentin in November 1989. Over 500 men occupy the prison's section reserved for condemned convicts. Appeal to the state supreme court is automatic, but as with a majority of the men on Death Row, appeals for Ramirez, hadn't yet begun as of March 1999.

Horoscope for Richard Ramirez
Born February 28, 1960, 2:07 A.M. MST, El Paso, Texas
Source: Birth certificate

News media photographs of Richard Ramirez depicted pure evil in the shackled serial killer's repulsive grin. His reign of terror over Los Angeles terrified millions of residents, who collectively exhaled in relief when he was finally captured.

The evil his face reflected, and the ostentatious show of devil worship, was not a phony performance for photographers. Ramirez's ninth house of religion is not only the abode but also the place of worship for Pluto, the planetary ruler of Satanism. He really believed in his reverence to the underworld. Pluto, associated with obsession, is negatively aligned in opposition to the Sun, an aspect inflicting Ramirez with pathological, sadistic traits, including a compulsion to torture to death his pagan sacrifices.

His eighth house of death is occupied by Uranus, the planet of eccentricity. This planet's alignment in opposition to Venus saddles Ramirez with the negative traits of Uranus—irrational, erratic behavior. The murders he committed, involving mutilation and rape, were unpredictable and bizarre. Two other planets, the Moon and the Sun, also exert influence over the eighth house. The Moon, symbol of women, suggests that his primary targets were females, no matter what age or shape. But Ramirez also killed men, mostly because they were nothing to him but obstacles in the path to his real objective, raping the women. The Sun, representing men in his chart, sits in a dangerously negative alignment to Pluto, the planet of obsession and torture. This arrangement predisposes Ramirez to be brutally dominant and dictatorial over his victims. Without question, he dictated whether they lived or died.

While strongly influencing the eighth house, the Moon and Sun, accompanied by Mercury, occupy the third house of mental processes and short trips. The Moon's presence reveals that Ramirez spent a great deal of time thinking about women, and that his short trips throughout Southern California were to seek out female victims. The Sun, in a negative aspect to Pluto, suggests that his mental processes involved thoughts of torture and the obsessive desire to commit rape, then kill his victims. Mercury is the planet of mental thoughts. Combined with the mental traits intrinsic to the third house, the thought processes of Mercury are strongly reinforced, making the horror rooted in Ramirez's mind even more deadly.

The disturbing thoughts festering in Ramirez's head were filled with a desire for violent sex and death, heated to fever pitch by his drug usage. Neptune, the ruler of drugs, is in the sadistic sign of Scorpio. Another frighteningly negative alignment shows up in the relationship between Neptune and Mars, ruler of weapons, violence, and cruelty. The Martian effect of drugs lit up his brain like fireworks on the fourth of July.

Mars, by its abrasive rule of the fourth house of home and father, began its invasion on the psyche of Ramirez early in his life. Hostility and aggression, along with lethal weapons, are legacies of the violent planet, and these traits were liberally distributed among young Ramirez's family. Among the Martian weapons are guns and shooting, relating to the traumatic incident Ramirez experienced when he saw his sister-in-law shot to death.

Yet another appearance is made by Mars in its own residence, the second house of money and possessions. Both Mars and Venus, an odd couple, occupy the second house. In his quest for money, Ramirez started burglarizing homes. But the burglaries, under the influence of Mars, escalated to murder. Venus, not to be outdone, rules the fifth house of sex, so the two planets' presence allowed the crimes to take another twist. Ramirez's home invasions graduated from robbery, to rape, to murder.

After Ramirez's wild spree came to a crashing halt and he landed in jail, the Moon and Venus stepped in again. His mid-heaven, ruler of reputation, is in Libra, the sign associated with love and affection. The Moon, ruler of women, activated its power in his third house of communication by making Ramirez the recipient of letters from female admirers. The Venus influence turned the communication from a few of the smitten women into love. Ramirez married one his ardent admirers. Jupiter, in rulership of his twelfth house of prisons, exerted its beneficence by allowing the marriage.

The twelfth house of prisons is ruled by Sagittarius, the sign of good luck. Ramirez's luck has held so far by being locked up in California, where the death penalty is imposed so rarely. But the Martian influence in his chart will eventually win out, and the barbarous acts committed by this "Child of Satan" will send him to hell.

James Earl Ray

Saturday, March 10, 1928, 3:00 P.M.
Alton, Illinois • Time Zone: 06:00 (CST)
Longitude 090° W 11' 03" • Latitude 38° N 53' 26"
Placidus Houses • Tropical Zodiac

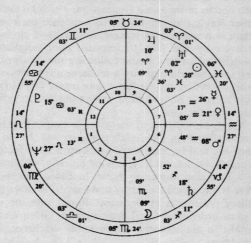

The murder of Dr. Martin Luther King, Jr., on April 4, 1968, is shrouded in controversy. Despite a confession by James Earl Ray, who admitted firing the fatal shot, only to later recant, vehement arguments still rage today.

In his restless pursuit of equality, King made a visit to Memphis, Tennessee, to organize a march of striking sanitation workers. While standing on the balcony of the Lorraine Motel with a group of supporters, he leaned over to speak to the Reverend Jesse Jackson. A single gunshot boomed, and King hurtled backward, his spinal cord ripped apart. Ironically, the peace advocate's death lit the fuse to a series of riots, violence, arson, and killing across the nation.

A photo snapped seconds after King fell would be branded into the world's memory. The image showed King lying face up on the balcony, with one man kneeling at his side and four other members of his entourage raising their arms, pointing to the apparent source of the shot. They had zeroed in on the window of a rooming house adjacent to a littered vacant lot across Mulberry Street.

James Earl Ray, 40, had rented a room on the building's second floor that same afternoon, using the name John Willard.

Ray's early life was a struggle from the very beginning. The first of nine children born to poverty-stricken parents, he experienced the depths of the Great Depression, which hit the country shortly after Ray's birth in 1928. His existence on a worn-out Illinois farm was marked by hunger, filth, ragged clothing, and rejection even by the family's equally poor neighbors. His mother sought solace in a bottle following the death of one of his sisters in a fire during Ray's tenth year. A schoolteacher added to his misery by calling Ray's appearance "repulsive." The only family member Ray admired was an uncle who worked the outer margins of the law.

Even though his IQ was in the average range, Ray had progressed no further than the eighth grade by age 16, so he quit school, left his family, and found work in a shoe factory. His destitute childhood scarred Ray, leaving him shy, withdrawn, and speaking with a slow stuttering drawl. In 1946, after the end of World War II, he joined the Army and learned to drive in a jeep as a military policeman in Germany. Bored with the duty, he ignored some orders and faced court-martial. Given a choice of three months in confinement or honorable discharge, Ray accepted discharge.

Back in Illinois in 1949, he found his family still mired in misery, so he moved north to Chicago. When a menial job there ended, he caught a freight train to Los Angeles, but soon landed in jail for a bungled burglary. A pattern of discontent kept Ray constantly on the move. Working temporary jobs, performing petty thefts on the side, he marginally survived the next few years and frequently returned to Chicago. Ray's clumsy botching of criminal efforts in the Windy City drew him a two-year stay in Illinois State Prison at Joliet.

Upon his release, he attempted to reunite with his family, but they'd scattered into gutters and jails across the state. Perhaps the least talented burglar in history, he was caught again after losing his driver's license at the crime scene and running right out of his shoes, which stuck in a muddy street. Waiting for trial, he fled and joined a pal in spending stolen U.S. postal money orders in several states. The federal rap for that crime cost him nearly three years at one of the county's toughest prisons, at Leavenworth, Kansas. Drifting again after his 1958 release, he roamed through the South, into Mexico, and back to Illinois. Accused of participating in a St. Louis robbery, Ray fled to Canada to hide, but soon returned to the place of his roots. Within a few months, he became a suspect in several supermarket armed robberies, all with accomplices. The incompetence of the thieves bordered on comedy. They made every goofy mistake possible. Once again, Ray found himself behind bars with more serious charges. Adding to the farce, Ray chose to defend himself at trial, even though he had confessed. The jury didn't laugh, at least out loud, but needed only minutes to find him guilty. Now regarded as a career criminal, Ray was slammed with a 20-year sentence.

Locked in prison during the first half of the 1960s, the decade of social upheaval, Ray remained a quiet, solitary loner. He worked at self-improvement and increased his vocabulary by extensive reading, but spent much of his time thinking about escape. One early attempt at scaling the wall sent him to solitary confinement for six months. By April 1967, he'd earned a move to a lower-security honor farm, where he leaped from a bakery truck and vanished.

Using an alias for employment, Ray saved a few bucks, obtained an old car, and lay low in East St. Louis. Later rumors suggested he heard whispers there, among outlaw cronies, of a hefty bounty on the head of Martin Luther King, Jr. Resorting to his old drifting habits, he inhabited the underworld shadows of Montreal, Canada, where he used the alias Ray S. Galt. It was there, Ray later claimed, that he met a man named Raoul who spoke with a Spanish accent. Raoul, Ray said, was actually responsible for killing Martin Luther King, Jr. Whether this mystery man ever truly existed is still debated by conspiracy theorists.

In Ray's recollections, he and Raoul transported contraband across the U.S.–Canadian border, and later over the Mexico–U.S. border. With the profits, Ray lived well in Mexico, but left for Los Angeles in November. Deciding to change his image and lifestyle, Ray hoped that plastic surgery might prevent recognition and recapture, so he had the tip of his nose altered. It did little to change his appearance. His goal, he said, was to resettle on the other side of the world.

During the next few months, in the early spring of 1968, according to investigation records, "Eric S. Galt," driving a white

Mustang, seemed to show up wherever King traveled.

On April 2, Ray said, he met Raoul near Memphis, and gave him a rifle he'd recently bought. As Galt, Ray checked into a Memphis motel on April 3, then, as John Willard, rented a room across Mulberry Street from the Lorraine Hotel on April 4.

Immediately after the shot that killed King, a man left the rooming house; dropped a bundle containing a scoped rifle, binoculars, and a bag filled with travel items; then drove away in a white Mustang. James Earl Ray's fingerprints were found on the rifle and binoculars.

Ray fled back to Canada, while police searched for someone named Eric S. Galt, the registered owner of a white Mustang abandoned in Atlanta. Within a few days, investigators realized that Galt was actually escaped convict James Earl Ray. But the fugitive had obtained a passport in the name of Ramon George Sneyd and had flown to London; then to Lisbon, Portugal; and back to London. Short of cash, he robbed a bank, netting a little over $200. Desperate, Ray made a run for Brussels, Belgium.

Meanwhile, Canadian sleuths, using photos of Ray, had identified the passport issued to Ramon Sneyd as being in the possession of Ray. At Heathrow airport, officials had been alerted. They detained Ray on June 8, just two months after King's murder.

Brought back to the United States, Ray faced trial for murdering King. Famed attorney Percy Foreman reportedly persuaded Ray to plead guilty. He complied and was sentenced to serve 99 years in prison. Ray soon recanted and appealed for a new trial. The U.S. Supreme Court twice turned him down. In 1977, Ray made good another prison escape, but was recaptured in a couple of days. He married while in prison in 1978.

Consistently denying that he shot Martin Luther King, Jr., Ray convinced the Congress to hold a special hearing. They decided that Ray had pulled the trigger, but probably in connection with a conspiracy.

As the years passed, Ray's health deteriorated while he continued his denials of murdering anyone. In 1998, new investigations revealed little. A test-firing of the rifle allegedly was inconclusive. The son of Martin Luther King, Jr., visited Ray in prison, came away convinced that Ray might not be guilty, and called for a new trial.

But it was too late. Suffering from liver disease, Ray waited for a possible transplant. He died on April 23, 1998, still surrounded with controversy.

Horoscope for James Earl Ray
Born March 10, 1928, 3:00 P.M. CST, Alton, Illinois
Source: Birth certificate

Death took James Earl Ray before a host of questions could be answered. Did he kill Dr. Martin Luther King Jr.? Ray's chart offers some possible answers.

Ray appeared to the world to be a slow-speaking hillbilly, but a man of considerable cunning may have been hidden under the facade. His eighth house of death is occupied by a weak Sun residing adjacent to Uranus, planet of eccentricity. The flagging Sun indicates a small ego, which is consistent with his outward personality of a bumbling, soft-spoken country boy. His confidence was undermined by eccentricity that sent him spiraling off in the wrong direction when attempting any endeavor. Because his Sun is in the sign of Pisces, planet of delusions and fantasies, Ray would tend to face away from reality in order to pursue unrealistic goals.

Ray's personality and temperament are matters of the first house, which is occupied by Neptune in Leo. The Neptune influence endowed Ray with a tendency to constantly change his stories, especially when discussing his crimes. Using Neptunian-bred deception, Ray probably invented the story in which he said the mysterious "Raoul" was the real assassin of Martin Luther King, Jr., although Ray may have had a real person in mind.

Weaving such half-truths became Ray's pattern. Leo governs his ascendant, which affects Ray's personality. With the Sun in rule of arrogant Leo, it became natural for Ray to believe he could fool anyone with a convincing lie. He developed this skill and became a cunning liar.

Many of Ray's problems were rooted in his miserable childhood. His fourth house of home and father provides residence to the Moon, ruler of emotions. Mars, while occupying the sixth house of police, co-rules the fourth house. So Ray's family life was a hotbed of trouble and a thorn in the side of law officers. The unfortunate mix is heated up by both the Moon and Pluto, the fourth house's other co-ruler, extending their reach to the twelfth house of prisons. With these alignments, Ray and several of his male family members were no strangers to prison cells.

Poverty in the Ray family motivated the generally petty crimes they committed. Ray's second house, governing money and material possessions, is quite weak. This supports the fact that neither Ray, his father, nor any of his brothers ever made much money through law breaking. Their main legacy turned out to be the scars left on Ray's emotions. The Moon rules emotions, but is negatively aligned with Mars, which liberally dosed his feelings with pain and heartbreak. He showed no ostensible signs of it, though, with one exception. Mercury, which rules speech, makes a powerful aspect to the Moon. Ray's speech was afflicted with chronic stuttering.

The wheel of Ray's chart is severely imbalanced by most of the planetary weight being accumulated on one side. This effect predisposed Ray to become the victim of circumstances.

One of the major planets occupying the chart's nearly empty side is compulsive Pluto in the twelfth house of prisons and self-undoing. Its contribution is an albatross around Ray's neck, dragging him in and out of prison all of his life.

After the assassination, Ray fled to Europe and came close to escaping permanently. Foreign countries are ninth-house matters. Jupiter in Aries dwells in Ray's ninth house. Aries dispenses initiative, and Ray made good use of it by adopting aliases and obtaining fake passports along with phony identification cards. Neptune, planet of deceptions and disinformation, continued to influence him. But fickle Jupiter, planet of luck, occupying his ninth house of foreign travel, finally deserted him. Ray was arrested to face murder charges. He pleaded guilty to avoid the death penalty.

But he couldn't avoid death. The largest planet, and one of the most influential in Ray's destiny, is Jupiter, which not only endows luck, but also happens to rule the liver. Mars rules alcohol. Ray suffered from liver disease, exacerbated by a lifetime of alcohol abuse. Cruel Mars, the resident pharmacist in Ray's sixth house of health, filled a lethal prescription from Doctor Jupiter. Ray died in prison. All of the unanswered questions surrounding him remain clouded by mystery.

John Wayne Gacy

Tuesday, March 17, 1942, 12:29 A.M.
Chicago, Illinois • Time Zone: 06:00 (CST)
Longitude 087° W 38' • Latitude 41° N 53'
Placidus Houses • Tropical Zodiac

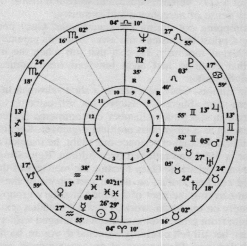

John Wayne Gacy was the polar opposite of the immortal actor for whom he was named. Short—about 5 feet, 8 inches tall—chubby, devious, loquacious, and filled with hidden depravity, Gacy became not a star but a notorious sex killer. Gacy's life was a kaleidoscope of conflicting images: prosperous business-man versus night stalker on skid row, twice married versus sexually attracted to young men, painted clown entertaining sick children versus a sexual predator of teenage boys. The murders he committed are among the most gruesome in criminal history.

Conflicts started early for Gacy. Born in Chicago on March 17, 1942, he didn't meet the standards set by his macho, homophobic father. The child became a mama's boy to his pharmacist mother and an object of scorn by his father. Sexual confusion may have been planted in Gacy as a toddler when a teenage girl molested him. Soon after the boy's ninth birthday, homosexual fondling by a grown man added to his dilemma. The mortification continued when, at age 18, he fainted during his first prurient fumbling with the only girl who would date him.

Trying to compensate for his homoerotic feelings, young Gacy immersed himself in work—delivering papers, mowing lawns, and accepting any job. In high school, he spearheaded the establishment of a civil defense squad and wore a uniform that gave him a new sense of acceptance and authority.

After dropping out during his senior year, Gacy considered becoming a priest but instead ran away from his parents to work in a Las Vegas mortuary. He lost that job when the mortician noticed that clothing had been removed from bodies during Gacy's night shift.

Back in Illinois, Gacy excelled as a shoe salesman in a major department store. Success bolstered his self-esteem, so he became active in the junior chamber of commerce (Jaycees) and gained respect as a gregarious political organizer. Keeping secret a drunken homosexual experience one night, he married a female co-worker in 1964 and fathered two children. Relocating to Waterloo, Iowa, workaholic Gacy became the manager of three fast-food fried chicken stores, an active participant in the Jaycees, and a gun-carrying member of a police auxiliary group.

Seemingly on top of the world, Gacy's forbidden sexual urges toppled him from grace. Not satisfied with alleged wife-swapping encounters, he still felt morbidly attracted to young, blond males. One such lad, age 15, the son of an acquaintance, accepted a ride home from Gacy, who offered to show the boy some porn films at his house. There, he persuaded his young guest to engage in mutual oral sex. When the victim informed his father, a subsequent police investigation turned up other teenage employees of Gacy who told similar stories. Gacy had taken one boy home and enticed him into a pool game in which the loser would give the winner oral sex. When the youth reneged, Gacy tried to collect at knifepoint but failed, and the lad escaped. A few days later, Gacy fired him. Another victim told police that he, too, had played pool with Gacy for different stakes. If the boy won, he would be rewarded by having sex with Mrs. Gacy. The woman allegedly lured him into bed, and Gacy "caught" them in the act. Feigning anger, he demanded equal treatment from the youth.

Charged with sex crimes against minors, Gacy was arrested. Psychological exams of Gacy in jail revealed classic symptoms of antisocial personality disorder. He felt no remorse for any of his behavior—rationalizing every act, finding excuses, and blaming the victims for seducing him. An unsympathetic judge sentenced him to ten years at Iowa State Reformatory. Gacy's wife, not charged, promptly divorced him and took both children out of his life.

In prison, Gacy resumed his manipulative ways—working, organizing and joining rehabilitation groups. He earned a high school diploma and passed some college courses. Ostensibly a model prisoner, Gacy earned parole after only eighteen months behind bars.

Starting over while living with his widowed mother, Gacy worked as a cook, then built up a business called PDM—, painting, maintaining, and decorating of homes and businesses. It prospered so well that he moved to a new, two-bedroom brick and yellow wood home on Summerdale Street in Norwood Park, a Chicago suburb.

Remarried, Gacy attended a New Year's Eve party, drank heavily, and left without his wife. Cruising around a downtown bus station, he picked up a teenager, Tim McCoy, and took him to the house on Summerdale for sex. Afterward, Gacy stabbed the boy to death, dumped the body down a trap door to the crawlspace, and subsequently buried him there. Gacy would one day admit that he experienced an orgasm while repeatedly plunging the knife into his victim's body.

Following the first murder in January 1972, the urge to seduce, torture, and kill youthful victims obsessed Gacy. Meanwhile, his business continued its spiraling success, along with corollary political and organizational activities. He threw lavish parties for business associates, impressed neighbors with gregarious assistance, and painted himself like a circus clown to entertain children in hospitals or at picnics. But his dark side grew with malignant vigor.

Luring teenagers to his home sometimes backfired. One youth, 19, gave him a beating for his trouble, and another managed to seize handcuffs Gacy tried to use, snap them on the assailant's wrists, and escape. Before long, Gacy took steps to prevent escapes. In July 1975, John Butkovich, 18, wound up buried beside the first victim. Within two years, a dozen more young decaying bodies occupied graves in the muddy earth of the crawlspace 30 inches below the wooden floor. As they decayed, a putrid gaseous odor seeped into the house, but Gacy didn't seem to notice.

A few of his intended conquests were allowed to live. One

boy told of being anally raped and tortured, and having his head
repeatedly dunked in a full bathtub until he almost drowned.
After forcing the victim to play a nerve-racking session of Russian roulette, Gacy let him go.

Divorced again in 1976, Gacy plunged into heavy use of booze
and amphetamines but managed to continue the facade of successful businessman and community activist. One day, in 1978,
he even posed for a photo with Rosalynn Carter, U.S. President
Jimmy Carter's wife. At night, the bodies continued to fill
earthen pits beneath the house on Summerdale.

Most of Gacy's victims came from bus stations or sleazy sections of downtown Chicago. But on December 11, 1978, he
chose a wholesome boy of 15, Rob Piest, an excellent student
who had nearly completed requirements to become an Eagle
Scout. Piest worked part-time in a drugstore that Gacy had
started remodeling. When the lad's mother came by to pick him
up on that day, Rob asked her to wait a few minutes while he
went outside to meet a contractor who'd offered him a much
higher-paying job. The mother waited, but her son never returned. Sick with fear, she contacted the police. They traced the
contractor, Gacy, and heard denials, anger, and alibis. With no
hard evidence, they released him but continued surveillance. The
investigators had no way of knowing, yet, that Gacy had raped
the youth, strangled him with a rope, and thrown his body from
a bridge into the Des Plaines River because the putrid ground
beneath Gacy's home had been filled to capacity.

Within a few days, police located several young men, some
of them Gacy's employees, who claimed they'd been lured to
his home for sex. One lad told of helping to dig trenches beneath
the house, understanding they were for new sewage pipes, since
terrible odors seeped from the muddy earth. Gacy, confident and
cocky, taunted the investigators. He made a puzzling statement
to one, saying, "Clowns can get away with murder!"

To search the house without interference from Gacy, police
arrested him on a minor drug charge. In his rooms, they found
pornographic tapes and sex magazines, mostly gay oriented, and
finally a receipt for development of a roll of film. It had belonged
to Rob Piest. With that thin evidence, the sleuths obtained a new
warrant, and started to dig under Gacy's house. The discovery
of putrescent flesh and rotting bones sickened the searchers and
stunned an entire nation. Underwear filled the mouths of fleshless

skulls, and other objects had been jammed into body cavities. Layers of lime had hastened the decomposition, but pathologists eventually pieced together 29 bodies buried under the house, the driveway, and the garage. At least four more of Gacy's victims had been dumped in the river. Six of the 33 bodies would never be identified.

In a detailed confession, Gacy rationalized that he'd never forced any of the victims to have sex, and that they were worthless street trash who deserved to be killed. Furthermore, he'd acted in self-defense. Another personality, he insisted, had taken over his will and body, forcing him to commit acts abhorrent to him. Later, Gacy repudiated the entire confession, arguing that someone else had committed the murders.

A jury in 1980 didn't believe him. They found him guilty and recommended the death penalty. While confidently waiting on Death Row for the verdict to be overturned, Gacy became a prolific artist, often painting garishly colored circus clowns.

On May 10, 1994, the State of Illinois used a lethal injection to end John Wayne Gacy's repugnant life.

Horoscope for John Wayne Gacy
Born March 17, 1942, 12:29 A.M. CST, Chicago, Illinois
Source: Birth certificate

The image of John Wayne Gacy concealing himself in a clown's makeup is a perfect symbol for his whole life, a life full of deception and the masking of his hideous true nature. His chart virtually turns over a stone to reveal the murky, crawling truth underneath.

In Gacy's Sun sign Pisces, which sets the stage for fantasy, dreams, and delusions as well as deception and lies, the Sun and the Moon play important roles. The Sun represents not only his ego, but also the male sex. In Gacy's third house of the mind, the masculine Sun resides in close conjunction with the feminine Moon, ruler of women. With these two planets locked together in such intimate space, Gacy was cursed with extreme confusion regarding his own sexuality.

Attempts to hide his dual sexuality show up in Gacy's Sagittarius-governed first house, which rules his appearance, temperament, and disposition. Sagittarius brings to his personality the gregarious and friendly countenance he used when playing the clown. In addition to projecting likable personal traits, Gacy wanted desperately to have an image of success and social status. His midheaven, which disseminates reputation, is ruled by Libra, the sign of law-abiding, respected, solid citizens. Venus, which endows charm, affection, and harmony, governs Libra. So, on the surface, Gacy appeared to be a prominent pillar of success in his community. But underneath lurked dark sexual urges that led to murder.

Actually, Gacy was bisexual. His seventh house of marriage, occupied by abundant Jupiter, set in motion Gacy's two matrimonial ventures. Jupiter is in Gemini, the planet of duality, so Gacy experienced not only dual marriages, but also double-gaited sexual activities.

Gacy's fifth house of sex is occupied by Saturn, which shadows his libido with depression, thus afflicting him with feelings of sexual inadequacy. Venus and Pluto conspire to turn this sexual confusion into disaster. By its rulership of the fifth house, Venus yields promiscuity and dissipation. These disagreeable traits take control due to Venus's negative alignment with Pluto, which looms in Gacy's eighth house of death. Sex and death became synonymous in his mind. One more bias is introduced by Venus, from its seat in the second house of money. Being the planet of valuables as well as ruling the house of sex, Venus clouded Gacy's mind with a mixture of money and sex, which equates to prostitution. So Gacy sought to satisfy his confused sexuality by cruising in search of boys, offering to pay them for sex. But Pluto, leering from the eighth house of death, blended kidnapping and murder into the complicated mindset of John Wayne Gacy.

Most of Gacy's victims were lured to his home, where the sex and murder took place. The planet of violence, Mars, rules his fourth house of home. He brought his prey there under false pretenses of jobs or payment. Mercury in Pisces gave Gacy the ability to lie convincingly and perfect his talents as a successful con man. As the planet of mental pursuits, Mercury joins the Sun and the Moon in the third house, which represents Gacy's mind. He relished playing mind games with his victims before killing them. Mental acrobatics were a fascination to Gacy, as a means of manipulation.

Gacy's sixth house, the domain of employees, is the residence of Uranus and Mars. One of the ploys Gacy used to lure young men was the offer of employment. Uranus, the planet of eccentricity, is next to Mars, the planet of violence. So, when Gacy had his "employees" under control, his eccentric urges turned to violent murder.

The ninth house rules the court system, relating to Gacy's long and involved dealings with justice. Neptune, the planet of deception and confusion, lies in the ninth house. Its negative aspects to Gacy's Sun and Moon show that even with overwhelming evidence against him, confusion reigned, and he managed to delay his execution date for fourteen years.

The twelfth house, ruling prisons, is ruled by Scorpio, but is heavily influenced by Pluto, from the eighth house of death. During Gacy's long wait on Death Row, he sold clown paintings, a Venus pursuit. In his motions to overturn the death penalty, he offered varying alibis for his perceived false imprisonment. They changed almost hourly. His attempts to shift the blame and play the victim are Sagittarius/Pisces qualities. The myriad stories he concocted were ridiculous, yet he presented them with a straight face. He was finally executed, proclaiming his innocence to the end.

James Mitchell "Mike" DeBardeleben II

Tuesday, March 19, 1940, 4:36 A.M.
Little Rock, Arkansas • Time Zone: 06:00 (CST)
Longitude 092° W 17' 22" • Latitude 34° N 44' 47"
Placidus Houses • Tropical Zodiac

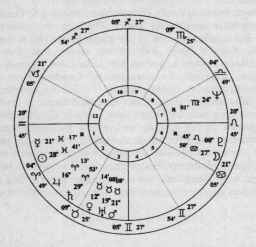

It is quite possible that Mike DeBardeleben got away with murder. A sexual sadist, he was convicted of kidnapping several young women whom he raped, tortured, and forced to pose in explicit sexual postures while he photographed them. However, despite strong evidence that he may have murdered at least two women, DeBardeleben was never tried for the homicides. Investigators in a dozen southeastern states suspected him of killing up to 20 female victims.

In an odd twist, he was finally captured not as a suspect in the rapes or murders, but as a prolific counterfeiter. The U.S. Secret Service, tracing the source of a batch of phony $20 bills, finally cornered DeBardeleben in a Knoxville, Tennessee, shopping mall. They charged him with printing and distributing approximately $165,000 in bogus money across the United States over a period of eighteen years.

With search warrants, the federal sleuths discovered a staggering volume of evidence against DeBardeleben, most of it stored in boxes he'd kept. As officers opened each container, they grew increasingly appalled at what they found. They saw lewd photos of obviously terrified women in humiliating poses, apparently being sexually assaulted, and heard audio tapes of female voices, begging not to be assaulted any more. In addition, it also became clear that DeBardeleben had been involved in kidnapping bank executives' wives to extort ransom money. Incredibly, his detailed records of his activities helped seal his fate.

The strange enigma of Mike DeBardeleben began in Little Rock, Arkansas, where he started life in March 1940, sandwiched between an older sister and a younger brother. Early on, he showed a tendency to be rebellious and disobedient to his strict parents. DeBardeleben's father, a career Army officer, moved his family around the country and across western Europe. His alcoholic mother reportedly sought solace in bars with other men, causing her boys to have a love-hate relationship with her. Exceptionally bright, DeBardeleben fared well in school until about age 16, when he was twice arrested for rowdy behavior and subsequently expelled from high school. At 17, he joined the Air Force, where his conduct landed him in the stockade twice. A psychiatric examination recognized his intelligence, but called him egocentric and antisocial. In August 1958, the military ushered him out under less than honorable conditions.

Back with his parents in Fort Worth, Texas, DeBardeleben arrogantly quit a string of menial jobs and failed to complete stabs at further education. His first marriage, at 18, lasted less than a month. Needing money, he turned to car theft and was soon caught, but received only probation instead of prison. Vain about his personal appearance, he attracted naive young women, and entered into marriage again with a teenager he impregnated in 1960. They divorced a year after the birth of a second child.

Still troubled in 1961, he had an argument with his younger brother, who committed suicide the next day. Stunned and furious, DeBardeleben blamed the emotional turmoil of their childhood.

In 1962, a judge revoked the scofflaw's probation for auto theft and sent him to Huntsville Prison for eight months. He came out angry and obsessed with revenge. A physical brawl with his mother resulted in 45 days of extensive mental exams at a Virginia institution.

Taking his third teenage wife in 1964, DeBardeleben gradually forced her into posing for sexually explicit photos, then into helping him defraud elderly women out of their money. The depressed wife would later reveal that her cruel husband even told her of his fantasies to kidnap, rape, and kill women. After being compelled to help him kidnap a banker's wife in order to extort money, DeBardeleben's unhappy mate couldn't tolerate the treatment, and left him.

He responded by marrying a fourth time, finding another gullible teenager just out of high school. The same pattern of sexual abuse and coercion into criminal activities followed. With the money from another kidnapping-ransom, DeBardeleben opened a nude modeling studio in Washington, D.C., but it soon failed, as did his marriage.

After a fifth wife fled, DeBardeleben finally gave up and remained single.

Meanwhile, he had been deeply involved in printing funny money and spending it. In 1976, the feds nailed DeBardeleben and sent him prison for nearly two years. Not long after his 1978 release, he began living out his fantasies about sex with captive women. In some cases he picked up pedestrians, bound and blindfolded them, and drove to his own house where he abused his captives, often photographing them. Real estate agents were particularly vulnerable to a well-dressed man, about 6 feet tall with bespectacled brown eyes, who seemed harmless. Some of them escaped after sexual assaults, while others met a worse fate. In Barrington, Rhode Island, a vivacious agent left her office to show a man some expensive homes. She was found the next day in a basement, strangled to death. An attractive agent, age 40, in Bossier City, Louisiana, turned up dead in a new home in April 1982. Witnesses later identified DeBardeleben as the prospective customer of both victims.

Using countless aliases and continually on the move, DeBardeleben passed his counterfeit money in 65 different cities, and cleverly evaded arrest until May 1983.

In four different trials, juries quickly found him guilty of offenses against the women he abducted and abused, and for his counterfeiting activities. When judges listened to the horrific audio tapes DeBardeleben had recorded, in which females screamed for mercy, and viewed the incredible array of brutal sex depicted in pornographic photos he had snapped, they felt no mercy for the convicted felon. The accumulated sentences added up to 345 years in prison for DeBardeleben.

Perhaps swayed by the fact that he would never again be free, and by the passage of time since the two murders, prosecutors in Louisiana and Rhode Island decided not to pursue homicide charges against him.

So, pale, in ill health, and hated by fellow inmates because of his crimes against women, "Mike" DeBardeleben no longer passes fake money. Instead, he passes countless hours, days, months, and years in dreary confinement. When he reaches the age of 109, he will become eligible for parole.

Horoscope for James Mitchell "Mike" DeBardeleben II
Born March 19, 1940, 4:36 A.M. CST, Little Rock, Arkansas
Source: Lethal Shadow, *by Stephen G. Michaud, p. 155*

Forgery and fantasy occupied Mike DeBardeleben's troubled life until he turned his prurient dreams of kidnap and rape into reality. Then he became obsessed with lustful abuse of female victims.

As a young man, DeBardeleben realized he had a smooth way with women. Venus, the planet of love and charm, lounges seductively in his third house of communication, in close proximity to Uranus. This aspect blessed DeBardeleben with the ability to charm women and, at least initially, to persuade them to like and trust him.

The Moon, ruler of women, floats frighteningly close to Pluto in DeBardeleben's chart. Pluto, in this ominously negative aspect, introduces obsession along with compulsive thoughts of kidnapping and torture. Because Pluto is in the forceful and dominating sign of Leo, these traits gripped him with even more power. The Moon is in Cancer, an emotional and moody sign. This combination forms a foreboding cloud over DeBardeleben's destiny in regard to women.

Violent Mars, in Taurus, bristles anger in the chart. Mars is the planet of cruelty and forced sex. The added Taurus influence shows his interest in sexual bondage and control of the women he captured.

Sex, in the domain of the fifth house, became an important factor in DeBardeleben's schemes. Mercury rules the fifth house. With Mercury's placement in Pisces, the sign of deception, DeBardeleben's sexual excitement would be stimulated by conning and deceiving women. The mental manipulation fed his ego, particularly when he used the deceit as a prelude to sexual assault.

DeBardeleben's ascendant is Aquarius. This sign gives him personal magnetism, or the power to attract. Aquarius falls under the rulership of Saturn, which is in a negative alignment with the Moon. This configuration activates an unpleasant trait of Saturn: taking advantage of people, or, in this case, women. Aquarius is also influenced by Uranus, which is negatively aligned with Mars, creating a dangerous and violent aspect. Both Uranus and Mars are in Taurus, the sign that darkens the personality with compulsions and a relentless drive to attain goals.

The goals DeBardeleben set for himself stemmed from a massive ego. His strongest planet is the Sun, ruler of ego. With his Sun in Pisces, the sign associated with fantasy and deception, he is not only endowed with a huge ego, but also an overweening sense of pride and self-confidence. The term *confidence man* is an apt description of DeBardeleben. His forgery skills are also connected to the Sun, which is adjacent to Mercury, the planet of writing and drawing. With Mercury in deceptive Pisces, the graphic skills turned into forgery. Since both the Sun and Mercury are in DeBardeleben's first house of personality, he not only created his "funny money," but passed it around with assurance and audacity. This same Sun/Mercury aspect gave him the forceful ability to speak convincingly when scamming his victims.

The second house of money takes on importance due to the residency of two planets, Jupiter and Saturn. They are often called the business planets. Jupiter rules abundance while Saturn is practical and organized. Together, they facilitated De-Bardeleben's ability to make money, in both meanings of the word, *make*.

If DeBardeleben succeeded in money matters, he failed miserably in marital success. Marriage is in the domain of the seventh house, which is occupied by Neptune, planet of deception and lying. Utilizing these traits, he persuaded five women to marry him, but when they discovered his obsessive lust and domineering ego, the bonds of marriage dissolved. DeBardeleben forced a few of his wives, and later his female captives, to luridly pose for his camera. Neptune also rules photography.

The photos DeBardeleben took came back to haunt him when he faced trial. Evidence presented by the prosecution included the Neptunian pornographic snapshots, along with audio tapes on which he had recorded his victims' pleas for mercy. Neptune also rules audio taping. Into the ninth house of courts strutted Mars and Pluto, bearing yet more influence. Violence belongs to Mars, while obsessions and torture are Plutonian traits. DeBardeleben's use of bondage, cruelty, and torture, unfolded before the jury, helped convict him.

Prisons are in the domain of the twelfth house, which is ruled by Saturn. This lonely and depressed planet of restraint and restriction served up to DeBardeleben 345 years of imprisonment. Considering the lost freedom to travel anywhere and the curtailed opportunities to manifest his ego-driven obsessions, the tight confinement imposed on DeBardeleben is a particularly harsh and difficult punishment.

Randy Steven Kraft

Monday, March 19, 1945, 2:18 P.M.
Long Beach, California • Time Zone: 07:00 (Pacific War Time)
Longitude 118° W 11' 18" • Latitude 33° N 46' 01"
Placidus Houses • Tropical Zodiac

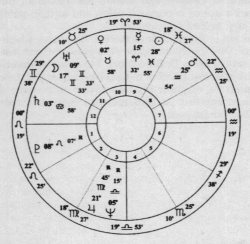

Probably California's most prolific serial killer, Randy Kraft targeted young men to sexually abuse and kill. During the late 1970s and early 1980s, he picked up and slaughtered at least sixteen victims, and is suspected of snuffing out the lives of many more.

Born on March 19, 1945, to a middle-class family in Long Beach, California, Kraft lived in loving comfort with his three older sisters. His father worked in the lucrative aircraft industry and his mother supplemented the family income with part-time jobs. After Randy's third birthday, they moved to Westminster, in Orange County, when the citrus groves still covered most of the fields that are now industrial or residential tracts. Raised in the Presbyterian faith, Randy and his sisters actively participated in church activities. He earned high academic marks and became profoundly interested in politics at an early age, but didn't mix well socially, preferring the company of a small group of intellectuals. During high school summers, he worked flipping burgers near the Huntington Beach pier. Pretending to admire the hordes of bikini-clad beach girls, Kraft later said he knew quite early that he was homosexual. Openly admitting it in the early 1960s, though, was just not done and could be dangerous.

Kraft graduated from Westminster High in June 1963 near the top of his class, and worked at Disneyland that summer before enrolling at Claremont Men's College in northeast Los Angeles. There, he was isolated from the social and sexual revolution sweeping other campuses in the decade of hippies and flower power. Kraft became an active member of the ROTC, but quit when the Vietnam war heated up. During the first summer vacation, he made love with an African American youth, whom he awkwardly introduced to his unsuspecting family. They still didn't make the connection. At night, Kraft tended bar in a gay watering hole.

Back in school, he developed the odd habit of vanishing from the dorm for long unexplained stretches at night. He also began to suffer from migraines and stomach problems. The following summer, during nocturnal cruising of beach restrooms, he inadvertently solicited a vice cop, but lucked out with just a warning. Afterward, Kraft made a show of dating women and mixing socially. He became exceptionally skilled at playing bridge and changed from a right-wing political conservative to an actively liberal Democrat.

In 1968, having obtained his degree, Kraft enlisted in the Air Force. Picturing himself as a glamorous officer, he was disillusioned by a lesser assignment: painting airplanes and weathered buildings in the dusty desert heat of Edwards Air Force Base. Now more openly gay, he spent weekends visiting homosexual hangouts in L.A. His family tried to hide their embarrassment when Kraft allowed his homosexuality to become evident, and the Air Force dumped him with a stigmatic general discharge for "medical" reasons after he'd served only thirteen months.

In civilian life, Kraft bounced from job to job, dissatisfied with the routine of meaningless work. His masculine behavior and rejection of effeminate posturing affected by many gay men certainly gave no hint of Kraft's sexual preference. He shared an apartment with a gay roommate in a Long Beach suburb called Belmont Shore. In March 1970, Kraft convinced a runaway boy, age 13, to accompany him home. After drugging the lad, Kraft raped him. The humiliated boy later reported being drugged, but failed to say anything about being used sexually. The police filed the case without taking any action against Kraft.

Bodies of sexually brutalized young men, many of them nude, began turning up along Southern California roads and freeways, most of them emasculated and strangled with a wire ligature. Some of them remained nameless and valueless, written off as street bums who solicited the wrong homosexual trick. One anonymous victim had been carved into multiple pieces and scattered for miles.

Kraft labored at unchallenging jobs until he discovered the burgeoning field of computer technology. He sharpened his natural aptitude in classes at Long Beach State, and thereafter was easily employable in a high-tech career. At night and on weekends, he discovered the added pleasure of picking up young men from the Camp Pendleton Marine Corps base. One of them turned up dead and mutilated near the Long Beach campus.

In March 1975, Kraft gave a ride to two high school boys, drugged them, and dumped one out. The other one's severed, decomposed head was found on a marina jetty. The rattled survivor described Kraft and his classic Mustang, which detectives promptly spotted in the parking lot where Kraft had picked up the boys. They questioned Kraft, who admitted giving the dead victim a ride, but said he'd dropped him off later. A deputy D.A. decided that the surviving boy's word was inadequate evidence to support prosecution.

After a brief hiatus, the body count accelerated again in 1976. The first one, in January, turned up in the Saddleback Mountains of south Orange County, with an extremely high blood alcohol level. The victim's mouth and throat had been packed with muddy leaves, which had suffocated him. Round burns from a cigarette lighter left marks all over his nude body, including his eyes. After sodomizing him, the killer had sliced off the victim's genitals and stuffed them in the anus.

The new crop, extending into 1977 and 1978, included not only Marines, transients, and gay prostitutes, but younger boys who'd been shot instead of garroted. The killer expanded his selection of disposal sites into the Southern California desert. More than a dozen sexually mutilated young men were found in 1979. In June 1980, William Bonin, the Freeway Killer, was arrested and later convicted for fourteen of the murders. (He and Kraft would one day become pals in prison.) Investigators knew, though, that another predator was still out there.

In 1980, Kraft acquired a new Toyota Celica and a new computer job that included traveling. During his business trips to other states, bodies turned up in the locations he visited. Oregon lost at least a dozen young men. The killer also struck in Michigan, Connecticut, and central California. And when Randy Kraft stayed in Long Beach, more violated bodies turned up in the southland.

On May 14, 1983, just after midnight, a pair of California highway patrol officers pulled over a 1979 Toyota Celica on the freeway. The driver, who had been steering erratically, jumped out and strutted toward the cops, which aroused their suspicion that he had something to hide in the car. While one officer gave Kraft a sobriety test, the other tapped on the Celica window to get the passenger's attention. But the motionless Marine remained slumped down in his seat. Within minutes, the cops realized that the young man, who had been bound with shoelaces, with his pants bunched at his ankles, had been strangled to death.

With Kraft in jail, a thorough search of his car produced a piece of lined paper from a legal pad that contained 61 neatly lettered, short, cryptic entries such as "TEEN TRUCKER," "2 IN 1 BEACH," and "PORTLAND HEAD." Investigators realized they had stumbled on a coded list itemizing 61 of Kraft's conquests, and they wondered whether all 61 had been murdered. But the suspect laughed it off as a list of gay acquaintances. The prosecutor would later refer to it as Kraft's "scorecard."

From the date of Kraft's arrest in May 1983 to the date of his conviction on May 12, 1989, six years of astronomically expensive and frustrating legal wars unfolded. Finally, a jury found Randy Kraft guilty of murdering sixteen young men between 1972 and 1983. The penalty phase concluded in August, resulting in Judge Donald J. McCartin sentencing Kraft to die in the gas chamber at San Quentin.

Two decades later, Randy Steven Kraft remains on Death Row. On most days, he meets a foursome for bridge in the exercise area. Two of the players are Lawrence Bittaker, a serial rapist/killer who tortured young women with pliers, and Douglas Clark (also a Pisces), who, with his female companion, killed and raped blond prostitutes in Los Angeles. The fourth recently had to be replaced. He was William Bonin, the Freeway Killer, who accounted for several of the victims during Kraft's rampage. Bonin was executed in February 1996, only the third condemned man to face the supreme penalty in California since reinstatement of capital punishment in 1976. More than 500 still wait their turns.

Horoscope for Randy Steven Kraft
Born March 19, 1945, 2:18 P.M. PWT, Long Beach, California
Source: Birth certificate

Serial killing becomes an addiction for some murderers and often the cruelty involved begins to increase with each victim. The fact that Randy Kraft became a living manifestation of this phenomenon is evidenced in his chart by the ominous alignment of two powerful planets. The presence of Pluto, planet of sadism, compulsion, and torture, lodged in his first house of personality, gives ample warning of Kraft's evil potential. Mars, planet of violence, in his eighth house of death virtually shouts a warning of the dangerous threat posed by this man.

Kraft's strongest planet, the Moon, ruler of his subconscious mind, shares close space in the eleventh house with Uranus, the planet of eccentricity. Since Uranus rules the eighth house of death, bizarre, offbeat visions of killing swirled through Kraft's subconscious thoughts. The Moon also beams rays of influence next door on his twelfth house of hidden agendas. So Kraft's deadly visions remained in the dark recesses of his mind during ordinary social functions, but surfaced when he ventured out to search for homosexual liaisons.

Kraft felt intellectually superior to the men he picked up. His first house of personality is occupied by Pluto in Leo, the sign of haughty arrogance. Leo is also Kraft's ascendant, and this double dose of the Lion endows Kraft with an incredible sense of pride, self-assurance, domination, and control. Evil Pluto injects Kraft's feeling of superiority with an interest in sadism and torture.

As Kraft singled out each potential victim after cruising beaches and bars, he subtly began to exert control. The placement of Venus, planet of comradeship and promiscuity, suggests that Kraft first approached his targets with overtures of friendliness, followed by hints of homosexuality. Venus is in Taurus, a sign associated with control and determination, so when the victim agreed to go with Kraft, the predator knew he had full authority over the man's destiny. Then sex took over.

The sign of manipulative Scorpio governs Kraft's fifth house of sex. Scorpio is ruled by Pluto and Mars, so the negative traits of those two planets infiltrate the fifth house. Mars, from its throne in the eighth house of death, sends violence and cruelty to the fifth house. Pluto, as noted earlier, contributes thoughts of sadism and torture, which bloomed into obsession. Sex and death, then, are linked in Kraft's mind.

Drugs were often involved in Kraft's modus operandi. Neptune, planet of trickery and deception, is the ruler of drugs. Kraft used narcotics to lull his victims into a haze of confusion and helplessness in order to assault and kill them.

Two key planets in Kraft's life, Sun and Mercury, sit side by side in his ninth house. The Sun is in Pisces, another sign associated with deception and lies. Its unfortunate alignment with Neptune only adds to his ability to dupe his prey. Mercury in Aries, a volatile and aggressive sign, rules speech and is associated with intellectual matters. Kraft is quite intelligent and mentally quick. Mercury is adjacent to his midheaven, ruler of the tenth house of careers. A high IQ paved the way for his employment in the early stages of the computer industry. The same mental agility unfortunately guided him along the darker path of murder and mutilation.

Kraft killed his victims by strangling them. Uranus, a ruler of his eighth house of death, is in Gemini, and the part of the body Gemini rules is the hands.

The ninth house of courts is influenced by Neptune, planet of confusion. The convoluted trial, fraught with delays and disruptions, was one of the longest in California's history. Saturn, as ruler of his eighth house of death, in which violent Mars dwells, had the final word. Kraft was eventually convicted and sentenced to death.

The twelfth house of prisons is partially ruled by Mercury, the planet of writing and communications, which resides in the ninth house of law and legal matters. This planet's influence expresses itself through Kraft's voluminous writings about his case, in which he endlessly explains all the various reasons why he should not be executed. Saturn, though, by dwelling in the twelfth house, and ruling the eighth house of death, clearly ordains that Kraft will die in prison, whether or not he ever faces capital punishment.

Sirhan Bishara Sirhan

Sunday, March 19, 1944, 2:00 A.M.
Jerusalem, Palestine • Time Zone: –02:00 (Eastern European Time)
Longitude 035° E 14' • Latitude 31° N 46'
Placidus Houses • Tropical Zodiac

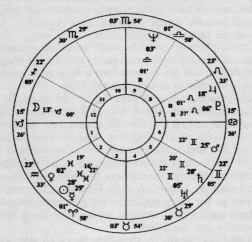

Four years and eight months after President John F. Kennedy fell to an assassin's bullet, his younger brother, Senator Robert Francis Kennedy, 42, traveled the country in his own campaign to win the U.S. presidency. On the evening of June 5, 1968, he ended a ballroom speech at the Ambassador Hotel in Los Angeles with the final words his public would ever hear him say: "On to Chicago. Let's win there," referring to that city's pending Democratic nomination convention. Kennedy waved to the crowd, exited the podium, and joined the flow of his entourage through an anteroom into a narrow pantry, en route to the kitchen.

Several shots echoed through the cramped room, accompanied by screams and men scrambling to grab whoever fired the weapon. A news photographer caught a photo that would be seared into the public imagination, of Kennedy lying on his back, surrounded by standing figures, right arm outstretched with a closed fist, while a young white-smocked busboy cradled the wounded leader's neck in one hand. Kennedy's eyes seemed to stare at the ceiling with a dazed sightlessness. He reportedly asked, "Is everybody all right?" Then, as medics tried to lift him onto a gurney, Kennedy groaned, "No, please don't." Although he lasted another full day, he would never speak again. Of the four bullets that hit Kennedy, the one that tore into his brain ultimately caused his death.

In the mad scramble immediately following the deadly burst of gunfire, several men, including author George Plimpton and retired football star Roosevelt Grier, struggled with the diminutive shooter but couldn't prevent him from squeezing the trigger again and again. Five more bullets ripped into members of the crowd, but none caused serious injuries.

The shooter, who stood only 5 feet, 4 inches and weighed 120 pounds, carried no identification and remained extraordinarily calm while being transported under heavy guard to jail. Speaking very briefly in an odd accent the police couldn't recognize, he refused to answer any questions. A dozen hours later, two of the suspect's relatives showed up at the police station and gave investigators the name of the man whose face occupied every television screen in the country. Sirhan Bishara Sirhan, age 24, was an immigrant Palestinian who had lived in the United States for more than a decade.

Born March 19, 1944, to Jerusalem parents who already had five children, Sirhan spent his childhood as a Christian in a population of Muslims warring with the Jewish population. His little brother died in 1947 when a British truck, swerving out of the line of fire, slammed into the child. By the time Sirhan reached 12, he had witnessed more violence, destruction, and death than most soldiers see at war. In 1957, his parents and most of his siblings immigrated to Pasadena, California. Sirhan's father searched for employment during the next six months, then deserted his family and eventually returned to his homeland. With his mother and siblings working, Sirhan and his family survived.

In school, Sirhan received average grades, but didn't seem to adapt socially. Small, dark-skinned, and harboring a simmering anger, he made no friends and felt completely rejected by girls. He showed an interest in history, and especially assassinations, once expressing the opinion that many more will come. He graduated the year President Kennedy was murdered.

At home, Sirhan joined his family in sticking to the food, customs, and traditions of Palestine, rejecting the culture of their adopted land. Sirhan worked hard, but failure to hold jobs and being forced to drop out of junior college embittered him. His stunted size led Sirhan to attempt a career in horse racing with hope of becoming a jockey. But an accident unnerved him and in 1966 he walked away. Other jobs petered out due to his bitter refusal to adapt to management policies.

Caught in the center of his own mental tornado, Sirhan turned to mysticism and a belief that he had psychic powers. He tried his mind control at a racetrack by willing that trouble befall a specific horse. Victory swelled in Sirhan when the horse hit the rail and finished last. He wondered if he could possibly use this new strength to force the death of people he imagined were his enemies. He began making entries in a journal about the ongoing struggles in the Mideast, imagining himself as a budding savior of Palestinian causes and a tool against American forces whom he considered biased against his homeland. On June 5, 1967, the Six-Day War between Israel and Arab nations began, and the Israelis attained quick victory. The date etched itself in Sirhan's mind, and he identified himself as an instrument of revenge.

In his journal, Sirhan identified Robert Kennedy as a political sympathizer with Israel who should be sacrificed to the cause. "RFK must die, RFK must be assassinated," he repeatedly scrawled on lined paper. The final straw may have been when Kennedy visited an L.A. synagogue and wore a yarmulke while making a speech. Sirhan intensified his goal by practicing marksmanship with an eight-shot .22-caliber revolver.

At the Ambassador Hotel on the evening of June 5, 1968, he mixed with the crowd and had a few cocktails, which he would later say caused his memory of the night to blank out. Witnesses noticed Sirhan, though. One woman asked him twice to leave the pantry area. While Kennedy spoke to the crowd, Sirhan reportedly asked kitchen personnel if the Senator would exit through the pantry.

Then, in one blinding moment, he changed the course of United States history.

At Sirhan's 1969 trial, a parade of psychiatric experts, all of whom had examined his handwritten journals threatening to kill RFK, took the witness stand. They used terms such as *disassociative, schizophrenic, paranoid*, and *psychotic*. No one except Sirhan denied that he had shot Kennedy, but the defense focused on the goal of keeping him out of the gas chamber. One expert said that Sirhan, in an "accidentally induced twilight state, accidentally executed the crime. . . ."

The jury, perhaps aghast at such comments, found Sirhan guilty and recommended the death penalty. But, just as had happened with Charles Manson and his "Family" of killers, the penalty was changed to life in prison when the U.S. Supreme Court ruled in 1972 that the death penalty on the books at that time was unconstitutional. Technically eligible for parole, he remains in prison.

Just as with Lee Harvey Oswald, conspiracy theorists believe that Sirhan acted as a puppet of an organized plan to kill Robert Kennedy. Even though his journals reveal longstanding plans and personal reasons to commit the murder, some groups argue that powerful mob figures who hated Kennedy for trying to wipe them out during his tenure as U.S. Attorney General found Sirhan, trained him, and paid him to assassinate the presidential candidate. The real truth may never be known.

Horoscope for Sirhan Bishara Sirhan
*Born March 19, 1944, 2:00 A.M. Eastern European Time,
Jerusalem, Palestine
Source: Family member*

Sirhan Sirhan suffered from a delusion that convinced him that a violent murder, committed in the name of patriotism, would make him an international hero. For this reason, he assassinated Senator Robert F. Kennedy.

Delusion and dreams have dominated Sirhan's life. The planet Neptune plays an extremely important role in his destiny. Ensconced firmly in the ninth house, Neptune is associated with deception and confusion. Its significance beams from the chart like a lighthouse beacon, illuminating the astonishingly appropriate traits of the ninth house, which include foreign countries, distant travel, courts, and dreams.

In the matter of foreign countries, Sirhan's fantasy of Palestinian independence, with him at the forefront of this political cause, is clearly a Neptunian delusion. Venus, the planet of affection and the other ruler of the ninth house, relates to Sirhan's love of his native country. But since Venus is in Pisces, sign of delusions, it only adds to his warped conception of reality. The issue of distant travel, of course, relates to Sirhan's unrealistic goal of returning in triumph to Palestine. Neptune's influence on courts reflects the subsequent trial, when Sirhan attempted to use his confused mental state as a defense, claiming he couldn't recall the events of the assassination. The dreams seen in his ninth house circle back to Sirhan's fantasies of being a political hero.

His Sun, Venus, and Mercury, being in the sign of Pisces further reinforces the delusional characteristics in Sirhan, since delusions and confusion are also the key traits of Pisces. Despite his confused and addled state, signs of lucidity in Sirhan are quite evident. His first house, representing his personality, is ruled by Capricorn, the sign associated with cunning, planning, and calculation. Even more support for his insidious guile becomes evident in the alignment of Sirhan's Moon in Capricorn, residing in the twelfth house of secrets. Saturn, Capricorn's ruler, is in Gemini, the sign of mental agility. All of the astrological signs indicate that Sirhan's assassination of Kennedy was carefully constructed. This is strongly supported by the influence of Capricorn and Saturn.

Mars, ruler of guns and shooting, is also in Gemini, negatively aligned with both Mercury and the Sun. These two planets rule his eighth house of death. So Sirhan thought of death as the only solution to the political problems he thought existed. Violent death was a strong influence on his life from the very start and left its mark on his impressionable imagination at an early age. Having an impressionable imagination is a Pisces characteristic.

Sirhan alleged that he couldn't remember the actual shooting. This is interesting because it was later determined that he practiced self-hypnosis in order to be able to commit the assassination. Therefore, he could have been in a "trance" at the time, explaining his lack of recall. Hypnosis, self-administered or otherwise, is a Neptune association. With the overpowering astrological emphasis on Neptune through most of his chart, it is not surprising that he was attracted to hypnosis as a means of assuring his success. It was also a convenient excuse to use in an attempt to avoid responsibility. The avoidance of culpability by playing the part of the helpless victim of an outside influence is another trait of Pisces.

The ninth house of courts, as stated before, is the residence of Neptune, which is consistent with Sirhan claiming to have been in a confused mental state at the time of the crime. This ploy did not work. He was convicted and given the death penalty.

Prison is ruled by the twelfth house, which is occupied by the Moon in Capricorn. This sign of constriction and confinement represents Sirhan's present and future situation. The other ruler of this house is Jupiter, the planet of beneficence. Jupiter's influence came into play when the death penalty was overturned and Sirhan was sentenced to life with the possibility of parole. This slice of good luck keeps him alive, but other signs indicate he will never be released. His midheaven, representing reputation, is in Scorpio. This sign of violence and obsession keeps the bloody image of a dying senator in sharp memory. The same fixed sign of Scorpio, which influences Sirhan's continued incarceration, is ironically the Sun sign of his victim, Robert Kennedy.

Appendix

How to Read a Chart
by Dana Holliday

The word *horoscope* means "chart of the hour." To prepare an accurate chart and horoscope, I must have the following information:

1. Place of birth.

2. Date of birth, including year, month, day, and time within four minutes. I prefer a birth certificate as a source, but if one is unavailable, I will use hospital records, baby books, or other reliable documents. I would rather not rely on memories of relatives or acquaintances, since they can be inaccurate.

The fact that charts are now usually done on computers eliminates much chance of error. The information is entered into the program, along with the latitude and longitude of birth taken from the city and state and the correct type of time, such as Standard Time, Daylight Time, War Time, and so on.

There are four factors I use in astrology: planets, signs, houses, and aspects. The combination of these four factors makes up a horoscope.

- The ten planets used are the Sun, the Moon, Mercury, Venus, Mars, Jupiter, Saturn, Uranus, Neptune, and Pluto.

- The twelve signs used are Aries, Taurus, Gemini, Cancer, Leo, Virgo, Libra, Scorpio, Sagittarius, Capricorn, Aquarius, and Pisces.

- Aspects are the angles or relationships between the planets within the circle. Some are positive, some are negative, and some are neutral. If the aspect is positive, the positive sides of both planets and the signs in which they fall are activated. If the aspect is negative, the negative sides of the planets and signs are activated. If the aspect is neutral, only the power of the planets and signs are shown.

- The houses and the areas that they rule are as follows:

First house	Physical body, appearance, and personality
Second house	Personal material possessions, including money
Third house	Everyday thinking and communications, siblings, short trips, commuting, writing, talking
Fourth house	Home, home life, father
Fifth house	Children, sex, hobbies, heart's desires, love, romance, creativity
Sixth house	Health, service to others, employees, working environment, police, small animals
Seventh house	Marriage partners, equal partnerships, open enemies
Eighth house	Death, partner's money, inheritance, insurance
Ninth house	Religion, philosophy, publication of ideas, the courts, long-distance trips, higher education

Tenth house	Reputation and career, mother, status in the community or world, honors
Eleventh house	Friends and platonic relationships
Twelfth house	Secrets, places of confinement, prisons, hospitals, laboratories, suicide and self-undoing, hidden enemies

The twelve houses are divided into sections. The lines between the sections are called the *cusps*. The line before the house is the cusp of that house. There are two other factors used. The *ascendant*, or rising sign, is the sign on the cusp of the first house. It is literally the sign rising or coming up over the horizon at the date, time, and place of birth. It reflects the personality and personal appearance along with any other planets in the first house. The other cusp used is the cusp ruling the tenth house. It is called the *midheaven*. This sign acts as a transmitting tower and sends the qualities of that sign, along with all the planets that aspect it, into the public. This is why people with strong tenth houses should not go in for criminal activities, as they are much more likely to be caught.

Each sign is ruled by a planet or planets, as follows:

♈ Aries is ruled by Mars ♂

♉ Taurus is ruled by Venus ♀

♊ Gemini is ruled by Mercury ☿

♋ Cancer is ruled by the Moon ☽

♌ Leo is ruled by the Sun ☉

♍ Virgo is ruled by Mercury ☿

♎ Libra is ruled by Venus ♀

♏ Scorpio is ruled by Mars and Pluto ♂ ♇

♐ Sagittarius is ruled by Jupiter ♃

♑ Capricorn is ruled by Saturn ♄

♒ Aquarius is ruled by Saturn and Uranus ♄ ♅

♓ Pisces is ruled by Jupiter and Neptune ♃ ♆

In general, the houses containing the largest number of planets are the most important in a person's life. If a house is unoccupied by planets, it is ruled by the sign on the cusp. For example, in Ted Bundy's chart, his first house is empty of planets. His ascendant is Leo. As the Sun rules Leo, it is the ruler of his first house. The Sun is in Bundy's fifth house in Sagittarius.

The Sun rules the ego, and the fifth house rules sex. Sagittarius is an outgoing and indiscriminate sign. His Sun (ego) is next to Mars, the planet of violence. Therefore his ego would tend to express itself violently and indiscriminately through sex.

Finally, each of the ten planets rules an emotion, feelings, or things, as follows:

The Sun	Ego, men
The Moon	Emotions, women, subconscious mind
Mercury	Conscious mind, communications
Venus	Affections, love, and beauty
Mars	Aggressions, initiative, violence, guns, knives
Jupiter	Abundance, overdoing, overdosing, overly optimistic

Saturn	Restrictions, law and order, repression, depression
Uranus	The unexpected, bizarre, eccentric, unusual, odd
Neptune	Vague, dreamy, idealistic, poisons, cloudy
Pluto	Coercion or cooperation, kidnapping, group activity, gangs, Mafia

The astrodyne sheet on Ted Bundy (below) demonstrates the relative power and harmony of each of the planets, signs, and houses, with the most powerful at the top of the list and the weakest at the bottom. (The example in the astrodyne sheet may be used to visualize the chart described in Bundy's horoscope on page 226.) These are calculated from the positions in the birth chart. They are given numerical weights and are added up for totals. This is a great help in reading a chart, as it sometimes is difficult to see which planets are strongest.

Power and Harmony of the Planets for Ted Bundy Individually Sorted

11/24/1946, 10:35 P.M.
44N28, 73W12

	Power	Hrmy + Disc		Hrmy		Disc		Neut	
Moon	87.35	Pl	6.15	Pl	21.87	Mi	-29.05	Mo	41.05
Pluto	81.85	Ju	3.57	Ma	20.08	As	-26.72	Pl	32.33
Mars	81.09	Ma	3.55	Mo	15.68	Me	-23.75	Ur	31.99
Uranus	69.45	Su	-.18	Ju	13.50	Ur	-23.20	Ma	31.29
Mercury	66.63	Mo	-1.33	Ve	8.99	Mo	-17.01	Me	24.73
Midheaven	59.26	Ne	-1.94	Ne	8.58	Ma	-16.53	Ve	15.50
Venus	55.08	Sa	-3.99	Sa	7.99	Pl	-15.72	Su	12.65
Ascendent	50.54	Ve	-5.93	As	7.11	Ve	-14.92	Mi	10.14
Sun	38.81	Ur	-17.04	Ur	6.16	Sa	-11.98	Sa	3.10
Saturn	38.81	Me	-18.16	Me	5.59	Ne	-10.52	Ju	2.91
Jupiter	34.36	As	-19.61	Su	5.57	Ju	-9.93	As	.31
Neptune	30.57	Mi	-29.05	Mi	.00	Su	-5.75	Ne	.00
Totals	693.80		-83.96		121.12		-205.08		206.00

Your Dominant Planet is Moon

Power and Harmony of the Signs Individually Sorted

	Power	Hrmy + Disc		Hrmy		Disc		Neut	
Sagittarius	224.43	Sa	3.83	Sa	48.08	Le	-57.30	Sa	86.45
Scorpio	196.81	Ar	1.78	Le	39.77	Sc	-56.67	Sc	59.04
Leo	190.60	Pi	.41	Sc	38.57	Sa	-44.25	Ge	44.35
Gemini	102.76	Ca	-.67	Li	13.08	Ta	-36.51	Le	42.07
Taurus	86.80	Cp	-1.99	Ar	10.04	Ge	-35.08	Ca	20.53
Libra	58.11	Li	-4.90	Ge	8.96	Li	-17.98	Ta	17.89
Cancer	43.67	Aq	-5.26	Ca	7.84	Vi	-11.88	Ar	15.64
Aries	40.54	Vi	-9.08	Pi	5.52	Aq	-8.80	Vi	12.36
Virgo	33.32	Le	-17.53	Ta	4.50	Ca	-8.51	Aq	8.77
Aquarius	27.06	Sc	18.10	Cp	4.00	Ar	-8.26	Li	7.75
Capricorn	19.40	Ge	-26.12	Aq	3.54	Cp	-5.99	Cp	1.55
Pisces	16.23	Ta	-32.01	Vi	2.80	Pi	-5.11	Pi	.73
Totals	1039.73		-109.64		186.70		-296.34		317.13

Your Dominant Planet is Sagittarius

Power and Harmony of the Houses Individually Sorted

	Power	Hrmy + Disc		Hrmy		Disc		Neut	
Fourth	369.70	5	1.79	4	66.41	4	-86.03	4	141.13
Twelfth	164.33	9	1.78	12	37.71	10	-59.71	12	55.96
Tenth	156.25	12	1.50	3	17.99	12	-36.21	10	49.88
First	69.95	3	.60	2	11.38	1	-29.59	9	15.64
Second	63.89	8	.41	10	10.66	2	-22.40	11	12.36
Third	61.90	6	-1.99	9	10.04	3	-17.39	2	12.36
Ninth	40.54	7	-5.26	1	9.90	11	-11.88	3	10.66
Eleventh	33.32	11	-9.08	5	6.75	7	-8.80	7	8.77
Seventh	27.06	2	-11.02	8	5.52	9	-8.26	1	6.64
Sixth	19.40	4	-19.62	6	4.00	6	-5.99	6	1.55
Fifth	17.18	1	-19.69	7	3.54	8	-5.11	5	1.45
Eighth	16.23	10	-49.05	11	2.80	5	-4.96	8	.73
Totals	1039.75		-109.63		186.70		-296.33		317.13

Your Dominant House is Fourth

It is significant that the Moon (women) is the strongest planet in Bundy's chart. All of his victims were women and his whole life revolved around women, even when he wasn't killing them. He is one of the most prolific serial killers. Exactly how many women he murdered is unknown. Sagittarius, his strongest sign, is ruled by Jupiter, the planet of overdoing, abundance, and excessiveness. Sagittarius/Jupiter also governs long-distance travel; thus, he traveled all around the country on his killing sprees. Sagittarius and Jupiter are connected with good luck. He escaped from jails twice and evaded the executioner for many years, despite his murder convictions.

His fourth house is his strongest house. He was born illegitimate, but found out late in life. His mother remarried and gave the child his stepfather's name, Bundy. She stood by him all his life and attended his final trial in Florida. It is suggested by some psychologists that the absence of Bundy's real father (the fourth house rules home and father) was a strong factor in his psychological makeup. He lived with his mother and stepfather during his childhood. He did not grow up in extreme poverty and orphanages, as some killers did.

Bundy's eighth house of death is ruled by Pisces. There are no planets in it. Therefore the rulers are Neptune and Jupiter. Neptune is in his second house of money and Jupiter is in his third house of communications. His thoughts (third house) would be of death and money (second house).

The fourth house, his strongest, contains five planets. In order of importance, they are Venus, Mercury, Sun, Mars, and the Moon. He also has Mars and Pluto ruler of Scorpio on the cusp. The planet nearest the cusp is the strongest, with the next planet, second strongest and on down the line with descending influence. The planets ruling the sign on the cusp are last in influence.

Bundy's twelfth house, ruling secrets and prisons, is ruled by Saturn, Pluto, and the Moon, as it rules Cancer on the cusp. Saturn also rules his sixth house through Capricorn and his seventh house through Aquarius. The police (sixth house) and law and order (Saturn) were his open enemies (seventh house). They also put him in prison (twelfth house).

Pluto also rules his fourth house of the home. He kidnapped (Pluto) some of his victims from their homes (fourth house) and killed them. Again, this put him in prison (twelfth house).

The Moon, ruler of Cancer, also rules women. The Moon, his

strongest planet, rules his twelfth house. The killing of women put him in prison.

Bundy's tenth house is ruled by Uranus, the planet of the unusual and eccentric. His reputation (tenth house) was certainly that. His midheaven is Taurus and is ruled by Venus. Venus is in his fourth house of the home and also rules his third house of communications and travel. Many people who met Bundy saw him as a nice guy (Venus) with a great deal of charm, also a Venus characteristic. He used this charm to lure his victims. He had a smooth way of talking (third house). Venus is in Scorpio, the sign ruling kidnapping and coercion.

Each house is read in this way, involving the planet, sign, and house, as well as any aspects they make to each other. It is the combination and blending of all of these factors that makes up a horoscope.

Index

DON LASSETER is an expert in the field of true crime. He is the author of *Dead of Night, Going Postal, Cold Storage,* and *Property of Folsom Wolf.*

DANA HOLLIDAY is an astrologer who has spent the last twenty years researching the astrological aspects of criminal behavior.

PENGUIN PUTNAM INC.
Online

Your Internet gateway to a virtual environment with
hundreds of entertaining and enlightening books from
Penguin Putnam Inc.

*While you're there, get the latest buzz on
the best authors and books around—*

Tom Clancy, Patricia Cornwell, W.E.B. Griffin,
Nora Roberts, William Gibson, Robin Cook,
Brian Jacques, Catherine Coulter, Stephen King,
Jacquelyn Mitchard, and many more!

Penguin Putnam Online is located at
http://www.penguinputnam.com

PENGUIN PUTNAM NEWS

Every month you'll get an inside look at our upcoming
books and new features on our site. This is an ongoing
effort to provide you with the most up-to-date
information about our books and authors.

Subscribe to Penguin Putnam News at
http://www.penguinputnam.com/ClubPPI